Love Immortal

Kit Vincent

SKY HOUSE

Published by Sky House Publishing LLC.

Library of Congress Cataloging-in-Publication Data is available upon request.

ISBN 978-1-959052-13-5 (paperback)

978-1-959052-06-7 (ebook)

978-1-959052-07-4 (audiobook)

First edition: October 2024

For my Chu.
Thank you for writing this book with me till the end.

AUTHOR'S NOTE

Dear reader,

This book contains vampires. You know what they eat. Other content warnings may include: violence, death, gore, sexual content, drug and alcohol abuse, disturbing dreams, confinement, bullying, mentions of suicide, racism, homophobia, misogyny, abandonment.

Enter freely and of your own free will.

"What do you mean my letter went missing?" Clay asks, his blue eyes wide with a fear I've never seen in him before.

My insides wrench, and I press my back against the cold, brick wall.

We're behind the school building. I've waited here for more than an hour for Clay's football practice to finish. I had to let him know as soon as possible. "Someone stole my backpack during PE," I confess. "But I...I found it later. It was just a prank. They dumped everything into a trash can..." I hate how normal I must make my voice sound so I don't make him panic. What happened wasn't out of the ordinary for me. Unlike Clay, I've been taunted like this for all of high school.

Clay's lips tighten. Sadness flashes across his face, but then fear overtakes it. "So what happened to my letter?" he asks again.

I look down at the ground, which feels like it's quickly disintegrating beneath my feet. "The letter...it wasn't there."

"Jonathan!" Clay's voice breaks. He rakes his fingers through his dirty-blond hair, still slightly damp with sweat. "Do you understand what you've done? If anyone reads it, they'll find out about us!"

"I know!" I yelp as the wave of Clay's despair crashes into me. But what can I do? What can I possibly say to fix this? It's not completely my fault. Clay and I have been dancing on the edge of this abyss for months now, exchanging these letters. We both knew the risks: what our parents would say, what the school would do if they discovered that a silly pen pal assignment had turned into a secret love affair.

We've always known the consequences, but it felt like as long as we were careful, there was no real threat.

"Nobody will find out," I say, steadying my voice. "I probably just misplaced it, Clay. Maybe it's in my locker, and it fell behind something." I don't know who I'm trying to convince more, but I take a step closer to him. "I'll check again first thing tomorrow."

I reach for him then, just to touch him, to tell him everything is going to be okay. For the briefest moment, I feel the warmth of his cheek against my chilled fingertips. But then Clay flinches away.

"Burn them," he says through gritted teeth.

"What?" My outstretched hand freezes in midair.

"Jonathan, if you ever loved me, if you ever cared about me, I want you to burn them all. Tonight."

My hand drops to my side, Clay's words slashing like knives through soft flesh. Burn them *all*? His gentle confessions that made me swoon, our inside jokes and hidden dreams, the proof I'm not alone? That I can be loved? That despite what the world tells people like Clay and me every day, it is possible to be happy?

"Promise me you'll do it." Clay urges, breaking my stupor. He's crowding me back against the wall. "Say you will, Jonathan."

As I stare at Clay's demanding expression, my eyes sting, and my lungs seem to be filled with ice. Soundlessly, I nod. Because what else can I do?

But in the end, I can never bring myself to burn our letters.

And by then, it's already too late anyway.

Part One
In The Absence Of Light

ONE

My green Chevy Nova makes a series of pitiful popping noises as I pull the rusty clunker into the parking lot in front of West Hall. I guess that's to be expected from a car that's almost as old as I am. Except nineteen in car years is ancient; I'm lucky it's still kicking at all. I won't have money to fix it anytime soon.

A shoebox filled with letters sits safely on the passenger seat beside me, and the back seat and trunk are loaded with the rest of my earthly possessions, which amount to exactly two boxes and a laundry hamper filled with clothes and bed linens. At least the dorm room is furnished, and I won't have to sleep on the floor anymore like I have all summer.

I snag a spot not too far from the entrance and head inside.

West Hall is one of Camden's five residence halls, a three-story red brick colonial with white windows and deep-green shutters. This will be my dorm for my sophomore year. True to its name, it sits on the western edge of campus. Baseball and football fields and the adjacent athletic buildings are the only things that lie between it and the sprawling, luscious woods of Vermont's Green Mountains.

Once inside, my first stop is the resident assistant's room located on the first floor. There's a small line outside the door, but it moves quickly, as most students already moved in earlier this weekend. Unfortunately, I couldn't do that. Perpetually short on cash, I tried to squeeze in as many hours as I could at my summer job in the valley town south of here.

As I wait, I see familiar faces bustling about the hall, some accompanied by excited or teary-eyed parents helping them lug boxes of their belongings. Unlike most of these students, I have no family to help me move in, and no home to return to during school breaks.

Instead, this past summer, I rented a dingy studio apartment above someone's garage and worked long hours at a shitty gas station, because even full-ride scholarships don't cover summer housing—or clothes, or ridiculously expensive textbooks, for that matter. But I'd rather starve and sleep in my derelict car than go back to the people who made my life a living hell. I promised myself that much a long time ago.

"Name and student ID," the RA says.

"Jonathan Evergreen," I say, flashing her my card for a quick inspection.

"Signature here." She points to the ledger on her desk. After I sign it, she retrieves a manila envelope with my keys and hands it to me. Judging by the number written on it, my room is on the third floor. Not too bad.

Even without help, it takes only three trips to carry my things from the Chevy to my room. As expected, the room is small, and I'm sharing a bathroom with six other students. But the space still has some of the charming original details from when the dorm was built in the late 1800s, like the oak wainscoting on the walls and the heavy cast-iron radiator under the window. I'm a bit disappointed by the absence of a fireplace—I've heard some rooms have those, though they're no longer functional because it's a fire hazard. But I'm not about to complain. I've finally gotten what I want—a *single*.

Starting a new life in a new place looks so much smoother in movies. In reality, however, you put on a brave face and change locations, but people are still people. Sure, being accepted to Camden and moving to Vermont from North Carolina was a vast improvement, except for one little thing: Camden has a policy that all students must live on campus during their freshmen year and have a roommate. The assignments are supposed to be random and nonnegotiable, and of course, it was my "luck" to be paired up with a legacy because *look at how inclusive we are at this elite institution*! Everyone gets the same opportunities, whether you're a scholarship kid or someone with so much inherited wealth and privilege that it should be illegal. Never mind that there's an unbreachable chasm between people like Madison Jr.— the youngest son of the senator whose family has owned huge swaths of Vermont for the past four generations (I don't even know why they bother to run for office, they might as well just declare themselves kings)—and people like me, whose families have disowned them.

I lost count of how many times I was locked out of my own dorm room because Mads Jr. was having "fun" with a new girlfriend. Sometimes, I came home and found the place completely trashed because his clique, a bunch of rich and spoiled legacies like him, had thrown another raging party. Having nowhere else to go, I spent an awful lot of time in the library. Full disclosure: I do love libraries, and my GPA is a solid 4.0, which was the one silver lining of this whole situation. Mads Jr. and his buddies, on the other hand...I honestly don't know if I ever saw any of them holding a book. None of them got a failing grade in a single class, though. Because when your family name is on a college building, or you're the sole heir to a real estate empire, you're not beholden to the same set of rules as everyone else. I plan to interact with them as little as possible this year.

Relishing the much-desired solitude, I begin to unpack. Carefully, I put the letter-filled shoebox on my bedside table before I move on to the large boxes. There isn't a lot in them: a reading lamp, a few of my favorite books that I brought with me when I left North Carolina, a clock radio, and some school supplies. I empty the laundry hamper and hang my clothes in my small closet. Lastly, I make my bed.

My room is sparse but neat—I can live with that. The window could use some curtains, but I don't have any. At least nothing will obstruct my view of the mountain range, which is quite nice.

I open the window and let in some fresh air. Below me is the back courtyard of West Hall. It transitions into a patch of mostly green lawn studded with occasional maple and aspen trees. Many of their leaves are already spotted yellow and rust-red. I'm still not used to how much earlier fall comes in this place than in North Carolina. I hope I've acclimated enough by now that I won't need to bundle up in all three of my sweaters the moment the skies turn gray and the temperatures drop below sixty, which is bound to happen by the time October rolls in.

Camden University is by far the most remotely located of the elite institutions. Last year, we even got snowed in, and the power was out for three whole days. The blizzard was so bad they couldn't plow the roads to allow the electric company to fix the downed power lines. Of course, classes were canceled, and the entire campus turned into a party. Mads Jr. had enough stashed alcohol to outlast the entire blackout. I holed up in the student center—reading, of course—as it was one of the few buildings with a functioning generator.

But honestly, I don't mind the occasional snowstorm or the wilderness or the isolation. Even if Camden hadn't offered me a full ride, I still would've fought tooth and nail to go here. Because

Camden has something no other campus in America does: the biggest university library of rare books in the country.

It's a special collection that houses titles from as far back as the eleventh century. Scholars and researchers from all over the world visit to study these books. I'd like to join them someday. Once I graduate, it is my dream to work in book conservation and historic document archivism. This past summer was supposed to bring me closer to that dream, but at the very last moment, the opportunity that was meant to be mine was snatched away from me by none other than a damn legacy student.

I grip the windowsill angrily. These past three months could've been so different. I could've avoided the embarrassment of working at a shoddy gas station that smelled like spit and gasoline fumes. I could have been learning about old books. I could've done so much more if not for that stupid—

A familiar voice carries through my door, which I left ajar. "I'm gonna give you exactly three seconds to explain why you ghosted me all summer. One—"

I whirl around, startled. "But I called last week!" I say defensively as Fiona Onayemi leans against the doorframe with her arms folded and her eyes narrowed.

"To kindly inform me that you were still among the living and that you got your room assignment? Wow, Jonathan. Sometimes, I wonder if you even consider me a friend."

Fiona is wearing a turquoise silk bomber jacket with a denim bell skirt and tall socks. There's a satin bow which matches her jacket that's holding back her curly brown hair. And from the fierce look on her face, I can tell she is not in the mood to buy any of my bullshit excuses.

So I don't try to sell her any. "Sorry. That wasn't cool," I say sheepishly.

She stares at me for a moment. "No legitimate excuse, then?"

"Other than the fact that my summer was pretty pathetic, and I didn't want to ruin yours by talking about it?" I shake my head. "Not really, no."

Fiona's eyebrows fall as she sighs. "You know, acting as a receptacle for venting is a part of being someone's friend. You let your pals spill their rage and heartbreak and commiserate with them, and in return, they do the same for you when you need it. It's mutually advantageous." She steps forward, opening her arms for a hug.

"I know," I say apologetically, squeezing her back.

The truth is, I'm really happy to see Fiona again. It would've been nice to hang out with her this summer. She's the one soul in Camden who knows about my situation, and she generously invited me to visit her family in Albany. But the way my summer plans went south—and the fact that I never have enough money —squashed my desire to see anyone, or even talk to my best friend.

"Your hair's longer," she says when she pulls away.

I brush my floppy mess of brown locks out of my face. "I need a haircut."

"It's very rock 'n' roll. You should keep it."

I snort. "Can't believe you're accusing me of looking cool." With my faded jeans and my collection of stretched-out T-shirts and old sweaters, I'm hardly fashionable.

Fiona grins. "Well, they say even a broken clock is right twice a day. This might be your year to shine. You even lucked out and got a single."

"Wait, you didn't?" I ask, surprised. I know Fiona applied for one too, and her academic standing should be good enough for her to qualify.

"Nope. Got assigned to East Hall." She shrugs, disappointed but not overly so. "I'm rooming with this freshman girl, Becky, from California. She's nice. Total airhead, though. At least I don't have to share a bathroom with the entire floor."

"That was the worst," I say.

Besides not being allowed to choose their roommates, most first-year students are assigned to Allen Hall, which is the oldest dorm with the tiniest rooms and only one coed bathroom per floor. Whoever approved that building plan should've been forced to live there for the rest of their life as punishment. Too bad they're long dead by now.

"It was disgusting," Fiona grumbles. "The toilets were always a mess. Oh, by the way, did you hear that Mads Jr., Callahan, and Eric Stockton moved off campus? Rumor has it they're renting a giant mountaintop mansion. Lucky jerks. I can't believe anyone would let a bunch of nineteen-year-old douchebags live in a mansion by themselves. They're so gonna destroy the place."

I laugh humorlessly. "I'm sure their parents will pay for the damages. And if this means we won't have to see Mads Jr. on campus anymore, I fully support it."

"True. I'm still jealous, though. They probably have private bathrooms with bathtubs," Fiona says, her voice full of yearning. "So, are you done unpacking?"

"I think so," I reply, taking a cursory glance around the room.

Like the future badass lawyer she is, Fiona sees an opening and pounces on it. "Then you have absolutely no excuse to ditch me. Whether or not you wanna vent about your woes, I'm telling you all about my summer, Jonathan Evergreen. Pancakes?"

I grin. There isn't much entertainment in the small towns surrounding Camden. The nearest movie theater is a thirty-minute drive away. But there's a tiny bookstore (that had no job openings left by the time I inquired at the beginning of the summer), a bar, a country club, and a diner off Route 7. Getting late-night pancakes there is our version of therapy. I've spilled most of my life story to her over half stacks and strawberry shakes. When I got unbearably lonely over the break, I caved and drove down there for a solitary midnight vanilla malt. It improved things a little.

I hesitate for a moment. Money is tight, as always, and I don't know what astronomical prices they're going to demand for my textbooks this year, but I haven't eaten since yesterday, and there's no way I can refuse the invitation. "If you're driving," I say.

"Of course I'm driving," Fiona says confidently, already on

her way to the door. "I'm not gonna force the last living dinosaur into extinction, assuming it still runs."

I chuckle. "I wouldn't call it running. More like puffing along at a leisurely pace." I grab my room key and wallet and scramble after her.

Two

Day one of the fall semester is nothing like the pandemonium of my first day of freshman year. To avoid the student stampede at the registrar's office, I took care of my class registrations back in April. My major is self-designed, and I tried to squeeze as many courses as I could into my schedule, which was one hell of a logistical nightmare.

Now, the only thing that remains unsolved is my work-study arrangement. I've left multiple messages for my advisor, Dr. Kowalski, but I haven't heard back from him, which is unusual. I don't know how old he is—he's gotta be in his eighties at least—but he always answers questions about class assignments and my major promptly. I hope he's all right. Although it's possible that he simply couldn't reach me since my shitty apartment had no landline.

In any case, I'll see him later today in my Gothic lit class. And there's a chance I can catch him even before that—the dean of the School of Arts and Sciences is giving her annual address at noon. All students are required to attend, and most professors show up as well. I head there after intermediate Latin, which is my only Monday morning class.

The Royall Tyler Theater, where the assembly is being held, is one of Camden's landmarks from the mid-1800s. It's gone through several major renovations since then, but some elements of the original decor remain. The lobby is dark, illuminated only by the glow of two brass chandeliers. It gives off a very New England vibe. The walls are painted a deep oxblood, and the ceiling is supported by rows of ornate mahogany beams and pillars.

The auditorium is nearly full by the time I make it through the crowd of chattering students. The inside is a sea of red velvet —the heavy curtains framing the stage, the runners, and even the seat upholstery are the same invitingly plush scarlet fabric.

I don't see Fiona, so I take an empty aisle seat in the back row. It's not that I'm poorly socialized or don't know how to make friends; it's just that I prefer to be alone. Fiona is the only person I've allowed to get close to me. We both took Dr. Kowalski's class during our first semester and bonded quickly over our mutual love of books. But it's more than that. Fiona's parents are hugely successful lawyers in upstate New York—unlike me, she doesn't need scholarship money to attend Camden—but being the only Black student in the entire prelaw program doesn't exactly make it easy to fit in. It's the unspoken knowledge that neither of us will ever belong in the rich boys' club that makes us allies.

Still, Fiona does most of the work to keep our friendship alive. I know it's unfair. She deserves better, and I feel guilty about it, but I don't know how to change.

Ever since Clay, there's been a crack in my world: me on one side and everybody else on the other. Although maybe it was there even before him, and I just pretended not to see it. After him, I simply stopped trying. I don't trust people anymore. It's futile trying to connect when you're forced to hide major parts of yourself. Although in that regard Camden is much safer than a small town in North Carolina. We even have a Gay and Lesbian Alliance. Fiona goes to their meetings sometimes—she's interested in advancing equality for every Camden student. She tries to get me involved, too, but I always find reasons to politely decline.

The thought of cracking open my chest and pouring out my life story to a bunch of strangers makes me want to run as far away as my legs will take me, no matter how sympathetic Fiona promises they'll be.

Instead, I prefer the company of books. It's a perfect relationship, really. A book will always open and let you in. You can close it anytime you wish. There's no need for awkward social interactions, and the words inside won't judge you or ask more of you than you can give.

I suppose books can lie or mislead, too, but you can't blame them for it. It's the fault of the people who wrote them—or edited them, especially after the fact. We form our opinions on books based on their most recent available edition, even when those editions might differ greatly from what the author originally intended. Books aren't really written in stone; they change all the time. That's why conservation is so important. It's the only way to preserve all points of view, to protect narratives from meddling by anyone with a quill and an agenda. An archivist wields a lot more power than people realize. While they cannot travel back in time, they *can* change the way history is viewed by future generations, elevating certain figures and their accomplishments and completely erasing others, like their existence doesn't merit even a footnote. Sadly, all too often, the same kinds of people get pushed beyond the margins of history, their stories truncated, their identities rewritten. Without our society putting in the extra effort to protect them, nothing will change.

Speaking of protecting books, I scan the crowd for Dr. Kowalski—I really need to talk to him before all the library jobs are filled. But I don't see him. Instead, my gaze is drawn to a solitary figure standing by the wall at the far end of the theater, half engulfed in the shadows. I squint, curious.

He looks to be in his mid-twenties—a new grad student, maybe? Camden is not a big school; after a while, most faces become familiar, and I wouldn't have forgotten his. There's a sharp grace to his features, like that of a wolf. An untamed wildness that doesn't belong here, which creates the illusion of movement even though he's standing still.

His right shoulder leans against the wall as he gazes into the crowd, seemingly searching for someone as well. For a moment, I have this deranged idea that it might be me.

Just as that thought crosses my mind, as though I've pulled some invisible string, the stranger's head whips in my direction—and no matter how embarrassed I should feel for being caught staring, I can't look away from him. A peculiar feeling whispers across my skin, a hushed sigh against my throat.

The shadows must be playing tricks on my eyes because it feels like the distance between us has shrunk, and I find myself impossibly closer, pulled toward him by an irresistible force. I can even make out his features as though someone had magnified them. Dark eyes, slender nose, a wisp of jet-black hair grazing his high cheekbone. His lips part in silent surprise, and he tilts his head, birdlike, examining me. His stare is so intense that I wonder again if it's me he has been searching for this whole time—although of course that isn't possible because I don't know this out-of-place, strikingly beautiful person. How *could* I know him?

Suddenly, the house lights go out, and his face is obscured. Distracted, I glance at the stage; Dean Wilkins is walking up to the lectern. I turn back, wanting to sneak another look at this strange man, but with profound disappointment, I realize that the space where he stood is now empty.

I exhale with a shudder, weirdly dizzy. What the hell was that? I feel like I just had a particularly vivid daydream.

At the lectern, Dean Wilkins tests the microphone by tapping it unnecessarily loudly. The resulting shrill makes me wince.

"Good afternoon, everyone!" she says cheerfully, satisfied that the microphone is indeed capable of damaging the hearing of the entire school. "Let me start by saying how excited I am to welcome both our new and returning students, as well as our esteemed faculty, back to Camden, our elite institution and the top university in the state of Vermont. For two hundred and three years, Camden has been home to generations of scholars and researchers aspiring to reach new frontiers of knowledge. But of course, while academics are important, they aren't everything. We want you to have a fulfilling experience in your studies *and* extracurriculars during your time with us."

Occasionally interrupted by applause, Dean Wilkins prattles on about the events the school has planned for the fall semester, such as homecoming, family weekend, and a variety of academic competitions. Most of them are the same as last year. Few things change in a place where even the walls are older than the state of Vermont. I can't help but tune out the twenty-minute speech, letting my thoughts drift back to the mysterious man. Who is he? He certainly looked too young to be a professor. If he's in grad school, chances are I'll see him on campus again. We might even be in some of the same classes.

I shake my head. Why am I suddenly so excited about the prospect of being in the same room as some guy who caught me staring at him? I tell myself that would be awkward, that it would be best to avoid him. Or I try to, but it doesn't work because when I recall his gaze, the space-warping intensity of it, I feel a shiver at the nape of my neck.

"And last but not least," Dean Wilkins says, finally wrapping up her speech, "student safety remains this institution's utmost priority. Drinking on campus will not be tolerated. Buying alcohol with a counterfeit government ID is a federal crime and will result in expulsion." The message seems to be aimed mostly at the crop of wide-eyed freshmen, away from their parents' supervision for the first time and ready to party till they're dead. But nobody seems to take the dean's words seriously. There's a reason Camden is known as a party school. What else is there to do when you're surrounded by mountains with no entertainment and no major cities within an hour's drive? Campus security never does anything worse than wag their fingers. Mads Jr. and his cohort are prime examples of that. If Camden ever got serious about enforcing the no-drinking rule, they'd put every liquor store in the valley and the sole bar downtown out of business.

"And," Dean Wilkins continues, "I strongly urge you not to throw any parties in the woods, either. I know some of you have romantic notions about escaping into the wilderness to have private intimate liaisons"—several students snicker at that choice of words—"or to partake of illegal substances, but I must remind you that black bears are very active during the fall. Local authorities are still on high alert after a hiker went missing in the mountains last week. We will keep that person in our prayers, but for the sake of yourselves and this school's two-hundred-year-old reputation, do *not* get mauled by a bear."

Some students begin to whisper, disturbed by the news of a person going missing near Camden, but quite a few of them laugh as though getting eaten by a hungry bear is hilarious. Dumbasses.

After Dean Wilkins dismisses the assembly, I finally link up with Fiona on my way to Gothic literature. Sadly, it's the only class we're taking together. I have too many art history courses to get through, and her prelaw curriculum is insanely packed. Together, we cross the large green space in the center of campus until we reach Kinnell Hall, which houses the humanities departments. It has a copper roof, bright green with a patina, and a maroon brick facade, although most of it is invisible under vast swaths of verdant Boston ivy. There's a bit of a commotion in the adjacent parking lot. Several students are eyeing a brand-new car, a Jaguar blacker than a raven at midnight. Even I do a double take. Given the number of wealthy students here, there's no shortage of cool cars in Camden. Mads Jr. drives a Firebird, and his buddy Grady Callahan has a fiery-red Testarossa. But honestly, both of those look cheap and pretentious compared to the timeless elegance of this Jag.

Fiona snorts beside me, and I realize I've totally frozen on the steps of Kinnell Hall, ogling the car. "Didn't know you cared about fancy whips."

"I don't," I say, making a show of hurrying to the massive

green double doors under a white gabled portico. "I've just never seen one of those before. I wonder who it belongs to."

"Some privileged asshole," Fiona replies sardonically.

My admiration for the Jag deflates a little. She's probably right. Still, I sneak one more glimpse at it before pushing the doors open and stepping inside.

We look for the room for Gothic lit, which turns out to be a big amphitheater-style auditorium on the first floor—way bigger than needed to accommodate the dozen or so students. Gothic lit is an elective, and no major is required to take it. Only language geeks and people who like Dr. Kowalski will have signed up for it. It's strange that they put us in this room. I honestly prefer the smaller and cozier spaces most of my other classes are in, with oval tables and wood paneling on the walls and old paintings of people in ridiculous white powdered wigs.

As Fiona and I decide where to sit, I spot a familiar figure in ripped jeans and a varsity jacket all the way in the corner of the top row, slumped in a chair and dozing off. Eric. Fucking. Stockton.

Anger flares up in me. "What is *he* doing here?"

Fiona frowns. "I don't know. But don't let it rattle you, Jonathan."

Don't let it rattle me? Like that's possible. Eric Stockton is the number one reason for the utter misery that was my summer.

The story goes like this: Camden's Rare Books Collection has a prestigious internship that takes place during the historic research symposium that is held every summer. I became eligible for the position after finishing my freshmen year, so of course, I applied immediately. It wasn't just perfect for my résumé and my future career; it also—amazingly—paid money. Book conservation is largely an apprenticeship-based industry. It's hard to find jobs without knowing the right people—collectors, researchers, and museum curators. The internship would've been a great way to start making those vital connections.

Dr. Kowalski assured me that the job was all but mine. I was the most qualified candidate, and I had his recommendation, which was key. Or so I naively thought. Because then, at the last moment, the internship went to Eric Stockton, a mind-boggling travesty of a choice. Eric couldn't care less about any books, let alone rare ones. There was absolutely no way he was qualified for the internship, and yet...

"Why?" I asked Dr. Kowalski, shell-shocked by the news. I was sitting across the desk from him in his office.

Dr. Kowalski shuffled the papers in his hands for a moment, then glanced at the door to make sure it was closed. Looking apologetic and uncomfortable, he said, "I'm sure you know that Eric's parents are major donors to this institution." He let the sentence hang in the air meaningfully.

I let out a bitter huff. Who could miss the giant bronze plaque with their name on it hanging right by the entrance to Kinnell Hall? It was just the tackiest possible thing to stick next to the name of a Pulitzer-winning poet.

Dr. Kowalski continued, "I hope I can count on your discretion, Jonathan. Please don't repeat this to anyone, but Mrs. Stockton thought spending a summer surrounded by books would do Eric a world of good."

I nearly choked on a laugh. Being *near* books doesn't make you smarter! You have to actually *read* them, which wasn't something I'd observed any of the legacies do during my tenure as Mads Jr.'s roommate. They partied, they drank themselves into oblivion, and they slept with every pretty girl who sought to improve her social standing by hooking up with elite jerks.

I hung my head but couldn't muster anything to say.

Dr. Kowalski's voice softened. "You're right to find this unfair, Jonathan," he said in a way that felt more parental than anything I'd heard in a long while. "I know how hard you've worked for this. But it's done; we can't change it. Take this advice from someone who's been steeping in academic circles for half a century—not everything is based on merit. There's always money and internal politics at play. You're going to have to navigate both if you intend to continue on this path. You understand?" He waited until I slowly quelled the raging storm of resentment inside me and nodded.

"Don't take any of this to heart. There's always next year. I'll certainly recommend you again, and I can help facilitate a work-study arrangement with the library in the fall semester. You will be eligible for it based on your financial situation. I know it's not quite as prestigious as the internship, but it will look good on your résumé and will get you closer to your career goals. All right?"

I nodded again and tried to be a little more optimistic. But by the time I lost the internship, all the decent summer jobs in the valley were already spoken for. That's how, instead of living my dream, I spent last summer behind a register at a grimy gas station, consoling myself with hopes of a brighter future. Next semester. Next year. All I had to do was wait for my second chance...while the rich pricks of the world took whatever they wanted from whomever they wanted.

"Why the hell is Eric here?" I repeat through gritted teeth as Fiona and I claim two neighboring chairs in the middle of the second row.

She shrugs. "If I had to guess, the same reason I am. It's an elective, and Dr. Kowalski teaches it. Stockton probably thinks he can coast through his class."

Unlike Eric, Fiona doesn't expect an easy A from Dr. Kowalski; she genuinely likes his classes. That's why she added Gothic lit as an elective, even though her schedule was already full. I really like Dr. Kowalski too. The man knows endless obscure literary anecdotes, making books seem less like out-of-context abstract creations and more like extensions of the authors' lives. Not like Eric Stockton cares about that. Even now, he's still passed out in his chair. Probably partied all weekend. I grimace at the gross injustice of it all but bite my tongue and pull my notebook out of my backpack.

For the next five minutes, more students trail in—as expected, there are just over a dozen of us total. I thought Dr. Kowalski would be here by now, but when the clock above the blackboard ticks past one p.m., the professor's desk remains empty. I start to feel a little nervous.

Then, moments later, the auditorium door swings open, but it's not him who walks in. I gasp—it's the strange man I saw in the theater earlier. He looks even more striking in broad daylight. He's wearing all black, a chic tailored ensemble that looks like it's come straight off the cover of *GQ*. His sharp cheekbones, raised chin, and confident stride all contribute to his air of prideful authority.

"Who is he?" I whisper to Fiona.

"No idea. A student?" she suggests, a curious wrinkle between her eyebrows.

Except the stranger doesn't take a seat among us. First, he goes to one of the big, sashed windows on the left side of the room and opens it. The old wooden frame creaks and a cool breeze rushes in, carrying with it the smell of early fall. Then, still without saying a word, he glides over to the blackboard, picks up a piece of chalk, and writes a name in the most exquisite, elegant cursive I've ever seen.

"Good afternoon," he says, turning around to face us. There's a melodic, almost noble quality to his voice, and an accent— British, I think, though it sounds mixed with something else. Wait... Why is he introducing himself? Briefly I wonder if maybe he's Dr. Kowalski's graduate assistant. That would explain his presence here. But then he continues, "My name is Dacian Bathory. I will be teaching Gothic literature this semester."

My jaw drops. Did I miss an instructor change announcement? But how could that be? Dr. Kowalski has taught this class for years! Shocked, I glance at Fiona, but she only shrugs, not nearly as surprised by the situation as I am. Meanwhile, Mr. Bathory strolls over to the professor's desk, takes a sheet of paper from his shiny black briefcase, and begins roll call.

A din of worries erupts in my mind. Did something happen

to Dr. Kowalski? He never picked up the phone, even though I called his office several times. I haven't seen him around campus today, and now he's not even teaching his class. This is not good news for me. With difficulty, I force myself to calm down. No point in agonized speculation—I'll just have to find out after class. There's got to be a reasonable explanation for this.

I shift my attention back to Mr. Bathory as he makes his way down the list of students, calling each name and then staring at each face for several uncomfortably long seconds in an apparent effort to memorize who is who.

Despite my sudden despair, there's also a part of me—a small, treacherous part—that is unexpectedly delighted by the chance to be near this man. We ended up in the same class after all, just not the way I thought. And I'm not the only one who's feeling this way. Three girls whose names come before mine on the roster don't even bother to hide their excitement from him as they chime, "Here!" and "Present!" It's like their interest in Gothic literature has suddenly quadrupled because of the hot new professor who is a lot younger and more attractive than Dr. Kowalski.

To his credit, Mr. Bathory doesn't dignify the extra attention with any kind of reaction. He doesn't even appear to notice it. Despite the quiet, unbreakable intensity of his gaze, there's an air of aloofness about him. Although it's not that he seems arrogant or bored; it feels more like an intentional barrier, like a moat around a medieval castle. You can come in, but only if you've been invited by the lord. Otherwise, into the water you go.

It won't be long before he gets to my name. The inexplicable thrill at the prospect of him saying it, of him looking at me, catches me off guard. My cheeks heat in anticipation. Why am I reacting to him like this? He isn't the first good-looking guy I've met. Although, to be honest, good-looking is quite an understatement. I don't think I've ever seen anyone this attractive before. To my embarrassment, Mr. Bathory's gaze flickers to me, just for a breath, as though he somehow knows what I'm thinking. Of course, I realize that isn't possible, but my pulse flutters nonetheless. Our eye contact is brief, and then he looks down at his paper.

He pauses. He stares at my name for several unbearably long seconds, and then, for some unfathomable reason, his striking features form a grimace of displeasure as though my name has deeply offended him. The hostile reaction is so obvious and swift that it completely takes me aback. I am instantly confused and self-conscious.

"Mr. Evergreen?" he finally says without looking up at me, sounding like he's struggling to hold back anger. No *Jonathan*. Just *Mr. Evergreen*, even though he called everyone else by their first and last name.

A heartbeat passes. I squirm in my seat like a bucket of ice water has been dumped over my head. I can't believe this. He still won't look at me. What on earth did I do wrong? Is he allergic to my name? Beside me, Fiona nudges my elbow to bring me out of my spiraling thoughts.

"I'm here," I reply belatedly.

Mr. Bathory schools his expression into something neutral, but he still doesn't glance at me before moving on to the next student, as though he doesn't need to remember my face. I wrack my brain for what I could've done to provoke such an unkind reaction. Did I anger him when he caught me staring in the theater? He didn't seem to mind it at the time. He even held my gaze. Like we had a moment. I recall that strange whispering sensation that swept over my skin. His eyes felt like they were so close to mine. I was completely enthralled, like I could've fallen into them with the slightest push, eager to enter his abyss...

Now I'm mortified. I don't know what came over me. I guess this is what happens when you read too many books: your imagination spins out stories that have no basis in reality, and then they come crashing down like a house of cards. How long could we possibly have stared at each other across the giant orchestra section, anyway? I was just caught up in my own musings, and he probably decided I was rude to gawk at him like that. Or worse, he was bothered because, well, I'm a guy. Still, isn't it a bit much to not even call me by my name? There is no way he isn't used to people's attention with the way he looks.

As I stew in my ruined expectations, Mr. Bathory goes through the rest of the class roster like nothing has happened. Like my very existence is insignificant to him. Finally, he calls on Eric, who has yet to lift his head off his desk. "Mr. Eric Stockton?" For a second, there's no reply, only a muffled giggle in the row behind me. "Mr. Stockton?" Mr. Bathory repeats louder, directing his words at Eric's slumbering shape.

One of the students hisses, "Hey, Stockton, wake up." More giggles follow.

That jerks Eric out of his afternoon siesta. "What?" he drawls, his voice grating. He pushes his spiky blond hair, à la Billy Idol, out of his barely-awake face. With nearly comedic slowness, his eyes focus on Mr. Bathory, and a realization dawns. "Who're you? Where's Dr. Kowalski?"

Unbelievably, Mr. Bathory remains impassive at Eric's complete lack of decorum, save for a tiny sharp glint in his eyes that's gone as quickly as it appears. "Dr. Kowalski has retired," he informs the class in a flat tone.

Eric's mouth drops open. "No freaking way!"

And as much as I detest him and his entitled attitude, I can't help but agree with the sentiment. What the hell? How could Dr. Kowalski retire? Why didn't he tell me he wasn't planning to come back? He was my advisor! Come to think of it, the dean mentioned nothing about this in her speech, either. She always gives honorary send-offs to retiring faculty members, especially those who've been with the school for several decades. Maybe Dr. Kowalski's retirement was sudden, and no one was expecting it. But what could've brought it on? Is he ill?

Ignoring Eric's rudeness and maintaining the same aloof demeanor, Mr. Bathory confirms my suspicion. "From what I know, it was a last-minute decision motivated by personal reasons that I am not privy to. I was merely invited to teach this class in the wake of Dr. Kowalski's departure. Now, if there are no more questions—" he stands up and rounds his desk as his dark gaze sweeps over the auditorium with the authority of a ruler establishing his domain "—I shall begin. Gothic literature has fascinated readers since the late eighteenth century, with its looming castles, haunted red rooms, and inescapable dungeons, its ghostly apparitions, flying helmets, and monsters born and made. But why are we so drawn to stories of the macabre? Is it the mystery of the unknown? Of supernatural occurrences our rational minds cannot explain? Is it the pleasure of a thrill that makes the hair on your neck rise with a tantalizing shiver? Or is it perhaps the allure of the darkness, the secret desire for the forbidden that mesmerizes the soul and ensnares the heart? 'Words have no power to impress the mind without the exquisite horror of their reality.'"

Mr. Bathory leans against his desk, effortlessly quoting famous literary works and authors in that melodious voice of his, but I'm having a hard time following. My mind is in a tailspin. Dr. Kowalski is gone. My one faculty ally at this institution is no more.

I sink deeper into my chair. This year was supposed to be different, a new beginning for me. I was supposed to get my foot in the door and get my dream internship and a work-study job at the library. But once again, my plans crumble before I can turn them into reality.

THREE

"That was amazing," Fiona says as we exit the auditorium after class.

"Was it?" I say dejectedly.

"He was quoting entire passages *from memory*. I don't even think he had notes. I've never seen anything like that."

Mr. Bathory didn't have notes. He spent an hour talking about decades of Gothic works like he'd memorized entire texts. When someone asked him about the reading list for the semester, he was surprised, like he didn't know we needed one—then made one up on the spot. It was like this teaching job had been sprung on him at the last moment. Maybe the school has had a hard time finding a replacement for Dr. Kowalski.

"He might have a photographic memory," I say, unimpressed, as we continue down the hallway toward the back exit, which is closest to the dining hall. I'm done for the day, while Fiona has a free hour before her next class, and neither of us has had lunch yet. Although I really don't feel like eating right now. I'm just tagging along until I figure out what to do with my life.

"What was he quoting, anyway? I think I caught something from *Jane Eyre*," Fiona says.

I furrow my eyebrows. "The first one was Poe. But I'm not

sure about the others." There were too many quotes and literary references to keep track of, and I was too distracted to pay attention.

I open the doors, and we step out of Kinnell Hall.

"Mr. Bathory has gotta be some kind of literary genius," Fiona muses as we weave through crowds of students, following a tree-lined path toward the dining hall. "He seems so young, too—not to mention hot."

"I knew it!" I say accusingly. "It's not his intellectual ability you're really impressed by, is it?"

"Who says one has to negate the other? You can be both hot *and* smart." She grins.

I sigh. Everyone in the class, even her, is fawning over Mr. Bathory. I would be, too, if it wasn't for his intense, inexplicable dislike of me. And I'm still thinking too much about him when I should be preoccupied with my employment prospects.

My gloom must show on my face because Fiona asks, "Are you worried about Dr. Kowalski?"

"Don't you think it's odd that he retired so suddenly?"

"Well, he *is* old," Fiona says, not overly concerned.

I frown. "But shouldn't he have said something to me? He's my advisor."

Her tone turns sympathetic. "I know you really like him. I'm gonna miss him too. But if he decided it was time to go, there's nothing we can do. I'm sure the department has assigned you to someone else by now."

They probably have, but that offers little consolation to me. Fiona doesn't understand how big of a deal this is. It will be a complete clusterfuck trying to explain my self-designed major to whoever takes over for Dr. Kowalski. Besides, he was supposed to help me land the work-study at the Rare Books Collection. Without his help, I'll probably end up working in the cafeteria again, or in the mail room. Neither of those will do anything for my résumé, or my post-graduation employment prospects.

But the work-study isn't the only reason I'm so upset. Dr.

Kowalski was more than an advisor to me. He knew my situation, and I thought he genuinely cared. When I told him about my dreams of working in book conservation and that I had no family to fall back on, he seemed really moved by it...but now he's gone without a word.

Why am I even surprised? Doesn't this always happen to me in the end? People I care about just leave.

Fiona adds, "I'm sure whoever your new advisor is, they'll help you figure it out. It's their job."

I nod without conviction.

So much for trying to avoid the registrar's office on the first day. When I arrive there after lunch, the line stretches out the door and loops around the building. After half an hour of trying to stave off a headache from the crowd's noise, I wait at the counter as a tired-looking lady quickly flips through my file. Then my already-bad day goes completely to hell.

"Looks like you've been assigned to...oh, there it is. Your new advisor is Mr. Dacian Bathory," she says.

The room tilts sideways.

"What?" I ask, not comprehending.

"Dacian Bathory. His office is in Kinnell Hall, room 207. Would you like directions?"

I shake my head numbly. I don't need directions to that room —he even took Dr. Kowalski's office!

"This has to be a mistake," I plead, leaning on the counter. "Mr. Bathory can't be my advisor. He just started teaching here."

The woman's face turns annoyed. "I'm sorry, but we don't make these decisions. If you have concerns, you should take it up with your department." She shuts my folder with a little too much force and shouts "Next!"

There is no point in arguing with her. I swallow my objections and force out a bitter thank-you before shuffling away.

Dismayed, I cut through the crowds and march out of the building to get some fresh air. What am I going to do now? Keeping Mr. Bathory as my advisor is out of the question. He doesn't even know the school, let alone my curriculum. But replacing Dr. Kowalski's replacement means I'll have to make an appointment with the head of the department or the dean. Either option will take days, if not weeks—at which point I can pretty much say goodbye to work-study at the library. With a sour feeling in my stomach, I realize that I don't have much choice. I'm going to have to deal with this new professor. But remembering the barely-contained anger I felt from him makes me want to shrink inside myself. What are the chances I just imagined it, or that he'll treat me differently if he knows he's my advisor? I'm not bursting with hope, but I'll have to try.

I trek all the way back to Kinnell Hall and climb the stairs to the second floor, where Dr. Kowalski's office is. As luck would have it, Mr. Bathory is still around. I find him standing by his office door in conversation with the Dean. He doesn't see me immediately, his black-clad shape turned away from me, a striking vision against the plain whiteness of the walls. It would be rude to interrupt them, so I wait just out of earshot.

I lean against the wall, trying to keep my gaze on an old portrait of some guy in a gray wig—probably one of the school's first professors—but it fails to hold my attention. It's like trying to ignore a ringing phone; all I can think about is picking up the receiver. I give up resisting and once again find myself drawn to watching Mr. Bathory.

His body language is approachable but reserved, like it seemed in class. He's listening to Dean Wilkins intently, and there's a polite, exquisite smile on his face, expertly placed there as though to entice the dean to tell him everything. And the dean...well, Dean Wilkins is having the same reaction to him as every student in class, including myself. I wonder if Mr. Bathory knows hypnosis. Or does he command such rapt attention simply by being so attractive?

Or is it something else, something deeper? Even though I'm not his intended audience, the more I watch him, the harder it is to look away. It's like I'm being pulled toward him by some sorcery. My gaze traces the lines of his mouth, the sharp angle of his chin, his long, dark eyelashes. The oversized cut of his blazer, although stylish, somewhat obscures his physique, but it's still easy to imagine the lean muscle underneath that silky black fabric, the strength concealed within. Unmoored, my thoughts drift to him, seeking, wandering—

I snap out of it once I realize that a pair of dark intense eyes is now boring into mine—the same eyes that just a moment ago were focused on the dean. While I was daydreaming, Dean Wilkins left, and for the second time today, I've been caught unabashedly ogling Mr. Bathory. A swift succession of emotions flashes across his face, too quick and complicated for me to decipher. It doesn't warrant the labor anyway because he presses his mouth into a hard, furious line, slams the door to his office, and, without saying a word, strides down the hall away from me.

For a heartbeat, I'm too stunned to say anything. What on earth did I do? Why is he so mad at me? My lips open and close soundlessly like a fish as he continues to move farther from me. But then I remember why I came to his office in the first place and take off after him.

"Mr. Bathory, I need to talk to you," I say to his back. But he doesn't slow his step. It's an effort to keep up with him.

"I have an urgent matter to attend to," he says brusquely.

"It'll only take a moment!" I plead, but it's in vain.

His shoulders stiffen as though he's holding back some unspeakable anger, and he just keeps walking. "Not now," he grits out, seething. Then he rounds the corner and patters down the stairs, the hem of his silky blazer fluttering behind him, while I'm left to watch his disappearing silhouette, utterly speechless.

If I had any doubts left after class, they've now been burned in a blaze and turned to ash. For reasons I can't even begin to comprehend, Dacian Bathory positively hates my very existence.

FOUR

I have a recurring dream that started after Clay's letter went missing.

Although maybe it's more accurate to call it a nightmare.

I'm asleep in my bed when I feel someone's cold presence beside me. When I open my eyes, my room is dark, but I can see Clay standing quietly at the foot of my bed, his beautiful silhouette framed by a translucent glow. My heart twists, and I want nothing more than to reach for him, to tell him how much I miss him, how some days I want to howl from all the emptiness in me, a human-shaped crater in my soul. But Clay doesn't see me. His gaze is stubbornly fixed on the box of letters on my bedside table. *His* letters. That's what he's here for. Then, slowly, without saying a word, he turns to face me. I shudder. His eyes, which used to be so warm, are now lifeless and utterly devoid of emotion. Like there's barely any Clay left in them.

I wait, my body leaden, even though I already know what's coming.

The most unsettling thing about this dream that haunts me night after night is that Clay never says anything to me. He just stares. And stares. And stares. And the box continues to lie on the table between us, an all-seeing judge in this silent standoff, as minutes tick away, swallowed by the void of eternity.

It's me who eventually breaks. Always me.

"I'm not giving them back!" I tell him for the millionth time. My lips tremble. But he doesn't take no for an answer. Instead, the room becomes so cold that my breath turns into clouds of icy vapor. Tremors rattle my body as I press my back into the headboard, but there's nowhere to hide from him. A chill starts to crawl across my neck like someone is winding an invisible rope around it with gentle but determined fingers—not tight enough to choke, but firmly enough to remind me of the price of keeping these letters. The price I didn't pay.

I wake up. My mouth is open, and my throat aches as though I've been screaming for hours. For one blurry moment I swear he's still standing there, right by the foot of my bed, watching, waiting. I snatch the box with letters off the bedside table and cradle it in my arms. "I won't burn them. I won't," I repeat over and over again.

I keep my eyes on the box and count my breaths until they slow, until the mad thrumming of my heart ebbs. Only then do I dare to peek at the space in front of me. I exhale. Clay is no longer there, just the moonlight streaming through the window. *It was only a dream*, I tell myself as I work on unclamping my arms from the box. Gently, I place it back on the side table next to my clock radio.

It's barely past five a.m., but I doubt I'll be able to fall back asleep. So I flick the lamp on and drag my sluggish body to my desk, where I pull my heavy art history textbook off the shelf and open it to the first chapter. I need a distraction. I rub the last dregs of sleep from my eyes and force them to concentrate on the lines of text, trying not to glance at the spot where Clay stood earlier.

"ARGH, I feel like my brain is melting," Fiona grouses, shutting her gigantic psychology textbook with a thump. We're sitting on a blanket on the university's big green, the grass a soft cushion underneath. There's an early autumn bite to the breeze coming down from the mountains, but the afternoon sun is warm on our faces. Fiona likes to take advantage of this space to have lunch or catch up on reading before the weather starts to turn. There won't be any studying outside once there's a foot of snow on the ground or buckets of rain pouring down every day.

"Do you wanna go scope out the library and the bookstore to see which books from Mr. Bathory's reading list we can find? Whatever the library doesn't have we can split—you buy half, and I'll get the other half, and we'll trade. We always read ahead anyway. I think it'll be easy to coordinate," Fiona says.

I can't help but feel moved by Fiona's valiant attempt to help me. She knows that buying a dozen books for an elective class is not financially feasible for me. She really is a good egg, but...

"I think I'm gonna drop out of his class," I say, keeping my gaze on a couple of students playing Frisbee by the large maple tree in front of us. Its canopy is already covered in splotches of bright red, a sign that there won't be many more sunny days like today.

"What? Why?" There's shock in Fiona's voice.

"It's just..." I pause, unsure how to explain without sounding too melodramatic. "I'm pretty sure he doesn't like me," I confess.

Fiona's eyebrows rise. "You think Mr. Bathory doesn't like you? Based on what?"

I repress the sudden urge to curl up on the blanket, squeeze my eyes shut, and forget the world exists. "A lot of things. He didn't call me by my name. He said everyone else's first and last names when he took attendance, but he only used my last name." I feel slightly ridiculous admitting that out loud. "Then, when I went to talk to him about being my new advisor, he totally blew me off."

Fiona rolls her eyes in disbelief. "That's it? Are you serious?"

I nod.

"He was too busy to talk to you and stumbled over your name, and now you're convinced he hates you?"

When she puts it that way, it sounds rather insignificant. But it wasn't. I was there. I saw the way he regarded me like he could barely stand the sight of me, like he found my presence deeply offensive.

Fiona sighs. "Ever tried having a Nigerian last name?" she deadpans. "Do you know how many people get it wrong or just downright refuse to try and pronounce it? If I assumed they all hated me, my life here would be exponentially more difficult, not to mention miserable."

I feel a stab of guilt. Fiona's mother, Angelina Onayemi, kept her last name after marrying Fiona's father and insisted on passing it on to her daughter because she wanted Fiona to grow up a strong, independent woman who was proud of her Nigerian heritage and took no shit from men. My parents' only inspiration for my name was the Bible, unless you count Uncle Jon on my mother's side, whom I personally never saw sober. And my last name is as straightforward as you can get: Evergreen. We're named after a tree.

"I'm sorry," I say quietly. "Mr. Bathory pronounced it right, though."

Fiona huffs out a laugh. "And he's literally the only professor who has gotten it on the first try! So by your logic, the entire Camden faculty hates me."

"Of course they don't," I say. I should have known not to debate with Fiona—she always wins. And she doesn't even have her law degree yet. I'd be terrified to encounter her in the courtroom.

"Then why would you make assumptions about whether people like you?" she asks.

"I don't know." I shrug dejectedly.

"I'm guessing you haven't tried to talk to him since?"

"Nope," I say. In fact, I've spent the last couple of days

avoiding the section of Kinnell Hall where his office is like the plague.

Fiona lets out a long sigh. "Jonathan, I swear, you're hopeless sometimes. I know you've got a lot going on, and you're basically starting your life over, but it doesn't benefit you to be so defeatist when it comes to people and their opinions of you. You can't just bury yourself in books and assume that nobody likes you. Books are great, but they don't talk back. You have to talk to people."

"Yes, Coach Onayemi," I agree with a mock salute.

"Then start with Mr. Bathory," she says, not letting me off the hook so easily. "You want that library job, and you need an advisor. You've gotta go talk to him. I promise he isn't gonna bite you."

"You don't know that," I protest weakly.

"Yes, I do. If he tries, he won't keep this job for very long."

I chuckle at the silly turn our conversation has taken. But Fiona is right. I can't let something I worked so hard for collapse just because Dr. Kowalski left.

"Thanks," I say, grateful for the mental shake-up.

Fiona offers to walk with me to Mr. Bathory's office so I don't chicken out, but I swear to her that I won't. Of course, that's easier said than done. I avoid going there for at least another hour after we part by coming up with various errands that I absolutely must do right this second, filled with the anxiety that Dacian Bathory's wicked glare induces in me. But in the end, I run out of both excuses and time if I want to make it before his office hours are over. So, with dread, I trudge over to Kinnell Hall.

It's an unsettling feeling, approaching Dr. Kowalski's office but knowing that he isn't there. It's like déjà vu with a surprise twist ending. They haven't even changed the name plaque yet.

The office door is open a fraction, and I peek inside. Sitting at Dr. Kowalski's desk, clad in another black, tailored suit, is none other than Dacian Bathory. The top button of his shirt is undone, revealing his graceful throat and Adam's apple. Dangerously, my eyes want to linger. At this point, I'd wager his entire wardrobe is black, not that it doesn't look exceptional on him. Black is such a strange color—people wear it both to blend into the background and make themselves stand out. I wonder which one Mr. Bathory is trying to do. Although I can't imagine any circumstance in which all heads in the room wouldn't immediately turn toward him, whatever he wears.

His dark gaze is fixed on a book. My eyes widen in surprise—it's Ursula K. Le Guin's *A Wizard of Earthsea*. I suppose just because he teaches Gothic lit doesn't mean he can't read fantasy. And that story has plenty of Gothic elements too. It's about a man with great magical powers whose own dark shadow chases him across the world. Mr. Bathory is so engrossed in it that he doesn't even notice my arrival. I'm awfully tempted to just watch him read for all eternity, but I know better. So I knock.

"Mr. Evergreen?" His eyelashes flutter—I've caught him off guard, and for a moment, he doesn't seem to despise me at all. Or maybe he's just forgotten that he does, distracted by a good story. But that moment doesn't last. He tears his gaze away from me and closes the book with a tense, controlled motion. "May I inquire what brings you here today?"

I can't help but feel that he's holding back anger again, and I have to suppress a desire to run away and avoid this baffling standoff with him. But I can already hear Fiona's voice, chiding me and reminding me why I came here. So I step inside.

The room is emptier than I've ever seen it. Gone are all of Dr. Kowalski's family photos and the framed articles that used to hang on the wall. The air is unusually crisp too. I swear Dr. Kowalski always kept his office at ninety degrees—old people and their arthritis. But now, the big window behind Mr. Bathory is propped open a few inches, letting in the late afternoon mountain breeze. Open windows seem like a quirk of his. I wonder if he does this in the dead of winter too. I clear my throat; I need to focus and not let myself wonder about Dacian Bathory's odd habits.

"Hi, Mr. Bathory," I say, battling to keep my voice steady.

"You've been assigned to be my academic advisor." Whether he likes me or not, advising is part of his job, so I'm hoping he'll at least hear me out.

His perfect dark eyebrows arch slightly. "Have I?"

My stomach quivers. "Yes," I say, trying to not panic. "There should be a folder with my records in one of the drawers over there." I point at the shelves in the lefthand corner, hoping that since they haven't yet changed the name plaque next to the door, they haven't moved Dr. Kowalski's files either.

"Let me take a gander. Do sit down," Mr. Bathory says. He puts aside his book and stands up to search for my records, pointedly avoiding looking at me.

I shuffle to the cushioned chair in front of his desk as his long fingers flip swiftly through the rows of folders. I can't help but release a shaky breath of relief as he retrieves mine. I know Dr. Kowalski took detailed notes; there should be enough in there to fill Mr. Bathory in until I can get a different advisor.

The atmosphere couldn't be more awkward as he returns to his chair and studies my folder. It's strange to be in such close proximity to him. The Gothic lit auditorium is big; there were a good twenty feet between the second row, where I was sitting, and the front of the room. But now, even though I am close to him, it still feels like there is a chasm between us, one he always seems to keep between himself and other people. Even when he was talking to the dean, I could sense it. He's like a dark castle at the top of a snowy mountain, so high that the sun never melts the ice caps, no matter how warm the summer's day. I might as well be gazing at him from another jagged peak. I can almost sense the coldness emanating from his skin. I shiver. I can't make sense of him at all. Where did he come from? Why was he chosen to replace Dr. Kowalski?

I stare at the gold signet ring he's wearing on his left pinkie finger—it's engraved with a figure that has the head of a wolf and the body of a dragon. Such a peculiar symbol. It seems like something that belongs in a fantasy book not unlike the one he was reading before I interrupted him.

"Old family heirloom," he says in his melodic voice as he notices my curiosity.

My gaze snaps up, and his eyes catch mine. "I'm sorry, I didn't mean to—" I don't finish the sentence because there's no denying that I *am* staring. Sometimes, I find it difficult to maintain eye contact, especially with strangers. But for some reason, it's impossible to look away from him. In his eyes, there's an absence of light that I like. It calls to me.

"Your records show that you have a self-designed major. What does this mean?" he asks, not releasing my gaze.

"I—" I feel suddenly tongue-tied, like I'm wading through fog. It takes a moment to hunt down my scattered thoughts and form them into sentences. "I want to preserve and restore rare books, but no U.S. college offers a major in that for undergrads. So Dr. Kowalski helped me design my own curriculum."

As I explain this, something sparks in Mr. Bathory's lightless eyes; the ice caps still don't melt, but for the first time since I glimpsed him in the theater, he looks genuinely curious. "Is that so? And what made you wish to preserve books?" he asks, leaning in.

Something happens then. Maybe it's the quiet, overwhelming intensity of his voice. But I feel lightheaded, like the whole room has blurred and slowly begun to spin, all except for him and me, inexplicably tethered to him.

I don't usually talk about why I chose to pursue book conservation. Only a few people have cared enough to ask, anyway. But for some reason, I want to tell *him*. I want to tell him all my secrets.

Words pour out of me. "Because truth matters. It gets lost if we don't protect it. Books are fragile things, and we must carefully choose who we put in charge of keeping them safe. If an archivist has biases, facts can be distorted or omitted. I want to help preserve the truth, even if what's written in some books is ugly, I want all sides of every story to be represented, not just a privileged few."

"That is…admirable," Mr. Bathory says slowly. It feels like my skin is being wrapped in velvet. *Admirable.* Dimly, in the back of my still-spinning mind, I realize that no one has ever called anything I've done admirable.

"I—" I lick my lips, which are suddenly dry. But before I can utter anything coherent, he looks away again, and just like that, his hold on me is broken.

"So, what advice might you need from me in this noble endeavor, Mr. Evergreen?"

With surprise, I realize that he's giving me an opening and that he isn't going to come up with some crazy excuse to boot me out of his office. Dare I claim victory? I clench my fists, battling anger and embarrassment as I recount the story of the stolen internship and explain how much my future employment depends on having a work-study job at the Rare Books Collection.

A frown creases Mr. Bathory's eyebrows. "If you don't mind my asking, who received the internship in your stead?" I sense a note of discontent in his voice—and more genuine interest.

"Eric Stockton," I reply.

"The one I caught sleeping in my class?" he asks, baffled. "The gentleman who thinks that reading a book a week is too great a burden?"

"Yes, that's him," I confirm with a sigh. "His family wanted him to have the position," I add by way of explanation. I don't repeat what Dr. Kowalski told me about Eric's mom thinking that being surrounded by books would make him smarter, but it's clear Mr. Bathory understands the forces at play.

He glances down at my records again, deep in thought. When he finally sends me off, he no longer sounds like he's holding some terrible, unforgivable grudge against me. "I understand. I will see what I can do," he promises.

Dismissed, I stumble out of his office, still feeling oddly dizzy.

My heart is hammering. That wasn't the horrible disaster I thought it was going to be. Maybe I've even managed to convince him to help me.

I feel so hopeful that I go to the bookstore and fork over four bucks for a new paperback copy of *The Mysteries of Udolpho* by Ann Radcliffe, the first reading assignment for Mr. Bathory's class. All the library editions are checked out, and there's no way Fiona and I can manage with just one copy. It's a massive, six-hundred-page tome. Usually, I wouldn't agree with Eric Stockton on pretty much anything, but it is a big book to finish in just one week, especially considering my late start. So I dive in immediately, trying not to think about what's going to come of my meeting with Mr. Bathory. I don't expect that one conversation has reversed his uncomplimentary opinion of me, but on Friday morning I get a surprise when I check my campus mailbox. In it, I find a letter addressed to Mr. Evergreen, rendered in the most beautiful handwriting I've ever seen.

FIVE

"Guess what?" I say when I meet up with Fiona in the dining hall for dinner on Friday night.

"What?" she asks before taking a bite of a golden, delicious looking grilled cheese.

I can barely contain myself. "I got the job at the Rare Books Collection! Mr. Bathory talked to them on my behalf."

Fiona's mouth stretches into a grin. "Oh my gosh, congrats! Also, I told you so."

I set my tray on the table and sit, looking down. "I can't believe he did that for me."

"I can," Fiona says confidently. "It's his job to help you. Hopefully, this will teach you not to quit before trying. I think this monumental accomplishment calls for a celebration. There's the Welcome Week party tonight. You should come."

"Nuh-uh, I think I'm good." I always try to weasel out of plans that involve being surrounded by a lot of loud, drunk people.

"Come on. It'll be good for you," Fiona insists. "Maybe you'll even meet a cute guy." She wiggles her eyebrows conspiratorially.

The glow of happiness that came from Mr. Bathory's letter

dims a bit. I pick up my fork and stab my spaghetti. "I really don't think that's a good idea."

Fiona narrows her eyes at me. "Don't tell me you're still moping about that prick who broke your heart in high school." As always, she cuts straight to the heart of the matter. But she doesn't know everything.

"No," I protest. "It's not that. You know I'm not a party person. Anyway, since when are you so interested in the Welcome Week booze fest? Isn't it mostly freshmen who go?"

"Yeah, but I already kinda promised my roommate I'd chaperone her," Fiona confesses, putting air quotes around *chaperone*. "But it's also good to be social and have fun once in a while. Also, look at you! You're cute. You're smart. You should have a hot new boyfriend every week!"

My face flushes.

"I mean it, Jonathan. Give yourself some credit. This whole vintage book nerd thing is very charming. Guys would be lining up to date you if you'd just let them."

I want to sink under the table from embarrassment. "It's not really a style choice. I just don't have money for new stuff," I say, conveniently omitting the fact that I'd probably still wear old sweaters and torn jeans even if I won the Megabucks lottery today. "And why don't *you* have a hot new boyfriend every week?"

She gives me a sly look. "Because *I* had plenty of fun on my summer break. And please stop trying to change the subject," she says gently but sternly when I open my mouth to interject. "And before you say that there aren't enough gay or bi guys at this school, you should visit a Gay and Lesbian Alliance meeting and take a good look. There are a lot more members than last year. Chandler is doing a great job organizing."

"I know. I've seen their posters around campus." My cheeks go hot as I remember the image of two guys scantily clad in leather, posing suggestively under the slogan HOMOSEXUAL LIBERATION. I guess that's what happens when an organization is filled with mostly arts majors, half of whom are into punk culture.

"They *are* provocative," Fiona concedes. "But you have to be. Otherwise, everyone will ignore you. Remember how people tried to protest the AIDS lecture they organized last year? And now the school is asking them to host it again for the freshmen. Their initiative for free condoms in the Health Center also caused quite a stir at first, but now that's where everyone goes. Anyway, just stop making excuses and come to the party already. I promise it will do you good."

I sigh and poke at my spaghetti a few more times before reluctantly acquiescing. "Fine."

THIS YEAR'S Welcome Week party is hosted by South Hall. By the time Fiona, her roommate, Becky, and I arrive, it's already packed. The alcohol is flowing, and Def Leppard is blasting from the speakers.

"Wow, they really outdid themselves this year," Fiona shouts, trying to be heard over the music. The common room has been transformed into a dance club. There's even a disco ball and colorful lights hanging from the ceiling. I already want to leave. I know I'm supposed to like this—the obnoxiously loud music, the abundant free alcohol that tastes like paint thinner, all the drunk people dancing like there's no tomorrow—but I don't. I didn't like it as a freshman either. I think I only agreed to come because I was so happy about the letter—and, well, because Fiona insisted.

Fiona is wearing a cute, tight dress with a jean jacket and a sparkly bow in her hair. Becky is also dolled up with teased bangs and neon-pink hoop earrings. She looks so California with her golden tan and wavy hair, like she just came in from the beach. I haven't seen a beach in years, which you could probably tell by looking at my pasty white face as well. And I'm wearing the same red plaid shirt and jeans from earlier today.

We're weaving through the dancing crowd, searching for some friends Fiona is supposed to introduce Becky to, when she spots someone of interest. "Ooh. Look, there's Cody," she tells me conspiratorially and points at the guy next to one of the bowls of spiked punch.

"Cody who?" I ask, confused.

"Cody is a member of the Gay and Lesbian Alliance I keep telling you about," she says with a meaningful look. "He's in the theater program—and he's openly gay *and* single."

Clarity dawns on me. This was Fiona's plan all along.

"Oh my god, he's so cute," Becky chimes in. "You should totally talk to him, Jonathan. He's all alone." She winks at me. I can't believe Fiona roped her roommate into this scheme too.

"I don't think—" I start to say.

But Fiona is already beaming at some girl with a heap of raven hair and a miniskirt. "Hey, Erica!"

"Oh, *heeey*!" Erica waves. Fiona swiftly loops her arm around Becky's and ushers her toward Erica and her group of friends before I can finish my protest. I think all those girls used to live in the same house as Fiona and me when we were freshmen, but this year's housing assignments have spread us all across campus. This party is her opportunity to catch up.

Fiona turns around to mouth *"talk to him"* before getting invested in discussing everyone's party clothes.

I sigh. She's been saying for a long time that she'll help find me a boyfriend should I need a push in that direction. I guess she's decided it's time to start making good on that promise.

But I don't know anything about Cody except that he's gay and in the theater program, which Fiona just told me. I guess she thinks that's enough to make him a perfect candidate, at least to hook up with.

I watch him for a minute. Blond wavy hair, soft manners, preppy pink cardigan in a slim fit. He ladles punch from the bowl into a red plastic cup and holds it gingerly with the tips of his fingers like it's a delicate stage prop. He's very good-looking.

There's no denying it. I should *want* to meet him. Right now, I should be nervously wondering how to approach him, planning what to say so I won't seem awkward and unappealing. But instead, for some reason, I try to imagine what his fingers would look like holding a pen, what his handwriting is like. I doubt it's ornate and elegant like Mr. Bathory's penmanship. Who even writes in cursive anymore? All class assignments have to be typed up these days. Handwriting is a fading art form that belongs in the worn pages of old journals, in hidden compartments of antique secretary desks—not something that makes sense in this century.

I huff out a bitter little laugh and turn away. I'm not talking to Cody. I don't even know why I came here.

Fiona is still chatting with her friends. She seems excited. I don't want to rain on her parade. I can just dip out without her noticing...but I'd feel bad leaving her so soon. Maybe I'll just get some snacks and pretend to give this party a shot so my conscience will be clean when I scamper off back to my room alone.

I locate the snack table at the far end of the common room and make my way toward it. There is another punch bowl and a couple of party-size bags of chips on it. I grab a handful of chips, put them on a paper plate, and lean against the wall to observe the crowd.

You can always tell who the freshmen are—they get drunk the quickest. Released from the tyranny of their parents' watchful eyes, they descend on cheap alcohol like they'll never be allowed to drink again, and most of them have no idea what their limits are. But they seem to be having fun. Good for them, I guess.

There are even more people dancing now. Someone cranks up the volume when "Tainted Love" starts playing, and the heavy synth beat rattles the windows. Most of the armchairs and sofas are occupied by couples making out.

I wish it were that simple for me. I don't know why it's so easy for others to find someone to like and be liked by them in return.

I knew that I was into guys by the time puberty hit, but it was all pretty hypothetical—like knowing what love was from seeing it in movies but without having experienced it myself. Even with Clay, it wasn't instantaneous. We went to the same high school for three years before anything romantic happened. I guess that's to be expected after growing up in the closet, surrounded by small-town small-mindedness and Christian dogma. Clay was everything I was not: the school's star athlete, attractive in every conventional sense. All the guys looked up to him, and all the girls swooned over him. He was worlds away from a quiet book nerd like me until our English teacher assigned us to be pen pals for a senior class project, and our worlds collided. We were supposed to write letters to each other twice a week in order to pass the class. I thought there was no way Clay was going to take it seriously. He didn't have to. The school would never let him fail, even if he didn't write a single page.

But he did write to me.

He was timid at first, which was surprising because he seemed so confident, so sure of himself in front of others, never showing a vulnerable side to anyone. But it didn't take long for him to open up. The assignment was graded on the honor system; we didn't have to turn in any of the letters, so privacy and discretion were guaranteed. Maybe that helped him be honest with me.

When I read his letters, it was like I *knew* him. Like I'd discovered a hidden door that led to the secret garden that was the real Clay, whom nobody else met or even glimpsed. It was all mine. *He* was all mine. And so I poured all of myself onto those pages too.

By the end of September, we were sneaking out to kiss in the abandoned parking lot until my lips were bruised. In October, he climbed through my bedroom window one night when my parents were out of town, and I let him bruise the rest of me.

I was so naive, living in a dream world, like a dashing lover from a forbidden romance novel. But life is different from books. Because in December, we got caught.

I turn to the punch bowl, suddenly feeling a strong urge to down the spiked red liquid, let it scorch my insides. That's the only thing alcohol is good for—reckless annihilation of self. I should know. I tried it last year, the only other time Fiona convinced me to go out. In the throes of heartache, I bought into the idea that it would help me forget. And it did. For an hour.

I think I danced. I even made out with another freshman. It was only when we stumbled into his dorm room and he pressed me against the door, eager to get off before his roommate came back, that my alcohol-induced ability to fake it ran out. Out of the corner of my eye, I saw Clay's pale face watching me from the darkness, and I felt sick to my soul. I shoved the guy away and spent the rest of that night gripping the toilet bowl, vomiting long after there was nothing left inside me.

Forgetting Clay did not work. Replacing Clay did not work either.

I look at the couples around me—they aren't all madly in love, are they? So why can't I be like them and not care? Or be content with caring only a little, just enough not to be alone? But I can't. I don't want crumbs that will never satisfy the hunger I feel inside. I'd rather have nothing at all.

But what if what I want doesn't exist? I was so sure it did when I was with Clay. I *believed* we would have eternity together, that our love was the kind people write about in novels. Instead our forever lasted only slightly less than four months, and then our love crumbled into dust.

Still, even if all that's left of us is a box of letters that haunt my dreams, a memory that aches on rainy days like a broken bone that fused back together wrong, it is mine to carry. And I swear I'll keep it safe inside my own private library of rare things, no matter how much the world wants to destroy it.

I stuff the last greasy, salty chip into my mouth instead of drinking the punch. The momentary urge to self-destruct has passed. It's time to leave.

I push myself off the wall and toss the paper plate into a nearby trash can, but just as I turn for the exit, I catch sight of Grady Callahan, one of Mads Jr. and Eric Stockton's legacy buddies. He's hard not to notice, as he's six feet tall with a raging black mullet and a studded leather jacket. He's by the punch bowl with two full cups, and he's slipping some kind of powder into one of them. You've gotta be kidding me. Why is he here? Didn't the legacies rent a fancy mansion for their fucked-up parties?

I take a deep breath. I really don't want to get involved in this, but my conscience won't let me walk away. Grudgingly, I trail after Callahan as he cuts through the dancing crowd to where Mads Jr. and Eric Stockton are. They are laughing, flanked by some girls. Being the senator's kid, Mads Jr. hasn't managed to ditch the preppy button-up and cardigan for Callahan's edgy rock 'n' roll look. But this year he's bleached his hair and pierced his left ear, probably to rebel against his father's wholesome American family image. I only recognize one girl in the group: Alessandra Lucente. I think she's the daughter of some famous magazine model. She always dresses like she just got off the runway. Maybe she's finally been promoted to Mads Jr.'s chief girlfriend; she's been pining for him since last year. The other two girls are probably freshmen, judging by how tipsy they are. And lo and behold, Callahan is handing the drugged drink to the one with the neon-green scrunchie in her ponytail, the one who looks like a pixie because she's three-quarters of his height.

This time, I don't need punch to make me want to puke. What is wrong with this guy? He look like he's in a rock band, and he can swim in money like Scrooge McDuck. He doesn't *need* drugs to make girls want to sleep with him. He's just using them because he can. For fun.

I grit my teeth and march straight up to them.

"Hey," I say to the girl with the drugged drink, not acknowledging the trio of legacies whose very existence I despise. The faster I get this over with, the faster I can leave. "I saw him slip something in your punch. You really shouldn't drink that."

"Huh?" she asks, confused. I've clearly underestimated how inebriated she already is and how loud the music is blaring.

"He drugged your drink," I shout, pointing at Grady.

I don't bother to look at his face; I just turn to leave the scene, letting the pixie girl and her friend process what's happening. Callahan can deal with the fallout.

"Oh my god!" I hear her squeak behind me. Good. It's dawning on her.

I stuff my hands in my pockets and start to walk away when a large hand grabs my shoulder and yanks me backward. I spin around, nearly losing my balance, and find an acutely pissed-off Grady Callahan towering over me.

"What the fuck, Evergreen?" he barks in my face.

I jerk away. I should've expected that it wouldn't be so easy to extricate myself from this. "Are you seriously asking me that?" I shout back. "Why don't you go back to your mansion instead of trying to drug some naive freshman?"

Despite Grady's intimidating look and our height difference, I'm not that afraid of him; it's probably because he spent so much time in the room Mads Jr. and I shared. We had many verbal spats in the beginning, back when I thought I could maintain some control over my living situation, but eventually, I quit wasting my time. Anyway, none of our altercations ever transitioned into anything physical.

"What did you say to me?" he snarls, his face turning red with fury.

"You heard me just fine," I say defiantly. Then I wrench my shoulder out of his grip and try again to leave. I'm done with this stupid party and these entitled jerks.

But I don't get far. In fact, I don't manage to take a single step because my feet lose contact with the floor. Before I can figure out what's happening, the room tumbles around me like I'm on a roller coaster, and then I crash into a foldout table ten feet from where I started. It topples under me, spilling chips and plastic cups onto my chest and shoulders.

I blink dizzily. What the hell? A pulsating ache spreads across my lower back where it collided with the table. I'm so shocked that for a moment, I'm speechless. Did Callahan just fling me across the room?

I'm still struggling to process what happened when I notice Grady isn't done with me yet. His face contorts into a heinous grimace, and he stalks toward me like a wild beast cornering its prey. The hair on the back of my neck stands up. This doesn't feel right. A Depeche Mode song thumps from the speakers, but the people closest to the scene have stopped dancing and are scrambling to get out of his way. Callahan looks deranged. I've never seen him like this. Is he on drugs?

In a panic, I try to crawl backward, but the overturned table stops me from going anywhere. Callahan continues to advance like he wants to rip my throat out, and when the swiveling party light flickers over him, I swear his eyes flash red. My heart jumps. I'm bracing myself for whatever might come next when suddenly, Mads Jr. pops out from behind Callahan and puts a hand on his forearm.

"Grady, you need to calm down, my man," he says in that magnanimous, charming voice that girls like Alessandra swoon over. He must've inherited it from his politician father. For a moment, Callahan doesn't react, just keeps staring at me, breathing heavily. "Grady," Mads repeats.

"What?" Grady finally growls through gritted teeth.

"Let's not let some government moocher spoil our fun." Mads' arrogant green eyes slide to mine for just a second to bask in my reaction. But I'm still too rattled by what just happened to give a damn.

"Yeah, it's all cool, bro," Eric chimes in, emerging on the other side of Callahan.

Grady's mouth twitches, and he gives me one last *I will kill you* look before Mads Jr. and Eric all but drag him away.

I exhale with a shudder. What in the holy hell was that? Was Grady seriously going to murder me in a room full of people? I don't think even being filthy rich would save him from prison, although I wouldn't want to test that theory. With a grunt, I push myself to my feet. My back aches. At least none of my bones seem broken.

Fiona must have heard the commotion because she rushes up to me. "Oh my god, Jonathan! Are you okay?"

"Yeah, just got in a fight with Callahan." I brush potato chip crumbs off my shirt.

"I saw!" She scowls. "What the hell is his problem?"

"I don't know," I say honestly, shaking my head. "I think I'm gonna head back to my dorm."

Fiona's face falls. "I can't believe that prick ruined your night after I finally convinced you to go to a party." That triggers a twinge of guilt in me, but there's no point in telling Fiona I'd given up on the fun even before Callahan attempted to murder me for ratting him out. "Are you sure you're okay to walk back by yourself, though?" she asks with concern. She glances over her shoulder to check where Callahan's clique is, but they are nowhere in sight.

I give her a small smile. "Don't worry. He isn't gonna chase me across campus to settle the score. They're probably drunk racing his Testarossa in the mountains by now." Which is something the legacies are known for doing during their wild parties. Anyone else would have their licenses stripped by now, but of course, those assholes are immune.

"All right, well, let me know if you need anything." Fiona gives me a tight hug, and I try not to wince.

I wish her a fun rest of the night, leave her with friends, and trudge back to West Hall. I know I told her not to worry, but as I step into the chilly September night, a shiver crawls up my spine. Other than a few students smoking cigarettes outside the dorm, the campus looks deserted. Everyone must be at various parties or the bar downtown. The echo of the music in South Hall fades, and shadows stretch around me as I head down the small walkway that winds past the tree-lined courtyard. I try to stop my brain from replaying the image of Callahan's vicious glare, but the whole thing still feels so surreal. How could he have lifted me off my feet like that? Maybe it was just inertia carrying me—that, or he spent the entire summer lifting weights.

A rustling noise to my right jerks me out of my thoughts. My nerves must be frayed because I jolt to a stop. The noise came from the direction of the dining hall, which is odd. It should be closed at this hour; the lights are off. Despite my better judgment, I peer into the darkness surrounding it. My pulse ticks up. Even though I don't see anyone, an unnerving feeling that someone is watching me latches on to my skin like a cold, wet leech.

"Get a grip, Jonathan. No one's coming after you," I tell myself after an eerie moment of silence, and resume my walk back to my dorm at a much faster pace.

In the distance, I hear the screech of tires against asphalt as a car races away.

Six

As expected, my weekend is uneventful. I spend it nursing my sore back and catching up on my coursework. Finishing the Gothic lit assignment takes up most of my Sunday. I should start reading ahead whenever I have free time to keep up with the long list Mr. Bathory has given us.

I'm almost looking forward to his class now that I know he spoke with the library staff for me. Maybe he doesn't hate me after all. Perhaps he just despises my name. I sigh at the hefty copy of *The Mysteries of Udolpho* in my hands. Jonathan is such a common, boring name. What is there to hate? Maybe it isn't Gothic enough for Mr. Bathory. Would he cringe the same way if I were named Valancourt instead, like the love interest of the kidnapped heroine from this novel? I chuckle to myself. Dacian Bathory, on the other hand, sounds very Gothic. Too conveniently Gothic, if you ask me. Is that even his real name, or did he pick it to match the class's aesthetic? I like the sound of it, though: *Dacian*. Especially the way he said it, with his aristocratic accent.

I wonder what it means. Maybe I could find its etymology in the library, along with something about that wolf-dragon symbol on his signet ring. I don't recall seeing anything like it in any of my art history courses. I make a mental note to investigate before powering through the remaining seventy pages of Ann Radcliffe's novel.

"HOW STRANGE IT IS, that a fool or a knave, with riches, should be treated with more respect by the world, than a good man, or a wise man in poverty!" These are the words that Dacian Bathory opens our Monday class with. He's quoting from the book I just finished reading—*The Mysteries of Udolpho*. Once again, he hasn't brought any notes with him, just a stack of library books. They must be ones he intends to read for pleasure, as none of them are related to this class.

"Did you know that in her time, Ann Radcliffe was compared to the Bard himself?" he continues with a flourish, standing in the center of the auditorium. "She was no less famous than Shakespeare, I assure you. Reverently called the Mother of Gothic, Ms. Radcliffe was the highest-paid and best-selling writer and poet of her time, which was quite an accomplishment for a woman in the eighteenth century. With her fine language and vivid imagination, she held enormous influence over not only her contemporaries but also those who came long after her, including the Bronte sisters, Jane Austen, Lord Byron, and even the master of the macabre himself, Edgar Allan Poe. So why, then, you might ask, is Ann Radcliffe so little known now?

"After publishing five vastly popular novels in the span of just nine years, Ms. Radcliffe suddenly disappeared from the public eye, sparking wild rumors about her fate that could rival the fantastical plots of her own stories."

"What happened to her?" a girl in the front row asks with a mystified frown.

Dacian's mouth curves up into a devious smirk. "No one truly knows. Some speculate that she was driven mad, haunted by ghostly apparitions from her own novels. Others suggest it was the evil doings of her husband—perhaps he forbade her from publishing any further. After all, when she died, he burned Ann's papers as though he didn't want the world to see what was in them."

When Mr. Bathory says this, he glances in my direction. There is exhaustion in his face, as though he didn't sleep well either; perhaps he's plagued by nightmares of his own. But with enormous relief, I see that there's no hostility toward me in his tired eyes.

I honestly wasn't sure what to expect from class today; would he ignore me, or treat me like I did him some terrible injustice? But now I'm convinced that what I said to him at the meeting last Wednesday has changed his mind about me. I need to thank him for speaking to the library on my behalf.

After a brief moment, his gaze returns to the rest of the students, who listen with rapt fascination as he continues to lay out the mystery of Ann Radcliffe's life.

"But perhaps it's the third theory that is most plausible. Despite the abundance of supernatural phenomena in Ms. Radcliffe's books, at their core, her novels interrogate the unfairness of the power structures dominated by men and the abuse of women. It is no wonder they faced heavy criticism from those whom such power imbalances benefitted most. At the time, Gothic romance novels were painted as both frivolous and dangerous to the young and impressionable. Women writers, who now were not only paid for their books but, in some cases, paid more than their male counterparts, were a source of envy and a sign of societal change that many fought to extinguish before it became a blaze of revolution. By the mid-nineteenth century, Gothic romance was almost entirely replaced by Gothic horror, and Ann Radcliff's works slowly descended into obscurity. Now, let us discuss what was so dangerously corrupting about *The Mysteries of Udolpho*."

After class, a line of students, mostly girls, wants to talk to Mr. Bathory. I tell Fiona I'll see her later at the dining hall, resigning myself to waiting patiently. Even though a couple of people dropped the class, probably intimidated by the amount of reading, six enthusiastic new students have signed up. Shockingly, Eric Stockton didn't join the ranks of the dropouts. The jerk once again slept in the back row as Mr. Bathory lectured. He's got to be delusional to think that he can coast through this class without doing any of the work.

After ten long minutes of waiting, it's finally my turn, and I approach Mr. Bathory's desk.

"Mr. Evergreen," Dacian Bathory says with a light lilt in his melodic voice that suggests surprise. It does strange things to my thoughts. I almost forget why I'm here.

"I...I wanted to say thank you for putting in a good word with the library," I manage, amazing myself by not stumbling over the syllables.

"Oh." His perfect eyebrows arch, and he smiles slightly with just the very corners of his mouth. "Do not mention it. Seems to me you are the one who truly deserves the position."

Unexpected warmth spreads through my chest. After everything that happened last semester, it's nice to get some validation. I want to thank him again, but before I can say any more, he adds, "Maybe if you'd been there last summer, a book wouldn't have gone missing from the Rare Books Collection."

I blink, startled. "What do you mean, a book went missing?"

Mr. Bathory's dark gaze flickers briefly to the side. "Regretfully, I was informed that one was stolen from the collection, a truly one-of-a-kind book," he explains.

"That's horrible," I say, appalled.

"I quite agree, Mr. Evergreen."

"Do they suspect who took it?" I ask, hoping that perhaps the perpetrator has been caught.

But Mr. Bathory shakes his head somberly. "Local police and campus security don't seem to have made much progress in their investigation. If it were up to me, such crimes would be punishable by—" He pauses suddenly, and there's a glint in his eyes that bears the sharpness of a thousand blades. My heart skips a beat. His silence stretches for another moment as he sits frozen, consumed by his thoughts, and then he continues, "Whoever the thief may be, they should consider themself lucky that such punishments are not for me to deliver."

I clear my throat. "Well, I definitely won't let anyone steal any books while I'm there," I promise a little too eagerly.

"I trust you will not," he agrees, a surprising fondness smoothing the dangerous edges of his words. It's probably because we're talking about books, which he seems to be quite passionate about, not because of me or my daring declaration. But I quite like hearing him talk this way. It's such a relief that he isn't glaring at me with hatred anymore.

Now that I'm standing in front of his desk, my curiosity about what else this man reads gets the best of me. I glance down, spotting Hesse, Toni Morrison, and even Tolkien in his stack of books. That's quite a variety. Is he reading all of them at once?

"Shouldn't you be somewhere right now, Mr. Evergreen?" he asks.

Right! Fiona is waiting for me at the dining hall, and it's at least a fifteen-minute walk from here. "Sorry. Yes. I should get going," I blurt. "I just...I wanted to tell you that I'm meeting the library director today so she can show me around."

"Then I wish you luck on your first day, Mr. Evergreen," Dacian Bathory says with an enigmatic smile.

A flutter of nervous excitement hits me as I approach the library later that afternoon. Sure, I've been here many times before, but this feels like taking an important step toward getting my dream job after graduation. Most positions in conservation and archiving are based on carefully built relationships. That's why it's so important for me to have this experience on my résumé. It will be an invaluable opportunity to make connections within the industry, as Camden's Rare Books Collection is one of the most visited in the United States. Not to mention that it hosts several annual events that attract scores of researchers and scholars from all around the world.

The special collection takes up the entire east wing of the main library. People often call it the glass box because it's a room within a room: a three-level glass-and-aluminum enclosure that was built in the 1960s to keep sensitive books and manuscripts in a temperature- and humidity-controlled environment.

I make my way across the main floor, furnished with rows of heavy wooden tables, cozy armchairs, and green reading lamps, toward the special collection's circulation desk. A girl with a Duran Duran T-shirt and a side ponytail is working the desk. She dials the special collections director, Ms. Tarnow, who comes out to greet me several minutes later.

Ms. Tarnow is a tall woman with a mop of curly red hair, likely in her late forties. She's dressed in a checkered suit with a little gold pin on the lapel in the shape of an open book. I like her immediately.

"Nice to meet you, Jonathan." She shakes my hand, smiling. "Mr. Bathory spoke highly of you."

A flush creeps up my cheeks. "He did?"

"Indeed. You are very lucky to have such a charming advisor. So young, but he already possesses such a deep knowledge of literature," she says dreamily.

"He certainly does," I murmur, still blushing over the fact that he spoke highly of me. I wonder what he said.

"Shall I show you around?" Ms. Tarnow asks, interrupting my musings.

"I would love that," I say eagerly.

She gestures at the round circulation desk. "You will mostly be stationed here, answering calls and assisting patrons when they need a particular item brought out. For security reasons, only library staff has access to the glass box. We do not allow items in our collection to be checked out, and all research must be done in this reading room. It's part of your job to make sure the materials are handled with due care. Jessi, our other student employee, will fill you in on proper handling procedures and teach you how to use our computerized cataloging system once you officially start."

Jessi, the girl in the Duran Duran shirt, gives me a thumbs-up. I smile at her in return.

"I don't have a lot of hours," Ms. Tarnow continues somewhat apologetically, "so for now, it'll just be three days a week. Are you able to work evenings?"

"Absolutely," I say. "I can take the closing shift if you need me to." In truth, there's no place I'd rather be. Besides, I want all the hours I can get.

"That's great!" She beams. "This time of the semester is a bit slow, but many researchers are coming for this fall's symposium, and we have several classes and exhibits scheduled to start in October that are open to the community, so it'll get a lot more crowded. Now, let me show you the glass box."

Ms. Tarnow leads me to the entrance and shows me the key card entry system. I will be issued my own card once I start. Ms. Tarnow scans hers, unlocking the door, and we go in. Inside, it's noticeably colder and the air smells like old books. It instantly gives me a feeling of comfort, like I've finally returned home after a long journey.

"We have more than eighty thousand manuscripts and documents here, about three linear miles of archival materials collected over the last twenty years," she says proudly. "As you probably know, we have some very special books here: autographed first editions, illuminated manuscripts, rare photographs, and materials related to the history of Camden itself, of course."

"That's amazing," I say, gazing at the rows of shelves.

"It will take you a while to get familiar with where things are located, but the cataloging system will help. Besides, we always have librarians on duty who specialize in various disciplines, and they'll be happy to assist patrons with their research. Just dial them from the front desk if you have any questions."

"Will do," I say dutifully.

"Mainly, your job is to make sure that at the end of each day, every item is undamaged and back in its place."

"Um, Ms. Tarnow," I ask, recalling what Mr. Bathory told me after class, "is it true that a book recently went missing?"

Ms. Tarnow's mouth twists in disappointment. "Yes. It is very unfortunate—the first time something like this has happened since I took this job almost ten years ago." Judging by the tone of her voice, it's clear that Ms. Tarnow considers herself partially responsible.

"Was it very valuable?" I ask.

"You know, not particularly," she says, surprising me, "which makes it all the stranger that someone would steal *that* one. Don't get me wrong, it was one of a kind, but we have titles here that would fetch hundreds of thousands of dollars if they were auctioned off to private collectors. Fortunately, they are not for sale, and we get to keep those books in a place where citizens of any means can read them. Provided they've made an appointment with us, of course. Preferably at least two weeks in advance." She laughs.

I chuckle too. "Do you have any clue who stole the book?" I'm not sure why I'm so curious about it. Maybe it's the fact that Mr. Bathory expressed interest in it.

Ms. Tarnow sighs. "Sadly, there's no real way to investigate."

I frown. "But isn't there security footage?"

"We do have cameras," Ms. Tarnow says, "but the tapes get deleted every two weeks to save money, and we didn't realize something had gone missing until it was too late. You see, the title wasn't on display. It was deemed of modest interest to our patrons and therefore kept in the vault, which is underground, a level below us. So we didn't find out it was gone until someone asked for it. Just between you and me, the contents were a little scandalous."

"What do you mean?" I ask, puzzled.

"Well, the title in question wasn't strictly a book. In fact, it was more of a diary. It seemed to have belonged to a nineteenth-century nobleman, most likely from Eastern Europe, based on the dates and places mentioned in it—although oddly enough, the owner wrote it in English. We never successfully identified who he was, exactly. But a lot of it was centered around a forbidden affair. The nobleman, you see, had a gay lover," Ms. Tarnow clarifies conspiratorially.

"Oh," I say, as my gaze instinctively falls to my shoes.

She mistakes my reaction for embarrassment. "I know, right?"

For a moment, I'm afraid that my face might give too much away. While a fair number of people in Camden know I'm gay, I don't necessarily want to tell the person who just hired me, even if Ms. Tarnow doesn't seem to have a moral objection to it judging by her carefree attitude toward the diary. "Have you read it?" I ask, trying to keep my voice level.

"Oh, no," she says, waving her hand. "As I said, there are thousands of books here; a whole lifetime wouldn't be enough to read them all. I'm merely going off its catalog information and the sample I reviewed back when it first arrived here. But the gay affair wasn't the only controversial aspect. While it was structured like a personal journal, it was full of such occult, fantastical stuff that either the aristocrat who wrote it was an aspiring fantasy author or a true madman."

"Wow. I must admit, I'm really curious," I say, trying to process this information. I've never encountered a book like that before. It's the kind of niche historical stuff that belongs in museums, otherwise it will never survive the brutal churn of history. Not to mention that it's *gay*. "Is there a digital copy I could look at? Even a sample?" I ask.

Ms. Tarnow shakes her head. "Unfortunately, it was never digitized. I keep bugging the IT department to devote more resources to our library. It's the rarest items that should take priority in terms of preservation, but alas, it's already too late for that book. The only thing we have left is a short description of it. Hopefully, whoever has it now will take proper care of it so it may see the light of day again. Speaking of the light of day—or should I say, rather, the absence of it," she adds with a chuckle, "let me show you the vault before I let you go. It's mainly used as additional storage for whatever we can't fit on the shelves in the box, but you will need to access it from time to time. Now, don't be scared—I know closed-off underground spaces make some people uncomfortable, but it's just a room like any other. As far as I know, no one has ever died in it, which cannot be said about some other basements on this campus."

I follow Ms. Tarnow down a set of stairs as she tells me an unsubstantiated but nevertheless juicy legend of a haunted passage that connects the old chapel with the administrative building. Supposedly, it served as a secret meeting space for those who wanted to keep their illicit affairs discreet. That is until some lady turned up dead inside it. I struggle to pay attention to the story, though, because my mind is on the mystery of the missing diary. Who stole it, and why?

Seven

That night I have a peculiar dream, and for once, it isn't about Clay.

I'm wading through a thick fog. I can't see anyone around me, but I know I am not alone. It's as if someone is calling me from deep within the fog, a gentle whisper on my skin that tugs at the yearning in my rib cage. I find myself unwilling to resist and follow it into the silver shadows that swirl invitingly in the moonlight, beckoning me, waiting. My anticipation builds as I get closer.

Finally, I can see the silhouette of a man. He's hidden behind the misty veil, but I'm so close. Warmth flushes my throat; my pulse quickens. I reach out, overcome with a craving to touch him, to make that ethereal presence solid. But before my fingers make contact, I wake up.

THE NEXT MORNING, my elation over working at the library is somewhat tarnished when I walk into my eight a.m. intro to accounting class and discover Mads Jr., Eric, and Grady Callahan there, sitting three rows back. And here I thought I had avoided taking any classes with them. They must have skipped the first week—probably partied every night and couldn't be bothered to wake up so early. Today, Mads looks like a zombie, and Grady is wearing dark sunglasses—like that's going to fly when the professor sees him. I growl inwardly, wishing they had ditched the class again so I wouldn't have to be in the same room with them.

As I walk to my desk, Mads leans over and whispers something to Callahan, and even though Callahan's eyes are hidden behind the dark lenses, I feel his gaze snap to me like a hunter stalking its prey. The skin on the back of my neck prickles. I battle the instinct to shrink away and stubbornly proceed to the first row to take my seat. As I pull my textbook out of my backpack, reluctantly turning my back to them, I try to convince myself that my jitters are irrational. These creeps aren't likely to harass me out in the open. Even legacies can't get away with starting a fight in class. At least, I hope not. But the tension in my shoulders doesn't relax. I swear I can feel three pairs of eyes burning holes in my back, which is still sore from my run-in with Callahan at the party.

The seconds stretch on endlessly as I wait for the professor to arrive. As I contemplate leaving and switching my schedule around to avoid these three stooges, a girl walks in and passes me. She looks familiar. Her eyes are glued adoringly to someone behind me. When I hear a sugary-sweet "Hi, Grady!" I do a double take over my shoulder. I recognize her now—she's the girl I warned about the drugged drink at the party.

I blink as though that can erase the disturbing image from my mind. I thought that after finding out the disgusting jerk was trying to drug her, surely she'd hate him. Both she and her friend sounded appalled at the time, if my memory serves me, so what the hell happened? I'm tempted to get up and ask her if she's okay, but the professor finally arrives and I'm forced to pay attention to the small business ledger he projects on the screen. But I have a hard time keeping my thoughts in check for the next hour and a half, puzzling over what the heck that girl's deal is and imagining Mads Jr. and company staring daggers at my back. When the class is over, I don't stick around and give them an opportunity to corner me—better to avoid dealing with the legacies and their fucked-up relationships altogether.

AT LUNCH, I meet up with Fiona and her very sociable Cali roommate in the dining hall. Apparently, Becky's also in the psychology class Fiona has been complaining about.

"I don't understand. How can it be this hard? It's just an intro class," Becky whines, looking sullen.

"Some professors don't believe you deserve an A unless you've memorized the textbook from cover to cover," I say, putting my tray on the table. The cheese pizza looks particularly good today, so I grabbed two giant slices. When I bite into it, I almost forget the unpleasantness of the morning. The cheese is hot and golden and exactly the right kind of gooey.

"The professor acts like we're all PhD candidates," Fiona says with a sigh. She looks down at her salad, then at my pizza. A sudden longing clouds her eyes. "Is it any good?" she asks hopefully.

"Very," I practically moan with my mouth stuffed.

She considers her salad for another brief moment, then decides it's time for radical change. "Want me to grab you a slice?" she asks Becky, sounding like the mere prospect of pizza has lifted her mood.

"Nah, I'm watching my figure," Becky drawls.

I try not to laugh. Becky definitely does not look like someone who needs to count calories. It must be a California thing.

I continue to indulge in my heavenly pizza, but not five seconds after Fiona leaves, Alessandra Lucente enters my peripheral vision. Teased bangs, high heels, and full makeup—one would think it's a Friday night party and not a Tuesday lunch in the dining hall. I fully intend to ignore her, except I can't—she's strutting straight toward our table with that tiny pixie girl Grady tried to drug. They stop a step away from me.

Alessandra folds her arms, then speaks loudly, clearly aiming to attract as much attention as possible from people at the nearby tables. "I would appreciate it if you stopped spreading vile rumors about Mads and his friends," she says to me.

When I was rooming with Mads last year, Alessandra was a frequent guest in our dorm, but she always acted like I was an empty space not worth acknowledging. Suffice it to say I did *not* expect her to approach me today.

"Excuse me?" is all I can manage after a moment of blankly staring at her.

"You heard me," she says, and then elbows the girl next to her. "Trish, tell him."

Pixie Trish sneaks a nervous glance around, looking like she's giving herself a mental pep talk. I take it confrontations are not her forte.

"You said Grady put something in my drink, and that's a total lie," she finally says, crumbling under the pressure from Alessandra. "You should be ashamed of accusing a good guy like Grady of something so terrible."

If Alessandra striking up a conversation with me was a shocker, this leaves me practically scraping my jaw off the floor. "A *good guy*?" I ask, dumbfounded. "Are you kidding me? He tried to drug you."

"No, he didn't," Trish says defiantly. "You made it up."

I can't believe I'm hearing this. I tried to help this girl and got beaten up for it, and now she's accusing me of lying in front of a whole bunch of people. "Why on earth would I do that?" I demand, trying to curb my anger.

"Because you're clearly jealous of him," Alessandra butts in.

Fiona has just returned with her pizza, and upon hearing the absurdity of that statement, she bursts out laughing. "Are you off your meds, Lucente? Why would Jonathan be jealous of some stuck-up jerk who drugs girls at parties?"

Alessandra doesn't hesitate; her response is fast and full of poison, like a viper. "Nobody asked for your opinion, affirmative action."

"Hey!" I snap. The temperature around us plunges.

I'm ready to give Alessandra a piece of my mind, but Fiona doesn't need a knight in shining armor to defend her. She puts her plate on the table and fires back, "Let's see who has the right to express their opinion here. You show up at our table, spouting garbage on behalf of your loser boyfriend and his bestie, who would be kicked out of this school for failing every class if not for their rich donor parents. Where is Grady, by the way? Is he not even man enough to speak for himself? Then again, when do any of the legacy boys ever deal with the consequences of their actions? Those cowards always hide behind someone, even if it's just a pair of skirts."

"Grady is not a coward!" Pixie Trish squeaks in protest. "He's dangerous and rad and drives a Ferrari. So what if he has weird kinks and a bit of a temper?"

"Ummm, TMI?" Becky chimes in, grimacing. I can't help but agree. How much denial is this girl in?

Alessandra throws a nasty scowl at Trish.

"I think it's time for you both to leave. You're ruining our lunch," Fiona says icily.

Alessandra scrunches her nose, seething, but she doesn't try to prolong her stay. "Let's go, Trish," she says, flicking her long hair back arrogantly. "Like anyone would wanna eat at this trashy place anyway. It stinks in here."

The two of them leave, strutting toward the exit.

I look around. Students at the nearby tables are whispering, pointing, and sneaking glances at us.

"Oh my gawd, this drama is, like, worse than high school," Becky grouses as Fiona reclaims her seat.

"Why the hell did she do that?" I say, frowning.

"Wait, you didn't hear?" Becky asks.

Fiona narrows her eyes. "Hear what?"

"It's damage control," Becky replies sagely. "Half of South Hall saw Callahan fight Jonathan last Friday. Some of them heard him accusing Callahan of slipping something into a girl's drink. News spreads fast. Even the girls in sociology were talking about it. I think there was some kind of a fallout at their mansion party afterward. Now Alessandra is trying to fix their reputations, I guess."

"By publicly accusing me of lying?" I deadpan. "Also, there is no fixing those jerks' reputations. You'd have to invent a time machine to unbirth them."

Becky shrugs. "There are plenty of girls who are eager to believe Callahan did nothing wrong because they want to hang out with him. Someone just has to reinforce that fantasy. It's called confirmation bias."

"Sucks to see women undermining other women, though," Fiona says with disappointment. "Makes me sick."

I nod and get back to my pizza. I find Alessandra's behavior atrocious, too, but sadly, it's very common. People do all kinds of things to fit in.

I remember when Clay said that we should start being extra careful not to be seen together. We never hung out to begin with, only exchanged letters, but Clay grew increasingly paranoid about even those few short moments when we handed them off. I understood why he'd said what he said. We belonged to completely different strata of the high school hierarchy. Being pen pals gave us an excuse to interact in the open, but that was only twice a week, and otherwise, I had to keep my distance. No matter how much I wanted to go cheer for Clay's team or linger in the hallway to say hello when he was leaving class, Clay thought it would be too suspicious, so I was never allowed.

I felt so jealous of all those couples who could drive to school together or walk around holding hands or sit at the same damn table at lunch. Clay and I had to live by a different set of rules.

Clay said some of his teammates made fun of him for taking the pen pal assignment too seriously. He didn't give details of what they said, but I bet the words *loser* and *dweeb* were in heavy rotation. They probably laughed at me. And Clay probably laughed with them. I understood why he felt pressured to do that, but a part of me still felt like it had been clawed out and left to bleed on the floor.

That was when I realized something profound: every person who keeps up appearances, who goes the extra mile just to be a part of a group, has something to hide. Maybe it's just their own diminished view of themself, or maybe it's something darker, something that would destroy them if it were ever forced out into the light. A person like that has no choice but to hide their secret, shove it deep within themself until it starts to corrode them like acid. When you have nothing to hide, you don't care whose company you are seen in. You simply want to be seen.

In the end, Clay and I wanted opposite things.

<h1 style="text-align:center">EIGHT</h1>

I guess the altercation with Callahan caused a bigger stir than I thought because since it happened, I've begun to notice people looking at me oddly. Even at the start of my shift in the library today, I saw two students whispering to each other while pointing at me. But I'd rather concentrate on books than all that drama. Jessi, who's wearing a Megadeth shirt (don't ask me how one goes from Duran Duran to death metal), is giving me the how-to on handling antiques. Turns out she's doing a master's in library science, and working here is part of her graduation requirement.

"You see those heavy chubsters?" she asks, pointing at the pair of two-foot-tall, six-inch-wide illuminated manuscripts sitting on a shelf inside the glass box. I nod. "If someone asks for one of them, you have to give them this pillow display to keep the manuscript from touching the table. The binding is ancient, so you want to protect it as much as possible."

"Got it," I say.

"And I'm sure you already know this, but absolutely no gloves," Jessi continues. "They can actually get stuck to the pages and damage the old ink. Bare hands only."

"I know we're not supposed to let anyone bring pens inside,

only pencils, but do people actually try to mark up the books?" I ask skeptically.

Jessi gives me a side-eye. "Don't ever underestimate human stupidity, Jonathan. People have climbed the pyramids in Giza to graffiti their initials. They definitely try to write in books, even knowing some are hundreds of years old. Like, I get it, some books are more valuable because of the notations left by someone famous. For example, we have a rehearsal script of *Sweeney Todd* with original cast autographs, but that's from its debut Broadway run in 1979. It's not valuable because some idiot thought to doodle on it for fun."

"Wow. Do we really have an original *Sweeney Todd* script here?" I ask.

Jessi chuckles, amused. "You should save your wows for stuff like Shakespeare's first folio. There are only two hundred and thirty-five of them in the entire world."

Actually, I saw the Shakespeare folio during the exhibit the library hosted last year, but it still blows my mind that we have it. "How did we even get it?" I ask in awe.

Jessi's forehead wrinkles. "I think the way we get most items —it was donated by the estate of some rich collector after they died."

"Does that happen often?"

"Which one, rich people hoarding relics, or dying and not being able to take their hoard with them to the netherworld?"

I laugh. "I guess both."

"Then the answer is: All. The. Time," Jessi says with a smirk. "At least most of our collection was purchased with grant money or donated and didn't involve anyone invading other countries and stealing their artifacts, unlike most museums. Although some items here do have questionable provenance." She smacks her lips in disapproval. "I'll show you how to use our cataloging system in a bit. You'll see that the origin of every item is listed as far back as the library can trace it, but sometimes, there's just no record of how a collector procured a particular book. It might have been stolen or plundered in war, and we'll never know." She sighs. "Anyway, we're getting off-topic. Back to book handling: always make sure to inspect the materials after someone works with them. If you notice any new damage, even if it wasn't directly caused by the patrons, report it immediately. Bookworm might sound like a cute name, but it ain't so cute when you see the holes they make."

"Yikes," I say, grimacing. There is just so much to know about this stuff. I feel all giddy just being in the vicinity of these fragile, ancient things.

After Jessi is done quizzing me on proper procedure, she takes me back to the front desk and shows me how to use the electronic catalog on the computer, which is so much more efficient than navigating the card catalog. But it still takes me a second to learn all the different directories. Jessi leaves me to practice on my own for the rest of the evening.

Out of curiosity, I look up the stolen book. After a few seconds of processing, the entry pops up in bright green letters. As expected, it doesn't say much that I haven't already heard from Ms. Tarnow, but after my conversation with Jessi, I want to check the book's provenance. The catalog says it came from the estate of Mr. George Druckenmiller—a wealthy collector who bought it from a European antiques dealer in the early 1920s—but before that, its origin is unknown. I wonder if this book could be a part of some shady transaction or if it was obtained illegally by the dealer. Or maybe Mr. Druckenmiller was simply terrible at maintaining records of his purchases. Sadly, there's no one to ask anymore.

All in all, my first library shift is a success, and hanging out with Jessi improves my mood greatly. I don't even care when I get completely drenched on my way back to the dorm. That's New England weather for you—when I started my shift, it was pleasant and sunny, and now the sky is dumping buckets just to spite the weather forecast. My high-tops are sloshing with water by the time I enter my room. I take them off, empty them in the shared bathroom, and place them on the radiator to dry.

Leaning against the window frame, I peer out into the dark forest looming past the edge of campus. The pathways and benches are deserted because of the dreadful weather. Shrouded by dense black clouds, the moonlight is faint, but the endless curtain of rain creates a strange, silvery halo around the treetops. It looks like fog, and for a moment, I'm reminded of the dream I had the other night, the one in which someone was calling out to me. The memory is so vivid that I'm suddenly gripped by an intense feeling that I'm still in that dream. I feel the hypnotic longing, the ephemeral whisper of the voice on the back of my neck. Disoriented, I whip around, expecting to find the owner of that voice standing behind me, but I am alone in my room.

Of course there isn't anybody here, I tell myself in the most rational, calm manner I can muster. I latch the window securely, trying to shake off the thought that someone in the woods is watching me, concealed by the darkness and the rain.

That night, I don't dream of the mysterious voice. Instead, my dreams are a confused, fractured mess, alternating between being haunted by Clay's absent gaze and cold fingers and the snarling, vicious faces of the legacies, who are causing havoc at another party and trying to pin the blame on me.

When I finally wake up, groggy and barely rested, I hear the howling of police sirens outside.

NINE

After the night of heavy rain, the small river that runs through Camden has overflowed. During her morning run, one of the track and field athletes discovers a naked body that has washed ashore. The incident shocks the community, sparking a chain of wild rumors. All classes are canceled, and within hours, the dean calls another mandatory assembly.

"I heard she was tortured!" I overhear a student murmur to her friend on the way to the theater.

The rain has stopped, but the day is dreary and cold, and there are a lot of fallen leaves sticking to the pathways. I adjust the hood of my sweatshirt, trying to shield my neck from the chill.

"Tortured? How?" the friend asks, terrified but also eager to hear the gruesome details.

Her face turns two shades paler when the first girl replies, "Get this—she was drained of all her blood. Carey, who knows a guy who knows the girl who found her, says that the woman's body was covered in all these weird puncture wounds. And she was totally blue and swollen."

"Oh my god," the friend gasps, now looking like she might puke into the hedge along the pathway.

I scowl and speed past them, trying not to slip on the wet

leaves; I don't need to hear this nonsense. What is wrong with people? This isn't some medieval torture story. Even if there's some psycho on the loose, I've never heard of anything like that happening in a peaceful town like Camden.

But when I finally catch up with Fiona in the crowd filing into the theater, she echoes the same story, and unlike those girls who heard it through the grapevine, Fiona got it from her psychology professor.

"I missed the announcement about classes being canceled, so I showed up to psych at eight a.m.," she says in a low voice as we enter the theater lobby. "I'm pretty sure my professor wasn't supposed to mention anything, but he couldn't help himself. The circumstances of that woman's death are way too creepy. She had actual bite marks, Jonathan. Like someone gnawed on her. And guess what?"

"What?" I ask automatically, even though I'm not so sure I want to hear. My brain is already conjuring up a set of disturbing images that belong in a horror novel.

"They're trying to keep it under wraps, but the victim worked in the dining hall. She didn't come to her shift on Monday, and her neighbor hasn't seen her since last Friday."

A shiver of dread grazes my skin. My work-study job last semester was in the dining hall. I wonder if I knew her.

Fiona and I take our seats as Dean Wilkins walks onstage. She seems rattled, but she does her best to reassure everyone that the suspected homicide of Ms. Anita Hernandez has nothing to do with the university and that no students are in danger. But the crowd isn't so sure.

"Is it true she was a dishwasher in the dining hall?" someone shouts before the dean can finish.

A wave of whispers sweeps across the theater. Of course, that information has already been leaked; the dean never had a shot at keeping it contained. My mind reels, because I do recognize the name Anita Hernandez. We didn't speak much, as I worked the front counter scanning meal cards while she washed dishes in the back, but I do remember her. She was a quiet, older woman who mostly kept to herself.

It doesn't take much time for people to start jumping to outrageous conclusions. My blood boils when I hear some guy in our row loudly declare, "What were they even doing hiring an illegal? Next, we'll have them living here with free room and board!"

Another student, sitting four seats to my right, decides to inject her own unsolicited opinion. "I bet the Mexican cartel got her. A drug deal gone bad!"

Like wildfire, an uproar spreads through the auditorium. Fiona and I exchange disgusted glances. For starters, Anita was from Guatemala, not Mexico, and she definitely wasn't smuggling drugs into the country. How crazy do you have to be to churn out that kind of crap? She was a nice and hardworking lady. She didn't deserve to be killed, and she definitely doesn't deserve to be talked about like this.

"Everyone, please calm down." The dean raises her voice over the din of the crowd. "We're cooperating fully with the authorities to locate and apprehend the suspect as soon as possible. I encourage anyone with helpful information to come forward. In the meantime, local police will be patrolling the area around campus to ensure the safety of students and faculty. In addition, the board has decided to institute a nine p.m. curfew, including on *weekends*," she adds with emphasis.

There's a cacophony of groans. I want to smack my forehead in frustration. Just moments ago, these people were outraged about the dangers of nonexistent, bloodthirsty Mexican cartels, and now they're complaining that their parties are being canceled.

"Classes will resume on Monday, and we will have counseling services available all through the weekend for those who need it. Please remember, your safety and well-being are always our top priority at Camden," Dean Wilkins concludes before dismissing us.

"That poor woman," Fiona says as we exit the theater. "Not

only was she a victim of a ghastly murder, but now her name is being dragged through the dirt."

"Those idiots watch too much TV," I grouse.

Fiona exhales angrily. "Yeah, this is freakin' Vermont. There are no cartels here. Just a whole lot of race-baiting white folks."

"What do you think happened to her, though?" I ask.

Fiona's anger deflates a little, and now she just looks sad. "Honestly? It was probably just bad luck. Some psycho saw her as an easy kill. It sucks, but chances are she was in the wrong place at the wrong time."

"But how did she end up here, washed up on campus?"

"I'm no forensic expert," Fiona says cautiously, "but whoever did this likely dumped her body upstream or left it close to the bank, so when the river overflowed, it took her down with it. Our murderer is either bad at hiding their crimes or just didn't care."

I shiver in the damp autumn air. It always freaks me out a little when Fiona goes into detective mode, which happens whenever we watch thrillers together or discuss some disturbing piece of news she caught on TV. She gets coldly rational and detached while theorizing about killing sprees and serial killer motives. Although I think that's probably a skill one needs to have while working in criminal law, the same as the way surgeons need to be desensitized to blood gushing out of wounds.

"You think there could be more victims?" I ask anxiously.

Fiona stares absently at the line of trees on the path ahead. "It could be a one-off, or it could be the start of something bigger. Only time will tell."

"That's awful," I say.

"I know," Fiona agrees, snapping out of her daze. "But I'm sure the police will have some leads soon. Someone must have seen something. Meanwhile, what should we do for the rest of the day since classes are canceled? Go for pancakes?"

Unlike Detective Fiona, I'm not particularly hungry; my brain isn't as capable of brushing aside the spine-chilling image of a bloodless body with chunks of flesh bitten off. But my work shift is canceled as the library is also closed for the day, and I could use a change of scenery, so I tag along.

To everyone's shock, campus security actually enforce the curfew that weekend. Even the party at my dorm gets broken up by the R.A. A grim sense of dread settles over Camden. I see police cars circling our streets, their red-and-blue lights reflecting off my windows in the dead of night. But honestly, their presence comes off as nothing more than window dressing, a way for Camden to feel good about itself as the authorities fail to make any real progress in their investigation.

I still dream of Clay, but in these new dreams, his eyes are red instead of blue. It's both Clay and not Clay at all. I can't help but stare into them as they glow like two pools of liquid scarlet until it seems like there is nothing in the world but those eyes and an infinite, dark void. Called by their hypnotic pull, I tumble into them and keep sinking—endlessly and willingly—until the morning breaks my fall.

TEN

"I am glad to see everyone here today, safe and sound," Dacian Bathory says as his solemn gaze sweeps over the auditorium the following Monday. It's only for a moment, but he pauses on me as though making sure I am indeed here, unharmed, and not floating downstream with my blood drained or drowning in my nightmares.

A curl of unexpected pleasure at being singled out by him brushes my skin. I haven't seen or talked to him since last week, when I thanked him for speaking to the library on my behalf, but that doesn't mean I haven't thought of him. I wonder what he said to Ms. Tarnow that she considered "high regard." I'm not fishing for compliments, but after the ice-cold reception he gave me the first week of class, I'm dying to find out what changed his mind. Does he see something in me now that he didn't see before? The very thought kindles a spark in me, a desire to know more about him. If I'm not careful to tamp it down, it very well may turn into an all-consuming inferno.

Mr. Bathory's gaze shifts to the slumbering shape several rows behind me, and he sighs in annoyance. "Although it seems some still prefer the embrace of Morpheus to talking about literature... isn't that right, Mr. Stockton?"

Unsurprisingly, Eric does not wake up when his name is called.

Fiona rolls her eyes in the seat next to me. "Seriously? Again? I can't believe this dude."

There's a murmur of low voices in the auditorium, and I find myself awash in embarrassment on Eric's behalf since he's clearly not capable of feeling any himself.

By this time, Mr. Bathory is fed up with Eric's lack of decorum as well. In a few steps so swift and graceful that I wonder if his shiny black shoes even made contact with the wooden floors or if he simply glided up the steps like an apparition, he makes his way to Eric's seat in the top row. "Mr. Stockton," he repeats, gazing down at Eric like an owl zeroing in on a mouse. "WAKE UP."

I jolt. It's not that Mr. Bathory's voice is particularly loud, but somehow, it rings out like a bell struck in a tower. It resonates inside the walls of my mind like he spoke the command directly into it.

Eric jerks upright. "What?" he yelps, startled.

There is a look of panic on his face that the circumstance doesn't quite merit. Falling asleep in class and being called out by the professor is no joke, but Eric doesn't have a sense of shame, as we've established. Yet he looks positively mortified, as though he was expecting to see the devil himself upon opening his eyes.

"Late night?" Dacian asks with a cold intensity that would make a grown man cower.

"Um..." Eric opens and closes his mouth several times but fails to produce a coherent response. He looks like he barely knows where he is.

Dacian grants him no mercy and continues to pin him down with the crumbling power of his glare. "Perhaps you should ask your generous family to invest in a wonderful modern invention called an alarm clock."

Eric's bloodshot eyes blink stupidly.

Mr. Bathory, however, doesn't wait for a verbal response. He turns around and smoothly descends back to his desk. "Let us embark on today's discussion, which involves monsters." He addresses the rest of the class in his usual alluring yet aloof manner, as though he has already forgotten about Eric's existence or considers it completely insignificant. "And this time," he adds meaningfully, "it concerns a *real* monster made of flesh and blood —not merely a ghost, or an illusion, or a figment of someone's troubled imagination. '...If I cannot inspire love, I will cause fear,'" he quotes from Mary Shelley's *Frankenstein*, which is the assigned reading for today's class.

I let my shoulders slump against the back of my chair as the music of Mr. Bathory's voice fills the room, lulling my senses. What just happened with Eric was *weird*. I can't believe Mr. Bathory didn't kick him out of class. That's what I would have done. But perhaps Dacian Bathory is too cool for that. It would mean admitting that Eric's rudeness ruffles him, and he seems so above that. But seriously, what's going on with Stockton?

I sneak several glances back at him. He looks fidgety. His spiky blond hair is a limp mess, and there are dark bags under his eyes. Is he on drugs? That would explain the jitters. The idiot is throwing his life away, not to mention thousands of dollars in tuition and whatever his family is spending to rent that mansion in the mountains. Mads Jr. and company are probably going to level it; over the weekend, everyone rushed to party at their place to avoid the campus-wide curfew, the drugging incident all but forgotten. I grit my teeth. I guess that standoff with Alessandra in the dining hall achieved what she intended.

"Now, why would he do that, Mr. Evergreen?" Mr. Bathory asks suddenly. I'm so distracted thinking about the stupid legacies that I almost miss his question. Of course he's chosen to call on me when I wasn't paying attention. Just my luck.

"I...uh—" I stammer, trying to execute the old-age maneuver of quickly rewinding the last bit of someone's speech while assembling a response that makes some semblance of sense. I think he was talking about the violence Frankenstein's creature inflicted upon Victor's friends and family for rejecting him. "Because he was lonely?" I venture hesitantly.

Mr. Bathory's eyebrows rise. There's a notable intensity in his voice when he asks, "And do you think loneliness is reason enough to commit heinous crimes, Mr. Evergreen?"

"Um..." He's standing no more than five feet away from me. We're still in the middle of class, of course, but there's suddenly a surreal quality to the scene. The soft white light coming from the window seems to bend around Mr. Bathory's dark silhouette, reminding me of artists' renderings of black holes in distant galaxies. Again I find myself caught in his eyes like they have the gravity of their own, stronger than the pull of anything else around us. It's so hard to think clearly when he looks at me like this. But what chances do I have at escaping him when even light eventually gets trapped inside black holes and time stops? I read *Frankenstein* in high school and reread it just before class; it's not an unfamiliar story. Yet my mind feels like it, too, is swirling toward the event horizon.

"I don't condone it," I finally manage to reply. "But I understand where his resentment comes from."

"I think the creature did it because he didn't understand that his actions were evil," Fiona adds, mercifully rescuing me. "Victor didn't teach him what was right and wrong before completely abandoning him to fend for himself."

Mr. Bathory tips his head, curious. "Do you consider Victor to be a good person, then, Ms. Onayemi?"

The question surprises Fiona. "Well, no, I wouldn't think so. He placed a lot of importance on someone's physical appearance while judging their worth as a person. That speaks of superficiality and a flawed value system. Plus, there's the whole unethical experiments thing, and let's not forget about the grave robbing."

"But you still expect him to make good, morally correct choices even though he is not a good person?" Mr. Bathory asks.

Now that his attention is on Fiona, my brain has regained the ability to function. "I don't think the results of Victor's choices have anything to do with him being good or ethical," I say, reinserting myself into the discussion. "The issue is that he created something, then refused to take responsibility for his creation until it was too late. Therefore, Victor shares the blame for what the creature did—and for his loneliness."

"What about free will, then?" Mr. Bathory folds his arms, still not satisfied with my answer. "Doesn't the creature possess it?"

"He does," I agree. "But if he doesn't know anything about the world or the extent of his own powers, can you trust him to exercise it properly?"

"As much as you can trust a child running with scissors," Fiona adds.

Mr. Bathory's eyelashes flutter in surprise at her metaphor, but his lightless gaze stays on me. "Then are you suggesting that the true monster of the story isn't the sad creature who murders out of rage and rejection, abandoned by a madman who wants to play god, but the madman himself, the *human*, who refuses to accept the consequences of his actions and bear responsibility for his blind ambition?"

"Yes," I say quietly.

The sharp angles of Mr. Bathory's face soften a little. "Perhaps you are right, Mr. Evergreen," he says, sounding oddly withdrawn. Like he's thinking of another time or place—a distant memory, another dark story of monstrous deeds and evil men. "I suppose in Victor's case, it wasn't too late for him to tame the monster and seek atonement for their shared crimes, however futile. If only all villains were so fortunate as to find a path toward redemption. But alas, therein lies the difference between fiction and reality."

There's a slight curl to Mr. Bathory's mouth when he says this, but the bone-deep sadness that permeates his words would hardly allow me to call it a smile.

ELEVEN

After several days of flashing police lights and officers making inquiries, their presence on campus starts to diminish. Not even a week later, the cruisers are gone, further convincing me that the patrols were mostly for show. Despite the fact that there's no public update on the murder investigation and no suspect has been apprehended, the palpable edginess in the air starts to dissipate as well.

Although the stupid legacies seem to have missed the memo to chill.

They all skip accounting on Tuesday. On Thursday, Callahan smashes his shoulder into me while pretending not to see me on his way out of the auditorium. I might believe his subpar acting if not for Trish and Mads Jr.'s snickers at my pained yelp of surprise. Those jerks! My banged-up back has barely healed.

Eric doesn't laugh, though. Something is still off about him. He looks even worse than he did in Gothic lit, like he's about to be sick and he'd rather be anywhere in the world but here. Still, he trails behind his asshole friends without protest like a loyal puppy. Whatever is happening to him serves him right, I guess.

On Friday evening I get my first closing shift at the library. Dean Wilkins hasn't officially lifted the curfew, and between that and the intensifying, chilly drizzle, the place is deserted by seven. I diligently hover around the front desk, but when no patrons show up for a solid half hour, I decide to spend some time checking out the glass box. If anyone needs me, I won't be far.

I swipe my key card and head to the third level, where we store our oldest texts. Usually, I'm too busy to browse the shelves, but this is my chance to touch history. I walk slowly down the row of bookcases, letting my fingers lightly graze the spines of old tomes, some leathery and smooth, some etched in gold and covered with a fine layer of patina. I inhale deeply and smile—I love the smell of books. There is something comforting and nostalgic about it. Seemingly so fragile, these pages have held history, have seen so much—wars, natural disasters, persecutions, burnings—and yet they've survived. If magic existed in the world, it would be in a place like this. If I close my eyes, I can almost hear them talking to me like a welcoming circle of friends.

I stop in front of one of the shelves and pull out a hefty illuminated manuscript. Inside, the pages are decorated with many colorful miniatures. I let my fingers gently trace the ink. There is so much I can tell about the book just from looking at it. For example, this one is written in black letter, a narrow, more economical style of handwriting developed to replace the round letters of Carolina minuscule, which was very labor-intensive and required more page space. The handwriting dates this manuscript to between the twelfth and fourteenth centuries. Its velum pages have yellowed with time—and yes, there is some bookworm damage—but the drawings and gold accents are well preserved.

I skim the pages, wondering if any of the drawings depict knights battling monster snails. I heard my professor mention this in my art history class last semester. Why on earth *would* there be pictures of monster snails in medieval manuscripts? Well, nobody knows exactly. One popular hypothesis is that snails were used as a slur for the Lombard moneylenders, who were starting to set up pawnshops around Europe. It was a type of business that skirted legality, as most types of loans were outlawed by the Christian church. Another less popular theory is that the snails were just a weird inside joke among scribes. Anyway, at a cursory glance, this book doesn't contain any. It does, however, have a drawing of a shaggy guy laying eggs into a basket like a chicken. Another head-scratcher courtesy of the scribes.

I chuckle and close the tome, but as I try to return the manuscript to its place, I spot a pair of black eyes gazing at me from the other side of the shelf through the gap between books.

Is that...?

Suddenly, the lights flicker, and a big, lithe shadow darts away. The movement is so quick that it's like there was never anything on the other side of the shelf at all.

Startled, I drop the book.

In a complete panic, I look down, terrified I might've damaged an invaluable twelfth-century relic, but instead, I find a graceful hand holding it in a sure grip.

"You'd best be careful with these." Dacian Bathory straightens up and offers the book to me. His dark eyes are as impenetrable as ever, but there's a hint of amusement in the curve of his mouth. I blink. I could've sworn it was him on the other side of the shelf just now. But how could that be? There is no way he could've gone around so fast—the shelves are at least ten feet long. I must be seeing things.

"I'm so sorry," I say, mortified about nearly damaging a book I'm supposed to protect. "I'm not usually this clumsy."

"It's quite all right. It will be our secret," he suggests smoothly.

"Thank you," I murmur, taking the book from his hand. Inadvertently, the tips of my fingers brush his. *Cold*, I notice briefly before a swell of warmth rushes up my neck. "Um, weren't you just—" I start to say.

"Wasn't I what?" he asks intently.

For a moment I feel confused, unsure if I'm still seeing things. Deep in the recesses of my mind, I realize that I often feel like this when I'm around Mr. Bathory. Like I'm not quite in control of myself. Like I'm treading on a frozen river and the ice under my feet might crack at any moment, plunging me mercilessly to my death.

"N-nothing," I stutter, shaking my head. He releases his hold on the book, and the tiny point of skin contact between us disappears. I put the manuscript back on the shelf. "Are you looking for something, Mr. Bathory?"

"Ah, I am indeed. I waited at the front desk, but no one was there, so I let myself in."

Another wave of embarrassment crashes over me. I swear I shut the door behind me, and only library employees are supposed to have access to this area. It's not like Mr. Bathory is any danger to these books, but still, I wouldn't want to explain this mishap to Ms. Tarnow. "Sorry," I say. "I thought I'd look at the books for a bit, but I lost track of time."

A small smile graces Mr. Bathory's lips as he glances at the shelves with a kind of wistfulness that tugs at my heart. "No need to apologize, Mr. Evergreen. I, too, find it treacherously easy to get swept away by ancient stories..." He trails off, still gazing at the books, and I'm suddenly irresistibly tempted to get lost in there with him.

"So, what can I help you find?" I ask.

"Oh, right." Mr. Bathory snaps out of his daze. "The first edition of Poe's *The Raven and Other Poems*, published by Putnam in 1846."

My eyes widen. "Really? I didn't know we had something like this. Let's find where it is."

I usher Mr. Bathory back to the computer at the front desk and search the database. I can't help but smile at the results. "We *do* have it!" I don't bother to hide my excitement as I all but run to the second level of the glass box and reemerge with a first edition of one of the most famous poems of the nineteenth century.

To my delight, the expression on Mr. Bathory's face mirrors mine. "Would you like to look at it with me?" he asks.

His invitation genuinely surprises me. "Would that be all right?" I ask.

"It *is* one of the works I chose for your upcoming assignment, so yes, it would be quite all right," he says coyly.

I try to hold back a grin as I follow him to a reading table near the window. The overhead lights are dimmed at this hour, but the table and the dark oak wainscotting are cast in the warm glow of a pair of green glass lamps, making the space feel like a cozy cocoon. Dacian pulls out two chairs next to each other and offers one to me. There's a swirl of anticipation in the bottom of my stomach as I sit down.

"The cover is not original," he says with a crease of disappointment between his perfect eyebrows.

"The catalog said it was rebound in the early nineteen hundreds and the spine was repaired. But it's a real Zaehnsdorf," I add, hoping that fact will make up for the absence of the original cover. Beginning in the mid-nineteenth century, Zaehnsdorf was considered one of the finest binderies in London. This book was treasured by whoever commissioned them to rebind it. The cover is a work of art—rich burgundy with elaborate inner dentelles, raised bands, black Morocco spine labels, and the title lettered in gilt.

"It is lovely," Dacian admits, letting his graceful fingers glide enticingly along the edges. My eyes follow the movement, mesmerized. "Just a shame the original pink wrappers haven't been preserved. I suppose they *were* rather delicate."

"Gosh, how do you know all this, Mr. Bathory?" I say, and instantly get embarrassed about it. I was stingy with praise when Fiona pestered me to admit I was impressed with how much Mr. Bathory knows about books, but I truly am in awe of him now. "I mean, not just what the first edition of *The Raven* looked like. You always quote novels in class like you have them memorized."

Mr. Bathory's dark eyelashes flicker. For a moment I have this strange feeling that he wishes to take back what he said, although I'm not sure why. "The truth is, I spent a long time in a very isolated place with nothing but a small library to entertain me," he says warily. "It seems I've read some of those books too many times. The words got stuck in my head."

This answer completely mystifies me. What does Mr. Bathory mean by spending a long time in an isolated place? Does he mean he was imprisoned? That just doesn't seem plausible. Besides, how many days would one have to spend poring over books to be able to recite them from memory? But before I can prod further, he continues, "And in the case of *The Raven*, I know what the first edition looked like because I was once in possession of one."

I try not to let my jaw hit the floor. From my quick glance at the catalog, I recall that only fifteen hundred copies were printed. How many of those survived? It must have cost a fortune. But the longing softness in Mr. Bathory's voice leaves me with no doubt that he's telling the truth. Then, a shadow passes over his face. "However, I lost it under the most unfortunate circumstances."

I simply can't comprehend the idea of owning something that valuable and then losing it. "I'm sorry to hear that," I manage awkwardly after several seconds of stunned silence.

A melancholic smile graces Mr. Bathory's lips. "I suppose that makes tonight's reunion all the more special."

With careful reverence, he opens the book, and once again, I'm magnetically drawn to the smooth movements of his long, elegant fingers. I was supposed to explain how to handle rare books, but I honestly forgot, vacillating between flustered and excited, as I so often feel around him. Although it doesn't seem like Mr. Bathory needs a lecture from me, since he has owned antique books himself. Gently, he flips the slightly yellowed but otherwise wonderfully preserved pages to the start of the titular poem.

"Would you like me to read this to you?" he asks.

The offer is so unexpected that I find myself speechless. I even replay it in my head to make sure I heard him correctly. No one has ever offered to read a poem to me. I sneak a glance at him. From this angle, his eyes are obscured by wisps of his dark hair, and he doesn't raise them from the book to meet mine, to trap me again in their endless depths. Something about this feels significant, though I cannot immediately grasp why.

"I'd love nothing more," I finally reply, my voice trembling a little for some reason.

If Mr. Bathory notices, he doesn't mention it. Instead, he nods and then begins to read. "Once upon a midnight dreary, while I pondered, weak and weary..."

As the words leave his mouth, something in me starts to unravel. He speaks with a slow, heavy somberness that makes me feel the weight of every line as it settles into the plush half-darkness surrounding us. Cold rain pounds against the arched windows of the library, seemingly cutting us off from the rest of the world as Mr. Bathory's voice fills all the available space. He still doesn't look at me—he keeps his eyes trained on the page—but it's obvious he's not *really* looking at it. He must know "The Raven" by heart, and he recites the stanzas with such a profound sense of loss that I want to weep from the overwhelming sorrow that drenches his words. Like a perfect key cut by an expert locksmith, they unlock the door to my own grief.

Scholars believe that Poe wrote "The Raven" in the aftermath of the death of his wife, who inspired the character of Lenore. In the poem, the narrator keeps asking the raven that haunts him where his Lenore is and if he'll ever see her again, but the raven gives no answer. Because Lenore is gone, and being visited by the ominous black bird—be it a messenger from the netherworld or the ghost of his beloved—is not enough to bring her back. Eventually, the narrator is driven to madness as he realizes that he will never overcome his loss and that the darkness and the raven are there to stay.

My heart twists. There is no raven in this room and no box of letters, but I don't need them to see the ghost that haunts me. All I need to do is let my gaze wander past the safe dome of lamplight and into the dim penumbra where the shadows start to claim their domain, and there he is, watching me with those glassy blue eyes, empty since that day. As Mr. Bathory continues to read the poem, memories start to pour through the unlocked door of my heartache and regret.

If you ever loved me, if you ever cared about me, I want you to burn them all. Tonight. Those were some of the last words Clay ever spoke to me. At that moment, I still had no idea that a mindless prank would soon spin into a tragedy that would change our lives forever. Earlier that day, during PE class, someone had stolen my backpack and dumped the contents into a trash can. Nothing was taken except for Clay's most recent letter to me.

I probably just misplaced it, Clay. Maybe it's in my locker, I said to him, forcing calm into my shaky voice. Like I could ever be so careless with anything he gave me. I'd hidden it in the inner pocket of my bag as soon as he'd given it to me so I could read it when I was alone in my room, where I'd be free to stare at each word, each lovingly handwritten dot and curve, and kiss the paper with Clay's name on it. I treasured those letters more than anything in the world; I still do. That's why I never burned them, no matter what Clay said. That's why they are still sitting in a box on my bedside table, where I can see them every morning when I wake and every night before I fall asleep. But when I broke the news to Clay, all I wanted was to erase that wretched worry from his lovely face.

My naive hopes never stood a chance. They disintegrated into ash when I got to school the next morning and saw photocopies of the stolen letter plastered around the entire campus. Even now, my throat spasms and I feel like I might choke, just like I did that day. Both our names were on those pieces of paper.

Miss you, Jonathan.

Love you, Jonathan.

Can't wait to see you.

Yours, Clay.

I remember wishing that the ground would open and swallow me whole, as if I could be allowed such mercy. I remember people jeering and pointing at me like I was a disgusting freak. I'd never wanted anything more than to run away, to never see that place or those people again, but I couldn't. I didn't. Because somewhere in that building, Clay was going through the same thing. My eyes burned as I sped down the hallway. I looked for him everywhere. I wanted to say I was sorry. I wanted to tell him we'd get through this together. That I'd be there for him even if the whole world turned against us.

But I never got the chance. Because that morning, Clay'd had football practice before first period. He'd come to school and seen the photocopies an hour before I did. By the time I arrived, he'd already gone home and hanged himself in his bathroom.

Jonathan. Oh, Jonathan. I see Clay's cold lips move as the apparition that wears his face stares at me from the dark corner of the reading room. There's an accusation in his eyes and a rope around his neck. *Why didn't you burn those letters, Jonathan? If you loved me, if you cared about me, how could you let this happen to me? You* promised *you'd burn them—*

"Mr. Evergreen?"

Mr. Bathory's voice reaches me from a faraway place. My gaze refocuses on him as I follow his voice back to reality, to the library, where I'm still sitting next to him, my chest heaving as though it is ready to collapse on itself as the rain pours down outside. Mr. Bathory has finished reciting "The Raven," and he's looking at me with the utmost worry, his hand hovering in the space between us as though torn between wanting to reach out and touch me and not daring to.

"Your eyes," he says quietly.

Dazedly, I put my hand to my face and find it wet. I didn't realize I was *crying.*

"I'm sorry. I didn't mean to—" I start in a panic, but I'm too shaken to continue. I haven't cried in such a long time, especially in front of another person. I thought I'd forgotten how.

"You have nothing to apologize for," Mr. Bathory replies, his voice like satin against the patter of the rain on the library's windows. He withdraws his hand, but his gaze traces the wet line splitting my cheek in two. I stifle a sob. "Poe himself said that 'if a poem hasn't ripped apart your soul, you haven't experienced poetry,'" he adds soothingly. "Great art has that effect on people, Mr. Evergreen. It brings the things we bury deep within ourselves to light so we can set them free."

My ragged heart gives another jolt.

When I left North Carolina, I buried my past along with my tears and hid what had happened from everyone. Even Fiona—I've given her only bits and pieces of the truth. She doesn't know that Clay took his life because of me. And I don't know if I'll ever be able to tell her when I can barely admit it to myself. I've guarded this secret like a stone gargoyle guards a crumbling tomb—in weathered stillness, undeterred by time. And yet, Dacian Bathory has drawn it out of me with just a handful of stanzas. Even if it isn't words yet, if it's only tears, I know he knows.

And just like that, I can no longer hold the truth inside me.

"What if there's no way to set them free?" I ask—no, I beg of him. "What if they're buried so deep that the light never reaches them? What if..." My breath catches as fear seizes me again, used to being the solitary ruler of my soul. I struggle to still myself. "What if I am buried along with those things, and no matter how much I try to dig myself out, to climb up this endless black tunnel, it still feels like I'm only falling deeper into the darkness?"

For a moment, Mr. Bathory is silent. My heart echoes in my ears, shuddering in my chest like a caught rabbit, and I'm suddenly worried that he might not understand me after all, that he might think someone like me doesn't deserve forgiveness or even a chance to atone. But then he leans in closer, as though he too has a secret he's been harboring for an eternity, one he's ready to release.

When he speaks, his words are a revelation. "Then it is best to make friends with the shadows, Mr. Evergreen. For if you're shrouded in darkness so complete, so all-consuming, that there's no telling the skies above from the ground below, then what is the difference between falling and flying?"

My lips quiver as his words shatter me, the full intensity of his lightless eyes on mine. A puzzle piece clicks into place. Now I know how he knows my secret, why he wanted to read "The Raven" to me. He knows because this poem means something similar to him. Because I'm not the only one who's been roaming in the shadows. We are alike, Dacian and me. I wonder who his Lenore is. There must be one for him to have read the poem the way he did—like his soul never left the funeral even though the grave has long been filled. And perched on this chair beside him, am I the raven that reminds him of his beloved who could never return?

I open my mouth to respond, but no words come out. I've been offered something of great importance—a private history, a piece of a secret that makes Dacian Bathory who he is—and if I'm not careful, if I ask too much too soon, I might break this fragile bridge between us. Still, I desperately want to know more about him, about this strange person with eyes like ancient abysses, who looks barely a few years older than me but speaks like he's carrying the weight of centuries upon his shoulders.

My heartbeat picks up once more. "Are you—" I start to ask, but the rest of the question never leaves my lips.

At the front desk, the phone begins to ring, reverberating through the empty library with its cathedral ceilings. Unable to tear myself away from Dacian, I let several seconds slip by, but the caller is persistent, and since I'm on the clock, I must answer it.

"I'm sorry, I have to get that," I say reluctantly, and no matter how much I want to preserve the moment, it breaks as soon as the words leave my lips.

"Of course." Dacian pulls back from me.

Maybe I'm just imagining it, but I think he regrets the interruption too.

To my further frustration, the phone call balloons into a lengthy research session as I help a grad student from another university find titles in our possession that are pertinent to her dissertation. Minutes tick by as I steal glances at Dacian's refined profile while skimming the catalog entries on the computer screen. When I finally—finally!—hang up, Dacian Bathory is back at my counter, handing me the book.

"Are you already finished?" I ask, unable to keep the disappointment out of my voice.

"I believe you're about to close."

I glance up at the clock. "Oh. Right." I didn't realize it was almost eight forty-five. The janitor is about to show up, and I need to get back to my dorm before curfew. Without that untimely phone call, I probably would've forgotten the rest of the world existed.

Dacian seems amused by how out of sorts I am. I clear my throat and take the collection of poems from him.

"Have there been any updates on the missing book?" he asks then.

I'd forgotten all about that. I shake my head, feeling oddly guilty for not solving the mystery. Although, how could I have possibly done that? I'm no sleuth. "None of the librarians have any idea how it could've disappeared. It was kept locked up in the vault underground, which only library employees had access to," I say.

"Hmm. That's regrettable," Dacian says. Something about this information seems to bother him, but he doesn't elaborate. "Well, good night, Mr. Evergreen."

My heart sinks a little; I'm loathe to let him go. Just half an hour ago, I was bearing my soul to him, and now the time we spent with "The Raven" feels more like a fantasy than a reality we shared. "Good night, Mr. Bathory," I force myself to reply.

Just before he turns to leave, he adds, "Be careful walking alone at night. Not all shadows are friendly here."

At first, I'm confused about why he'd say that, but then I remember the flashing lights of the police cars and the body of Anita Hernandez on the riverbank. "Uh, yes. You too, Mr. Bathory."

His mouth curves up. He gives a slight bow and walks out into the rain.

After the door swings shut, I suddenly realize that Dacian wasn't carrying an umbrella and that it's still pouring outside. Although, I don't recall seeing a drop of rain on his hair or clothes when he first appeared in the glass box. How odd.

***

THAT NIGHT, I have the most unsettling dream.

I'm running alone through a snowy forest. I don't know how I got there or where I'm going. All I know is that I'm being hunted.

It's freezing cold, colder than I've ever felt before. With each step, my feet sink deeper into the snow. A wet chill bites my limbs, turning them numb. It's hard to move, but I desperately keep pushing forward because somewhere behind me, there's a tremendous howling. It grows and grows as it gets closer to me. I whip my head around. Already, I can see shadows in the woods. The wolves will catch up to me soon. They will rip my flesh to pieces and leave them scattered in this desolate place where no one will ever find me. Inescapable terror wraps itself around my throat. I try to pick up speed, but I tumble forward.

Do not fear them, a voice says softly into my ear—a calm and steady voice that somehow drowns out the howling. *They will protect you from the ones who truly mean you harm.*

I scramble to turn around, searching for the source of the voice, but I don't see him or the wolves. Instead, I'm confronted by a crowd of people. My stomach lurches. I remember these faces. It's the kids from my high school, dozens of them emerging from the woods. Their eyes are cruel, their faces twisted with malevolence.

"It's him."

"The freak."

"Disgusting."

They whisper to each other, laugh, and point at me.

I want to curl into a ball to cover my ears, but my body won't listen to me, frozen from the cold and panic. This feels just like when Clay died.

My parents, teachers, our neighbors—everyone joins in. They all circle me as their voices spin around me like a mad carousel fueled by hate.

"He did it."

"Yes, him."

"Poor Clay."

"Because of him."

Whispers blur into laughter, into insults, into sneers.

Just when I can't take it anymore, the crowd finally parts, and Clay steps forward.

Everything stops; even my own heart feels suspended. But Clay isn't here to save me. He casts his silent judgment on me like he always does in my dreams, but this time, there's no box of letters between us. His blue eyes are focused on my neck. At once, I feel the weight of something wrapped around it.

Slowly, I lift my hands until my numb fingers touch the coarse fibers of a rope. Someone has wound a noose around my neck. I choke out a sob. "Is this what you want?" I ask Clay, my chest rattling.

He says nothing. He only stares.

But even if Clay won't say it, the rest of them are ready for the gallows. From the mob, a chant begins to rise.

"Hang the freak! Hang the freak! Hang the freak!"

A tear rolls down my cheek. Even as the vortex of voices spins out of control, I refuse to look at them. I look only at Clay.

"Is this what you want?" I whisper again.

An unbearable realization strikes me: maybe this is why Clay has been haunting me. Not because I refuse to burn the letters but because he thinks I deserve to die for everything that happened to him.

As though he's finally ready to speak to me, Clay's mouth

opens, stretching grotesquely wide, like he's not human at all but an emissary from hell wearing Clay's skin. Petrified, I forget how to breathe. But before Clay can pronounce my verdict and drag me to my eternal punishment, a big black shadow darts from the trees and sinks its teeth into his jugular.

I gasp. Blood gushes out of Clay's throat.

The howling returns, suddenly and viciously, as dozens of dark wolves spring from the forest and tear into the crowd, their eyes red, their movements so deadly and swift that they look like they're made of smoke and shadows. Screams of agony erupt around me. The wolves don't let a single soul escape.

Clay's body drops to the ground, and a wolf continues to gnaw through his muscle and bone until what's left of his head snaps off his spine with a wet, bubbly crack, and I—

I watch with wide eyes as Clay's red blood soaks the white snow, and the crowd is reduced to a pile of mangled limbs.

And then I wake up.

PART TWO

MAKING FRIENDS WITH THE SHADOWS

Twelve

The first six months following Clay's death were hell.

The school principal called my parents and told them everything. My mother became hysterical; my father turned my room upside down, searching for evidence that I'd abandoned God's righteous path. I'd hidden the remaining letters, but that didn't stop him from unloading more than a few hefty punches on me to try and force a confession, or perhaps merely to express his disappointment. My parents pulled me out of school for the rest of the quarter and permanently grounded me. But despite the constant abuse and threats, I never betrayed the location of the letters. They were the only things I had left of Clay, the only real things. My parents told me I couldn't even attend his funeral.

I didn't let them stop me, though.

It was held in a small Episcopal church that Clay's family belonged to. They never missed a Sunday mass, which was likely the reason Clay wasn't denied his last rites, as was usually the case with suicide victims. The priest made an exception for this one lost lamb. However, the rest of the town felt this was a step too far on account of the lamb being queer. It was one too many things for them to forgive.

On the day of the funeral, I snuck out of my house and went

to the church, thinking I could go unnoticed among the attendees, but other than Clay's immediate family, no one came. That sprawling circle of friends he'd tried so hard to belong to—not a single one of them risked showing up. Not one of his football teammates or coaches. None of the girls who had pined for him. The church was dark and cold while outside, just down the street, people were starting to hang Christmas lights on houses—the holiday season was already upon us. I'd never felt emptier in my life.

When Clay's mom found me huddled in the last row of the pews, she started screaming, her son's dead body lying in a coffin just a few feet away. Clay's older brother, an army sergeant, promptly grabbed me by the collar of my jacket and dragged me outside. He threw me down the church stairs, but not before shouting that I was going to rot in hell for corrupting his baby brother.

I don't know what I was expecting. Maybe for Clay's family to realize I'd lost him too? That my soul was being slashed to pieces by grief just as much as theirs were? Instead, they'd decided I was to blame for everything. All I wanted was to say goodbye to him, to see him one last time, but they didn't think I deserved even that. What *did* they think I deserved?

I didn't have anyone to talk to about it, so for months, I stopped talking entirely. Thoughts swirled and clashed in my head, but none of them reached my mouth. Even when winter break ended, and I had to go back and finish my senior year, I stayed silent despite the endless taunts and torment.

At school, a peculiar change had taken place. It seemed that in my absence, Clay's story had been revised. The school was split between those who wanted to punish me for existing and those who, like Clay's family, had decided I must suffer for seducing him and destroying his life. It was me, you see, who had lured Clay off the righteous path. All those people who wouldn't say a last goodbye to him were now whitewashing the truth, turning Clay into a martyr as though they weren't the ones who'd driven him to the grave. That was when I learned that people pick their own versions of history to ensure they aren't blamed for the outcome.

It's easy to say you loved someone when they're no longer around. After all, the dead can't speak. They cannot refute your self-serving delusions, and you can ignore the fact that you didn't stand up for them when it mattered. When they needed you.

Those kids barely knew the real Clay, but that didn't stop them from relentlessly scapegoating me as an act of "justice." Though if anyone cared about justice for Clay, how come nobody ever properly investigated who stole my backpack and exposed his private life to the school? No one was held responsible for that. None of the teachers or staff lost their jobs, and no students were expelled. As far as I could tell, the cops just swept everything under the rug. One fewer queer in their town.

Then Clay's ghost started appearing to me. Always silent, just like I was, simply staring at me with all his thoughts and unshed tears and ruined dreams.

Camden's acceptance letter arrived around that time. I had been interested in antique books ever since the summer job I'd had at a used bookstore in seventh grade. The owner was a collector of nineteenth-century chapbooks and penny dreadfuls. But after Clay's suicide, my hobby took on a whole new meaning.

I had always wondered why I never saw people like Clay or me as heroes of stories, why it was so difficult to find accounts of queer lives in libraries and museums. Clay and I weren't the only gay boys ever to walk the Earth. But given that people like us were routinely prosecuted for "indecent" behavior and outright censored by those who were supposed to preserve art, most writing about someone like us was concealed from the public eye. Museums and libraries display love letters from Mark Twain but not Oscar Wilde. Jane Austen's family tossed most of her correspondence into the fire. Our words to each other are snatched away and destroyed before anyone has a chance to feel them. If our writing is lucky enough to survive, it quietly gathers centuries of dust in archives and rich people's private collections. It might be naive of me, but I want to save them, to show our words to the world. That's why I want to work in conservation and why I can never burn Clay's letters. They are what remains of us, a truth that deserves to be known.

THIRTEEN

"Achoo!" I cover my mouth quickly to avoid sneezing all over Fiona's and my breakfasts. "Sorry," I say.

"Did you catch a cold?" she asks.

"Hope not." I pull a napkin out of the holder on our cafeteria table and wipe my nose. "I fell asleep with my window open. Woke up at three a.m., freezing and with a rain puddle on the floor. I could've sworn I'd closed it."

"That sucks," Fiona says sympathetically. "Wouldn't have happened if you had a California roommate. Becky is always cold, even when the blasted radiator turns the place into a desert." Fiona stuffs a piece of a waffle with chocolate chips and whipped cream into her mouth.

We have Waffle Saturday in the dining hall every other week, which is the only reason she is up this early. Unlike me, Fiona doesn't have trouble sleeping, but we always try to make it here before the popular toppings run out.

An unexpected swell of nausea hits me. I haven't told Fiona about the nightmare that woke me up, but vivid flashes of it suddenly burst into my mind, toppling my thoughts. The pile of mutilated limbs surrounding me in the snow, the wolves' jaws dripping with gore. Given that she's taking psych, Fiona would probably think I've lost it if I were to describe those images to her. I'm starting to wonder myself. In the dream, none of it bothered me. When the wolf attacked Clay, I didn't try to stop it. But now that I'm awake, this realization makes me queasy. Why did I do nothing as the person I loved more than anyone in this world got torn apart by a wolf? I still remember his frozen blue eyes staring at me as his bitten-off head rolled away in the snow. What the hell is wrong with me?

"So, how's the library gig? Everything you dreamed of?" Fiona asks with a grin.

I try to blink away the image of Clay's bloodied remains. *Get hold of yourself, Jonathan. It was just a nightmare.*

"I love it," I reply with an earnestness that is real—if a little forced at the moment—and spear a piece of syrupy strawberry with my fork, determined not to ruin my Waffle Saturday. "Yesterday, Mr. Bathory stopped by."

Fiona perks up with interest. "Oh? What did he want?"

I almost tell her about "The Raven," but I stop myself. What happened last night, the dreamlike moment Dacian and I shared... it feels too *intimate* to lay out in the open like that. "He was looking for a particular edition, and I helped him find it," I say. Then, remembering the strange sense of guilt I had about not investigating the missing book, I decide to pick Fiona's brain about it. "Hey, did you know someone stole a rare book from the library?"

Fiona's eyes widen. "No way! More Camden campus crime? I'm seriously starting to second-guess my decision to come here instead of Cornell. What happened?" There's a lilt of curiosity in her tone that I can only describe as professional interest.

"That's the thing—no one knows when or how the book went missing. It was kept in the vault, and no one has requested it since it came to the library as part of a large donation. They only discovered it was gone at the start of the semester."

"Hmm. What kind of book was it? Super valuable?"

I shake my head. "Apparently not. It was a diary of some guy from a century ago."

That surprises Fiona. "Why would someone steal an old diary if it's not worth a lot?"

"I don't know," I say, and take a sip of my coffee. "Maybe the culprit collects diaries of dead people?"

"Beats collecting chopped-up body parts," Fiona replies.

I nearly choke on my coffee. "W-what?" For a moment I wonder if Fiona somehow read my mind and got a glimpse of the gnarly nightmare I had.

But she waves me off. "Don't mind me. I've been reading some weird stuff for my psych class. Back to the missing diary— you said it was kept in the vault?"

It takes me a second to recover. "Yeah, it was," I say. "And that's the weird part—only librarians have access to it. You have to pass through the glass box first, and then there's a separate keyed entry to the vault."

"Sounds to me like it was an inside job, then," Fiona pronounces confidently.

I feel an instant flare of indignation. "A librarian would never do such a thing. They care about those books," I say. Besides, I've met everyone who works at that library. There are some odd ducks among the staff for sure, but they all seem like good enough people.

"Well, if no one checked it out and there's no way to get into the vault without a special key, who else could've done it?" she parries.

I really dislike that reasoning, but I must admit it's sound. That sours my mood. Fiona, still in full-on lawyer mode, presses her line of questioning even further. "To the best of your knowledge, is there anything in that diary that could shed light on the motive?" she asks.

"I only know that there's some 'controversial' content in it. The owner of the diary supposedly had a secret gay affair."

"Oh my! I didn't know Camden kept such books in its collection," Fiona says, her eyes sparking with interest before quickly dimming as she figures something out. "Wait...in that case, it was likely a hate crime. Someone probably didn't like that the library had a gay book and removed it."

My heart sinks. "You think so?"

"Wouldn't be the first time." Fiona sighs. "Did you know that when the Third Reich started burning books, the first library they went after was in the Institute of Sexology in Berlin, which specifically advocated for homosexual and transgender rights?"

"I didn't know that," I say, feeling deeply uncomfortable. The thought of some brainwashed neo-Nazi stealing gay books here in Camden makes my stomach twist.

Fiona continues, "For its time, it was a pretty progressive establishment. The founder was Jewish, too, which made them want to set the place ablaze even more. Fascists and dictators often rise to power by vilifying minorities to rile up the general population. It's a very effective tactic. And guess where the Nazis got their best ideas from?"

"Where?" I ask, but I think I already know the answer.

"Our very own land of the free," Fiona replies with a bitter kind of detachment. "The Nazis basically copied the way our government denied citizenship to Native Americans even though they were all born here. They turned it into legislation that allowed them to round up the Jews and send them to concentration camps, which were modeled after Indian reservations. Our reputation as leaders of the free world is hardly as pristine as some would have you believe..." She trails off, and for a moment, our table turns quiet.

I hold my mug of lukewarm coffee in a futile attempt to chase the chill away. All this only gives me more reasons to pursue book conservation. I might be powerless to stop a group of raging fascists from burning down a library, but if I can save even a few queer books from destruction, I'll feel my life has been a success.

Fiona returns to her waffle. "Anyway, aren't all the books being digitized just in case someone tries to burn or steal one?"

"Yep. About fifteen percent of the titles have been scanned. But the diary that was stolen hadn't been digitized yet, which means that if it's not recovered, it's most likely gone forever," I say.

Fiona muses as she chews. "Wouldn't it be so rad if someday we could just read stuff off a computer screen and say goodbye to hauling those heavy textbooks around?"

"That would be awful!" I protest with a frown.

"What? Why?"

"Because the two are not the same obviously. What about the smell of old paper? Or the cozy feeling you get from holding a real book? You'll never get that from a screen."

"Maybe not. But it's *convenient*, Jonathan. Nothing beats that," Fiona says.

That really riles me up. "We're gonna have to agree to disagree. Besides, you'd have to carry a whole computer with you if you wanted to read anything. How is that convenient?"

"True. But one computer could potentially hold thousands of books, and my backpack can barely fit one psych textbook. Have you seen that seven-hundred-page monster? My arms are gonna be like Hulk Hogan's after this semester. Besides, computers don't take up a whole room anymore. They'll probably invent smaller ones soon, like those hologram things in *Blade Runner*. Maybe they'll even have a robot voice that can read the books aloud for you. And you can just sit back, close your eyes, and relax." Fiona leans back in her chair, imitating her dream reading scenario.

"Right," I say skeptically. "Just don't forget that in that movie, the world had turned into a toxic wasteland because of all the technology."

Fiona's eyes open and narrow at me. "You just have to rain on my parade, don't you? I don't think our future has to be all apocalyptic like *The Terminator*. It could totally be more like Star Wars."

I fold my arms. "Where the universe is ruled by a dark

emperor who can blow up entire planets if anyone disobeys him? No thanks."

"He does get defeated in the end," Fiona points out.

"Tell that to the people from Alderaan."

Fiona rolls her eyes. "You know what? I think you need another waffle, Jonathan. You've been all rainbows and butterflies this morning."

"I'm just being realistic," I say defensively.

"I'd say you're being a grumpy curmudgeon. Go get your waffle."

"I am so not that!" I object immediately, but it's hard to hold back a smile. "I may take your suggestion about the waffle, though. And I'll get another coffee. But not because I'm a curmudgeon. I just hardly slept."

<hr>

LATER THAT AFTERNOON, when I'm alone in my room, my thoughts return to my nightmare. I attempt to distract myself with my accounting assignment, but my mind keeps flashing back to the dead crowd, to Clay's mauled corpse...and to the fact that I didn't protect him.

I still think it's shocking. But as I scour my mind for any modicum of shame or regret for my inaction, I'm unable to find any. Instead, what I feel deep inside is relief. For a long time after Clay's death, if someone had opened me up, all they'd have found was grief, every shade of it. There were days when it got so overwhelming that I wanted to claw my own heart out and stomp on it just to stop it from feeling anything. But at some point, that began to change. I don't know exactly when the sadness and despair ebbed and made space for anger. I will never know what Clay felt in those final moments before he took his life—if he blamed me or if he even thought of me at all. All I know is that, in the end, he left me *alone*.

What others thought of him was more important to Clay

than even his own life. Maybe being torn to pieces by shadow wolves is the fate they all deserve for pushing him to feel that way. Maybe Clay who has been haunting my dreams wasn't really Clay, but just my own misery and guilt, and this nightmare was my subconscious way of letting go. No wonder it was so violent.

If a poem hasn't ripped apart your soul, you haven't experienced poetry.

Dacian was certainly right about that. Except I'd read "The Raven" before, and it didn't have that same soul-shattering effect on me. So maybe it wasn't the poem that did it after all; maybe it was him.

I close my eyes and let my thoughts drift to last night—how close we were sitting to each other, how Dacian's voice seemed to fill every inch of space around us until the world fell away completely. I sigh. He could probably hypnotize me with that melodious voice. Not that he'd need to—I've already spilled all my secrets to him willingly. His voice had even entered my dream. It was Dacian who warned me not to fear the wolves and who tried to calm me when the angry mob was ready to execute me.

He was also there for me when I broke down crying at the library, his hand hovering just inches from my face. Did he want to wipe away my tears? Did I want him to?

These are dangerous thoughts, I tell myself sternly. He's a professor, and I'm a student. I shouldn't think of touching him. Of wanting to be alone with him. Of hearing him in my dreams.

But knowing you shouldn't do something and stopping yourself from doing it are two perilously different things.

I suddenly begin to wonder about the diary that went missing. Did Dacian inquire about it because he wanted to *read* it? Does he know that the owner had a gay love affair? The thought stirs something in me, something I don't dare give shape to, not even in the privacy of my own thoughts. Maybe Dacian and I are more alike than I thought.

I close my eyes and picture Dacian's hands again, the way his fingers flipped the pages, reverent and careful—just the way that book deserved to be handled, like the rare treasure it is. With a quiver in my heart, I finally let myself admit the indisputable truth.

I really want Dacian to touch me the way he touched the pages of "The Raven."

Fourteen

As the weekend dwindles to an end, a kind of desperate anticipation builds inside of me. It's not like my life has changed drastically since Dacian read me the poem, and yet there's been a seismic shift within me. I feel it in my bones. It has become easier to breathe, like a mountain has lifted from my shoulders. Finally, there's someone I don't have to hide myself from. Even if all I have inside of me is darkness, Dacian will understand.

Time and time again, I find myself daydreaming about how that night could've gone if I hadn't answered that stupid phone call. Something changed between Dacian and me on Friday. I can't rationally explain this, but it felt like he was looking straight into my soul.

Maybe it's because I'm thinking about him so much that I have another mystifying dream. In it, Dacian is standing outside my window. A spark of excitement ignites in me. He's alone, surrounded by a starless night so dark that I can't see anything else around him. Yet his silhouette is clearly visible, illuminated by a thin layer of silver mist swirling around him. He's so beautiful. Otherworldly, even. I rush to the window, eager to greet him, but just as I'm about to open the latches, Dacian takes a step back and covers his mouth with his hand as though he's trying to hide something. Confused and afraid he might leave me, I call after him, "Wait!"

But the turmoil in Dacian's eyes only becomes more pronounced. As I struggle to lift the uncooperative sash, he continues to back away from me until the darkness swallows him entirely.

I wake up with a deep sense of unease. What was that about? He looked almost panicked when he realized how ready I was to welcome him inside. And why was he hiding his mouth from me? That's so odd.

I groan and smush my face into the pillow, consoling myself with the notion that dreams are often nonsensical and should rarely be taken seriously. There's no way Dacian could stand outside my window—my room is on the third floor!

I drag myself out of bed and begin my Monday, but by afternoon, I can barely hold myself together. The need to see him, to confirm that my dream didn't mean anything, swirls in my head like the rumblings of a hurricane. But when it's finally time for Gothic lit, I nearly shatter into pieces when I discover the auditorium door is closed. Stuck to it is a note stating that class is canceled and that we should read Edgar Allan Poe's "The Tell-Tale Heart" before our next meeting.

The handwriting on the note is rather sloppy. Clearly, Dacian did not write it.

"Oh, that sucks," Fiona says, joining the chorus of disappointed groans. It seems most of the class was really looking forward to his lecture, though not as much as I was. "I guess it's early lunch for us," she suggests.

I follow her to the dining hall, but I keep thinking about the dream, unable to banish the dreadful notion that Dacian's absence has something to do with me, that the dream was a warning...but about what?

IN THE FOLLOWING DAYS, the campus-wide curfew is quietly lifted, and the murder of Anita Hernandez is swept under the rug like some inconvenience to be dealt with later—or not at all.

As the fall semester starts to approach midterms, I get buried in assignments and papers, but it's a welcome distraction. I throw myself into my Latin translations, despite the fact that I've never been a fan of the language and can't wait to move on to Greek with all its gay heroes and poetry. If only all this work would make me stop thinking about Dacian. Even in his absence, I can't get him out of my mind. I spend the rest of the week obsessing over every detail of the things he said to me. During my library shifts, I flinch every time the door opens, hoping it's him. But despite my wishful thinking, it never is. And eventually my despondency spirals out of control, not helped in the least by the fact that it's Family Weekend.

IT'S SATURDAY AFTERNOON, and I'm...hiding, sitting on a bench by the pond in the big green space by myself. There are crowds all over campus. Even Fiona's parents drove up last night and are currently having the full Camden experience by lunching in the dining hall. Generous soul that she is, Fiona invited me to join, but I didn't feel like going. Let the Onayemis do their family thing. I snuck a grilled cheese and a can of soda out earlier so I can eat alone. I wouldn't be good company right now.

Seeing all these proud parents makes me annoyed in a way that isn't rational. Of course, they should be happy for their children, who are living their dreams. These kids have made it into one of the most prestigious academic institutions in the world. Just...why is this enough to impress other people's families and not mine? I haven't heard from Mom and Dad since I packed up and left after graduation. Not once. They know I'm at Camden. It would be easy to contact me if they wanted to.

In my first few months here, my heart jumped whenever I

found a letter in my school mailbox, thinking it might be from them. I was incredibly naive. But hope can be stubborn, and deep down, I thought if I gave them time, they'd realize they didn't want to lose their only son. And that maybe they'd see how much they'd hurt me.

Naive, as I said.

I remember counting down the days till I could get out of that abysmal place. But once I left, it wasn't freedom I felt. It was another wave of loss, one I didn't expect. Somehow, leaving North Carolina behind cemented everything that had happened as truly permanent. Clay was dead. I was never coming back. And everything I knew was gone. Suddenly, I was terrified. I found I was willing to forgive the inexcusable things my parents had done to me if they only apologized. But of course, they never did. And on days like this, I'm reminded that, just like Clay, they didn't fight for me. They'd rather have an empty home than a queer son.

My hands curl around the edge of the bench until it feels like if I press any harder, the wood will splinter or my fingers will break.

"Camden is unusually lively today," a melodic voice says to my right.

I jolt, letting go of the bench in surprise. Dacian Bathory is standing next to me, clad as always from head to toe in black, like a vision from a Gothic novel, a mystical totem in the sea of golden leaves. Despite my current aversion to people, something in my chest unclenches, endlessly pleased about the prospect of sharing space with him, of being in his company.

"Good afternoon, Mr. Bathory," I say, trying not to let the whirlwind of feelings show on my face. "It's always this busy during family weekend. And the senator seems to be using it as a photo op." I tip my head at the big crowd congregating in the square to the left of the pond. I can just make out Senator Madison, his arm slung around his son's shoulder in an "attaboy" gesture.

Mads Jr. is flashing a delighted grin, his hair combed neatly for his father's benefit, but knowing him he probably loathes this charade. I won't be surprised if he lashes out later by doing something cruel to one of the groupies who follow his clique around. Being his roommate for a year, I learned quite a few tidbits about the utter dysfunction in his family. Although I still don't feel sympathetic toward the jerk. At least Madison Sr. finds some value in his son, even if it's only to bolster his reelection prospects.

"I see," Dacian replies, his eyes narrowing thoughtfully. "The Madison family is quite influential with the Camden board." As a professor, he's probably aware of a whole other side of things that I'm not privy to.

I huff. "That's ironic."

"Why so?" he asks, his interest piqued.

Dacian doesn't seem like he's been in Vermont for long; I suppose he wouldn't know. "Because the senator has been trying to defund public education at every turn," I explain. "But the board doesn't care as long as private donations keep flowing. And the senator's kids will always be able to afford to study here." Dacian's eyebrows shoot up at my acerbic tone, and I catch myself. Since he read "The Raven" to me, I don't feel like I need to pretend anymore because he knows things about me that nobody else does. But such carelessness could be detrimental. My anger has gotten the better of me. "Sorry, I shouldn't have said that."

He studies me for a moment. "No, you should speak your mind freely, Mr. Evergreen," he says eventually. I might be imagining it, but I think there's a ghost of a smirk in the corner of his sharp mouth. My face grows warm under his scrutiny.

"Thanks," I murmur, looking down and concentrating on Dacian's polished shoes. They're so clean that I seriously wonder if their soles touched the ground on his way here or if he just levitated above it. I expect him to excuse himself and continue on his way, but to my surprise, the wooden bench lets out a tiny creak as Dacian takes a seat beside me.

"May I?" he asks after he's already sitting.

My heart flutters. "Of course."

I can't believe he wants to stick around. A part of me was so convinced his absence from class had something to do with me. I know that's absurd. I'm no one important, and I doubt he spent every waking moment thinking of me like I thought of him. But after a week of unfulfilled expectations, I ache for his continued presence, and I want to know where he's been if only to dispel the preposterous idea that he's been avoiding me.

"Is everything all right? Class was canceled on Monday," I say, then hesitantly let myself look up again. Something seems different about him today. His eyes are less tired, maybe. The moment I get caught in them, I feel the familiar pull, the sensation of reality turning liquid. I want to tumble recklessly into them.

"I had to..." Dacian starts slowly, either searching for words or just gazing at me for what could be heartbeats or hours. "...settle some urgent affairs," he finishes somewhat stiffly, his eyes flickering briefly to my neck. "I hope my absence wasn't too much of an inconvenience."

"No," I lie. But I hesitate long enough that it triggers a small curl at the corner of his mouth. Something tells me he knows how bothered I was about not seeing him, how mad that silly dream has driven me.

It's strange sitting so near him again. I feel unsettled, but not in a bad way. It's like I'm hyperaware of him. He crosses his legs and places his hands gracefully atop them, his body relaxed, as though he's come here to catch a quiet moment away from the crowds. The wolf-dragon ring on his pinkie finger glints in the sunlight. This brings me right back to the night at the library. Except it is broad daylight, and we aren't alone, no longer hidden from the prying eyes of the world by a curtain of rain.

"Are you not joining the festivities?" he asks.

"No. Um...my family isn't here," I reply choppily as I try to suppress the resurgence of my anger.

"Does that mean you're far from home, then?"

"Yes," I say, and then add defiantly, "by choice." Even though I don't want to delve into details about how much I hate the place I'm from, I need him to know I'm here because I want to be, not because I'm running away. I'm worthy of this shot at a new life regardless of how my parents feel about me.

Dacian observes me with his dark, curious eyes. He doesn't try to prod, to make me explain what I mean. He just lets me go at my own pace, aware that I carry dark memories but not forcing them into the light. I'm grateful for this tacit understanding between us. But it should work both ways. This might be my chance to ask him something personal as well, to leave the door ajar and see if he'll step through it.

"Are you far from home too?" I venture cautiously.

His eyebrows rise slightly. "I am," he says, echoing my answer. "By choice."

I'd guessed as much from his accent, but hearing him confirm it feels like a reward. Greedily, I push further. "Very far?"

Dacian takes his time before he responds, "In more ways than you can imagine."

I recall what he let slip in the library: *I spent a long time in a very isolated place.* I still wonder what he meant by that. For some reason, I imagine a dark castle with gray stone rooms, so cold that they almost feel haunted, all except for one—a library filled with books. Given the way Dacian spoke of reading like it was his only reprieve, his home library must've been his favorite place.

"But I find that being able to travel is one of life's greatest treasures. Don't you?" Dacian adds, interrupting my musings.

This question surprises me. "I haven't really traveled all that much."

"No?" he asks, amused.

I huff out a small laugh. "Well, I went from a tiny town in the middle of North Carolina to this tiny town in the middle of Vermont. I mean, I'm exceptionally lucky that Camden offered me a scholarship," I add hastily. "And there's really only one other place in the world that I'd even consider being right now. But I don't think studying here qualifies as travel."

Dacian tips his head. "Which other place is that?"

I look down sheepishly. "I mentioned before that there's no university that offers an undergrad degree in book conservation—no university in the U.S., that is. But there's one in England, a very prestigious one. However, attending Oxford without a full scholarship that covers room and board was just never going to happen. So..." I shrug as I trail off.

"So, the two places in the world you would most love to be are full of dusty old paper?" Dacian finishes for me.

"Yeah," I admit with a laugh. I've already pretty much confessed to being a giant nerd—no use in downplaying it now.

I glance at Dacian, but I find no mockery on his face, only a wistful smile as he gazes serenely at the pond in front of us. "That is so very you, isn't it?"

"I guess it is," I say, suddenly bashful and giddy at the same time. "What about you, Mr. Bathory?"

There is a moment of stillness before Dacian responds, and as I wait, my heart does these tiny little flips in my chest.

"I've always..." he starts, but then silence moves into the small space between us again.

I watch as a golden maple leaf separates from the tree branch overhead and lands on the surface of the pond, creating a small ripple. "You've always...?" I nudge, afraid that the moment might pass, that Dacian might decide to close the door to the inner sanctum of his mind, leaving me stranded outside forevermore.

"I've always hoped that someone would come along and show me the world," he finally whispers, still gazing at the pond.

Whatever emotion is swirling in the depths of his eyes is hidden from me, but there's such longing in his voice, such sadness, that it leaves me breathless.

What a strange way to phrase it. Why would he need someone to *show* him the world? Isn't he free to go wherever he likes? The fact that he's here at Camden now, away from his homeland, is proof of that.

"It seems you've done quite well at seeing the world yourself." I try to sound overly cheerful to compensate for the soul-twisting melancholy that has taken root in me.

A smile graces Dacian's features, but it's a sad one. "I suppose so. I'm a modern man. I can go wherever I please." There's a strange bitterness in those words that leaves me even more confused. But before I can begin to decipher their cryptic meaning, this odd mood Dacian is in, he stands up. "Speaking of going places, there is a faculty function I am required to attend. The board is determined to impress the senator and his cohort, and I am sadly not exempt." He sighs a little dramatically.

"I'm sorry to hear that," I say, even though what I truly mean is, *I wish I could tell the Camden board to shove it so we could spend the rest of the day together. The rest of eternity.*

Dacian tips his head as though he finds something about my response entertaining. "I will live through it. Enjoy your evening, Mr. Evergreen. It would be a waste to spend such a promising night alone," he says meaningfully before he walks off into the crowd.

FIFTEEN

I don't know if it's because of Dacian's parting words, but I decide to join Fiona and her family for dinner. She has invited both me and her roommate, Becky, a fellow family weekend orphan since her mom couldn't fly all the way from California, and despite the shitty start to my day, I have a really good time.

The restaurant the Onayemis pick is one of those gourmet establishments that mills their own pizza flour and serves apple cider from the brewery next door. The pizza is to die for, and the bourbon maple pecan pie that comes with a scoop of homemade vanilla ice cream is probably the best dessert I've ever tasted in my life. Fiona's dad fills the evening with fascinating stories about all the corners of the world he saw while volunteering for the Peace Corps before he and Fiona's mom met in law school. I can tell how proud Fiona is of them both, and they of her, but I'm surprised to find that it doesn't make me feel resentful or envious, just happy for them.

At the end of dinner, I shamelessly pack up the leftover pie to take back with me, and when we're about to leave, Mrs. Onayemi gives me the tightest hug that makes me forget how awful my own family is. For a moment, I almost feel *loved*. And guilty for ditching them earlier. I promise myself I won't do that again.

The restaurant is in a small town along historic Route 7, a good forty miles from Camden, and I end up riding back with Becky, as we can't all fit in Fiona's car. Being the airhead she is, she forgets to drop me off and parks by her dorm, which is a fifteen-minute walk from West Hall.

"Shoot. Do you want me to drive you back?" she offers belatedly.

"Nah, I'm okay to walk." I wave Becky off and climb out of her convertible. Kind of a silly choice for a car, if you ask me, considering the amount of inclement weather we get in the mountains. Stylish, though.

I thank Becky for the ride and trudge back to my dorm.

Since the curfew has been lifted, my walk through campus is less creepy than usual, but it's also late enough that I encounter only a couple of students. The night is chilly but beautiful. *Promising*, as Dacian called it, whatever he meant by that. I look up at the sky and notice the moon is full, a large glimmering disk on a tapestry of dark blues. I wonder what Dacian is up to. Somehow, it's difficult to imagine him doing something ordinary, like having dinner with friends or watching TV. The idea of him spending the night with someone else irks me, though, so I abandon that train of thought.

I yawn, shivering in the brisk breeze, and decide to cut across the big parking lot instead of continuing on the windy path through the quad. As I emerge through the thick hedges that separate the lot from the lawn, I hear the screech of tires and someone laughing. Then I spot Mads Jr.'s blue Firebird and Callahan's Testarossa zooming in circles in the widest part of the lot, like dogs herding sheep, with Eric Stockton in the center.

"Bro! Come on, dude, let me in!" he pleads, trying to chase after Mads' Firebird. But the moment he gets close, Mads cruelly steps on the gas pedal and drives just out of reach. Eric jerks away, barely avoiding getting hit. He tries for Testarossa next. "Grady, my man!" he whines. "Let me ride with you guys!" But to no avail.

Mads Jr. laughs maniacally. "Nice try, Eric! But you know the deal. No rides for you until you do your part."

Eric looks positively miserable and dives for the Firebird again, only to be met with the same derision.

I halt at the edge of the lot. What kind of sick game is this? Not to mention, why are the legacies doing it to one of their own? I expected Mads to throw some kind of tantrum after being used as a prop for his dad's photo ops, but I can't believe he's taking it out on Eric, who always follows him like a loyal puppy. Not that it's any of my business or that I even care, but their mansion is far from campus, and Eric never got a new car after drunk-crashing his DeLorean. The idiot got away without a DUI, thanks to his parents' influence, but he didn't get out of the incident completely unscathed: they won't buy him another car, and he's forbidden to drive on campus. Since then, he's been hitching rides with Mads and Grady. And now, for some reason, they're refusing to let him in their cars. Do they expect him to hike miles through the mountains to get home? That's messed up.

Still, I'm not getting involved. I decide to cross the lot while they're distracted. I speed up, but before I can get to the other side and disappear under the cover of trees, I hear the loud roar of an engine.

"What the hell!" I scream and jump back as Grady's Testarossa zooms right in front of me, almost driving over the toe of my right sneaker.

Like an angry red demon, it screeches to a stop several feet past me, and Grady's head pops out of the driver's side window to leer at me. His mouth is all teeth, and he looks like he's barely holding himself back from flooring the gas and rear-ending me for fun. Several girls chortle in the back seat, highly entertained.

I clench my fists, my anger about to explode. What is this asshole's problem? I want to kick his stupid Ferrari, but I don't dare. Grady might very well run me over—he's that deranged. As I seethe, he revs the engine several times to taunt me.

From behind me, I hear another car coming. I whip halfway

around, not wanting to lose my visual on the Testarossa. The blue Firebird pulls up to me, swift and dangerous. Mads and Alessandra are sneering at me through the windshield.

"You should be careful what rumors you spread about us, Evergreen," Mads says, grinning like a horror movie clown. "Consider this your final warning."

I clamp my mouth shut to stop myself from lashing out. I've done nothing wrong, and it's been weeks! Why can't they just freaking let it go? But even as I think this, I realize that my telling Pixie Trish that Grady drugged her drink doesn't have anything to do with this. They're probably bored after dealing with their families all day, and they're using the stupid party incident as an excuse to take it out on me. I can only imagine what Eric has done to end up in the same boat. Now that Mads has stopped his car, he dives for the Firebird's back door. But to his further humiliation, it's locked.

"You know the deal, Eric!" Mads taunts mercilessly as both Firebird's and Testarossa's engines come alive again. From this close, their roar is so annoyingly loud that I have to cover my ears. Within seconds, they tear away several times faster than the fifteen-mile-per-hour speed limit.

I exhale heavily as their red taillights vanish into the night. Like an unwanted pet, Eric stands beside me, abandoned and miserable. He really doesn't look well. There are giant bags under his eyes, and his skin is the color of ash. I almost feel sad for him.

Almost. Because the moment our eyes meet, he snarls, "What do you want, Evergreen?" I instantly lose any charitable feelings toward him. Just because the legacies have a rift doesn't mean he and I are friends now.

"Nothing," I snap back and turn away, not sparing Eric another glance as I march back to my dorm.

I TRY NOT to let that encounter ruin my otherwise exceptionally good second half of the day. The dinner with the Onayemis and Becky was wonderful, and I even got to talk to Dacian. *Alone.* That was a dessert sweeter than even the maple pecan pie from the restaurant. I climb into bed, smiling. This weird push and pull between us is frustrating and confusing. But today was more pull, and I got to uncover more pieces of the enigma that is Dacian, even if I've yet to make sense of them. What did he mean about waiting for someone to show him the world? Whatever it may be, I'll be the first in line if called.

Before I close my eyes, I gaze at the moon hanging outside my window. *Promising*, Dacian's velvety voice says inside my head as I drift off to sleep.

The dream I have that night is perhaps the strangest one yet.

I dream that I awaken when I hear someone whispering to me. It's coming from the darkness of the trees beyond the western edge of campus, a distant voice I can't place. But it has a strange lulling quality that calls to me, compels me to rise out of bed and obediently follow it outside into the cold, moonlit night.

I'm on the path outside of the West Hall courtyard, halfway to the dark woods, when silver mist starts rolling across the grounds. It surrounds me, quickly obscuring my way. Alarmed, I stop. But then my wariness fades because the mist seems familiar somehow. It beckons me, whispers to me, makes me feel that it wants me nearer. In a daze, I take another step. Slowly, a tendril of silver extends toward me, shimmering faintly in the moonlight. It's beautiful, like a spell of midnight magic. When it grazes my hand, I sigh at how cool and soft its touch is. Entranced, I let it caress my skin—just the tips of my fingers at first, then my palm. I want to touch it back, but when I try, it slips through my fingers, ungraspable and ghostlike. Yet its effect is intoxicating.

Tentatively, as though asking for permission, it skims up my arm up to my exposed neck. My breathing quickens. As the mist brushes the sensitive skin under my ear, the touch becomes more sensual, and then I notice someone *watching* me. A glimmer of a silhouette concealed within the mist, or maybe one with it—I can't tell. But even so, I don't want the mist to stop. I let it whisper to me, let it drift over my throat, my mouth, slip under the neckline of my sweater and the loose fabric of my pajama pants. The feeling of being observed only makes my heart thrum faster, makes me want to lose myself in this phantom embrace.

I close my eyes and let the mist envelop me, let it touch me everywhere it wants.

Waves of pleasure explode in me as I gasp awake. I lie on my back, staring at the shimmery sliver of moonlight on my ceiling, panting, my body buzzing and warm. As seconds pass and my skin starts to cool, I gradually become aware of other things, such as the sticky dampness in my pajama pants.

Embarrassed, I squeeze my eyes shut. I haven't had a wet dream in a while, and this one was provoked by *a fog*. How can someone get aroused by fog?

There was someone hiding in it, though. Who was it? I furrow my brow, concentrating so hard on remembering anything about the mysterious stranger that splotches of white flood my vision. But there was no face, only a vague silhouette. Even so, I'm certain the presence didn't feel unfamiliar—so close, almost within my grasp, and frustratingly out of reach at the same time. Why wouldn't he come out? I wasn't scared of whoever was hiding in the shadows. Not once did I hesitate or try to draw back from the mist. I wanted to be touched. Wanted to be seen. Why did I have to wake up so soon?

I roll onto my side, and despite the immense need to sleep some more, I slowly coax myself out of bed. At least it's early enough that the shared shower should be empty.

It is only after I've washed myself in steaming-hot water and changed into fresh pants, devoid of evidence of any lascivious dreams, that I finally notice—I've left my window cracked open again.

"DESIRE AND TERROR," Dacian says as he writes the words on the blackboard in his exquisite cursive. A hush falls over the auditorium; the way his velvety voice curls around those words does something to the air in the room. Every girl in the class perks up, seemingly even more interested in his lecture than usual. But I don't have a brain cell to spare on them. My eyes trace the luscious flowing lines of the word *desire* over and over, and my cheeks flood with self-conscious warmth. Dacian doesn't glance at me when he turns around, but I have a hard time keeping my eyes on him. It's not like *he* was in my dream the other night. It was just fog that touched me, not a person. And yet, every inch of my skin seems to be reacting to him.

"As you know, we won't have a midterm in this class. Instead, I would like you to write a short essay exploring the connection between these two themes in Gothic literature," he announces. "You may use any of the works we've discussed or anything you've read outside of class to illustrate your points. You have the next two weeks to work on it. Don't shy away from the forbidden, from the monstrousness we might face if we follow our desire through the darkness. Does anyone have any questions?"

Slowly, his dark gaze glides around the room until it settles on me. My stomach feels like it's been hit with a cannonball of heat. I want to hide my eyes from him, but I can't look away. For a moment, time stops, and to my utter mortification, I become convinced that he knows what I'm thinking. It's not possible, but my heart stutters anyway. The heat spreads from my belly to my face like a raging inferno. I feel exposed right down to my bones. The images from my dream spark in my mind: the silhouette watching me from the fog, the sensation of being caressed, of being wanted. The dream hid the identity of the person in the mist, but try as I may to deny it, I know exactly who I wish it was. And just that acknowledgment makes me want to crawl under my desk and die of embarrassment.

"Ms. Onayemi?" Dacian says, and with a jolt, I realize I've been released from the captivity of his gaze.

Beside me, Fiona asks, "How many pages should we write, Mr. Bathory?"

"Hmm," he says, considering. "Five to ten will suffice. No more than that." Despite the emotional mayhem in my head, Dacian appears absolutely nonplussed. It's discombobulating. But why should he be rattled? He doesn't have the telepathic powers to read my horny thoughts; it's just me losing my mind over a dream. It's so stupid, that it's humiliating. I need to calm down. I won't survive the rest of class otherwise.

I look down at my notes, trying to concentrate on my barely legible scribbles—unlike Dacian's, my penmanship leaves much to be desired. But before I can stop panicking and get back to reality, Dacian adds, "I should also mention that some of you may choose to explore the subject of queer desire in this context—that would also be welcome."

If before I felt like my body was melting from shame, now it's like I'm about to be incinerated. How can he say that so openly? Why would he even bring that up? Perhaps, he really was interested in reading the missing diary. But if that's true, then what does all of this mean? Could it be a coincidence he kept mentioning it to me, or does he know something about me that I've never said to him aloud?

My frenzied thoughts are interrupted by a sudden disgruntled outburst in the back row. "Are you seriously saying you want us to write about queers?" Eric Stockton rasps, sounding exasperated.

I whip my head around. It's the first time he's been awake in class, and *this* is what he has to say?

Immediately I turn back to Dacian, anxious to see his reaction. His beautiful mouth twitches as though he's trying to suppress great fury. "Yes, I am saying exactly that, Mr. Stockton," he replies. His tone is controlled and even, but there's a current of danger crackling underneath. It makes the skin on my arms rise in goosebumps. "And why wouldn't I? It's as valid a subject as any. The queerness of many Gothic authors is well known. How can we judge these works if we disregard the lives of the people who created them?"

The class is utterly silent as everyone watches Dacian with stunned fascination. Most of the students seem uncomfortable with this topic; just the word *queerness* sends ripples of quiet gasps around the room. And yet Dacian delivers his speech with such bluntness and grace, like he's completely unafraid of what anyone might assume about him. Maybe it's my own history of being outed against my will, but I'm awestruck by him.

"William Beckford, the author of *Vathek*, one of the foundational Gothic texts, was chased out of England after his homosexual relationship became public," he continues matter-of-factly. "Lord Byron, who was directly inspired by Beckford, was also known all over Europe for his amorous exploits with both men and women. And I haven't even mentioned Oscar Wilde, who was forced to edit most allusions to homoeroticism out of *The Picture Of Dorian Gray* after its first edition was disparaged by critics for supposed moral corruption and 'effeminate frivolity.' Sheridan Le Fanu's *Carmilla* and Daphne du Maurier's *Rebecca* are other famous examples, full of repressed lesbian desire. Shall I continue?"

A heavy pause follows as the class processes what Dacian just said. Those are indeed a lot of notable works.

Then Eric shouts, "Who cares? I ain't writing no queer stuff!"

I recoil. It's always distressing to discover that the person next to you hates your very existence. Now that I have a few friends I can be open with, I sometimes forget what the rest of the world is like. Still, this level of disrespect is out of character even for Eric, regardless of what he believes.

If eyes could kill, blood would surely be spilled in Kinnell Hall this afternoon. "Mr. Stockton, you're in a place of high education," Dacian warns with unconcealed hostility. "If you cannot conduct yourself like an adult, I suggest you leave my class immediately."

Shocked murmurs fill the room as the tension that's been

building between Eric and Dacian for weeks finally comes to a head. Behind me, I hear a loud screech of a chair's metal legs against the wooden floor, then a furious patter of footsteps. As Eric storms out of the auditorium, he slams the door with so much force that it rattles the windows.

I stare after him, stunned and unsure of what just happened.

"JONATHAN? EARTH TO JONATHAN!" Fiona waves her hand frantically in front of me. I snap back to the present. We're having lunch at the dining hall, but I have no memory of getting here or piling a bunch of cheese pizza on my plate. "What's going on with you?" she asks.

"N-nothing," I stutter, feigning ignorance.

Of course, that doesn't work on her. "Right. You practically ran out of Gothic lit. Are you upset about what Eric said?"

"No." I shake my head automatically, then reconsider. "I mean, yes, I hated that he did that. Even if he wasn't talking about me, it still felt like he was. But him being a prejudiced asshole is old news. What I can't believe is that Mr. Bathory would discuss gay authors so openly." My cheeks flush again at the memory of the things Dacian said, the essay he assigned. I know he didn't specifically say to write about queer desire, but now that's on my mind, I can't stop thinking about it.

Fiona's eyebrows furrow. "I thought you, of all people, would be happy about that."

"I am. I just..." I feel the heat in my face intensifying, spreading down to my chest all the way to my groin. I mentally kick myself. If I'm not careful, I'll need a few minutes of privacy. "I had a weird dream last night. And this brought me right back to it," I blurt.

Fiona narrows her eyes. "What kind of dream?"

I lick my lips, wavering for a moment. I shouldn't have said anything, but it's too late to backpedal now. "The sexy kind," I admit in a hushed voice.

Fiona covers her mouth, trying to stave off a laugh. She quickly finishes chewing her spaghetti so she won't spray it all over the table before replying with glee, "Jonathan, oh, Jonathan. I can't believe you spent Gothic lit reliving your erotic fantasies!"

"Shh!" I practically jump out of my skin, waving my arms in an attempt to shush her and simultaneously checking if anyone at the nearby tables overheard us. I definitely don't want people to know that Dacian Bathory arouses erotic fantasies in me.

Fiona only laughs at me. "It's all good, dude. It's important to have a healthy stress release from time to time, if you know what I mean." She wiggles her eyebrows suggestively, and despite my embarrassment, I smile too. "Besides, I'm happy you're finally getting ready to move on from your old flame. You can't pine over someone forever. Life's too short for that."

My smile falters. I know Fiona only wants what's best for me, but this catches me off guard. In the last several days, I've barely thought of Clay. Ever since that nightmare with the wolves, he's stopped haunting my dreams, and my waking thoughts have been consumed by Dacian instead. I wonder if I should feel guilty about that. Am I using the first convenient excuse to get over Clay? Am I betraying his memory? But he's dead, and we'll never be together again. Maybe it's okay to feel something for someone else, even if that someone is completely unattainable and just plain wrong to pursue.

I put that thought aside, not ready to delve into it in front of Fiona. But as the day goes by, it keeps coming back to me. Finally, when I'm alone in my room that night, fresh out of distractions, I realize I will have to face this question head-on eventually. So I flick the lights off, climb into bed, and open the floodgates.

Am I really attracted to Dacian Bathory?

As my eyes adjust to the darkness, I try to give this question a thorough, critical examination.

Maybe I'm just projecting. Maybe it isn't specifically Dacian that I want. It could be my loneliness manifesting. Dacian is new and handsome and has given me a little bit of attention. It would be easy for the feelings I'd shoved down for two years to latch on to him.

But even as I list all these things in my mind, trying to convince myself that I can't possibly be feeling what I'm feeling, something inside me knows I'm lying.

I don't really know Dacian—

Lie.

During the moments we shared in the library and by the pond, I felt like he was looking right into me—like he could see inside my heart better than anyone I've ever met. And even though my understanding is nebulous and impossible to put into words, deep down in my core, I'm sure that I know him too.

But I can't like him, because that would be wrong, and it couldn't possibly go anywhere—

Also a lie.

Since the moment I saw him in the theater, I'd singled him out. I knew he was special. So how could it be wrong if I felt what I felt before I found out he was a professor, before I even learned his name? And Dacian—if he doesn't want anything to do with me, why does he continue to seek me out? Why speak to the library on my behalf? Why read "The Raven" to me?

Still, I should stop right there. This is a perilous path for my heart, and no good will come out of it—

Another lie.

What good has ever come of my feelings? My heart can't possibly get more broken. And even if I start trying right now to stomp my desire out before it blooms into something uncontrollable, that train left the station a long time ago. There is no chasing after it. I'm dangerously, hopelessly, and irreversibly falling for Dacian Bathory. And as I finally close my eyes, I wish the fog dream will return, and that the person hiding in it will reveal himself to me, and that it will be him.

Sixteen

I'm somewhat relieved that Gothic lit doesn't meet during the week of midterms. I ache for Dacian's company, but I also don't trust myself not to act like a fool in front of him. I'll have to learn to keep my cool. I can't let anybody know the effect he has on me. Not to mention that I haven't even started working on the essay he assigned. Every time I think of the theme, I get heart palpitations. I've no idea what I'm going to write.

I guess I'll have the four days of fall break to figure something out. There won't be much else to do, anyway. In the aftermath of Anita Hernandez's murder, all students are strongly advised to leave campus, so the place will be a ghost town. Having nowhere to go, I've applied for special permission to stay. I'll probably be haunting West Hall by myself. Last year, I spent both this break and Thanksgiving at Fiona's—her parents were very kind to host me—but this time, they are all traveling to St. Thomas for her cousin's wedding.

"I feel bad leaving you here," she confesses during one of our late-night midterm study sessions at the library. "But I can't miss Sasha's big day. She only picked this date because it was during my break. Are you sure you don't want to stay at our guest house? You can drive over with me."

"By myself? Without you?" I ask incredulously.

"Mom said you're welcome to. It's not fun being alone in an empty dorm. She also doesn't like that they never found who murdered that woman. She wants you to be safe."

I shake my head, touched. "Nah. Please thank your mom for her generosity, but I'm good. It's just four days. And don't worry about me. Enjoy the beach and the party!"

"God, yeah, I can't wait." Fiona sighs dreamily. "I could use some sunshine after all this dreariness." She gestures at the nearest window, which is being pummeled by endless streaks of rain. "But I'm gonna give you my hotel info. Call me if something happens, okay? And don't go hiking in the woods alone if you get bored. I don't think they ever found the missing hiker either."

I chuckle. "Nothing will happen." It's not like I ever venture out into the woods anyway. And I have plenty of reading to do, so boredom will hardly be a danger to me. But Fiona gives me a pointed side-eye until I acquiesce. "Okay, okay. I'll call."

In the end, something disturbing does occur that very week, but despite my assurances, I never get to tell Fiona about it.

MIDTERMS fly by faster than expected, and then it's fall break. My grades won't be posted till next week, but I feel pretty good about them. I spend most of Wednesday lunch trying to reassure Fiona that there's no way she failed her psych test with the amount of studying she did. She leaves that afternoon, feeling a bit more optimistic about it, and the whole campus clears out within hours.

I still have my shift at the library on Friday before it closes for the weekend, and I'm grateful since I don't have anywhere else to be. But it's a very slow day. Jessi is gone for the break, so I'm manning the front desk by myself. There's a total of three phone calls I have to answer, and a couple of professors stop by, but no students show up. Or so I think. I head down to the vault to return some works one of the language faculty requested and see a figure standing by the shelves, facing away from me.

I startle. "Eric?" What is he doing here, and more importantly, how did he open the vault? He couldn't have slipped past me at the front desk, and he certainly shouldn't still have his librarian's key from the summer.

For a moment, he doesn't respond, just continues to stare at the shelf, muttering something to himself. A foreboding sense of wrongness comes over me. I've never liked being in closed-off underground spaces with no windows and only one exit. Despite all the books around me, I can't help but feel like I'm locked in a tomb. In the silence, the fluorescent light buzzes and flickers above me, and the air feels cold, as though someone has cranked up the AC. There's nothing I want more than to get out of here, but it's my job to make sure Eric leaves too. I take a few steps toward him. "Eric, the vault is for employees only. You're not supposed to be here."

This finally catches his attention. But when he turns around, I wish he hadn't. Something is off about him, almost like when he had that outburst in Gothic lit but dialed up a few notches. His eyes are wide and red like he hasn't been sleeping, and he's still mumbling something dazedly as his gaze focuses on me.

"Evergreen?" he says, his voice gravelly, as though he didn't expect to see another person here. "What do you want?"

The gall. *I* should be asking *him* that. It's a Herculean effort to restrain my annoyance and repeat myself for the third time. "Eric, this section is off-limits. If you're looking for a book, I'll get it for you. Otherwise, please leave immediately." It's absurd to suggest that Eric wants a book, but what else am I to think?

Eric frowns, and his eyes turn absent again, drawn back into his own thoughts. "Books...yeah, it's the stupid books. It's all their fault." He shakes his head, his face twisting into a hideous grimace.

What the hell? Is he *drunk*? I need to get him out of here before he pukes on some antique manuscript. "Eric, I have no idea what you're on about, but you need to go." I move toward him, ready to escort him out by force.

But he doesn't even hear me. "I hate books!" he growls at the shelves instead. "Hate you! Hate you! Hate you!"

I stop in my tracks. The anger I've been repressing for months blazes up in me. This guy took away my internship and made my summer miserable. I know he never wanted the position, that he got it only because his rich family bought it for him, but to hear him say that he *hates* books?

"What is wrong with you?" I snap. "You show up here like you freaking own the place just so you can denigrate hundreds of years of intellectual labor? What does an imbecile like you even know about creating something of value? You live your spoiled little life where everything is handed to you. Get out of here before I—"

I gasp. In the blink of an eye, Eric closes the distance between us and shoves me into the nearest metal shelf, which knocks the wind out of me. He claws at my hoodie and snarls into my face. "What do you know about me, Evergreen, huh? You know nothing! NOTHING!"

Fear prickles at the base of my skull. Alarm bells start shrieking in my head. I've never been afraid of Eric. Unlike Grady, he just doesn't look menacing. But right now, there's a weird, disturbed energy about him. I swear it feels like I'm one wrong word away from him murdering me.

As calmly as I can manage, I say "Eric, let go of me."

For a moment, he simply heaves, his face manic.

Then suddenly, his arms twitch away, and he backs off, but a creepy smirk turns up his mouth. "It's you, then," he mutters under his breath like he's made some kind of decision. "Gotta be you."

"What?" I scowl, shaken. But he doesn't say more. Flashing one last murderous glare at me, Eric stomps out of the vault.

I exhale with a shudder. It takes a long moment for my muscles to unclench.

IT'S astonishing how deserted a place as big as Camden can look without the students milling about. In the time it takes to walk back to the dorm from the library, I don't encounter a single soul. The sidewalks and parking lots are all empty. I don't scare easily, but I feel a little on edge after the incident with Eric. I have no idea what any of it was about. I kick the dry leaves irritably. The silence that has taken over campus is eerie in a way that gets under my skin. I almost regret not taking Fiona up on her offer to stay at her place. But it's too late, and anyway, why am I suddenly such a scaredy-cat? I've spent plenty of time alone. The room I rented over the summer was above someone's garage out in the boonies, and the owners were often gone camping and kayaking. Being by myself didn't frighten me then. Besides, four days of quiet should be good for me. I'll take a stab at that essay and hopefully sleep. I haven't slept well in a few days. Despite how awkward I felt in front of Dacian, I've been secretly wishing the fog dream would return. That he'd be in it unconcealed, letting my eyes feast on him. There isn't anything wrong with just *dreaming* of Dacian, right? If those fantasies never leave the quiet chambers of my mind, they won't hurt anyone.

I kick my Chucks off by the threshold as I step into my room, which is awfully stuffy. The building's heat is on full blast again, and the radiator is clicking loudly. What a waste when literally no one but me is around. I crack open the window just a smidge to let some air in but tell myself not to forget to close it again, knowing my propensity to wake up freezing in the middle of the night.

I try to read *Jekyll and Hyde*, which is my next assignment for Dacian's class, but I quickly become drowsy and decide to call it an early night. I turn the lights off, gently pat my box of letters good night, and burrow snugly under the covers.

But peaceful sleep fails to come. For several hours, I toss and turn in my bed, unable to get comfortable. I open and close the window in a futile attempt to regulate the temperature before giving up and just leaving it open. As fresh, icy air fills the room, I finally manage to drift off. But my dreams are strange. I think Dacian is in them, except I don't see him—I just know that he's somewhere in the woods around campus. And there's someone else there, too, and a sense of danger. I feel it acutely. Worried about Dacian's safety, I try to find him, but I keep going in circles and getting lost in the trees.

Then I suddenly hear his voice calling from the darkness, and it sounds so real that I shoot into a sitting position, fully awake. Breathing heavily, I look around my room, my heart pounding. It doesn't make sense, but I swear Dacian's voice wasn't part of the dream. I strain to hear any noise around me—perhaps some students stayed behind and are throwing a party, or maybe the TV in the common room was left on. But West Hall is quiet. Oppressively quiet.

Prickly anxiety begins to crawl over my skin. What if Dacian really called me? What if a murderer is lurking outside, and Dacian needs my help? I know this isn't logical, but I won't be able to sleep again until I check. Rubbing my forehead tiredly, I crawl out of bed. I throw on my sweatshirt and sneakers and head outside.

The moment I step out of the residence hall, the October chill bites my skin, and I shiver. The nights have grown cold in the past week, the temperature dipping below thirty degrees. My hoodie isn't thick enough to protect me. But my head is instantly clearer, and that feels good.

I couldn't find Dacian in the incomprehensible maze of the dream landscape, but I know how to get to the woods in real life. I walk briskly through the back courtyard, making my way toward the looming darkness of the trees. It's quiet save for the crunch of fallen leaves under my feet. When I've walked for a few minutes without encountering anything or anyone, my erratic heartbeat slows and I calm down a little. The walkway bends around the athletic facilities, and after I pass them, I have an unobstructed view of the woods. There's a narrow hiking trail branching off from the path. I gaze at the twisted shadows of the tree trunks ahead. I think it's safe to turn back now. It was just a nightmare, intense but not real.

But just as I'm about to call it quits, there's movement in the trees. I stop abruptly. Is that a person? I squint, trying to make out the shape, but it's too dark. The sole streetlight nearby doesn't reach that far.

My heartbeat spikes again as I take a few steps along the trail. When my eyes adjust to the darkness, that's when I see it: a figure crouching under an old maple tree. No, not one figure—two. One is splayed on the ground, his body twitching as though trying to resist, his right leg bent unnaturally, probably broken. The second one is hovering above him, pinning him down. I can't see either of their faces, but there's a wet gurgling kind of sound coming from that direction.

Dread rolls over me. I need to get away from here and call security. But before I can force myself to take a step, I realize the silhouette on top looks familiar.

"Mr. Bathory?" I say, shocked that I actually found him.

The figure freezes. Slowly, he turns to face me. The hair on the back of my neck stands up. It is indeed Dacian; his striking face is unmistakable in the pale moonlight. Only his eyes...they aren't the two fathomless abysses I so often find myself lost in. Instead they are glowing bright red like some hellish creature from a horror story, and his mouth is smeared with something dark and wet. It's dripping off his sharp chin as though...as though he's been *drinking* it.

My mind goes fuzzy. My gaze falls to the grass below Dacian, and the person I find there, motionless, is Eric Stockton. Oh my god. I cover my mouth. Just hours ago, I saw him in the vault, but now there's a gaping hole in his neck that's gushing blood as though he's been mauled by a wild animal. No, not an animal—Dacian. He's the only one here.

My stomach roils. I stagger back a step. This breaks the silent spell.

Dacian's bloodied mouth opens. "Mr. Evergreen—" he says. His arm rises as though to beg me to stay. But my instinct to run finally kicks in. I don't fight it anymore.

I charge across the lawn to the back courtyard of West Hall faster than I've ever run in my life. I nearly lose my footing on the slippery grass and tumble through the hedges, but in my terror, I don't dare look over my shoulder, not once. I don't stop until I'm back in my room with my door shut and my key turned in the lock.

I force myself to stay by the door, listening. I have no idea if Dacian followed me inside or if he knows which room I live in. I strain for the sound of footsteps, any sign of pursuit, but all I hear is my own ragged breathing. Temporary relief washes over me, and I let my forehead fall against the wooden doorframe. As I close my eyes, images of what I saw swirl in my mind like pieces of a broken mirror.

Eric...he looked *dead*. Or soon to be dead, what with the severed jugular and that amount of blood pouring out of him. A part of me tries to conjure an explanation that isn't supernatural, that doesn't rely on Dacian being something I can't even say out loud, but it comes up empty. There was so much blood on Dacian's face, dripping from his mouth. And this isn't the first time something like this has happened on campus. I feel nauseated once the realization hits—this is how the woman who worked in the dining hall died. Once I discard all those garbage rumors about cartels, the only facts I know for certain are that there were bite marks on her body and that her blood was drained like someone tortured her. But maybe the blood was taken for a different reason.

My mind feels like it's about to explode. Was it Dacian who

killed Anita Hernandez and dumped her into the river to hide the evidence? But how is that possible? Dacian, who went out of his way to get the library job for me, who read me a poem like his heart was shattering, who looked at me like I meant something to him... has he been lying to me this whole time? Has he just been waiting for an opportune moment to corner me alone because he...he's...

I can't even make myself think the word.

Not daring to flick the lights on, I quietly pull away from the door, too afraid to make a sound. I'm alone, and he's looking for me. Whatever reason he had for not killing me earlier is surely gone now. I've learned his secret; he won't let me get away with it.

Tap-tap-tap. I hear a knock against the glass.

I jump. It takes a moment for me to realize that it came from the window behind me—the one I left open. Seized by terror, I turn around slowly. Bathed in shimmery moonlight, Dacian is outside—outside my *third-story* window—and his feet aren't supported by anything.

My knees wobble at the impossible sight. He's found me already. On instinct, I dive into a corner, hoping faintly that its shadows will conceal me. But on my way I crash into the sharp corner of my desk, hard.

"Careful, Mr. Evergreen," Dacian warns as I yelp in pain. "You don't want to hurt yourself." He's wiped the blood from his face, but that does nothing to erase my memory of him covered with it. The ominous red glow has yet to leave his eyes.

Shuddering like a rabbit about to be slaughtered, I back against the wall, but it's no better than a child hiding from a monster under their bed. Because the shadows are Dacian's friends. With unnatural swiftness, he zooms forward, right up against the window, peering through the open crack like an owl on a hunt. The crimson glow of his eyes casts light onto the white windowsill as they lock with mine. "You know I can still see you, Mr. Evergreen. You can't hide from me. Yours is the only beating heart inside this building."

A sickening wave of horror envelops me. Can he really hear that? He could be bluffing, trying to scare me, but what would be the point? In a frenzy, I wrack my brain for information about those who haunt the night in search of blood—anything I can remember from movies and books.

They don't reflect in mirrors, and they're scared of sunlight—I've never seen him near a mirror to know for certain, but that second one clearly isn't true. Sometimes, they can shapeshift into bats—I don't know about that, but Dacian can definitely fly. They can have extraordinary strength and healing abilities—again, I'm not sure. But Dacian killed Eric and took a chunk out of his neck with his teeth. What other abominable things is he capable of? If what he says is true, there's nowhere to run from him. He'll just break through the window and kill me too.

"Let me in. We need to talk," Dacian says again. For some baffling reason, he's not rushing in, just hovering outside like a black cloud.

I frown. Why is he bothering to ask permission? Is this some kind of sick game? Is he trying to make the food come to him?

"Mr. Evergreen, please don't be unreasonable," he says, more insistent this time. His scarlet eyes bore into mine through the crack. I can tell his patience is starting to wane. But still, he makes no move to lift the sash or break the window. This doesn't make sense.

Then, more trivia springs up in my brain. It takes a moment for me to piece it together.

When Dacian asks again, I shock myself by refusing him out loud—"No!" It's dangerous testing this theory of mine, but I've got nothing left to lose.

Dacian's long eyelashes flicker in surprise, casting odd shadows in the light coming from his eyes. But he doesn't lash out, and most importantly, he doesn't attempt to force his way in. His fingers tap the window frame impatiently. "Don't be stubborn, Mr. Evergreen. This is in your own best interest. Open the window. Now!" he commands. Then he unleashes the full intensity of his gaze on me.

I can feel the great churning pull of it, the trance I often find myself in when I'm alone with him. It lulls me. For a second, I wonder if it's best to stop resisting. I want to go to him. I want those eyes to look only at me. I want to feel his hands on me, corporeal and not just midnight imaginings. The desire is so deep and overwhelming that it's feral. I almost succumb to it. Almost.

"No!" I shout again and rise to my feet defiantly. How dare he use his vampire tricks on me? Yes, *vampire*—I can say it now. I know what he is beyond any doubt. A bloodthirsty, devious vampire who lied to me, who manipulated me. A murdering monster, and I—

I *liked* him. The hurt in my chest splinters into tiny little shards—and then spins into a fury. I liked him. I wanted him. How stupid was I? Led to the slaughter like a gullible lovesick lamb.

But I won't go down so easily. Of all the myths about vampires, I'm certain now this one is true—he can't come in unless invited, and I'm not inviting him, no matter how much he tries to dazzle me.

"Fine," Dacian hisses, no longer feigning politeness. In his mouth, I see two sharp fangs glinting in the moonlight. I flinch from pure shock, from this blunt confirmation of his identity. Dacian straightens and backs away from the window, watching me for a long moment as though debating something. Slowly, he schools his expression into submission, and the tension in his face seems to relax a little. "Resist all you want," he finally says, and there's a calm, unnerving confidence in his voice, one that borders on arrogance. "But you will let me in, Mr. Evergreen. One way or another. In fact, you already have."

My world goes topsy-turvy. But before I can demand to know the meaning of his words, Dacian's body transforms into silver mist and then dissipates like it was never there at all. Stunned, my mouth drops open. That mist—I know it. I've seen it before. I've *felt* it before.

You already have, echoes in my mind. *One way or another.*

My legs fold as the fight goes out of me, and I slide down the wall. The mad thudding of my heart drowns out the blast of panic in my head, leaving only one thought standing: Dacian Bathory doesn't need to break the window to get to me. For weeks, he has been visiting me in my dreams. And I welcomed him. Gladly.

SEVENTEEN

The odd nightmare about shadow wolves, the mist, my dorm window being open despite the fact that I couldn't remember opening it—it all makes sense now. Those dreams started only after Dacian showed up in Camden. Before that, I always just dreamed of Clay and his letters. All this time, he has been luring me in.

I press my hands to my face, wishing I could sink through the floor. What else has he been doing that I haven't caught on to yet? A clawing grip of hysteria seizes my windpipe. This can't be happening to me. Maybe if I fall asleep, I'll wake up tomorrow and realize that all of this has been an elaborate nightmare caused by all the trauma in my life. Heck, I'll even go to counseling. Or, per Fiona's advice, join the Gay and Lesbian Alliance to help me deal with my "issues." But as tempting as ignoring reality sounds, that's exactly what I mustn't do. Dacian will be waiting for me in my dreams, and I don't trust myself to resist him. I know I won't have the strength. I was barely able to reject him while I was awake.

So I don't dare approach my bed or close my eyes for the rest of the night, watching as the clock radio on my nightstand marks every passing minute with its glowing red digits.

When the day breaks, I finally work up enough courage to peer out of my window again. I examine the courtyard and the green plaza below. But both are empty. No parked cars, no students milling about. And no vampire literature professor.

I blow out a puff of air, emptying my lungs, and allow myself to sit down on the edge of my bed. There's a dull ache at my temples, and my backside feels like it's made out of bricks from spending the night sitting on the hard floor. I try not to think about the fact that I'm gonna be in this dorm alone until other students start returning on Sunday, and it's only Saturday morning. How am I supposed to survive that?

I can't have a meltdown, I tell myself. I must think clearly, and for that, I need coffee. I won't last the day, let alone another night, without it. My stomach grumbles treacherously too. My family used to have a Mr. Coffee machine. How I regret not snatching it when I packed. I barely took anything when I left, even things that belonged to me—I was so bitter then. But prioritizing anger over practicality has come back to bite me many times since. Without a coffee maker or a food stash, I've no choice but to venture out.

Is it safe, though? Clearly, not all pop culture myths about vampires are true. Dacian couldn't come into my room without being invited, but he doesn't burst into flame when exposed to sunlight, which means he could attack me at any hour of the day. Although I don't think he'll try to murder me in broad daylight; witnesses will complicate things for him. He'll bide his time and corner me when I'm alone or asleep. Being around people is one way to guarantee my safety for the time being.

Armed with that idea, I take a painfully cold shower to keep myself awake and then patiently wait for someone else to appear. It takes several hours before the school maintenance crew shows up to blow the leaves off the sidewalks and rake the lawn. That's when I make my escape.

I speed walk through the hallways, step outside, and bolt the short distance to my car. Luckily, I moved it to the first row since those spots were available for once. I don't care that I must look crazy to anyone who sees me right now. They don't know what I know. They haven't seen what I've seen.

My hands are shaking so badly that it takes several attempts to open my Chevy's rusted door. I cuss with relief when it yields and practically dive inside. Only after I merge onto Route 7 am I able to relax a little. I don't think Dacian will try to stage an ambush on a highway.

I want to put some distance between myself and Camden, so I drive north for a good twenty miles until I spot a large rest stop with a Dunkin' Donuts. There are several people sitting at the counter—an elderly guy with a newspaper and some commuters, enough watchful eyes to make it safe. Still, I double-check my surroundings before I claim a spot at the counter. I order a honey-dipped doughnut and coffee from the server lady wearing a bright pink hat and apron. She puts my donut in a paper bag and pours my coffee into a ceramic mug with a brown Dunkin' logo. I wrap my chilled hands around it and inhale the aroma. I couldn't stop shivering while I was driving—the Chevy's heating has been busted for years. As warmth seeps into my fingers, some tension finally leaves my body. A few sips and sugary bites later, my brain is revived enough to be reacquainted with logic.

This is one big, horrible mess, isn't it? I've witnessed a gruesome murder, but I can't call the cops because what am I going to tell them? "My Gothic lit professor is a vampire who drank my classmate's blood"? They'd put me straight into the loony bin! I have no proof, only what I saw and my dreams, which no one will believe.

A pit of acid swirls in my stomach. We have some kind of a mind connection, Dacian and me. He all but validated that when he said I'd let him in already. But how far does it go? All those times I looked into his eyes and "saw" or "felt" things, maybe those were just images he fed me to gain my trust. But that figure in the dream fog—that was him. I have no doubt about it. He watched me as the mist touched my body, as I let it roam unrestricted all over my skin... Despite everything, heat spikes in my cheeks, and it has nothing to do with the coffee I'm drinking. Did Dacian want me too, even the tiniest bit? Or was it all just a game to him?

I shove my traitorous desires away. I can't let my feelings get the better of me. I need tangible evidence that doesn't hinge on me confessing that I had a gay affair with a mist. The cops will never investigate that. Which means they can't protect me. Nobody can.

I finish my doughnut, trying not to plunge into despair.

I'm terrified to return to campus, but I don't have money for a motel. I could get in touch with Fiona; maybe I can still spend the rest of the fall break at her house. But what if Dacian follows me? I can't bring danger to the Onayemis' doorstep. They don't deserve to be killed for showing me kindness. And even if I find somewhere to lie low for a while, I can't run from Dacian forever. Camden is my life. I have no job prospects without it, no family waiting for me to come home. No matter how I look at the situation, I have no choice but to stay and confront him. But how am I going to do that?

I need a plan. Urgently. I have a few days at most before I'll have to sleep. How long did Nancy last in *Nightmare on Elm Street*? A week? But that was all movie magic and made-up sleep-suppressing meds.

My first priority is to survive until fall break is over. I'll be safer when the campus is crowded again. But what then? How can I possibly fight Dacian? I know abysmally little about him or vampires in general. Maybe that's where I should start.

Nervously, I check my surroundings again. Some customers have left, and a few more have come in, but there's no sign of a black-clad vampire stalking me...yet. So I indulge in a coffee refill and another doughnut—apple cinnamon this time, Dunkin's seasonal special. It's going to be a long day.

As I wait for my order, I start a mental list of things I do know about Dacian. He admitted he comes from far away—a desolate, snowy place, if his words and my dreams can be trusted. But why is he in Camden? What can he possibly want here? If he just needed a place to hunt without the authorities catching on, he would have chosen a bigger city with millions of people where he wouldn't be noticed so easily. Why go through the trouble of becoming a college professor? That doesn't make sense, much like Dr. Kowalski's abrupt retirement. Could Dacian have orchestrated that too?

A dark thought assails my mind, making me instantly regret getting a second doughnut: What if Dacian killed Dr. Kowalski to take his place? I suppress a wave of nausea and shake my head. No, that can't be. I'm sure there would've been an announcement and an obituary in the local paper. Dr. Kowalski had been a fixture at Camden for twenty-odd years; someone would've noticed his bloodless corpse. That makes me feel a little better, but not much. Even so, Dacian has murdered at least one person.

A memory from our first conversation pops into my mind: the signet ring he was wearing with the strange symbol. What did he say about it? *Old family heirloom.* A dragon with a wolf's head. How ominous. I want to kick myself for not looking it up earlier. It might've shed some light on his identity. It still could. A tiny spark of hope emerges amidst the rubble of terror I've been crawling through since last night.

I check my watch. Despite the fact that I feel like the day started an eternity ago, it's only ten a.m. Good—this should give me enough hours to investigate. I quickly finish my doughnut and gulp down my still-too-hot coffee, scalding my tongue, before exiting the shop and hurrying back to my car.

The wolf-dragon symbol is the one thread I can follow. Camden's library is closed, but there are plenty of good public libraries in Vermont. The one in Montpelier is big and a reasonable distance away. I pray my car won't quit on me. At least the weather is on my side, dull and gray with a wind that bites but no heavy rain.

So, I fill up my tank at the adjacent gas station and make my way to Montpelier.

Eighteen

The Kellogg-Hubbard Library is a gorgeous nineteenth-century building with a granite façade and columns and a marble-lined portico. The main floor has heritage golden-yellow walls with well-preserved oak wainscotting, carved stairways, and pillars. It's warm and welcoming and manages to lessen my anxiety.

At the service desk, I inquire where I might be able to find books on symbols in European art. It's impossible to tell Dacian's ancestry just from looking at him, but judging by his skin color and accent, that part of the world is a good place to start.

The librarian directs me to the second floor, where I find several encyclopedias and art history tomes relevant to my search. I bring my haul to a secluded reading nook and start skimming. Somehow, being buried in books makes me feel almost *normal*. This is how I planned to spend my fall break anyway. If only I could pretend I'm working on a class assignment instead of investigating the dark origins of my vampire professor...

Since I don't know what era I'm supposed to be looking for, it takes a good hour of randomly flipping pages before I stumble on a relevant image. My heart jumps at the discovery. I have to reread the caption several times before the information sinks in.

The wolf-dragon I've been looking for is in the chapter dedicated to the architecture of Ancient Rome, a close-up of a relief in Trajan's Column depicting a military standard. It's one of the most peculiar designs I've encountered in heraldry. The standard's long tail is made from fabric, meant to soar in the wind like a dragon, while the wolf head has sharp teeth and appears to be forged from metal.

The caption notes that the column was erected in the second century AD to commemorate Emperor Trajan's victory in the war with the Dacian people. My heart skips another beat. *Dacian.* And the wolf-dragon is known as Dacian Draco. Now that I know what dates to search, I quickly find a helpful volume about ancient Roman history. I discover that before the Dacians were defeated by the Roman Empire, they comprised a number of tribes who occupied the area around the Carpathian Mountains, including the region of Transylvania. They were fierce and proud warriors who covered their bodies in tattoos, wielded sickle-like swords and marched into battle accompanied by the howling sound that their wolf-headed standards made when air passed through them. Those warriors terrified the Roman Empire. They considered themselves one with the wolves, and the very name Dacian might have come from the Phrygian word with that meaning. A popular legend says that a wolf deity even fought alongside the Dacians, defending their capital from the Roman invaders.

Sadly, not much else is known about their ancient civilization. The last Dacian kingdom was wiped out in the first century AD when Rome decided the rich gold mines in Transylvania were an ideal source of funds to pay for their burgeoning military campaigns. After the bloody conquest, thousands of Dacians were forced off their land and subjected to ethnic cleansing, sold into slavery, or turned into legionnaires. And even though small factions of Dacians bravely rebelled against Roman rule for the next two centuries, they never gained full independence again, falling under the influence of Goths, Huns, and later Slavs. Eventually, what was left of them became the forebearers of modern-day Romanians.

I lean back in my chair and exhale with deliberate slowness. I recall the shadow wolves from my dream, their sharp teeth, and how violently they tore my classmates and Clay into pieces. There is no way that was just a coincidence. But can Dacian's family roots really go back two thousand years? Or can he himself be that old?

A cold shiver prickles my neck. One of the common beliefs about vampires is that blood can give them immortality. *I spent a long time in a very isolated place*, Dacian said. I thought it bizarre at the time because how could someone who looks twenty-five at most speak of time like it's an ocean he has crossed? But maybe he did mean centuries, even millennia...though something tells me that isn't right, even if I can't logically explain why. Besides, although he does come off as a little old-fashioned, Dacian doesn't look or speak like he's *that* ancient. But then again, how many two-thousand-year-old beings have I met to compare him with?

I sigh. What must it feel like to have so many memories, to have borne witness to so much change in the world? Wars, plagues, empires crumbling, and new ones rising from their ruins. Just imagining that makes my head spin. It must be so lonely. No wonder he gives the impression of being an impenetrable fortress surrounded by a moat. Why would he let anyone close when no one can understand what it's like to be him?

I shut the book with a loud thump—there isn't much else to glean from it. What am I doing, anyway? I can't afford to start romanticizing a vampire. He killed Eric and probably Anita Hernandez, and he was trying to lure me in too. I doubt it was so we could take an innocent stroll in the moonlight. The image of his crimson irises flashes in my mind, their wild, untamed hunger. Dangerous and yet so alluring. With effort, I drive the pining ache away. I need to stick to the facts and not indulge in fantasies. And there's one fact that stands out in the story of ancient Dacians:

the heart of their civilization, the source of their wealth, was the region of Transylvania, and there is at least one famous vampire who hailed from that corner of the world.

I know which book I need, but I hesitate. There's a reason I didn't start my search with horror novels or collections of myths and folk tales. This is a life-and-death situation—*my* life, and possibly my death, unless I can find a way to defend myself. How can I put my trust in some story? But there's sure as hell no scientific paper on the subject of vampires. In which case a fairy tale is as trustworthy a source as any. No matter how unbelievable this situation seems, I have to follow the only thread I have, and that thread is leading me to Transylvania and its lore.

I push myself up, return the books I no longer need, and visit the fiction section. The novel is so famous, I have no problem finding several copies on the shelf. My fingers tremble as they trace the black spine with ominous red letters. *Dracula.* I swallow and bring the book back to my research camp.

As I read the first page, a deep chill burrows into my skin. How did I not think of this before? I should've connected the names by now. *Jonathan Harker's Journal*, it begins...

SEVERAL HOURS LATER, I stare at the wall, my mind racing. I'm only halfway through the book, but I need to stop, or I'm afraid my brain will explode. This cannot be. Everything in me screams that it isn't possible. But pieces of what I know about Dacian spin through my head, perfectly aligning with Bram Stoker's book. The ability to transform into a mist, to visit his victim's dreams, the wolves, and the isolated castle in the mountains. How many "coincidences" does it take before one is forced to admit there's no such thing as a coincidence?

Dacian had a severe reaction to my name when he saw it on the class roster. He seemed to *despise* it, and me along with it. I'm certain now that I didn't imagine it. He still won't call me by my first name. Could that be because he has a history with Jonathan Harker? Because Jonathan escaped from his imprisonment in the count's castle and provoked the chain of events that eventually led to Dracula's destruction? Again, my rational mind wants to scream that this isn't possible, that a made-up character couldn't be walking the real world. But in the words of the greatest fictional detective of all time, "Once you eliminate the impossible, whatever remains, no matter how improbable, must be the truth."

Not everything in Stoker's book is pure fiction. Count Dracula was based on a real historical figure, Vlad the Impaler. There's extensive evidence that he existed, even if none of it claims he was a vampire. From the introductory note at the beginning of the book, I know that Stoker himself insisted his story was based on real events and that he was personally acquainted with relatives of the Harker family. Was that just clever book marketing, or was there truth to it too terrifying to accept?

I squeeze my eyes shut. I've read the encyclopedia entry on Vlad Dracula; I couldn't resist fetching it after finishing the first few chapters. His monstrous moniker, the Impaler, wasn't just for show. It's estimated that during his bloody reign, Vlad III, voivode of Wallachia, tortured and killed eighty thousand people, mostly by impaling them on wooden stakes. They were left to bleed out, and he refused to bury them for weeks. The entire country was one blood-chilling horror show. His other nickname, Dracula, originates from the word meaning dragon; he inherited the moniker from his father, who was a member of the Order of the Dragon. If I dig deeper, will I find references to mysterious wolves in his story too?

Nausea threatens to rise in my throat again. Could Dacian *be* Vlad the Impaler? Could he be the count? The awful things Dracula did to Lucy Westenra, Mina, and Jonathan—he was a gruesome killer, unburdened by conscience or remorse. He would've murdered his way through England had they not chased him out. But if this insane theory is true, then the ending of the story got twisted somehow. Dacian escaped retribution and is now hiding out at a university in Vermont, with at least two victims to his name. How many more will he kill before someone stops him? Can *anyone* stop him?

I let my forehead crash onto my folded arms and rest there for a moment. I feel like I'm stuck in a nightmare. Is any of this even real? It might just be a hallucination of my sleep-deprived brain.

My stomach growls pitifully. All I've had today are two doughnuts and two cups of coffee. I glance at the window. It's started to drizzle. It will start getting dark soon. I can't stay in the library overnight. As crazy as it sounds, there's no place I can be safe from him other than my dorm, into which he hasn't been invited.

So I check out a copy of *Dracula* and drive back, stopping for a grilled cheese and a bag of fries at a busy gas station along Route 7.

As I circle West Hall, I resist the urge to check the trail where I caught Dacian last night. I wonder if there are any stains from Eric's blood or if the rain has washed them away. The body is surely gone by now. Dacian would have disposed of it. He probably didn't throw it in the river, though. If another body washes up on campus, the police won't be so quick to bury the investigation this time. After all, this victim is a rich white boy. He must have buried it somewhere—

I shake my head violently. What the hell is wrong with me? This is not a sane train of thought. Lack of sleep is starting to get to me, and it's only been a day!

Fueled by anger and the inviting smell of fries, I make my way back to my room and manage to stay awake for a few more hours. But as night falls, I get increasingly paranoid that Dacian will pop up outside my window. I check it obsessively, not trusting myself to keep it shut and vampire-proof. My anxiety spikes, tormenting me with scenarios of the evil ways he could slither inside so he can hack a chunk out of my throat and gleefully watch me bleed out on the floor as punishment for uncovering his secret.

I pace around my room in endless circles, trying to shake

myself awake. I blast a rock station on my radio and set the alarm at regular intervals in case exhaustion gets the upper hand. This strategy gets me through the night and the better part of Sunday until students start returning in the afternoon.

But in the end, none of these tricks can keep me out of Dacian's reach.

Nineteen

I jerk awake to the shrill sound of my alarm clock. Shit, shit, shit. My gaze snaps to its red digits—it's seven a.m. on Monday. My stomach plunges. I must've passed out at my desk reading the final chapters of *Dracula*. There's a painful imprint of the book's edge across my cheek.

How long was I out? I don't remember resetting the alarm. An hour? Two at most. But that's enough time for Dacian to have gotten to me. Frantically, I try to remember my dreams, but my head feels full of syrup, thick and sluggish and impossible to think through. I take a deep breath and exhale slowly, trying to subdue my panic. I would remember if he'd come for me, wouldn't I? My window is closed, and I'm still here, alive.

I touch my neck. Temporary relief floods me when my fingers find no marks on my skin. I give it a thorough examination in the bathroom mirror to be sure, then allow myself to take a hot shower. As my stiff muscles relax a little, dreadful suspicion starts to overtake me. Why *didn't* Dacian visit me in my sleep? I left myself vulnerable, and he didn't take advantage of it. I didn't see him lurking outside my window either. Could he have left Camden? I doubt that my knowing his secret is enough to scare him off. But then why didn't he come? Is he playing some twisted mind game? Either way, it's only a matter of hours before I find out.

I've resisted for three days. My nerves are frayed; my brain is scrambled. I'm pretty sure I hallucinated the better part of yesterday. With students starting to return to campus, I felt a little safer, but it made it all the harder to stay awake. Not sleeping for two nights does bizarre things to your brain. I tried to stay coherent, tried to think of a plan to fight back, but still, I have no solution to this vampire problem. I won't abandon everything I've worked so hard for and leave Camden myself. Bleeding to death in his arms would be a better outcome.

And as such, I see no other choice but to confront him.

Despite finally getting some sleep, I feel like I'm stumbling through a haze. I barely hear a word my Latin professor says before he hands us a pop quiz. This will be the first one in my college career that I will fail. But I can't bring myself to care. Getting a D in Latin pales in comparison to facing an actual vampire in front of a dozen unsuspecting students.

My legs feel like they might deflate when I enter the Gothic lit auditorium two hours later. I can't help looking at the spot where Eric used to sit. It's empty. This simple confirmation makes me feel like vomiting. He wasn't a good person. In fact, he was always awful to me, up to the very last time I saw him in the vault. But he didn't deserve to die like that.

Fiona frowns when she sees me. "What happened to you? I thought *I'd* be a zombie after driving all night, but you look like you've survived an apocalypse. Are you sick or something?"

Is it really that bad? I guess a nap and a hot shower weren't enough to erase three nights of terror. "I'm okay. Just had a bad night's sleep," I mutter, taking my usual seat next to her. But my voice sounds like a badly scratched record.

Fiona's brow furrows even more. "I knew I should've insisted you stay at my house. Being alone can do a number on a person. You should've called."

My back stiffens. Calling Fiona is the one thing I *shouldn't* have done. But I can't tell her what grave danger it would've put her in, especially when a vampire is about to walk into the room —if he comes. I check the clock above the blackboard. Dacian is late, highly unusual for him. A familiar sensation of dread starts to slosh in my gut. "Sorry," I mumble unconvincingly.

Fiona shakes her head like I'm a hopeless mess. She's truly concerned about me. I clear my throat to ask her about the wedding. I hope she had a normal fall break that didn't involve any suspicions that her professor is freaking Count Dracula. But I don't get the chance because the door finally opens and Dacian strides in.

Despite days of replaying the image of his bloody mouth and wicked crimson eyes, of being terrified he'll rip out my throat like those wolves in my dream, the first moment I see Dacian again, my heart gives an unexpected jolt. And no matter how much I want to convince myself otherwise, it isn't out of fear or disgust. For a split second before my rational thinking kicks in, I'm incredibly glad that Dacian is still in Camden, that he hasn't disappeared into the mist where I'll never see him again.

Our eyes meet, and my throat clenches. I want to go to him, to be enveloped by his shadow. I must be sick in the head to want him like this. Or maybe he's making me feel this way, mesmerizing me with his vampire powers. I tear my gaze away from him in a futile effort to stave off whatever influence he has over me—but not before noticing that something about him is amiss today.

I try to steady my breathing as I hear the squeaking of his polished black shoes against the floor. He isn't walking toward me, I realize. Of course he wouldn't do anything risky in front of so many witnesses. When I dare to glance at him again, he's leaning against his desk, chin prideful and high, not even facing me.

"The subject of today's discussion is monsters, imaginary and real...as they pertain to Gothic literature, that is," he adds somewhat distractedly. "I hope you've all had a chance to review *Dr. Jekyll and Mr. Hyde* so we can compare it with Mary Shelley's

Frankenstein. It's often said that we fear what we don't understand. No other genre capitalizes on those fears more than Gothic literature. *Dr. Jekyll and Mr. Hyde* and *Frankenstein* are stories about beings who are perceived as monsters by society. Yet both are created by men and are, therefore, extensions of humanity, an exploration of the darker side of thought made into flesh and blood. Who would like to elaborate on the differences between Frankenstein's creature and Mr. Hyde?"

As Dacian initiates a discussion about monsters, of all things, he never once looks at me, acting like I don't exist. Is he mocking me? What the hell is wrong with him? As if the fear of Frankenstein's creature could compare to seeing a real vampire kill your classmate and then stalk you, invading your dreams and manipulating you into doing as he pleases! Eric's desk is still empty. Are we going to sit here and pretend that Dacian didn't murder him? My blood starts to boil. My mouth opens before I consider the consequences of what I'm about to do.

"If you want to talk about monsters, why don't we talk about vampires?" I demand, my voice rough and loud.

Dacian's eyes snap to me. His gaze bears the deadly glint of a raised blade, a warning before the strike. But after this past weekend, I don't know if I have any self-preservation left. I'm worn, frazzled, and pushed to the brink of insanity. I wouldn't know how to shut up if I tried.

"Speaking of which," I continue, "why are there no vampire books in our curriculum? Huh, Mr. Bathory? No *Carmilla*, no Polidori's *Vampyre*—and no *Dracula*, even though it's one of the most famous Gothic texts. You want to discuss real monsters? Why don't we talk about that book?"

Dacian's eyes flare. I don't miss the tectonic shift that name causes in him. He clenches his jaw.

"That book is not part of our curriculum," he grits out, his eyes narrowing dangerously before addressing the rest of the class. "Let's get back to *Dr. Jekyll and—*"

"Why not?" I interrupt. I won't let him ignore me. Several

heads turn in my direction, including Fiona's. But I don't care. "It's a perfect example," I continue. "That monster imprisons Jonathan Harker, then goes on to lure poor, innocent Lucy to the dark side so she can eat neighborhood children."

"Mr. Evergreen!" Dacian says sharply.

Everyone is staring now. Everyone except for Eric, whose bloodless corpse is rotting wherever this monster hid it. Maybe it's not sleeping for three days or being scared out of my mind, but something just snaps in me. "He even tosses a *baby* to his vampire groupies for them to devour. Probably partook of it himself," I continue at full volume. "How vile is that? And for what? So he can terrorize a small town and seduce Mina?"

Something flashes in my vision. In an instant, Dacian stands in front of me, looming over me like a black cloud.

"He. Did. Not. Eat. Children." Dacian's words are a series of staccato notes of barely contained fury. "And he was never interested in Mina. Or Ms. Westenra. It was never them. Never *them*."

His gaze locks with mine, and suddenly, I feel like I'm in the middle of a stormy sea. Water is pouring overboard, and I'm choking. What is this feeling? Sadness, so much grief that I'm drowning in it. *Unwanted. I made a mistake. I ruined everything.* A torrent of someone else's anguished thoughts bursts through me. I gasp as though my lungs are filling up with water. *He'll never forgive me. He'll hunt me. I made a mistake!*

Someone's familiar voice yanks me back to the present. Beside me, Fiona looks aghast.

"Jonathan, what is wrong with you?" she whispers.

I open my mouth, but no words come. My breathing is ragged, and my heart is pounding. Not waiting for my answer, Fiona turns to Dacian. "I'm sorry, Mr. Bathory. Jonathan has been under the weather today. Will you please excuse him?"

Dacian's tempestuous eyes flick from Fiona to me. Slowly, he backs away. "Yes. Mr. Evergreen, you do not look well," he says, forcing calm into his voice, but the storm in his eyes is still raging violently. I can feel its echo reverberating inside me. "Perhaps it's best if you get some rest. Sleep will do you good," he adds, with a distinct note of pleading in his voice.

That shocks me. I suddenly notice how wrecked he looks, exhausted in a way that shouldn't be possible for someone like him. Where has he been these past two days? What has he been doing? Just like that, regret pierces me. I feel awful for unleashing that barrage of accusations on him, of saying such cruel things to his face. That is, until his suggestion fully registers with me. *Sleep?* Is he joking? I want to laugh at this absurdity. I also want to scream at him for thinking he can put me through this, that he can twist my emotions however he pleases. I swear I'll wrench the truth out of him. Except after that vision, all the fight has gone out of me. I'm dizzy and wiped out.

I don't gratify Dacian with an answer as I yank my backpack off my chair and run out of the room, Fiona muttering an excuse and hurrying after me.

"Please tell me you're going to the health center," she says in the hallway.

"No," I grit out. The truth is that I have no idea where I'm going. I just need to get away. I can't think straight around Dacian. That feeling of drowning in despair—what the hell was that? A memory? A hallucination? Or something he *wanted* me to see, and like an idiot, I let him in again?

Fiona quickens her pace. In a few strides, she passes me and then halts abruptly, blocking my way. "Jonathan Evergreen, you will tell me right this second. What is going on with you?" I flinch at the anger in her words. "You know I care about you. You're my friend, but that was crazy! Why are you picking fights with our professor?"

A cold vise closes around my rib cage. I feared it would come to this, but I can't tell her the truth. What if Dacian kills her because of me? I can't put Fiona in his crosshairs like that. But I must warn her somehow. She's got no idea what that guy is capable of.

I lean in, afraid someone might overhear me. "Because he's

dangerous, Fiona," I say in a low voice. "Please keep away from him. For your own good."

Fiona's eyes bulge, and she actually laughs. "Dangerous? Jonathan, that's ludicrous. Are you talking about Mr. Bathory, the coolest freaking professor at this school?"

I grit my teeth. Of course, to Fiona, he's just a professor—a charming one with impeccable style and a superhuman, photographic memory. If only she knew what kind of monster hides behind that facade. "It isn't that," I grunt, frustrated. "He's not who you think he is."

"Then who is he?" Fiona demands.

For a long, tense moment, I simply stare at her, unable to utter a word. I can't answer her question directly. And would she even believe anything I say after the meltdown I just had?

Visibly disappointed by my lack of response, Fiona shakes her head. "I know you guys had a rough start, but I thought you'd cleared it all up. Mr. Bathory even went the extra mile to get you the job you wanted. And you repay him by throwing wild, baseless accusations at him behind his back? That's wrong, Jonathan."

My mouth is still clamped shut. Fiona knows nothing about the crimes he's committed, but there's no way out of this that wouldn't endanger her, is there? Perhaps ignorance is the safest option.

"You're right," I finally agree, deadly tired. "I was stupid. Staying on campus was a bad decision. I should've gone to your place. I'm just...all of this"—I throw my hands out—"the silence and being alone—it got to me. I'm sorry, Fiona. I think I need to take a breather."

"If you don't want to see a doctor, you should go back to your room and sleep," she says, also sounding exhausted and worried. She didn't sleep much last night either, since she had to drive from Albany after a late flight.

"Yeah. I will do that," I promise her before we part ways.

She goes back to class, and I stumble back to my dorm.

What am I supposed to do? No one seems to be concerned

about Eric being gone. It's day three, and I've yet to hear police sirens. Shouldn't his friends have reported him missing by now? Has no one noticed he's gone? For a moment, I wonder if maybe Fiona is right and I've lost it. Maybe I hallucinated the whole thing, or it was another one of those disturbing nightmares I've had lately...

No, I know what I saw. No matter how surreal, it did happen. I didn't spend my entire fall break cowering in fear because I made up a bloody vampire. And the way Dacian reacted to my mention of Dracula—that wasn't just him being ruffled by a student's rude behavior. What I said struck a chord in him. And while his response wasn't an outright confirmation of my theory, it only made me believe it more.

But if Dacian is an all-powerful, possibly ancient vampire who commanded kingdoms and killed Eric, why hasn't he killed me? He's had plenty of opportunities, even before I witnessed Eric's murder. I'm alone a lot. I shudder at how many chances I've unwittingly given him to target me. He could've gained my trust and lured me into the woods the night he read "The Raven" to me. He doesn't need to drag this out. Yet I'm still here. Why?

An unsettled feeling swirls in my gut, like biting into a fruit that tastes sweet and ripe, only to realize seconds later that it's rotting and the insides are bursting with maggots. I let him into my *dreams*, and I enjoyed it. I wanted him there. I wished to feel his nebulous touch on my skin. I check my neck again, feeling stupid, but there are no wounds on it, no scars. Maybe he's saving me for a special snack. Or he simply enjoys toying with me.

But then I remember his eyes a few minutes ago when I went off about Dracula, the way they flashed with hurt. Was it an act to fool me? Or is there a secret hidden deep in that dark abyss?

I've always wished someone would come along and show me the world.

Such a bizarre thing to say, but I don't think he was lying that day. There was no reason for him to fake vulnerability; I was already hopelessly falling for him by then. So what does he want from me?

Sleep will do you good. I replay the last words he said to me. It was as close to openly pleading as a prideful being like Dacian could get, especially considering we were in a room full of people.

In a daze, I make my way back to my room. My bed looks like the most seductive thing in the world after three nights away from it. I don't even have the strength to lift the covers. I fall onto the mattress, close my eyes, and let my head sink into the soft embrace of my pillow.

As sleep overtakes me, I realize there's a good chance I will never wake up again. But there's simply nothing to do but confront Dacian. Let him come to me this time.

TWENTY

I wake with a start.

My room is dark. My clock radio reads 2:57 a.m. Wow, I slept through the entire afternoon and dinner. At least I didn't have work—it would've been a shame to miss it. I guess this is what happens when you force yourself to stay awake for days. I rub my eyes. My body feels like I've been hit with a baseball bat. It's also freezing in my room. Slowly, I shift my gaze to the window—it's open again. I feel a shiver at the top of my spine. I roll out of bed to investigate. Everything is quiet outside. Patchy gray clouds obscure the moon. The back courtyard seems empty at this hour, as expected, except for...

A shadow catches my attention, a shadow shaped like a man, standing just outside the dome cast by the streetlight underneath my window. My chest flutters. I can't see the visitor clearly, but I know with undeniable certainty that it's *him*. It has to be him.

I don't hesitate; I've already made my decision. I jam my arms into the sleeves of my sweater and hurry outside.

By the time I reach the streetlight, Dacian is walking in the direction of the woods. He glances over his shoulder once but doesn't beckon me or stop walking—it's an open invitation. So I follow the black angles of his shoulders at a distance, through the grassy courtyard, past the baseball field, and onto the trail leading to the woods. It grows darker the farther from campus we move, and colder too. The air comes out of my mouth in little white puffs. Fallen leaves crunch under the soles of my high-tops, the only sound breaking the eerie silence around us as Dacian's walking seems to make no noise.

Just as the darkness becomes too thick for my eyes to make out shapes anymore, Dacian stops.

"Haven't I told you, Mr. Evergreen, that it is dangerous to walk alone at night?" He doesn't face me, and from his tone alone, I can't tell what he's thinking. Is this a warning to leave now while I still can? Or is it a reminder that I never should've come in the first place?

"You did say that," I admit as my heart gives a jittery thump. But I can't run from him anymore, no matter how much I wish I could convince myself otherwise. I'm in too deep.

Slowly, he turns to face me. "Aren't you scared of what might happen to you if you stay?"

At that moment, the shroud of clouds shifts, revealing a sharp crescent of the growing moon, the *hungry* moon. It shines through the web of craggy branches overhead to cast Dacian's features in pale light, and he...he looks stunning. Like a classic painting meant to immortalize a rare beauty—a true masterpiece, the glory of which will long outlive the artist. Except no renowned museum would feature this painting in its prized collection, would dare to show such blasphemy to its loyal patrons. Because around Dacian's pupils are two glowing rings of scarlet, a blood-chilling sight to behold.

The air catches in my throat.

He slides closer to me, smooth as a shadow. "Aren't you afraid of me?" he asks. His steps are so light that even the crunch of leaves on the ground sounds muted, as though he's barely touching them. A perfect predator, unmatched in his element. I have to force myself to stay in place, and even so, I'm afraid my soul might become untethered and flee my body.

"I am," I breathe, caught off guard by my own honesty. "I'm terrified of you."

But my admission does not faze him. He closes the remaining distance between us and leans in, his lips nearly brushing my ear. His breath caresses my skin just like the dream fog. "Then why are you still here, *Jonathan*?" he finally asks.

My knees go weak at the sound of my name, and warmth pools in my stomach. He's never once used it, and now he's saying it with such gentleness that I want to curl and wrap myself around his fingers. It's not at all the curse I imagined.

His mouth moves down my neck, hovering just above the pulse point. I don't know if it's his supernatural powers or just the effect his proximity has on me, but I have to concentrate to stop myself from swaying.

"Because I—" I swallow, trying to keep the upheaval in my chest contained. "I want to know the truth about you."

There's a lengthy pause before he answers. Maybe it's only my imagination, but I think I hear a deep note of melancholy in his voice. "But you already know it. You've figured it all out, haven't you?"

A wave of dizziness hits me. The impossible theory I concocted after my research—is he admitting it's true? *But it's just a work of fiction!* I want to argue. *Nothing more than the author's invention.* But my last-ditch attempt to cling to normalcy doesn't work because the proof is standing right in front of me in the flesh.

"Are you really Dra—" I start to ask.

"Shh." His fingers shoot up to cover my mouth—so swift, but at the same time, only the barest of touches. "Don't say that name," he whispers, then draws back a little so he can see my face. "It's Dacian now."

My eyes widen. He just confirmed my wildest theory, and somehow, that's not even the most important thing. Not when he's looking at me like that, standing so close, crimson eyes hooded by his inky eyelashes.

"Dacian," I whisper back before he has a chance to remove his hand. My lips graze the pads of his fingers, just a little cold from the night's chill. I can't help but wish them closer. I can hear my heart thudding in my ears. As scared as I am of the sinister red glow that makes his sharp cheekbones look even sharper, I can't look away from his eyes and the eerie, beautiful death they promise.

What starts as an idle thought in the back of my mind quickly spins into an uncontrollable desire. I want to kiss his fingers. I want to open my mouth and take them inside. We are alone. No one will see; no one will know. I want to push him down into the leaves and kiss the rest of him. I want, I want, I want—

Unhurriedly, he lets his thumb slide across my lower lip.

"Thank you," he says.

For what? I wonder deliriously. For saying his name? I'll say it as many times as he wishes. I part my lips in silent invitation, waiting, hoping, but his thumb doesn't dip inside. It moves to the corner of my mouth, then skims down my jawline until it stops on the side of my neck. It rests there along the collar of my sweater, unbearably intimate yet restrained. There are still things to be said and truths to be uncovered. I think Dacian is giving me permission to ask for the answers I want before I lose myself in him. Or maybe it's a condition I must fulfill before he claims me. Either way, I slog through my brain's haze, struggling to recall why I wanted to confront him in the first place.

"Did you kill Anita Hernandez?" I ask after some clarity returns to me.

Dacian's eyebrows crease in confusion. "No," he replies.

It occurs to me he could be lying, that he could easily mislead me with his mesmerizing power. Yet, with so little distance between us, surrounded by darkness, it's like we're inside our own private confessional. So I believe him. He's already admitted to being history's most storied vampire; what else is there to hide? Relief starts to wash over me, but I put a dam in its path.

"What about Dr. Kowalski?" I add.

Still frowning slightly, Dacian shakes his head. It seems he didn't expect that name to come up, either. "I promise I did not harm him. As far as I know, the old man is delighting in his retirement somewhere in the lush Caribbean. Which is a wise choice, considering the generous sum of money he received recently."

This time, it's my turn to be confused. Does Dacian mean he bribed Dr. Kowalski to leave his teaching job? Would Dr. Kowalski really have abandoned Camden for a bunch of money and let some stranger take over the Gothic lit course he taught for decades? So much for his loyalty. But I guess I should be happy he's alive and—more importantly—that Dacian is not as diabolical as I thought.

But I can't drop my guard just yet. There is one more victim, and that one will be a lot more difficult to explain. "What happened with Eric?" I finally ask.

Dacian is silent for a moment before delivering the brutal blow. "I killed him. As you witnessed."

I knew what to expect, and I still draw in a sharp breath. "Why?"

Dacian hesitates again before replying, as though deciding how much of the truth he's willing to give me. "Mr. Stockton...he was dangerous. More than you can imagine. Several months ago he took something from me, something of great value that I need returned to me by any means necessary. That night, I had no choice but to do what I did."

I don't try to hide my dismay. Eric? The not-very-bright, uber-rich boy whose favorite response to anything was "Cool, bro"? How could *he* be dangerous to Dacian?

"I don't understand," I say, fighting the instinct to pull away. I don't know what miraculous explanation I was hoping for, but hearing him justify killing Eric in the horrific way he did—a chunk of flesh missing, blood gushing from the jagged wound— forces me to relive the nightmare of that night. My pulse spikes and my mind starts crawling with anxiety.

"I know it is difficult to believe." Dacian's voice cuts through my panic, and I'm instantly reminded of his thumb resting on my neck, now warm from the skin contact. It anchors me in place. "I want you to know," he continues soothingly, "that it was never my intention to put anyone's life at risk. Especially yours. And before you ask any more questions, I must warn you that the more you entangle yourself in this matter, the more danger is sure to come your way. If it were up to me, I'd keep you as far away from all of this as possible." He gives me an intense look like he's hoping to convince me to back out. But he obviously knows it isn't that simple. "However, I understand that you're too stubborn for your own good and that none of my warnings will deter you. Thus, if you truly wish to know, I will not stop you. This Friday, come on a ride with me. You can ask everything then." He leans in again, his lips nearly brushing the shell of my ear. "But I implore you, my dear Jonathan—until that day, take caution and think things through."

As he says my name, the shadowy woods begin to ripple around me. I try to open my mouth, but a sudden, overwhelming exhaustion falls over me. I tip forward, my head falling onto Dacian's shoulder. The last sensation I register is his strong arms embracing me.

I have no memory of getting back to my dorm, but the next morning, I wake up snuggled in my bed, my window shut tightly, and my sweater slung over the back of my chair. It's like the midnight meeting with Dacian was just a dream.

A dream in which he finally called me by my name.

Twenty-One

The count never intended to let the human leave his castle alive. Some secrets were simply too dangerous to let them out into the world. But the danger wasn't what the count was thinking of just now as he strained his face to avoid bursting into laughter. He'd disguised himself as a coachman and was giving the young solicitor the fright of his life as he sped their carriage along the serpentine Carpathian roads, skidding around the bends and barely avoiding the cliffs' edges. And the way the poor human twisted in terror when the count summoned his wolves to chase them up the slopes! Of course, the human had no way of knowing that the wolves would never harm a hair on his head—not without the count's command, that is.

Later, the count would decide that the whole thing had probably been just a little unfair, but he simply could not pass up a chance for some amusement before returning to the gloomy hallways of his keep. Besides, he'd always found that terror looked ravishing on a handsome face, and if the shadows weren't lying, the young solicitor's face was handsome indeed.

If he was lucky, perhaps the count might find further amusement in this human's company. It had been decades since he'd had a willing visitor.

His castle used to be so much livelier even half a century ago, with months-long revelries marking each successful campaign against the Janissaries and endless processions of nobles who showered the dark voivode with hoards of gold and jewels. But that was when they still remembered why the count was here, why his fortress had been built in such an inhospitable place that only the people who had lived in these lands for generations would dare seek refuge inside its walls. When the castle wasn't just an ominous decrepit ruin staring down a snowy peak, a nightmarish legend to scare off the superstitious.

But the time of great wars and unceasing border skirmishes had passed, it seemed. The things that used to be magnificent were facing the inevitable fate of decay and obscurity. The nineteenth century had rolled in, and now the threat of invading Turks was but a sham excuse to keep the roads in a perpetual state of disrepair. There was no longer any use for a castle such as the one ruled by the count, nor a need for a terrifying being born of darkness and bloodshed such as him.

The locals had always feared him, even when they'd deemed the count's monstrous strength vital to their own survival. But in previous centuries, they hadn't shunned his mountain so completely. Truly, those humans were to blame for the abominable state of this place! These days, the only people who entered the count's employ of their own volition were the Travelers. They still remembered the price by which this land had been preserved: bones and blood. But they were no stonemasons. Or carpenters or textile makers, for that matter. All the treasures the count had accumulated over the centuries were useless when it came to quelling the primal fear he roused in the souls of the common folk.

That is how, to his great dismay, he found himself personally tidying the guest room and preparing supper for the human visitor. What did *he* know about making suppers? It had been ages since he'd tasted a vegetable. The sisters might still remember—their human days weren't as far behind them—but he had banished them to the dungeons for the solicitor's sake. His troublesome progeny had never quite learned to control their appetites. What else was he to do with them?

In the olden days, it hadn't been uncommon for the grateful and terrified locals to send the count maidens as gifts to mollify him after particularly vicious battles so that his bloodthirsty rage wouldn't spill over into the nearby villages. As if he'd ever had any interest in maidens. But the count found his hands were rather tied when it came to dealing with such "gifts." There weren't many choices left for a woman whose family had sent her to slaughter to save their own skins. Perhaps it was merely the endless silence that haunted the derelict castle that was to blame, but the count had shared his powers with three of them.

Alas, in the end, not a single one proved a suitable candidate for the insatiable demands of the shadows. None possessed a character strong enough to curb the ill effects the dark magic had on their minds. Instead of worthy companions, he'd gained a nightly headache trying to stop them from inciting terror in the villagers at the bottom of the mountain.

He supposed he could've snatched someone from Bukovina and made them cook supper for the human, but that might have stirred more trouble with the locals and interfered with his plans to leave this place.

He was noticing it more and more every day—the weakening of the hold this land had on him. For the first time in centuries, the count *felt* the invisible chain of ancient magic, which bound him to this place like nothing more than a Transylvanian guard dog, starting to crumble. And so a dangerous idea had been born in the tenebrous recesses of his mind. An idea that after years of serving the Order, after watching empires rise and drown in blood, after seeing countless bodies massacred and turned to dust, he too could be *free*. The count's plan to test that idea was already in motion, and he wasn't willing to risk it for anything.

Besides, as he raced his black steed with the carriage rattling in tow, he thought that just for tonight, he might want to have that human to himself. For what purpose? He couldn't yet explain.

There was something about him, this stranger in a strange land. He hung on to his seat for dear life, shaking like an autumn leaf, but he didn't beg the count to slow down or take him back to the train station. No, he stayed, and when the time came to disembark and enter the castle's grand hall, which used to host kings and queens but now looked like a glorified prison for one, the human went in *willingly*. And in the soft glow of the golden candlelight, the fortress inside the count shuddered. He didn't need candles to see; those were for the human's benefit. The count much preferred the lush embrace of darkness. In the shadows all his senses were sharper, his strength paramount. But the light did something to the human, to this *Jonathan*. The pulse trembled in his neck as he introduced himself to the count who had shed his coachman disguise—a tiny movement, a flicker of nervousness in unfamiliar surroundings, perhaps. But there was something else there, too, something warm and curious and fluttering, like the tiny birds in the spring when even the mountain snow had melted and the overgrown trees in the courtyard turned a lively shade of green.

The count opened his mouth to reply but froze. For a moment, he didn't want to be *this*—a member of the old guard with the powers of the gods of death and ruin, forgotten in this century that was all about science and progress. Just this once, he wanted to feel like he still had something to live for. And so he told Jonathan his old name, the one his mother had given him all those centuries ago when he, too, was still human.

"You may call me Dacian," he said, and shook the human's hand.

Jonathan's eyelashes dipped, and a flush spread across his

cheeks at the contact. To anyone with mere human sight, it would've been a faint color, but to Dacian, it may as well have been the blazing fires of the sunrise.

That night, in his diary, the count wrote: "Help me, great shadows, for today I met my own ruin and invited him in."

TWENTY-TWO

The four days that follow my midnight rendezvous with Dacian are unsettlingly normal. He doesn't visit my dreams, and Gothic lit meets only on Mondays, so I don't see him again other than once by accident in a hallway. We're walking in opposite directions and don't approach each other, but he glances my way and nods briefly, his expression unreadable. And then he disappears into one of the auditoriums while I continue on to art history, still seeing the afterimage of his enchanting eyes as though it is burned into my retinas.

The only thing that is markedly different from any other week is that Eric Stockton is still missing, and everyone is acting like nothing has happened. How can the son of a prominent businessman disappear without anyone looking for him? Especially after what happened with Anita Hernandez. But Eric does skip class often. Maybe that's why no one has sounded an alarm yet.

Neither of his legacy friends come to accounting on Tuesday, but the professor doesn't address their absence, either not caring that they ditched or not bothering to take points off because he's "obligated" to give them a passing grade. Despite how I feel about them, it's too bad—I want to see how they're reacting to Eric being gone. My time to make a decision about whether to join Dacian for a ride or heed his warning to stay away is running out, and I need to gather as much information as possible. What was so dangerous about Eric that Dacian had to eliminate him? And what did he take from Dacian that was so important?

The opportunity to dig a little deeper presents itself on Wednesday.

"So, are you cool with Mr. Bathory again?" Fiona asks as we exit the dining hall and head to our afternoon classes. She's checked on me several times since my breakdown on Monday, and I apologized for my behavior, weaseling back into her good graces by taking her out for late-night pancakes. I honestly needed some myself after the week I've had.

"Yeah," I reply, skirting the truth but sounding as upbeat as I can. "I talked to him after."

"Oh, good for you," Fiona says, surprised but genuinely relieved that I've gotten my act together.

"Yeah, he was very understanding. It's all resolved now." I don't tell her that my talk with Dacian may or may not have been a dream, and that I still have no idea if I can trust him.

As we take the bridge over the small brook shaded by the golden maple trees, I spot the fiery red of the only Testarossa in Camden sitting in the parking lot across from the green space, its owner and his legacy buddies standing beside it. An idea strikes me. "Wait," I say, stopping abruptly. "I just realized I left my art history textbook in my room. I'll catch you at dinner, okay?"

I don't think my bullshit acting skills are convincing, but Fiona doesn't call me out. "Sure, I'll see you then," she says, continuing down the path through the green as I turn around and wait for a few moments before darting across the lawn.

It's easier to be rational in the daylight, away from Dacian. No matter how much I'm compelled to believe him, I can't let him be my only source of information. I need to get to the bottom of what happened with Eric. But as I get closer to the legacies, I hesitate, remembering the night I saw Mads Jr. refusing to give Eric a ride back to their house. Eric seemed upset for days afterward and was completely deranged when he accosted me in the vault. What brought that on? Maybe the legacies had a falling out, and that's why they haven't bothered to report him missing. I might implicate myself by alerting them now. I'll have to be clever.

I clutch my backpack's strap as I approach Mads Jr., Callahan, and Alessandra, who's hanging on Mads Jr.'s arm like an expensive human accessory. I don't know if it's the drugs and constant partying or what, but the two guys have been acting more and more unhinged lately. I haven't exactly forgotten how they almost ran me over the night they ditched Eric. My stomach knots at the sight of the Testarossa. Grady straight-up growls when he sees me, his mullet so unkempt it looks like a crow's nest. His eyes are shaded, as they usually are these days, but I've no problem imagining him glaring at me from behind those black Ray-Bans. "What do you want, Evergreen?" he snarls.

I have to suppress the instinct to shrink into myself. Just the height difference between us is enough to intimidate me, but I'm not turning back now.

"Chill, Grady," I say. "I have no interest in talking to you either. I'm looking for Eric. He's my project partner, and I don't intend to fail Gothic lit just because he's decided to start ditching class." I'm surprised by how easily the lie comes and how calm I feel saying it. I'm banking on the fact that neither of them is in Dacian's class with me and that I doubt Eric ever talked about his homework.

I expect some kind of nasty remark from Grady, but the moment I mention Eric's name, I see alarm flash over all three of their faces. The panic doesn't linger, however, and Mads Jr. covers it up the fastest like the born-and-bred politician he is.

"Eric is sick. Cooped up at home on doctor's orders. Your professor should've told you," he says with an air of aloof arrogance, like talking to me is beneath him.

It's an effort to keep my face neutral. Eric is sick? With what? An acute case of blood loss? Even if Eric survived the encounter with Dacian, he would be in the ICU, hooked up to blood bags and recovering from the multiple surgeries it would take to reconstruct the chunk of meat missing from his neck. I struggle to tuck those horrible images into a tiny corner of my mind. I can't blank out here.

"It would've been nice to hear that from him," I say, feigning anger. "But I guess I should know better than to expect common courtesy from the likes of you."

I turn around to leave, not giving them an opportunity to respond. I desperately need a moment to process what I'd just heard. From the corner of my eye, I see Mads Jr.'s arm shoot out to stop Grady from lunging after me like a monster who has smelled blood. My whole body shudders. Mads and Alessandra mutter something to him urgently that I can't make out, but it's barely enough to restrain Grady. That guy needs a rehab facility and a psychiatrist. As I force myself to keep walking instead of breaking into a run, I can practically feel three pairs of eyes boring holes into my back.

I don't know what the hell just happened. But if these three have nothing to hide, why would they lie about Eric?

TWENTY-THREE

After everything that transpired during fall break, I expect my nightmares to resume their ceaseless haunting, but they don't. My dreams that week are not peaceful so much as empty—so empty, in fact, that some warped part of me wishes that a certain voice would call for me. But Dacian stays away, either to avoid frightening me or because he is respectfully giving me time to make my decision.

On Friday, I wake in the gray predawn light, my thoughts once again filled with Dacian. Even if he doesn't visit my dreams, I cannot keep him out of my head. And today is the day I must decide whether to follow him into the treacherous shadows or stay in the safety of the light.

I try to address my situation with clarity, but all my surreal interactions with Dacian make me question my own memories and conjectures about him. In Bram Stoker's book, the count had a way of confusing or hypnotizing his victims. But I already know that not everything in that book is true. I wonder who Stoker's sources were and how the truth got twisted. *He didn't eat children. And he was never interested in Mina. Or Ms. Westenra. It was never them.*

What did Dacian mean by that? Could he have been interested in someone else? Could it have been the person who started the whole story, my namesake? Or am I jumping to conclusions again? Is this merely wishful thinking?

I recall the way Dacian whispered *Jonathan*, his hand against my cheek, his thumb caressing my mouth. My face flushes. I never spoke about my fog dream with him or confirmed that it was his visitation, but just the thought of it makes me want to curl up under my comforter and never again show my face to the world.

I saw him dissolve into the mist with my own eyes. And if the dream fog was Dacian, if he was the one touching me, or if he took pleasure in simply watching, I—

I squeeze my eyes shut as heat coils under the suddenly tight fabric of my pajama pants. *Jonathan*, the memory whispers again and again. I can almost feel the soft hush of his breath across my neck, the sweet torture of the moment before his skin met mine.

My fingers skim the waistband of my pants, dithering. I shouldn't. What will I do when I see him in person? Will he know? But it's too late to stop my mind. I feel his thumb on my lip. Unrestrained, the memory extends into a fantasy—Dacian's thumb dipping inside my mouth and touching the tip of my tongue, my lips closing around it, drawing him in. My teeth graze the flesh of his knuckle. I'm filled with a greedy desire to take parts of him, all of him. Just like a vampire. How would Dacian even feel if he knew about this hunger inside of me?

I cling to the plausible deniability of it all as my hand reaches under the flannel of my pajamas. Dacian isn't here; I'm not dreaming, and in the privacy of my room, I can fantasize about him all I want. I can imagine being touched by him anywhere. Everywhere.

THAT AFTERNOON, as I step out of art history, I realize that I barely heard anything in the second half of the lecture as my nervous excitement mushroomed in anticipation of our meeting.

Who am I kidding? Of course, I'm going with Dacian wherever he wants to take me. I must know what's happening, what the real count is doing here on a college campus in the middle of Vermont. I cringe inwardly at the awkward title, but after Dacian's plea, I won't dare call him by that name he seems to hate even in my mind. He's Dacian now, and this drive is bound to lift the curtain on some of the mysteries that brought him to this place.

I reach my car in the parking lot and climb in. The details of our midnight conversation still seem like a dream, but I memorized the address before I blacked out. *Meet me at 29 Hollow Lane*, he whispered. I pull my weathered road atlas from the glove compartment and shuffle through it. It is a standalone property north of Camden, just off Route 7.

After about fifteen minutes on the highway, I turn onto a small road that winds through the woods until I find the ornate brass sign that reads 29 Hollow Lane. The property is tucked back from the road. I drive on loose gravel for several minutes before the trees finally part, and a lawn with a two-story dark brick Tudor comes into view. I gape. It looks like a castle—there are massive diamond-patterned windows, three gables under the slate roof, and a turret on the left side.

Dacian gave me his *home address*. I'm not sure how to process that, whether there's a meaning behind it other than the fact that he doesn't want people to see a student and a professor hanging out together. Not only would that be suspicious, it would be grounds for an ethics investigation. Still...this is his *home.*

As I park in the driveway, I am overcome with curiosity about the domestic situation and living conditions of the world's most famous vampire. I wonder if I'll be able to peek inside when he opens the door. But those thoughts are short-lived because, by the time I kill my Chevy's engine, Dacian is already outside, arms folded, leaning against a shiny black Jaguar.

I smile. Of course the fancy Jag I ogled on the first day of the semester belongs to him. They're a perfect match, down to the color scheme. Dacian is wearing a cable-knit sweater and jeans, stylish and all in shades of black, as always. Although I don't think I've ever seen him wear jeans. It must be his off-duty attire. It's impossible not to notice how good he looks in denim. They're neither loose nor skintight—just the right cut to show the shape of his hips and give me all the wrong ideas. My cheeks grow hot, and my mind is flooded with memories of what I did this morning while thinking of him. Shamefaced, I tear my gaze away before he can see right through me.

Stop daydreaming. This is not a date, I warn myself sternly, exercising all my will to banish the thoughts that will turn me into a puddle of lovesick slush. Then I open the door and climb out of the Chevy.

Dacian is always so composed, so hard to read, like he's wearing a facade he doesn't want others to peek under. But today, I sense uncertainty as I approach him. Perhaps he truly meant it that night when he said I should take my time deciding. Maybe he was worried I'd choose to stay away, to erase this mystery from my mind and return to the safety of pretending the world is normal, that dreams cannot be haunted, that bodies don't show up inexplicably drained of blood. To erase *him*...

I would never.

"Hi," I say, waving at him, which comes off as more awkward than I hoped.

"Hello," he replies, unfolding his arms. "Are you ready?" There's still a note of hesitation in his voice, as though he's giving me one last chance to back out. But I don't bite.

"I am," I say, even though I have no idea where he's about to take me. My remaining shred of rational thought is telling me that maybe I should be scared, but after fall break, my fear reserves are exhausted. My one consolation is that if Dacian Bathory wanted to kidnap me and turn me into his dinner, he would have already done so.

He gallantly opens the front passenger door for me, and I

climb in. The interior of the Jag is black, shiny, and spotless. How does he keep it so clean?

As he powers up his car, a quiet song begins to play from the speakers, and the engine roars to life like a fantastical beast, reminding me of the wolf-dragon on Dacian's signet ring. He performs his usual ritual of cracking the window open, and then he backs the beast up and commands it to follow the road back to Route 7.

Cool October air rushes in through the window, playing with wisps of Dacian's silky hair. The golden sun kisses his cheeks. I sneak furtive glances at him and think about how unreal it feels being so close to him in the light of day, both knowing and not knowing what he is, what he did.

The count died in the original story, and yet almost a century later, Dacian is here, driving in the mountains of Vermont with me. It makes my head spin with questions. Did the book lie about his fate, or did Dacian cheat death at the last moment, unbeknownst to everyone? Where has he been all this time? Has he eaten since Eric, and if he has, who was the source of his meal? And also, why is he driving so slowly?

Initially, I assumed he didn't want the loose gravel to scratch the pristine finish of his Jag, but now we're on the highway, and he's still going below the speed limit. A rusty pickup truck honks as it passes us. The audacity! I resist the urge to pop out the window and shout at the driver to have some respect. But I'm wondering the same thing as that driver. This ain't my twenty-year-old Chevy Nova. This is a *Jag*! We should be flying down this highway, not moseying along. Unable to contain my bafflement any longer, I clear my throat. "Is your car okay?"

Dacian's dark eyebrows crinkle in confusion. "Yes. Why?"

"Well..." I pause, thinking how best to phrase it. "You aren't driving very fast."

In an instant, Dacian's expression turns peeved—an uncharacteristically unguarded reaction for him. "Is that so?" he asks flatly.

I sense that I may have inadvertently hit a sore spot, but it's too late to backpedal now. "Um, well, the speed limit is forty-five, and you're going just above thirty," I say, cautiously watching Dacian's reaction. "If a cop sees you, you might get pulled over."

My words seem to have an effect on him. Looking very uncomfortable, he presses his lips into a thin line. His hands grip the steering wheel a bit tighter, making his knuckles white. After what appears to be a brief but tumultuous debate with himself, he confesses, "I...only recently learned how to drive."

For a moment, I'm at a loss for words.

"I didn't exactly need to do it in my former life," he adds, miffed. "I can cross vast distances much faster than any combustible engine. Unfortunately, you modern Americans expect me to travel inside a metal box, so I do my best to keep up the charade."

I hide the smile that threatens to make an untimely appearance on my lips. His feathers are really ruffled. "Have you asked anyone to help you practice?" I ask innocently.

Dacian relaxes a little. "I could, I suppose. But I don't keep many friends."

That makes sense, considering who he is. I wonder if he lives in that gigantic Tudor all by himself. That must be lonely.

As though sensing my curiosity and choosing to indulge it, Dacian adds, "I do keep several staff at my true residence. I could've asked them. But I've been traveling for a while, and I haven't brought any of them with me."

He doesn't tell me where his real home is or the reason he had to leave it. Judging from his accent, I bet it's somewhere in the UK. If it was still in Transylvania, there would be no need to hide it from me, as that information is already widely known thanks to the novel. Although the moment I think that, a pang of fear prickles my chest. If Dacian's real home is not the Tudor I just saw, does that mean his stay in America is only temporary?

Quiet descends between us again. I need to fill this silence with more questions. I want to know everything about him. I ask the first thing that comes to mind. "Do you like The Smiths?" A mixtape with songs by The Smiths, New Order, and Bauhaus has been playing quietly in the background since we left 29 Hollow Lane. If Dacian doesn't have many friends, I wonder if he made it himself. What a strange thought—Count D making mixtapes.

"Yes, I do enjoy them," he replies, smiling unexpectedly. "Bowie too. I'm glad I didn't miss him."

This puzzles me. How could he have missed Bowie? Was he not around for a period of time? And why didn't he learn to drive until *now*? It's not like cars were invented recently. Presumably, he's had decades to practice—unless, of course, he's always employed a chauffeur. I can't imagine Dacian using public transportation. But before I can pursue that train of thought, Dacian continues, "This is by far my favorite thing about the twentieth century—how easy it is to capture music. The Walkman has got to be mankind's greatest invention. I can't believe you can just carry it with you."

"You have a Walkman?" This time, I don't hide my grin as I imagine Dacian with headphones over his ears, bopping along to a catchy beat.

"I do. You find that humorous?" he asks, shooting a quick glance my way before returning his full attention to the road.

I shake my head. "Just, most people would say that something like penicillin is mankind's greatest invention. Or the airplane," I say, letting out a laugh.

Dacian looks momentarily befuddled as he ponders my comment. "I suppose most people would. However, my body is not susceptible to human afflictions, and I don't need a plane to fly. So, for me, it is the Walkman."

I smile again. "I could tell you loved books, but I didn't know you were into music too."

"Of course I love music," he says with a hint of pride. "How hollow would my soul be if I didn't? Even a being like me couldn't face the torture of such emptiness. If I had to endure an eternity without stories and songs, I would've given up on this immortal existence a long time ago."

There is a certain melancholy about Dacian's face when he says that last part. And I may be wrong, but I think I sense a hint of fear too. What is there to be afraid of if you cannot die? Although maybe that's too simplistic a question. How long has Dacian been alive exactly, wandering through endless shadows? For all I know, he's had lifetimes of experiences. They can't have all been pleasant. The way he reacted to my name, how guarded he is around me, and the broken fragments of memories he's revealed make me think fear must be a feeling he's intimately familiar with. Loneliness as well. *I spent a long time in a very isolated place with nothing to entertain me but a small library.* When Dacian told me this, I didn't realize how literally he meant it. Did anyone ever keep him company in that cold, dark castle, or has he been on his own for centuries? What really happened between him and Jonathan Harker? Where was he all this time that the world believed him dead? It's maddening how little I know about him when he's sitting right here, within arm's reach.

I fidget in my seat, but before I can gather the courage to ask him more, Dacian says, "We're nearly there," and merges into the exit lane. Out my window, I spot a sign that says, SCENIC TRAIL NEXT 10 MILES.

We drive down a narrow one-lane road for several minutes, and then Dacian pulls into a small parking lot next to a camping area. There are several shaded wooden tables with benches and a board with a trail map. Dacian looks around carefully before killing the engine, but we seem to be the only people here.

"Are we going on a hike?" I ask, half-joking. But the serious look on his face stumps me.

"Not exactly," he replies.

We exit the Jag, and I follow him to one of the three trails I saw on the map. He stops me before I step onto the path.

"It isn't prudent to travel further on foot," he says. "I do not wish for us to leave any trace behind."

I frown. There are plenty of tourist-trodden hiking routes in the Green Mountains—especially in the fall, when everyone and their cousin comes to Vermont to watch the leaves change—but this isn't one of them. There's not a soul around, just a yellow-red sea of trees. Why is he so worried that someone might know we were here? "What do you suggest?" I ask, perplexed.

"That I carry you."

My mouth falls open. Surely he must be joking. But Dacian keeps a straight face, and before any incoherent words tumble out of me, he adds, "Are you ready, Jonathan?"

My knees go soft at the sound of my name coming from his lips. Perhaps he starved me of it on purpose so that now he can mold me however he likes simply by saying it. Still, this is crazy. I look around awkwardly.

"Yes," I murmur, trying not to burst into flame from the spark of anticipation as he steps closer, puts his arms around me —one behind my back, the other under my knees—and swiftly lifts me off the ground. My eyes widen. I'm not heavy by any means, what with never having enough money for groceries and working double shifts over the summer, but I'm still a fully grown person! Yet Dacian's muscles show no strain holding my weight; he might as well be lifting a feather.

My head is pressed against his chest as he tightens his arms around me. And then he takes a step forward, except his feet are no longer touching the ground. I gulp.

The world around me tilts up. Dacian carrying me like his bride is already a shock to the system, but now we're *flying*. Instantly, my mind goes back to that night when I saw him hovering in the air outside my window. It's no less dizzying to see him do it in broad daylight—and now I'm flying with him!

"Breathe easy; I will not let you fall," he whispers as he levitates higher. As though my fear of falling is the reason my heart is about to thump out of my chest. I wonder if he can hear it, if he feels my blood running with his vampire senses. *You can't hide from me. Yours is the only beating heart inside this building.* My face grows hot at the memory. His words sounded so sinister then. Terrified as I was, I missed what he was really telling me—that he was *listening* to my heart, to my blood, as he's doing now. I feel a swirl of warmth under my sweater. I wonder if he's always listening to it. If he thinks of it when I'm not around. If he *wants* it.

I try to calm down for both our sakes, but it's easier said than done. I don't know what to do with my hands or whether I should keep my head resting against his collarbone. His hands were cold at first, just like the touch of his fingers on my lips when he called me by my name for the first time, but now they don't seem so anymore; my skin has grown hot where Dacian touches me. I try to sneak a glance up at him, but from this angle, I can't see his expression and can't even begin to guess what he's thinking. It's torturous to have him so close and not know, yet I welcome this torment, and he does nothing to stop it.

Unhurriedly, Dacian veers through the branches of golden-bronze beech trees and orange sugar maples. I can smell the chill in the air, the musky sweetness of the decaying leaves on the ground, and the sharpness of an occasional hemlock. But more than anything, I smell *him*. He smells like a memory, a feeling. Like a frozen, lonely place in faraway mountains, like a thousand desperate words, all unspoken. Like a millennium of yearning.

I let my cheek press against the fuzzy fabric of his sweater. I want to keep breathing him in. *This isn't a date*, I remind myself, but part of me is desperately hoping it is. A date that would only make sense in a book about an ancient vampire pretending to be a literature professor and his student, who's fallen for him beyond saving. Right now, he could carry me to the edge of the world and I wouldn't resist. I just want to stay like this, gliding through the woods in his arms, and if he wants to look inside my mind like it's an open book and read these feelings, I will happily welcome him in.

Dacian follows the trail for a while before turning sharply west. He still doesn't tell me where we're going or why, but I begin to sense a slight shift in him as we approach our destination, his body getting tense. This feels ominous. Dacian is not someone who scares easily—except apparently when it comes to driving above thirty, of course. Maybe it's me he's worried about. Reluctantly, I shake off the remnants of the daze I've fallen into and finally start to take note of my surroundings. Something seems wrong about this place. I can't pinpoint it, but it feels too quiet. Too empty. As though living beings are instinctively avoiding this part of the forest, leaving it dreary and stale, allowing shadows to take permanent residence here.

Dacian slows his flight, and my gaze zeroes in on something below, about fifty feet ahead of us—a slumped shape surrounded by white markings on the ground. I squint. "What is that?" I ask uneasily.

We rise a good fifteen feet before he brings me closer to the scene.

"Oh god." I gasp and cover my mouth once I manage to make out the shape below.

There's a body lying naked in the center of a pentagram drawn on the ground with white paint, like a summoning ritual from a budget horror flick. The body has clearly been rotting for some time. All that's left of it is a yellowish-green mass of skin and muscles clinging to a visible skeleton. It must have been here for weeks, a festering kingdom for maggots. Once I'm close enough, the putrid smell hits my nostrils and sends a stinging pain through my head. It is then, with a sudden inexplicable certainty, that I realize these half-decomposed remains belong to the hiker who went missing at the beginning of the semester.

I recall the photograph of him printed in the local paper. I think the man's name was Jeremy. He was smiling, posing in front of some picturesque vista. There was a sweep of luscious blue mountains in the background and bright sunshine glowing around him like a halo. He wasn't just a hiker—Jeremy was a forest conservationist visiting this part of Vermont to study the Green Mountain ecosystem. "His wife and one-year-old son miss him dearly and hope for his safe return," the newspaper had read. But this body on the ground looks nothing like that man, all his light robbed from him, leaving behind only a putrefying carcass.

"What happened to him?" I push out, my tongue too thick to cooperate properly. Why did Dacian bring me here? Dean Wilkins mentioned a bear attack, but bears don't draw pentagrams.

Dacian's tone is oddly flat and emotionless when he replies. "This person was killed as part of a ritual sacrifice."

Sacrifice? The word ping-pongs in my mind. I feel sick. My breath gets stuck in my throat like someone has smashed a fist into it. I turn away, desperate to escape the corpse, but there's nowhere to go; I can only hide my face in Dacian's chest and the smooth, dark wool of his sweater.

His arms tighten around me. His voice suddenly gentler, he whispers, "Let yourself breathe, Jonathan."

"I'm trying," I wheeze. But it's still a struggle to get the air in and out. "Who would do such a thing?"

Instead of providing me with relief, Dacian's reply feels like another sucker punch. "Your former classmate, Mr. Stockton."

Wait. What? "That's...that's impossible," I argue. "How would you even know that?"

With a calm that reminds me that Dacian is not human, no matter how much he may appear to be, he explains. "I know because I saw it in Mr. Stockton's blood when I drank it. Many things remain unclear to me, but this was at the very top of his mind. I saw this place and the body as vividly as I see it now."

I try to stay coherent, but my voice sounds like a helpless little whine. "You saw it in his *blood*? I don't understand."

"Let us return to the car," Dacian offers softly. "There, I will explain everything."

I don't object.

He carries me back to the Jag, soundlessly floating between tree branches. But it doesn't feel magical anymore. My hands are clammy, and I keep remembering the stench of corporeal rot, the fallen leaves obscuring the crudely drawn pentagram. *Eric sacrificed him. A real person. A husband. A father. For a ritual.*

Dacian opens the Jag's door for me and helps me into the front seat.

"Remember when I told you Eric Stockton took something from me?" he asks, joining me in the car. Dazedly, I nod. "It is the book that went missing from the library. It used to belong to me before it was sold off and eventually donated to Camden. Mr. Stockton was the one who stole it."

My brain scrambles for clarity, trying to arrange these pieces of information into a picture that makes sense. Ms. Tarnow said that the missing book was the diary of a nineteenth-century European nobleman—a "madman," as she referred to him, because of the bizarre writings that filled those pages. Of course! How did I not see this sooner? The journal was Dacian's! No wonder it sounded like the ramblings of a lunatic to a modern woman who likely doesn't believe in vampires. I don't know if I'd have believed it myself before I saw Dacian bite Eric...

"That book is *your* diary," I repeat aloud for confirmation.

"Yes," he says simply. As though admitting that he kept a journal almost a hundred years ago, even though he looks no older than twenty-five, is perfectly normal.

Numbly, I ask, "So why would Eric steal it? What did you write in it?"

"Mostly stories from my life, my private thoughts." Dacian's gaze briefly turns pensive before he adds, "However, among my writings was a detailed explanation of the ancient ritual that created me."

My stomach drops. "Created you? You mean..."

"Yes, it's a ritual that turns a human into a vampire. Mr. Stockton sought to replicate it."

Dacian's reply sends my thoughts reeling once again. Eric stole Dacian's diary and killed Jeremy...so that he could become a vampire? And not just Jeremy. Anita Hernandez's body was also covered in puncture wounds and bled dry, no bullshit cartels or hungry bears to blame. Both people were murdered for this ritual.

Still, it's unbelievable to think that Eric could do such a horrible thing. He was a spoiled, rich brat who treated me like dirt, slept through his classes, and spent his time at drug-filled parties with Mads Jr. and Callahan, but I'd never have pegged him as a cold-blooded killer or an aspiring vampire. "Are you *certain* Eric did this?"

Dacian's face remains impassive. He's not shocked by any of this. "I am certain," he confirms. "That night when you saw me with him, Mr. Stockton was *hunting*. For the next sacrifice."

I shake my head in disbelief. But then I remember the incident earlier that evening when Eric assaulted me in the vault. He sounded paranoid and incoherent, rambling about books being at fault for something. In fact, he'd been acting off for weeks. Was that behavior the result of becoming a vampire?

"As I mentioned, when I drank Mr. Stockton's blood," Dacian continues—I can't help but shiver at how openly he admits to this—"it allowed me to glimpse some of his memories. It's one of my abilities. I wanted to find out where he'd hidden my journal, but I was distracted."

"By me?" I ask.

"Yes, by you," he says softly.

There's an odd expression on his face that I can't quite parse. "There is a connection between us," he adds, confirming what I've suspected all along. "That night, when you saw me, I didn't know what to do. I couldn't decide if I should chase after you and lose my chance of finding my journal, or keep extracting the knowledge from Mr. Stockton drop by drop. In the end, I accomplished neither. I hesitated and let you escape, and by the time I returned to the woods, Mr. Stockton was already dead. Blood memories can only be taken when they flow from the living. Once there's no pulse, the current stops."

That explains why Dacian never caught up to me, letting me reach the safety of my dorm. He must've been scared I would out him, forcing him to flee Camden and killing his chances of ever finding his journal. Of course, I'd never do that. Even when I was terrified that he might kill me, I never considered exposing him. This affair has always been between the two of us. And now, because of my interference, Dacian has no way of discovering where his journal is stashed. It could be buried under a tree in the mountains, for all we know.

A silly hope springs to life inside of me that maybe we can put all of this behind us, that Dacian and I can return to being student and teacher again. Or something *more*, if only he'll allow it...

"I guess it's over, then." I sigh, ready to let the weight of this supernatural murder mystery slide off my shoulders. "Since Eric is dead, there should be no more victims. Maybe we can find a way to tip off the police about Jeremy's body without implicating ourselves."

But when I glance at Dacian, he doesn't look even the tiniest bit relieved. He gazes back at me with the kind of apologetic discomfort one might feel while explaining how the world really works to someone very naive.

"It is far from over, Jonathan," he says quietly. "Eric Stockton wasn't the only person involved in the hiker's death. In his memories, I glimpsed others. They wore masks, so I couldn't see their identities. You see, during the first stage of the ritual, each participant must kill one sacrifice. It seems that while Mr. Stockton partook of the hiker's blood, ultimately, he was someone else's kill. As was the woman. I stopped Mr. Stockton when it was his turn to bring a sacrifice of his own, but his companions still possess my journal. As they are not my progeny, I cannot distinguish them from regular humans. It is likely they will continue killing until the ritual is complete, but now they're going to be far more careful. They know someone might be watching them."

I stare at the trees surrounding the small rest area. Their bright, golden glow has dimmed—gray clouds have now shrouded the sky, blocking the sun. I can barely wrap my mind around Eric being an accomplice to two gruesome murders, and now Dacian is telling me there are a whole bunch of soon-to-be vampires running around Camden, looking for people to sacrifice?

"I apologize," he says, observing me cautiously. "Perhaps I shouldn't have subjected you to seeing that body. It was quite grotesque. But I wanted you to know that Camden is a lot more dangerous than you realize."

I understand that very well. I think of all those nights I walked alone after a late library shift, unwittingly tempting fate. I'm the perfect candidate for a sudden disappearance—no family and only one friend who cares about me. No wonder Dacian warned me on that rainy night in the library. He's known all along.

"We need to report this to the authorities. It's too serious," I say. "Three people are dead already. How many more will there be if this isn't stopped?"

Dacian's body tenses. "I'm sorry, but we cannot do that."

Something snaps in me. "Of course we can. And we must! Or are you suggesting we let that guy rot up there? He's an innocent person. He doesn't deserve this, Dacian." I think of Jeremy's corpse, used up and discarded like trash, decaying on the mountain while his family cries themselves to sleep every night, praying that he'll come home. And the poor immigrant woman whose death no one seems to care about. It's not right.

"No, he does not deserve this," Dacian agrees. "And neither did the woman. But I can't let you go to the police."

"Why not?" I demand, my nerves stretched to the point where I'm not sure I can hold it together anymore.

"Because I cannot be discovered," Dacian says, visibly frustrated.

I recoil from him. "Are you saying you'd rather save your own skin than stop this madness?"

Dacian's expression ices over, and it feels like the distance between us grows a thousand miles. "You have no idea what you're asking for. You don't know what it's like to be *caught,*

Jonathan," he says, his voice carrying a chill that hits me right in my bones.

An image of a small box flashes in my mind. A box hidden away in a tiny dark room where no one ever goes and no sunlight reaches. Something inside it rattles. Something inside it calls. Something—

I snap out of it. Is this somehow connected to why Dacian never learned to drive? Why he disappeared after the events described in the novel? Why he keeps a window open in every room he steps into?

"You might not understand this, but I'm severely compromising my personal safety by searching for my journal," he says sternly. "The nineteenth century was perilous enough with its arrogant Dutch doctors turned vampire hunters. What do you think the U.S. government would do if they found out about me? My imagination may be lacking when it comes to modern methods of torture, but I wager they'd start by determining exactly how immortal this body of mine is."

This stuns me into speechlessness. I haven't truly considered the consequences of Dacian being revealed for what he is.

"But worse than that would be them finding my journal," Dacian continues, not waiting for me to respond. "It was sheer luck that it spent a century gathering dust in some collector's private library, the ritual never taken seriously or tested. But if someone in power were to find it, what do you think they would do with the knowledge of how to create vampires? Imagine an army of immortal soldiers. I must prevent that from happening. Those who have the journal now haven't completed the ritual yet. They remain within my grasp. But if they get frightened by the police, they may escape and continue murdering their way across the country." Dacian exhales as though trying to reassert control over his emotions and then adds more quietly, "Besides, how would you explain to the authorities how you know where the body is? People like Mr. Stockton can afford to be reckless. They don't need to worry about plausible alibis. They have family lawyers ready to get them out of trouble. But you, Jonathan—who will protect *you*?"

One by one, Dacian's words sink to the bottom of my gut like stones in a lake. As horrific as the murder of two innocent people is, it pales in comparison to what might happen if the secrets in his journal become widespread knowledge.

"How long before they complete the ritual?" I ask quietly.

"I do not know. There are two parts to it, and the second part...it requires preparation," Dacian says. He doesn't elaborate, but his tone is grim.

After a moment he leans back in his seat, his gaze slightly unfocused. The weight of centuries seems to have settled on his shoulders once again. "Forgive me. I should never have put this knowledge into writing. In my arrogance, I never imagined that my words could be taken from me, that *anything* could be taken from me."

I hate this situation, but I do understand where Dacian is coming from. The journal must be retrieved and hidden where no human can be tempted by it again. There is no other way.

But there's one thing I still don't understand.

"Why did you bring me here? Why tell me all of this?" I ask. By showing me that someone else committed these murders, Dacian must have been trying to clear his name, but wouldn't it have been easier not to involve me at all? If his true intention is guarding the secret of how to make vampires, then why trust me with any information about this?

"Being what I am, there are places I cannot enter without invitation," he replies, watching me intently. "As you know, some of the legends about us *are* true. I'm hoping you can help me locate what belongs to me before more people die."

That seems fair. If a vampire can't enter a dwelling uninvited, then Dacian's ability to conduct his search is limited. He needs a willing human on his side.

Still, something about his answer makes my heart stutter treacherously. Dacian was haunting my dreams before I ever suspected anything about his true nature, before I even knew sinister rituals were taking place in the shadows of the woods.

Did he get me the work-study job at the library just so he could recruit me, or was there another reason? The way he looked at me that very first time at the theater—I *felt* it. The instant connection was unlike anything I've experienced in my life. And why did he touch my lips so gently when I confronted him? If this is all just a ploy to find his journal, isn't it too cruel to toy with my heart like that? To lead me on? Doesn't he know the effect he has on me?

"Is that the *only* reason?" I ask, feeling like I'm balancing on the edge of a cliff. One word from him could save me or doom me. Just one word.

But Dacian does not reply. Instead, he fumbles for his car keys in his pocket. "It's getting late. We shouldn't linger here."

He starts the engine and reverses the Jag out of the small parking lot, driving us away from the scene of the crime and further from the answer I so desperately need.

TWENTY-FOUR

"I'm not expecting you to make a decision right away," Dacian says once we're back in his driveway. "Take your time." The heavy implication of danger hangs in the air between us.

I nod and turn to open the door, but he stops me. His hand lands on my shoulder and for a moment, I have a burning hope that he's done holding back and that he'll say the words I crave hearing. I can barely breathe. "What?" I ask.

"Are you all right to drive back?" His concern sounds genuine —and that hurts even more.

"I'll be fine," I mutter, shoving the jagged shard of disappointment further down into my rib cage.

I don't look back as I exit his Jaguar and climb into my much-less-attractive Chevy. But I feel his eyes watching me.

For the next few hours, my brain is too shot to process what I saw in the woods. I simply go through the motions of my day. I drive back to campus. I clock in for my library shift. I listen to Jessi grumble about working Friday night when she could be at the movies with her boyfriend. Apparently, there's a drive-in theater not too far from Camden that's showing the new Nightmare on Elm Street sequel. I tune out most of her complaints and nod in between her sentences so as to appear invested in our conversation, but I'm not. Unlike Jessi, I've never been to the movies with a boyfriend. I've never done anything fun with a boyfriend. My only boyfriend had to be a secret.

And my day with Dacian turned out to be a date with a corpse instead of a romantic getaway. I wish I had the authority to let Jessi go early so I could wallow in my misery alone.

By late evening, the secrets Dacian revealed to me start to crop up in the background of my mind, grabbing hold of my thoughts and not letting go. It doesn't help that it's a slow night, and there isn't much to distract me from thinking about him.

Fiona's hunch proved correct in the end: the stolen book was an inside job. But I stand by my faith that a true librarian would never have done such a thing. Eric wasn't one of us. He only got the internship because he stole that, too—from me.

I would never allow a book to go missing. But what would I have done when Dacian eventually came looking for it? Would I have tried to stop him from taking it? Is it even possible for me to say no to him, or would he just have mesmerized me with those lightless eyes of his? I'm so helpless against them. It might not even have come to that, though. Dacian likely would have decided that dealing with humans was too much trouble. With his vampire powers, he could've snuck in and taken his diary without me ever knowing.

The cart full of returned books that I'm rolling between the shelves screeches to a stop. With unexpected fierceness, that thought wrenches at my heart: *I could've lived my whole life without knowing that Dacian exists.* And that's a fate much worse than seeing a thousand rotting corpses or being tormented by Clay's ghost. Was it Dacian who sent his shadow wolves into my dream to tear the ghost to pieces, to protect me? I've never asked. But something so cruel and so merciful at the same time sounds just like him.

He did confirm the mind link between us, though. Rationally,

I understand that I should be freaked out by the revelation that a vampire can peek inside my mind and unearth all my secrets. And yet some twisted, savagely lonely part of me rejoices at the idea that Dacian and I are tethered to each other. That he can haunt my dreams. That maybe he wants to know the *real* me, with all my guilt and sadness and anger.

But then again, maybe he only got close to me because he needs an ally in his quest for the missing journal. But is that really all he wants from me?

I think of his arms around me in the woods, carrying me. It makes sense now that he didn't want my feet to touch the ground. If rangers ever find Jeremy's body, they might spot my footprints in the dirt, and their canines could pick up my scent. It's unlikely that I could be implicated, but the chance isn't small enough to disregard. Still, why did Dacian choose to hold me the way he did —his arm around my waist, his breath in my hair? He was so quiet the whole time, as though he didn't want to interrupt the moment.

Surely, he knows he doesn't need to seduce me to get my help looking for a stolen book, even if it involves going up against a bunch of rabid vampires. So why visit my dreams? Why seek me out to tell me how much he wants to see the world? Why let his touch linger if this is all just business? Could he be holding back because of what happened between him and the other Jonathan? Well, I'm not that other Jonathan. I don't want to be pulled in by the dark vortex that is Dacian, only to be pushed aside because I remind him of someone who's been dead for decades!

I push the cart forward again a little too forcefully—a sign of my building frustration. So many damn questions, so few answers.

I wish I'd kissed his fingers that night in the woods; then, maybe, I'd be certain about some things. Or that he'd haunt my dreams not as a silver mist but in the flesh, so there would be no denying what we'd done in the morning...

But Dacian doesn't visit me again despite how badly my heart aches for him.

———

I WAKE up Saturday morning feeling unusually rested. Maybe it was delayed shock from seeing Jeremy's corpse, but as soon as my head hit my pillow, I passed out and slept for fourteen hours straight.

I glance at the box of letters on my nightstand—even Clay's ghost didn't visit me. The entire night feels like a giant black hole. Outside, the sky is leaden gray. Seems like it's going to be one of those days when the sun never makes an appearance. By the time I drag myself out of bed and trudge to the dining hall for brunch, a thin drizzle starts to break through the clouds.

Fiona isn't here, so I fill my bowl with cornflakes and take a seat at an empty table at the far end of the room. I chew my cereal, watching students mill about still in their pajamas, some clearly hungover from last night. I've no desire to scan the tables for familiar faces or find someone to sit with. I can't relate to any of these people, especially after recent events. My points of connection to the world are growing fewer by the day. What would I even say if someone asked me how my Friday was? *A vampire flew me out to the woods, showed me a decomposing corpse, and then asked me to help him uncover a vampire cult right here in Camden. Oh, and by the way, I'm hopelessly pining for him. How was* your *Friday?*

Exasperated, I drop my spoon into the bowl with a clatter. Milk splashes onto my tray. There is a serious possibility I might be losing it. Dacian has given me a way out, insisting I think things over before I decide, yet I stubbornly keep digging deeper, getting more entangled in this mess, in him. But I can't turn away now. He promised answers when he proposed that I take a ride with him, but all I got were more questions. Besides, there's something that bothers me about the story he told me—something I didn't catch right away, but it sticks out when I replay our conversation in my mind for the millionth time.

If Dacian wants my help, he will have to be honest with me.

So once again, I resolve to confront him and demand the truth.

TWENTY-FIVE

Thin gray mist settles over the mountains as I drive to 29 Hollow Lane that evening.

Dacian opens the door before I have a chance to knock—he must've heard me arrive—but there's a look of surprise on his face that he doesn't bother hiding. He is not expecting me.

He's wearing a loose black cardigan with a black V-neck T-shirt underneath and soft black casual pants. His hair is slightly disheveled, and there's a book in his hand—a fantasy, by the looks of the cover. This unbelievably attractive man is spending his Saturday night cooped up alone in the house with a book. I can't help the flood of warm fuzziness that observation brings.

If Dacian wanted to take someone to the movies or to dinner tonight, there'd be a line of candidates stretching all the way to Camden. I've seen the way girls look at him, the way everyone's head turns when he passes. And yet he prefers the company of books like a common nerd—a centuries-old noble vampire nerd. I resist the oncoming smile and remind myself why I am here.

"May I come in?" I ask.

Dacian's face blanks. Belatedly, I realize it must be a big deal that I, a human, have asked to be let inside the home of a vampire.

But unlike in Bram Stoker's book, Dacian doesn't give me a spiel about entering of my own free will.

"Of course," he says, stepping aside to let me in.

The Tudor's foyer is semi-dark, illuminated by the warm, inviting glow of two Tiffany lamps. The walls are paneled in mahogany wood, and a red Turkish rug covers the floor. Judging by the craftsmanship, this home must have been built for someone extremely wealthy. The furnishings are sparse but chic and expensive, just like most things Dacian owns.

We hover awkwardly by the door. Dacian might have invited me inside, but he seems to have reservations about allowing me in any further. The silence stretches between us for several long moments. I must have truly caught him off guard with my arrival.

Dacian places his book on the small table by the door. "So, what have you decided, Jonathan?" he finally asks.

I struggle to control my sudden nerves, and my words don't come out easily. "I have a condition. Or rather, I have more questions. If you answer them, I'll help you get your journal back."

"All right," Dacian agrees, slow and guarded.

I take a deep breath and exhale. Here comes the moment of truth. "You said Eric was hunting the night you caught him. Who was he hunting?"

The air in the room stills as soon as the words leave my mouth.

"I wouldn't presume to know. Could have been anybody," Dacian replies a little too quickly. I never thought I'd be able to catch him in a lie; his actions are so often indecipherable to me. But just now, there is a tiny flutter in his dark eyelashes that he doesn't cover up in time.

My heart lets out a thump. I knew it. *I knew it.* There were only a few people on campus during fall break. How did Dacian know to show up in the right place at the right time? Unless he was already there for some reason. Such as to watch someone sleep so he could visit his dreams.

I double down on my dangerous gamble. "When you realized

Eric was hunting, why did you stop him?" I keep my eyes on Dacian's, not letting myself miss a beat. "Wouldn't it have been easier to let him go through with it? You could've tracked him back to his little cult and found your journal, but you chose to stop him instead. Why?"

Dacian seems to have nothing to say, and that in itself is the answer I so desperately crave.

I throw all caution to the wind and step toward him. "Eric was hunting *me* for his sacrifice, wasn't he? And you protected me," I finally whisper.

The question rouses a storm in the dark depths of Dacian's eyes. Brazenly, I put my hand on his face. I let my fingers skim his sharp jaw as I draw closer to him. My mouth is mere inches from his. I want to kiss him so badly I could burn down. But I don't close the distance between us.

"Am I wrong? If you don't want this, tell me to stop, and I will," I murmur, my heart thrumming like a hot wire.

But Dacian still says nothing. Frozen like a corpse, he just stands there. I feel the first bells of panic chime inside of me. "Please say *something*," I beg. I wait for several agonizingly long seconds, but there's no response at all.

The fire in me sizzles out, and I'm overcome with tremendous humiliation. I misread our connection and made a fool of myself. I misjudged everything. How could he possibly want *me*, a stupid, insignificant human?

"I'm sorry," I blurt as my eyes begin to sting. How utterly idiotic have I—

I remove my hand from his face, but before I can pull myself away, my entire world jolts. I'm shoved against the wall with so much force that I swear the house rattles around me. My body is spared the impact because Dacian's arms wrap around me a moment before I collide with the wall, but his push is so strong that it knocks my breath out of me.

"What do you want me to say, Jonathan?" he demands, panting heavily as though he's struggling to hold himself back.

"That no matter how much I try to resist, I'm unable to keep myself from you? That the instant our eyes met in the theater, I saw our connection? Your heart called out to me, all ten thousand broken shards of it. How could I not answer when suddenly, in a room full of people, I could hear only you?" My eyes widen as Dacian's hand moves to my face. "Do you have any idea how rare this is?" he asks.

"Tell me," I whisper, my lips trembling.

"So rare," he says, "that I've only encountered it twice in four hundred years, but the first time I gave in to it, I lost everything, including my freedom. So I tried to deny it. Deny you. For my sake. For your sake. Yet despite all my efforts, here we both are. You said that night in the woods that you were terrified of me, but shouldn't I be terrified of you, Jonathan?"

There's a red glow blooming in Dacian's lightless eyes, only inches away from mine. The sheer intensity of them could stop a heart. For a moment, I can't speak at all. My skin breaks out in goosebumps as he challenges my courage. But as seconds tick away, I realize that underneath all the fear and the primal instinct to run from the deadly danger that is Dacian lurks an insatiable, uncontrollable need to be with him.

"Please don't be afraid of me," I whisper, trying to keep my voice steady, "because I am not afraid of you."

As the words leave my mouth, Dacian's head tilts like a predator about to attack its prey. But he doesn't bite. Instead, his lips crash into mine.

He kisses me ravenously, his tongue seeking the inside of my mouth with desperate urgency. It's like being hit with a gale-force wind; I feel simultaneously free and terrified that it will knock me off my feet. So I grab onto him, let my hands sink into his hair, pulling at the silky strands. He pushes me into the wall again, his body flush against mine. A fervor of excitement blazes through my skin as I sense how much he wants me, the loose, flowy fabric of his pants hiding nothing. Giddily, I press my hips against his over and over.

He parts his mouth from mine in a breathless whisper. "Upstairs?"

I have no idea what's upstairs, but I nod because I can't bear to be separated from him, even for a moment.

Without warning, the world spins again as he sweeps me away, traces of shadow mist melting in our wake as he carries me to the second floor.

After just one thudding heartbeat, my feet touch the ground again. Dazed, I try to take in my new surroundings. This room is dark, save for a faint strip of moonlight on the floor, and strangely chilly, as though someone forgot to shut the window. And looming behind me is Dacian's massive four-poster bed. A shiver skims down my belly, and it isn't from the cold.

Our bodies collide again as his mouth reclaims mine with renewed frenzy. One after another, our sweaters drop to the floor, then our T-shirts. I'm so delirious in my desire to touch all of him that I let my hands roam wildly over his chest and the muscles of his bare arms. I press my fingers into his shoulder blades and pull his body even closer to mine while his lovely fingers undo the zipper on my jeans.

He pulls them off, and then it's my turn. I kiss a path down his lean torso as my far-less-adept, but equally greedy hands fumble with his fly. I thread my thumbs through his belt loops once the zipper yields. But before my mouth can continue below his navel, he catches my chin, his hand gentle but insistent. He pulls me back up. Fear rumbles through me. Has he changed his mind? Are we moving too fast?

Anxious, I gaze up at him.

"Can I ask you something?" Dacian says quietly.

"Yes. Anything," I reply, and I mean it. He could wish for anything in the world, and I would burn my soul to ash to grant it.

"Keep your eyes open," he says unexpectedly. "I want you to *see* me."

For a moment, I'm at a loss for words. He wants me to see him? *Oh, Dacian, how could I possibly see anyone else?*

But a desperation seizes Dacian's features as he waits for my answer. It makes my heart twist wretchedly. Does he think I don't know who I'm giving myself to? Or that I'll abandon him? What absurdity. He could toss me out the window, and in this madness, I'd crawl right back to him, broken legs and all.

"I see you, Dacian," I whisper, with as much reassurance as I can.

Something unwinds in him then, like a knot that's been tied too tight. Red light rekindles in the depths of his irises, and this time, the haunting beauty does not frighten me at all.

Dacian holds me steady with his gaze as his fingers slide from my chin to my shoulder and nudge me in the direction of his bed. I ache for more of his touch, but he's in no hurry now as he removes the rest of our clothes. By the time he finally pushes me down on the mattress, I feel like my skin might catch fire unless it's united with his.

It's an excruciating effort to keep my eyes from squeezing shut as he takes me into his mouth. A moan tears out of me, desperate and raw. His face moving up and down is by far the hottest thing I've ever seen. I want nothing more than to lose myself in this ocean of him, but all the while Dacian keeps looking at me, the same plea in his eyes—*see me, see me*—and I can't look away. A shimmering red haze fills my mind. I bite my lip in concentration and grasp the sheets until my fingers vibrate from the strain.

My desire starts to crest, teetering on the brink of explosion, but he doesn't grant me release. Instead, he hikes my knee and moves his warm mouth to tentatively plant a row of kisses along the inside of my thigh. "May I—" he whispers.

"Yes," I mutter breathlessly before I even hear the rest of his question. I feel him smile against my skin as he presses his nose into the pulse point in my groin. He never lets go of me, but in my peripheral vision, there's a swirl of shadows followed by the sound of a drawer being opened and shut. The shadows drift over to his hand, and when they dissipate, they leave a small bottle in his palm. My heart thumps as I watch him open it.

I hold Dacian's face as he carefully settles inside me.

Just the feeling of fullness, of being complete, almost drives me over the edge. But I hang on, and then he starts to move, so unbearably slowly. I beg him to go faster in my mind, or maybe it spills into words—I can't tell anymore—but when he finally picks up the pace, I don't last very long at all. We roll and crash into each other like two waves in a storm, arching and falling again and again. His hand wraps around me and starts moving in sync. An unstoppable need swells in me. The world around us fades, dull and unimportant. Only Dacian remains, and the depthless, commanding scarlet of his eyes that bids me to see only him. I hold on to him desperately, his most willing captive, and shudder in his arms until every last drop of desire is wrung out of me.

Only then does Dacian release his hypnotic hold on me. He cradles my head and draws me in for a kiss that is as much a gasp for air as a sigh of relief. His eyelashes flutter shut, and after we separate, I notice his irises are black again.

I collapse, completely exhausted, onto the pillow, every part of me rearranged in a strange new fashion. He lies beside me, letting leisurely minutes pass as we catch our ragged breaths.

Now that the fever of being kissed by him has cooled a little, I shiver again. Curiously, I glance around and find that one of the windows to my right is open, just a crack.

"Are you cold?" Dacian murmurs contentedly.

"No," I deny, but scoot closer to him. He chuckles at my half-hearted deception but allows me to snake my arm around his waist. "Do you sleep?" I ask lazily when I notice his eyelids starting to get heavy. I've wondered this about vampires.

"Yes," he replies. "I have a body. It requires rest."

"But aren't you a creature of the night?" I ask, half-joking, half-serious.

"I am," he says, amused. "My powers come from the shadows; I am at my strongest when there is no light. However, this teaching occupation demands that I remain awake during the day, which has been very inconvenient, to say the least."

Well, that explains why his eyes often look tired when I see him in class. He probably feels like he's constantly jet lagged. He suppresses a yawn. "Any more questions, or will you let this old man sleep?" he asks teasingly.

I can't help but laugh. I want to make some witty comment about this "old" man looking twenty-five at most, but I am too worn out to think of anything worthy.

"I have one more question," I say hesitantly. "What happened between you and...the other Jonathan?"

Dacian never outright said it was him, the only other person he'd felt connected to, but from the way his body suddenly tenses next to mine, I know I've hit a bull's eye.

"Is this question a part of our bargain?" he asks somberly.

I shake my head. "Of course not." I'd never force someone to disclose such private matters. "Just wondering."

It's a long moment before Dacian replies. He stares at the ceiling, his eyes distant and his lips a hard, unforgiving line. I almost don't expect him to say anything at all. But as I start to feel the pull of drowsiness, every cell in my body sated and cozy with shared warmth, Dacian finally answers in a whisper, all the sadness in the world poured into two short sentences.

"He was a coward, and I was arrogant. We were doomed from the start."

Twenty-Six

The count paced around his quarters restlessly. Time was slipping away, and still, he was no closer to making a decision. He was departing in three short days, yet his human was still in the castle, and his previous plans to harm him now seemed unconscionable. But what was he going to do? Was there something he could offer that didn't mean separation for the two of them? Did he have the courage to? He didn't know, but maybe, maybe...

He knew where to find his human at this hour—and most hours, really. The library was his favorite place in the castle, as it was the count's. It was in that room that the count had learned the strange musical language named after angels and where, decades later, his favorite human taught him the intricacies of proper pronunciation. There was only so much the count could pick up from books; he needed someone to practice with. And practice they did.

"If I get it right, you shall kiss me," the count had said, dark fire molten in his eyes. That had been the first time they'd played what would soon become his favorite English-learning game. "And if I am wrong, I shall remove an article of your clothing."

His human had laughed and flushed a ravishingly deep shade of red. "So I'm the one being disciplined whether you're a good student or not?"

In response, the count had only grinned, all teeth and a little bit of danger. "Exactly right. Welcome to Transylvania, my friend." Then he'd pushed the human up against the shelves and shown him just how wicked the local Transylvanian customs were for misbehaving teachers.

The count's pronunciation had improved by leaps and bounds in just a few weeks. But it was nearly time to stop his lessons and put his knowledge to the test in the country he had dreamed of seeing for so long.

His human smiled when the count entered the library. "Are you here to play our game?" he asked, leaning suggestively against the writing desk and jutting out his hip in a manner most flirtatious.

For a moment, the count was tempted. But...

"Not today, I'm afraid," he said, folding his hands behind his back. He was uncharacteristically nervous. It had been a long time —decades, maybe—since he'd felt anything akin to this, and that in itself was disconcerting. "There is something I wish to discuss with you."

The human's eyes widened. Perhaps the seriousness of the count's tone had alerted him to where the discussion was headed. Or maybe he had simply guessed what the count was thinking, as he so often did.

"You asked me," the count continued, "how long you were required to remain here. As you know, I'm planning to travel to England soon—"

His human's face lit up. "Are you saying I can finally go home?" he asked with a little too much excitement, and the way he said the word *home* created an odd prickle in the count's chest.

This wasn't what the count meant, but he still didn't know

how to get the proper words out. He was severely out of practice when it came to being vulnerable, to asking for things instead of taking them.

His human continued, smiling unawares, "Mina will be so happy to see me. And there must be so much work piling up at Exeter for me. Not to boast, but Mr. Hawkins says I'm indispensable these days."

The rest of his human's words faded into a meaningless string of vowels and consonants as he babbled on about his delightful life back in England. Only one stood out.

"Mina?" the count echoed, stunned.

"Why, yes. We are supposed to be married when I return. She must be heartsick by now." His human let out an anxious laugh.

A strange coldness seized the count. This conversation was going disastrously wrong. "You still intend to marry her?" he asked.

His human nodded. "I am a man of honor. I cannot break Mina's heart. She loves me. You should meet her sometime. Maybe after you're settled?"

The count staggered a step back. "But what about...us?" he fumbled, still unable to name it, this fragile, aching craving between them that had taken over his soul, proving in a single sweep that he still had one, despite what the humans at the bottom of the mountain believed.

His human looked down, avoiding his gaze.

"What *about* us?" he asked quietly, his tone reflecting for the first time the desolate desperation that had been building in the air between them. "You know we can't go on like this. I have a life in England. A career. I can't be..." He licked his lips, stalling. "I'm not *you*, Dacian. There are rules for people like me. I can't disregard the whole of society. But you"—he stepped closer and put his hand softly on the count's cheek—"this month with you—I will never forget it. It was a wonderful dream," he added, solemn now. "But eventually, every dream must end. It is time for me to wake."

The count's lips twisted. The chill that had been spreading through his limbs suddenly turned to frost, plunging the temperature around them. He was being left behind after everything he'd done. Again. Used like a tool, not treated as a person. Not treasured. Not loved. Nobody cared about *his* heart being broken. It was meant to be used up and then forgotten for the rest of eternity.

Even though it was just past midday outside, the library darkened as though cloaked in dense shadow. Without realizing he was doing so, the count rose into the air.

"You're wrong, Jonathan. This is no dream. I am your nightmare!" His growl resonated off the library walls like a cathedral bell. As though struck, the human dropped to his knees, eyes wide with terror.

With shadows swirling around him, the count roared, "How dare you, human? Do you know what I am? I am the plague of Transylvania, the dark voivode who commanded legions. I sent the bravest to their knees to beg for my mercy. And you! *You* dare deny me?"

"Dacian, please!" Jonathan stuttered, his face white with horror.

In response, the count's eyes only blazed brighter, like hell's inferno. Towering above the human, he said with all the cruelty he'd cultivated for centuries, "Make no mistake: she does not love you. You have no one. No fiancée. No friends who care about you. I will prove it to you."

The human shook. "What do you mean?"

The count flashed his teeth victoriously. "You'll see. And don't you dare think about leaving here," he warned, snarling like a pack of ravenous wolves. "You will stay in my castle as long as I will it."

With that, the shadows slithered back into his body, and he retreated from the library, sealing the door shut behind him.

"Let me out of here!" the human screamed, throwing himself at the door. "Let me out!"

But the count continued down the dark hallway, never looking back. He'd order the sisters to guard his prisoner; he was too busy for that now.

The count was going to England, just as he'd planned, and by the time he returned, the human would surely change his mind.

TWENTY-SEVEN

Roused back to wakefulness by Dacian's confession, I wait. But despite my dire need to know more of what happened between him and Jonathan, Dacian won't utter another word. Soon, slumber overtakes me, but the dream that arrives makes me wish I'd never closed my eyes.

In it, I'm weak and fully surrounded. I never thought it would come to this. I'd always thought it would be legions of enemy soldiers who would destroy me, not one human—one *man*—whom I myself had turned against me.

Waves of grief and regret wash over me.

It takes me a moment to realize I'm dreaming as Dacian. I'm seeing the world through his eyes—or rather, I'm watching his memories, as vivid and brutal as though they're happening to me. His despair is inescapable.

The vampire hunter and his men are closing in, but I no longer have the strength to fight them. I am done. I watch as a crude stake is driven through my heart. I watch as my head is cut off with a sharp blade and thrown to the ground. I watch as they set my body ablaze, and the flames burn me to ash.

And he—my human—turns away as I burn, into the loving arms of his wife. Even as I am about to be sent into oblivion, I do not merit the kindness of his gaze, not after what I've done to him.

I close my eyes for a moment, naively thinking that Death is coming for me. But what awaits me is much crueler than the silent servant of the netherworld.

Dripping with blood, my head is stuffed into a small wooden box. The world plunges into darkness as the lid closes over me, and I'm carried far away. But I'm not able to die. Not like this. No matter how badly I yearn to return to nothingness, it's not easy to kill one such as me.

Even at this distance, I can feel the burnt remnants of my flesh rotting away as my castle is ransacked and pillaged by the Dutchman's surrogates. They kill my progeny; they take my books. I feel my domain crumble into ruins. And still, I remain alive inside the small wooden box.

I scream to be let out.

I scream and scream and scream, but no one hears me.

I keep screaming for a long, long time.

MY HEART JERKS like a trapped animal, unable to break free, finally waking me from the nightmare. For several minutes, I lie flat and motionless in Dacian's bed as I try to shake off its vise-like grip.

Were those really Dacian's memories? Or did my crazy mind conjure them up as revenge for all the macabre stuff I've put it through? The pale-gray light of dawn streams through the now-closed window, but I shiver regardless. When I finally dare check the space next to me, it's empty. Dacian is gone.

Panicked, I sit up and frantically look around the bedroom. I know it's irrational, but the hold of the nightmare is still strong. The mad beating of my heart calms only once I find him unharmed, his head blessedly still attached to his shoulders, eyes closed, and seemingly deep asleep, but it takes my mind a few moments to process what I'm seeing.

Some vampire myths claim they sleep in coffins, but I never took those seriously, chalking the belief up to religious superstition. But seeing Dacian now makes me reconsider. He's lying in a long wooden box, a human-size crate, really, filled with—I squint —dirt? Quietly, so as to not disturb his sleep, I climb out of bed and find my underwear and clothes in a heap on the floor. I shimmy into them and tiptoe up to the crate.

Dacian is dressed only in a pair of black pajama pants. I check his breathing: slow and even. He is sound asleep. What an unexpected sight. Dear heavens, he is so perfect that it's a sin not to admire him. Uninhibited, I let my gaze roam over his bare, sculpted chest, the taut muscles of his stomach, his navel, and the tips of his hip bones. I got to touch all of it last night, but it was too dark to see. Now, however... My blood rushes through my body as I try to align my tactile memories with what I'm witnessing. My skin tingles with how badly I want to touch him in daylight. I want to kiss him again. Suddenly I'm annoyed that I didn't get to wake up next to him, that some crate full of dirt stole him from me. I want to climb into it and curl up against him—

"Hasn't anyone told you that peeping is considered improper in polite society?"

My breath catches. I tear my gaze away from Dacian's navel and I find him awake, looking at me with hooded eyes. There's an indisputable tinge of amusement in them.

I bite my lower lip. "Has anyone told *you* that you're wildly beautiful and that polite society has no idea what it's talking about?" I must've lost all shame to say it so openly. But those bottomless eyes always manage to provoke the truth from me, however embarrassing.

Dacian's mouth curves up. "As I recall, most people think I'm an old codger with pointy ears, hair on my hands, and breath that reeks of death thanks to that book," he purrs.

"The book lied," I say, not breaking eye contact.

He chuckles. "About many things."

I watch his Adam's apple move up and down. But as my gaze falls to Dacian's neck, the memory of the nightmare flashes in my mind in all its monstrous cruelty. My body goes rigid.

The smile slips off Dacian's face. "What did you see?"

I swallow hard, trying to erase the gnarly sensation of my head being chopped off and stuffed into a box. "N-nothing," I stutter. "It was just a nightmare that felt a little too real."

Dacian studies me intently, his mood once again unreadable. "They often do," he says eventually. He sits up, his dark, silky locks obscuring his eyes.

"What is that thing?" I ask, gesturing at his crate. I'm genuinely curious, but my brain could also use a distraction.

"A piece of my domain. My homeland." He climbs out, carefully swiping loose dirt off his pants and back into the crate. When my eyebrows furrow in confusion, Dacian adds, "I will tell you everything as promised, Jonathan. I come from an era when bargains were thoroughly respected by both parties. If they wished to keep their heads on their shoulders, that is." His voice is so serious that it almost carries a note of warning. I gape, dumbstruck. "But first," he says, straightening up, his mood lighter again, "are you hungry?"

I wait for Dacian to change into his clothes—a cardigan and slacks similar to the ones from yesterday—before following him downstairs. His kitchen is nice; it has modern appliances but otherwise retains the charm from a hundred years ago. There are wooden beams supporting the ceiling, a big farmhouse sink, and a row of copper pans hanging above the stove. It's spacious and sparsely furnished, just like the rest of the house, but all the essentials seem to be here. There's even a drip coffeemaker quietly percolating on the counter. I wonder who furnished this place, as it looks to be set up for a human, not a vampire.

"How do you like your eggs?" Dacian asks, taking the carton out of the fridge, which also appears to be well stocked for some inexplicable reason. Maybe he's trying to avoid suspicion in case of unexpected visitors?

"Umm, sunny side up?" I say from my spot at the big wooden table in the center of the room, half-wondering if he even knows what that means. But to my surprise, he simply cracks two eggs into a hot pan and adds a piece of bread to toast beside them.

"What is it?" he asks, glancing over his shoulder at my awestruck face as the eggs sizzle, filling the kitchen with a mouth-watering aroma.

"I can't believe you cook," I admit sheepishly. "I mean, this isn't what you normally eat, is it?"

"Of course not," he says coyly. "But I was once human too. And believe it or not, there have been no drastic developments over the past few centuries when it comes to cooking eggs." With that, he scoops the eggs and toast from the pan and places them on a porcelain plate.

I chuckle. "I guess not. Are you going to eat anything?" I venture tentatively as he puts the plate and a mug of steaming coffee on the table in front of me and takes a seat at the opposite end.

"I'm...not hungry right now." Something flutters in my stomach at the way his eyelashes dip, and his eyes glaze over at the word *hungry*. I don't know if I believe him.

I take a few bites of my eggs. I'm not sure if I'm just ridiculously famished after everything we did last night, or if it's the fact that he has cooked breakfast for me, but they taste really delicious. "These are quite possibly the best eggs I have ever had," I say earnestly.

His lips curl into a smile. "I'm glad you're enjoying them."

"So...you used to be human?" I ask after taking a few more bites.

"A long time ago," Dacian replies, his tone shifting from playful to serious. "Have you ever heard of the Order of the Dragon?"

I rummage through my memory. I think it was mentioned in one of the history books I looked at in the library when I was investigating Dacian's identity. But I could barely string together a coherent thought at the time, let alone memorize a historical fact. "Does it have something to do with where you come from?" I ask.

"It does. I was accepted into the Order after I completed the ritual."

He doesn't need to clarify which ritual. A shiver skims the back of my neck.

"The Order of the Dragon was a secret society established in the fifteenth century to defend the Kingdom of Hungary, which controlled Transylvania at the time," he continues. "It later expanded its reach to the domain of the Holy Roman Empire as well. Of course, not everyone joined it for the noble purpose of protecting their kin; after all, the same people had no qualms about raping and pillaging their way through the later Crusades."

"Wait...you were in the Crusades?" I ask, astounded, forgetting for the moment to be horrified.

Dacian shakes his head. "No. That is one more inaccuracy perpetuated by that book. I'm not that old. I suppose I was lucky to avoid that particular disgrace. However, my predecessors did not." Dacian's gaze darkens, and a long moment passes before he continues. "I was a part of the Order, but not as a knight or a nobleman. Instead, I was their weapon."

My fork freezes halfway to my mouth. "Weapon?" Slowly, I put it back down without taking a bite.

"I told you the ritual is a kind of black magic capable of creating a superior being—a one-man army, if you will, one that can defeat hordes of enemies at once. The lands I hail from were the target of frequent and devastating incursions by the Ottoman

Empire. It was the Order's task to defend against them. Naturally, no small group of ordinary humans could fight thousands of the most brutal warriors the European continent had ever seen, so the Order resorted to using magic. For centuries they had possessed secret knowledge of how to bestow great powers on an individual in return for the sacrifice of blood. When a suitable candidate was selected, and the sacrifices were made, the ritual bound the chosen one to the land, establishing it as their domain. This made them nearly invincible within its borders so long as they continued to protect it. You asked about the large crate in my bedroom. It contains earth from my land, the domain I'm bound to, and I must rest in it every day. It isn't the same as being back in Transylvania, but it extends my powers."

"Like an embassy?" I ask.

Dacian tips his head thoughtfully. "In a way, I suppose—a piece of home in a foreign realm. The Order successfully created several such weapons throughout the centuries. When my predecessor ceased to perform that role, I was chosen to replace him."

"What happened to him?" I ask through the low hum of anxiety churning inside me.

A shadow passes over Dacian's face. "He went mad," he says bluntly. "He started impaling dozens of people, then hundreds, then thousands." Though he doesn't mention the man's name, I'm able to guess the identity of his predecessor immediately. "And while some 'extravagance' in terms of entertainment preferences was tolerated by the Order, eventually they deemed him too volatile and removed him. This power...it has an effect on you, Jonathan. It makes it hard to hold onto yourself, particularly in the early years after the transformation. When you're meant to kill hundreds in a single attack without a second thought or any remorse, it makes it difficult to draw a line that should not be crossed. That's why not everyone is suited for this ritual."

As Dacian says this, the space around us suddenly ripples. The kitchen with its table and pots and pans fades, and dark images flood my mind, too striking in their intensity to be merely my imagination. A lone man stands on a vast battlefield under ashen skies. Ominous black shadows swirl around him. Underneath his feet is a mountain of dead bodies, and he's gazing down at it. He has won. He has killed them all. But at what price? Blood flows in rivers of crimson from his fingers. His face is smeared with dark red. He is stained with death. It makes the hair on the back of my skull rise. Unstoppable. Unconquerable. He is the ruler of the darkness, his domain—the empire of bones. And in the black pits of his eyes lies such madness, such compulsion to ruin and destroy, that it will not be satisfied even if his homeland is soaked in blood.

The image flickers out, leaving me momentarily disoriented. Perhaps it's the proximity of Dacian or him lowering his guard that makes these visions so much more vivid than before. It takes me a moment to piece my thoughts back together.

"This ritual—you said it was to protect the land and its people, but where did the sacrifices that made you come from?"

The blackness in Dacian's eyes doesn't stir. "The common citizens taken by the Order."

I should've guessed as much; still, I find myself at a loss for words. How could someone's life hold such little value? Have regular people always been pawns in the careless hands of the corrupt and powerful?

Dacian says, "Things were different back then, Jonathan. The idea of sacrificing your own to repel a greater enemy was quite acceptable at the time—especially to the aristocracy, who never had to pay such a price. I myself was born a commoner, the bastard son of a nobody. But I had what the Order wanted—the blood of the ancient warrior race—and time and time again, I'd proven myself on the battlefield. That made me more than suitable. I was also the age that was considered a man's prime at the time. And lastly, I was willing." He lets out a sardonic laugh. "I believed I was being patriotic. The Order wanted to keep me on a tight leash, and thus, I was given a title, a castle with lands, and a pile of gold for my 'service.' But eventually, even the gold lost its sheen. After a few decades, most things lose their glow…" He trails off, distant again.

"What happened next?" I prompt.

Dacian exhales slowly. "Time happened next, Jonathan. The nineteenth century brought great changes to the continent. People were looking outward to new frontiers. Science replaced magic. The lands I defended lost their prominence. Even the Order faded away. And yet I remained.

"By the second half of the century, the magic that held me in its control had weakened enough that I thought I was finally free to leave my homeland. Unfortunately, I underestimated just how much of my power was still tied to my domain. In all my centuries, I'd never been away from it. By the time I realized just how vulnerable I was, it was too late. I'd made the most unfortunate of enemies."

There is a deep crinkle between the perfect arches of Dacian's brows, and I feel a prickle of something I know he's trying to suppress. No images come, yet it stabs at my heart all the same.

"What did you do?" I ask.

"You already know. You saw it last night, didn't you?" he says, his lightless eyes fixed on mine.

My insides go numb. I do know. I watched Dacian's body turn to ash and his head be cut off and shoved into a box. I feel a sudden swoop of nausea. Maybe I shouldn't have eaten before this talk. "Why would they do that to you?" I ask, dismayed. Everything I saw was quite close to the events described in the novel—everything except for the part about the box and the count's death.

"Keep me alive?" Dacian says tiredly. "I don't know. I fully expected them to end me. Perhaps the Dutchman, who was the mastermind behind the attack, wasn't convinced he could kill me, so keeping me incapacitated was his best course of action. Or perhaps behind his mask of righteousness lay the devious corruption to which the human species is so susceptible. Maybe he wanted to keep me as a source of power to be used one day.

"I will never know what his designs were. I never saw him again. He died within a decade, and his descendant took possession of the box. However, he did not release me or bargain with me. My head remained hidden in a small storage room beneath their family estate. But I knew as I waited that one day a corrupt descendant would seek power, and I'd be called upon again...and I was right."

"How so?" I ask, fully invested.

"Turns out, pilfering things from my castle was a profitable business. Who knows how many homes that family and their associates ransacked after they accused their owners of being monsters and dispensed punishment in the name of their god? I swear some tactics never change. Using the funds, the Dutchman's enterprising granddaughter built a financial empire, but five years ago, his great-grandson decided the bottomless well of money no longer satisfied him. He'd heard stories of an old wooden box buried deep in the basement of the estate, never to be touched under any circumstances, but this man wasn't raised with much regard for rules. So one night, he came to me to strike a deal."

There's a glint in Dacian's eyes, but the light isn't a warm reflection of the sun. It's icy and sharp, like the blade of a knife.

"What happened to him?" I ask.

"For a while, he was useful to me," Dacian says meaningfully, and I realize that everything around us—the house, the furniture, even the Jag outside—must've been purchased by that person. He must have helped Dacian get his body back too. Yet I can't help but notice that the guy isn't around, despite the kitchen being stocked to accommodate a human occupant as well as a vampire.

There's a barely-concealed hint of malice in Dacian's voice when he adds, "He lacked the fine talent that it takes to bargain with me. Let him be a warning to any family that believes it can take everything from me only to return later, demanding I serve up immortality on a silver platter."

On top of the table, Dacian's hands curl as though involuntarily, his nails leaving scratch marks on the polished wood. Again, I'm not privy to his memories, but there's a palpable fury emanating from him, a distant echo of the overwhelming desire to destroy that I glimpsed before. I fight the urge to shrink away from it.

As I wait for Dacian's emotions to settle, something he mentioned earlier comes back to me. He escaped from the box five years ago, but the events of the novel supposedly took place in the late 1800s. In my nightmare, there was no sense of time passing in the small wooden box. Everything felt like an eternal void with no beginning and no end, only my own screams echoing infinitely back at me. I know it went on for *a while*, but this would mean—

My voice comes out as barely a whisper. "How long did they keep you in that box, Dacian?" I don't dare to look up at him, as I don't know what horror I might find reflected in those eyes.

"Ninety years, seven months, and sixteen days," he replies quietly.

My breath catches. "That's..." The Dutchman may have been the one who orchestrated the ambush and took the box, but then there was the person who watched it all happen, who could've stopped it at any time but didn't.

Of course, Dacian can't bear to say his name. Of all the things that novel got right, I hoped and hoped this wouldn't be one of them. But I remember whose hands held my neck—Dacian's neck —as they plunged the sharp knife into my throat. The same hands that had held me—him—with such tenderness just weeks prior. They could've had the world, he and the other Jonathan, and yet...

"He never came back for you," I whisper, my throat constricted. The silence that pervades the room the moment I utter these words is louder than the screams of a thousand dying men. After a single glance at Dacian's face, I know I've dug too deep. "I'm sorry."

"No. He did not come back for me," Dacian confirms. His

voice is hollow, and his emptiness hits me like a wind howling over a wasteland.

"For the longest time, I thought I was in hell," he says. "I thought retribution had finally come for all the things I'd done. But as the years went on, I realized that even hell must not want me. I had simply been forgotten by the world that had made me, left to fade away in the slow drip of eternity. Stuck again. First in my castle, then in the box. Always stuck."

"They had no right to do that to you," I say, as oncoming tears sting the corners of my eyes. "No right to punish you like that."

Surprise registers on Dacian's face. "You don't know everything, Jonathan. Just because I didn't eat children doesn't mean I was a good person. I regret what I did to the Harkers and Ms. Westenra. And I killed thousands upon thousands of others. Some would argue that ninety years of imprisonment was hardly enough to atone for my crimes."

"And what about the Order? What punishment did they get?" I snap.

Dacian says nothing. I shake my head, extremely upset. He spent almost a century alone, abandoned in the dark. That's an entire lifetime! How could anyone allow that?

"I'm not him!" I blurt suddenly. Because I want Dacian to know. I *need* him to know.

Dacian's eyes widen. "I know you're not," he says.

"We may have the same name, but I swear I'll never—"

There's a flutter, a rustle of clothes maybe, and like a cloud of liquid smoke, Dacian appears before me, moving too fast for my eyes to properly register. I only recognize that he's near me when his thumb brushes my cheekbone.

"Don't worry, Jonathan," he says, holding my face. "But you are...how do they say it these days? You're *cute* when you're worried."

I huff, peeved. "Don't tease me like that."

"I'm not," he says, and when I catch his eyes again, there is a kind of intensity to them that leaves me breathless and strips me down to my bones.

Letting his thumb stay connected to my skin, I slowly tilt my head to place a kiss on his wrist. There's a flicker of a pulse there, an echo of Dacian's heart. Not human, but still alive, still feeling and real. I kiss his wrist again. "I want you," I whisper against his skin. "All of you. The way you are now and how you used to be. Good and terrible. You know that, right?" My lips trail across the heel of his thumb. I won't stop until I kiss every one of his fingers and then the rest of his body.

Dacian doesn't answer. I gasp as his strong arms lift me off the chair with that supernatural swiftness of his and push me down onto the table, his mouth already on mine and his eyes glowing scarlet, impossible to look away from.

TWENTY-EIGHT

By the time I return to campus, I feel like I'm walking on clouds, my body buzzing pleasantly. There's a stupid grin on my face, and I don't care who sees it. I climb to the third floor of West Hall, taking the stairs two at a time, humming under my breath, but I halt abruptly in the hallway when I see someone sitting cross-legged outside my door. There's a heavy book in her lap, and she does not look pleased.

"Fiona? What are you doing here?" I ask, puzzled.

"Are you serious?" Her eyebrows furrow as she frowns. I blink at her. Fiona groans. "We were supposed to meet for a study session, remember? I waited for you at the library, but you never showed, so I came here."

Oh shit. I feel like a bucket of cold water has been poured over my head. "I'm so sorry. I can't believe I forgot," I say guiltily.

Fiona sighs, closes her book, and stands up. "It's fine, as long as you're okay, I guess. You've been acting strange, Jonathan. You didn't show up for dinner on Friday, and I couldn't find you all day yesterday." She mercifully doesn't mention my complete melt-down during Gothic lit, but the implication is there.

"I'm sorry," I mumble again, feeling thoroughly awful for ditching Fiona when she's the only person who ever bothers to check on me. I don't think I'm in the right frame of mind to study, but I do want to make it up to her. "How about we postpone the study session and go for pancakes? My treat."

Fiona's eyebrow quirks up. "Wow. You feel *that* guilty?"

I shrug. "I stood you up. And also, I'm starving." As I say it, I realize how true that is. My stomach feels like an empty cavern. All the energy from the breakfast Dacian cooked for me has long been depleted, thanks to Dacian himself.

"All right," Fiona says, stuffing her heavy textbook into her backpack. "I'll allow you to work your way back into my good graces."

"SO...ARE you going to tell me what's been going on with you lately?" Fiona asks once the waitress leaves with our pancake orders. We're in a corner booth, away from prying ears, but I still feel like I'm sitting on needles. I have no idea what I can say to her that won't implicate Dacian or put Fiona in danger from deranged soon-to-be vampires.

"Um...I can't tell you because it doesn't only involve me," I say, stalling.

Unexpectedly, an amused little smirk appears on Fiona's face. "Jonathan Evergreen, are you telling me you're finally hooking up with someone?"

My jaw nearly drops. "Keep it down!"

"Oh my god, you totally are, aren't you!" Fiona is grinning from ear to ear now, and I feel like my cheeks are going to catch on fire. She totally misunderstood what I was trying to say, but also somehow hit the nail on the head.

"H-how did you know?" I sputter.

"You have *the look*," she says, all smug.

"What look?"

Fiona rolls her eyes before leaning in and whispering conspiratorially, "The sexed-up look, Jonathan."

"No, I don't!" I say it so vehemently that someone three tables down gives me a side-eye. But my protest is futile. It only makes Fiona more convinced.

"Dude, you look exactly like my roommate did this morning when she stumbled in at six a.m. after being gone all night. The rumpled clothes, the messy hair." She gestures vaguely at my body. "No smudged mascara, but ordering a double stack of pancakes with extra maple syrup is probably the male equivalent."

There's no denying that I'm still wearing my clothes from yesterday. And now that Fiona has pointed it out, my mind is flooded with images of Dacian's swift hands taking them off and throwing them to the floor, in his bedroom, and then again in the kitchen just a few hours ago. My skin still burns pleasantly where he touched me. Dear heavens, I must get a grip on myself.

"So spill it. Who is he?" Fiona asks. "Is he not out? Is that why you can't tell me?"

My stomach flips again. How is this girl so perceptive? She should switch majors and become a detective after she graduates. Being a lawyer is fancier, but I think she'd make a killer sleuth. Fiona is right—Dacian isn't out, just not in the way she thinks. I hate to mislead her, but I don't have the right to drag him out of the creature-of-the-night closet. Not to mention that he's my professor.

"He isn't out," I say reluctantly.

She nods somberly. "Don't worry, I won't pry. Good for you, though." She flashes a smile, all encouragement. "And if you or he ever feels like telling me, you know I'm safe. My lips will remain sealed." She makes a zipping gesture across her mouth.

"I know." I smile back. If only Fiona had any idea what she's encouraging. Mercifully, our pancakes arrive just then, providing me with an opportunity to change the subject. "Enough about me. How was your weekend? Anything exciting?"

She chuckles sardonically and spears a piece of chocolate chip pancake with her fork. "The only excitement I'm getting these days is from my psych book. You'd be amazed at all the crazy shit this class is putting in my brain," she says.

Somehow, I've already devoured half of my strawberry pancakes without even noticing.

I might need another double stack.

"Speaking of brains," I say carefully as an idea arises, "can I borrow your deductive powers?"

Fiona tips her head, intrigued. "Fire away."

I push a piece of syrupy strawberry across my plate to buy myself a moment to formulate a coherent thought. The night I spent with Dacian completely took over my mind, but now that I'm away from him, some of the unbelievable things he revealed are finally starting to sink in. I promised him I'd help look for his journal, and now that I know how serious the situation is, I need to make good on that. "So, remember how I told you about a missing book from the Rare Books Collection?"

"The one that seemed like an inside job? I remember," she says.

I lower my voice and glance around to make sure no one is eavesdropping on us. "I think it's connected to the murder of that woman from the cafeteria."

Fiona's expression darkens. "What makes you think so?"

I feel guilty that I'm about to lie again, but there's no way I can disclose the actual truth, so this is the best I can do. "Apparently there's a weird ritual in that book, one that involves draining a person of their blood."

"You mean like a sacrifice?" she says uneasily.

"Yeah. Remember what they said about Ms. Hernandez's body? I think someone might have been trying to do the ritual."

"Jonathan, if you really think that, you need to go to the police," Fiona says seriously.

Alarmed, I almost drop my fork. "Why?"

"Are you kidding? This is like those satanic cults they talk about on the news. A person is dead. It's not some hobby investigation for a college kid."

I panic. "I can't go to the police."

"Why not?" Fiona demands.

"Because—" I nearly trip over my words, trying to figure out how to dig myself out of this hole. "For one, I don't think anyone would believe me. And two, if they did believe me, they might think I'm involved. I often work in the library alone. What if they think that's suspicious?"

Fiona narrows her eyes doubtfully. "I don't think they'll suspect you of being in a satanic cult. It's more likely they'll write you off for lack of evidence. On the other hand, the police aren't exactly known for being unbiased. I'm sure they're looking for someone to blame, so maybe you're right—it may be best to keep your head down and forget about it."

"What if I can't forget about it?" I ask.

Fiona gives me a warning look. "You shouldn't be sticking your nose into something so dark, Jonathan."

"Well, someone has to do something. How hard do you think they're looking for the murderer? They don't care about some immigrant woman. They're probably happy to sweep it under the rug. But what if she isn't the only victim? Wouldn't you want to know if someone was out there planning to sacrifice more people in Camden?"

"That's really far-fetched," Fiona says skeptically. "We don't know if it was a ritualistic sacrifice to begin with."

"Let's pretend it was, for the sake of argument," I propose. "If someone did something so horrid, would they stand out somehow?"

Fiona takes a moment to ponder. "Not necessarily," she concludes hesitantly. "It would be much easier to catch them if they did. But those who commit heinous crimes are often great at masquerading as regular people. They also tend to keep someone in their circle who's willing to publicly defend them, or at least turn a blind eye to their actions—an enabler of sorts. Look at serial killers, for example. The Killer Clown was an upstanding citizen who volunteered to entertain hospitalized kids and had ties to local politicians. Even when his neighbors repeatedly heard screaming coming from his house, they didn't call the cops. The Interstate Killer had a professor friend who paid his bail and rented out an apartment for him after his first arrest. Some are even willing to defend those murderers after they find out the full extent of their crimes. The Night Stalker gets piles of fan mail from his followers, even marriage proposals. That's after he tortured and brutally murdered thirteen people in Los Angeles."

"That's sick." I grimace. "Who'd wanna marry a convicted mass killer?"

"Humans are twisted," Fiona replies with a troubled expression.

"Well, if murderers don't stand out from a crowd and there's no direct evidence pointing to them, what would you do to find them?" I ask as nonchalantly as I can.

Fiona stabs her fork into a pancake, musing. "Hypothetically? You would examine the circumstances under which the crime was committed, like if they used an unusual weapon or had access to a specific place where the murder happened. That could tell you something about the murderer. You can also investigate the motive and see if that produces a lead. But I'm sure the police have already gone over everything. The forensic scientists would've found something by now if they were going to."

They would, I think, *if they knew to look for people with fangs and a thirst for blood.* Out loud, I thank Fiona for her thoughts.

"Please promise me you won't go looking for satanic cults, Jonathan," she pleads, exasperated. "If you've got time on your hands, spend it hooking up with your secret lover. You look happy. Happy is a good look on you. Good sex does that. Go have more sex."

I stuff my face with the last bits of my pancake and mumble something that could be construed as agreement. Carefully, I file away everything she said to mull over later. I might not be Sherlock Holmes, but I have enough evidence to start putting this puzzle together.

TWENTY-NINE

I envy Dacian's ability to keep a straight face, because he barely reacts to my being in his class on Monday. As always, he looks like an aloof mystical shadow, if shadows wore stylish silk blazers and could quote classics in their sleep.

Maybe—*maybe*—there's a ghost of a smile on his lips when he sees me. But I might just be deluding myself. After he scans the room to see who's here, he breaks into a lecture about *The Picture of Dorian Gray*, and I...I'm just really glad I've read it before. Despite my honest attempts to pay attention to the words coming out of his mouth, all I can think about is, well, Dacian's mouth. It's absolutely maddening. I don't make a peep when he asks the class a question. It's too risky, attracting attention. What if my gaze lingers on him and someone notices? What if I blurt out something inappropriate? I feel dazed, my thoughts spinning round and round...

I don't know how I survive the lecture, and it takes all my willpower to go straight to the exit afterward. But even then, I can hardly banish him from my thoughts. The rest of the week is pure torture. Thinking that it might be easier to stay sane if I keep my distance from him, I avoid the section of Kinnell Hall where his office is. But I quickly discover how unhelpful that strategy is.

Not seeing him makes it infinitely worse. I miss the velvety sound of his voice, the hypnotizing, bottomless depths of his eyes, his hands on me. He's constantly on my mind. To make things worse, I can't recall any of my dreams, or if he visited them.

When Friday night finally comes, I can't take it anymore. We made no plans to meet again when we last parted. But Dacian did give me his phone number. *For emergencies*, he said. Well, I guess this is one.

Feeling like a criminal who might get caught at any moment, I walk to the phone at the end of my dorm's hallway and dial. It seems to ring forever, and my heart thuds impatiently until—

"This is Dacian Bathory. Who am I speaking with?"

"Hi," I breathe.

There's a long pause on the other end of the line. I don't think he was expecting me to call. But I *need* to see him. Besides, after my talk with Fiona, I've realized I still lack some crucial information I need to help him find his journal. Before Dacian can find some excuse to hang up and push me away, I say, "So, about those driving lessons..."

NOT EVEN HALF AN HOUR LATER, Dacian greets me from his doorway, looking like he still can't believe I have seriously suggested this. But serious I am.

"Got your keys?" I ask. I can barely contain a grin at how ruffled this gets him.

"Yes," he says, voice dead as a tomb.

But he follows me to his Jaguar without a squeak of protestation. Either he legitimately wants to get better at driving, or he really wanted to see me too. Whichever it is, I can't help feeling excited at the prospect of taking a night ride with him.

Under my careful supervision, Dacian drives on the highway for a while, heading north, away from Camden and possible witnesses. The night breeze flows through the open windows, and the radio is playing "Just Like Heaven" by The Cure. He's still intense and quiet, but I like this, being with him even if we don't say anything. For the first time since Sunday, I feel calm and at peace, like a lost satellite that has finally found its orbit.

Eventually I suggest we get off the highway and take the deserted country roads winding through the mountains, not aiming for any particular destination. Maybe it's the darkness or the absence of traffic, but slowly Dacian relaxes. At one point I even catch him zoning out.

"You know I have no idea where we are," he points out after some time. It's been a while since we passed a settlement or even a farm house.

"Oh. Do you have a map?" I should've checked before we went off into the wilderness. But Dacian only gives me a confused look. It has probably never occurred to a creature like him that getting lost in the mountains might be dangerous. "Let me check," I offer as he pulls over. Luckily, I find a current road atlas stuffed in my seat's back pocket. Dacian might be far removed from such trivialities as land navigation, but whoever bought his Jag was more practically inclined.

After studying the maps for a few minutes, I'm pretty confident I can get us out of here, but when Dacian asks if I'm ready to go, I hesitate. The mountains are cold but peaceful. Through the open window I can hear the night sounds of the woods—the rustling of leaves, the distant hooting of an owl. This place is perfect for a private discussion.

"Actually, I have more questions," I say.

Dacian heaves a sigh. "I should have expected as much." A little resigned, he leans back in his seat, seemingly settling in for the long haul. "Go on. Ask."

I nod. "About vampire food—"

Immediately, Dacian tenses. "Why would you need to know that?" he asks, guarded. Honestly, I suspected he wouldn't be too enthused to talk about it. He sounded evasive when I asked him if he was hungry when he was making breakfast. But still, I didn't expect this reaction.

"It's the main difference between humans and vampires, and it'll be easier to help you find your journal if I understand it," I say, treading extra carefully. "Like, how often do you eat and how much?"

It seems that question is the exact wrong thing to ask, because Dacian's expression frosts over. "I fail to understand the relevance of this. Next question." He folds his arms and pointedly doesn't look at me.

Why is he giving me the cold shoulder? It's not like I don't know what he eats; any illusions about that evaporated into thin air when I saw him bite Eric. I have to suppress the shiver that comes with the memory. Blood was spouting out of Eric's neck like a crimson fountain. There's no erasing that from my mind.

"Dacian, it *is* relevant," I insist gently. "You mentioned that those who stole your journal haven't finished the ritual yet, but do they still have to eat in the meantime, or can they abstain? Blood isn't something you can grab from a grocery store. Maybe we can find them if we figure out where their supply comes from."

There is a long silence, long enough for me to worry that I haven't convinced Dacian to talk. But just before I try again—

"That is a fair point," he admits with great reluctance. It takes several more moments for him to elaborate. "Their full powers won't manifest until they complete the ritual, but the moment they partook of the blood of the first sacrifice, they became vampires. They must eat blood to survive. Hunger is the great equalizer, Jonathan. It does not matter whether you're human, vampire, or wolf—when you're hungry, it's all you can think about." His gaze turns distant when he says that, making me wonder just how much time he spent starving while locked up in that box for ninety years. *"I thought I was in hell"* echoes in my mind.

"But you don't need a lot to survive," Dacian continues. "Just like with humans, your need depends on how much effort you exert. If you're not fighting, then a little is enough to get by. However, there are also circumstances that can make you crave it even when you aren't physically hungry." Slowly, he reaches into the inside pocket of his jacket and pulls out a small glass vial filled with red liquid.

I gape at him in shock. "Do you just keep that on you all the time?"

"Not always," he replies. "However, spending this much time around a certain human has proved more demanding on my body than I anticipated. I had to come up with a remedy."

For a few seconds, all I can do is stare. By "a certain human," does he mean *me*? Suddenly, I remember that dream I had about Dacian walking away from my window, covering his mouth as though afraid I'd see something he didn't want me to see, and the subsequent class cancellation. Is that why he was gone? Do I give him the munchies?

Mesmerized, I follow the elegant motion of his hand as he uncorks the vial and brings it to his lips. I watch with an indescribable feeling as the liquid travels into his mouth, staining it red. From under his top lip, I can just make out the sharp tips of his fangs as his tongue peeks out to lick up the last remaining drops.

"Ah..." He exhales contentedly and closes his eyes. There's a red shimmer coming from underneath his eyelashes.

I have to yank my mind out of whatever debauched fantasy it almost tumbles into.

"What does it taste like?" I ask. I don't mean for my voice to come out so breathless, but my senses are still rattled.

"Like *life*," he says simply.

"Does it...have to be fresh?" I ask awkwardly.

His eyes remain closed when he answers. "Yes. Blood doesn't keep very long, even with the modern convenience of refrigeration."

As the implication sinks in, I get nervous. "Where did that vial come from?" I ask, unsure if I actually want to know the answer.

"Local hospital," Dacian replies, unconcerned. "I can't draw attention to myself by hunting around here, so I had to find a substitute."

Oh. Well, it's a relief to know he didn't drain some stranger prior to my arrival. I mull this information over. This may be the answer I've been looking for. "Could the people who stole your journal be using that as their source as well?"

But Dacian shakes his head. "I watched the place for a few days back in September, but I don't think that's how they are getting their supply."

"Hmm," I murmur, disappointed. I guess I should've known better than to expect an easy solution. "What about..." I pause before continuing. "Does the blood have to be *human*?"

Dacian's eyelashes finally lift, and he glances at me from the side without turning his head. Embers still glow warmly in his irises. "Yes," he replies.

"But you drank Eric's," I say.

"A vampire's blood will suffice if circumstances demand it. They used to be human, after all. But it's not as nourishing. And Stockton's tasted like dirt and fear and a desperate obsequious need for peer approval," he says, with a grimace like he just ate something rancid.

His accurate assessment of Eric's character startles me. "Did you get all that from just a few sips of his blood?" I ask.

Dacian sighs, and for a moment, his gaze turns pensive. "You'd be surprised how much you can tell about the nature of people from the taste of their blood. It used to be that men went to battle for life and death, raised their banners in the wind and met the enemy head-on, steel clashing against steel, knuckles bloodied and bruised. You couldn't only taste it in their veins— you could smell it from miles away, the roaring strength of their spirits. Even the pampered nobility all trained with weaponry and would fight if they were called on to do so. But these days"—he purses his lips with disappointment—"such bravery is but a dusty memory. And why would men remember it when any lowlife with a handful of bullets can slay dozens in one breath? No need to see or remember their faces. The blood of men runs thin this century. Just like their spirits."

I've been itching to know this for a while, so quietly, I ask, "Can you smell mine too?" I almost immediately regret it, though. After all, I, too, have the blood of modern men Dacian holds in such low regard.

His piercing eyes turn to me. "Of course I can, Jonathan. You are human." He watches me for a long moment, letting those words hang between us.

I swallow and look away.

"Does that frighten you?" he asks.

"No," I hasten to correct him. "Just...I guess it would be nice if you had the option not to take human life."

Dacian's eyebrows crease. "I don't have to kill to eat if that's what you're worried about. Mr. Stockton and I were fighting, and that's why I had to do what I did. But I can stop short of draining a life completely. And as far as the blood being human, I don't know what you've been reading, but taking an animal's life is not the morally superior choice you might think it is. I've encountered many humans in my lengthy existence, and I can say with certainty that animals are better people than people. For one, they will never stab you in the back. They don't even understand betrayal."

"Sorry," I say, fidgeting uncomfortably. "I didn't mean it like that."

"No offense taken," he replies. "Now, let me ask you something."

I perk up, immediately curious. Compared to his, my life must seem so dull. What can he possibly want to know about me?

"Why haven't you turned in your midterm essay yet?" he asks.

My face all but bursts into flames. Oh god—that's the one I was supposed to write on desire and fear. I was embarrassed about the subject, especially knowing that Dacian was going to read it, so I never figured out what to say. But I have pondered over this situation, and I have a solution that will solve more than the essay problem.

"Actually, I've been thinking. I don't want to get you in trouble with the school," I say hesitantly. "I'd like to drop out of your class. It's a bit late in the semester, so I'll need your written permission."

"Oh," Dacian says, surprised. Something seems off about him, but I can't immediately decipher what it is. "I don't think you need to worry about that, Jonathan."

"I really do, though," I object. "I don't know how it was in the eighteen hundreds, but if anyone catches us together, you'll be dragged through an ethics investigation and probably lose your job, and I might lose my scholarship. It will be a huge scandal. Besides, it doesn't feel right that you have to grade me when I'm... when we're..." I trail off, feeling too self-conscious to name this thing between us. The Jag becomes quiet for a minute, save for the night sounds of the mountains.

"You won't have to do that," Dacian finally says. "With any luck, I won't be the one giving you your grade."

"Why not?" I ask. Little alarms begin to chime in my mind.

"Because once I locate my journal and deal with those who stole it, I plan to disappear from this town."

For a moment I just sit there, too shocked to say a word. Dacian is planning to go away. To leave. "But why?" I ask.

"You know why. I have already explained it to you. It isn't safe for me here."

"But...but what about your job?" I stammer.

Dacian's eyebrows arch. "My pretend job teaching literature?"

"It's not pretend," I argue, surprising myself with how defensive I sound. "You're doing great! Your students adore you. Can't you tell how captivated everyone is when they listen to you?"

He gives me a very unimpressed stare. "By *students*, do you mean those girls who are obviously infatuated with me?"

Wow, I didn't know he was aware of that. I always thought he brushed it off as something not worth his attention. "Fiona isn't," I say. "She definitely doesn't have any romantic designs on you."

"Are you quite certain?" he asks flatly.

"Yes, I am," I say, my voice starting to teeter on the edge of hysteria. Why are we talking about this? This isn't important. This isn't life or death. "You're changing the subject," I point out.

He doesn't respond, and I look away, unable to face him anymore. As seconds tick by in silence, I stare at the Jag's dashboard with its neat black dials and white numbers, their lines going blurry in my vision. My world is crumbling. He's leaving. He's leaving me.

"Jonathan," he says finally. "You know why I cannot stay here like this."

My throat quivers despite my effort not to cry in front of him. I know. Of course, I know. But knowing and accepting are two separate things, aren't they? And accept I cannot. My thoughts spiral. I'm going to be left alone again. Alone with the ghost of a memory, with a love no one can share with me or even understand, with a void instead of a heart. If I have to go through that again, no old books, no letters, no moving to a different state can save—

"*Jonathan*," he says again. There's movement in my peripheral vision, and a hand reaches out to touch my hair, lightly brushing a lock behind my ear. "Can we please not talk about this right now? You asked me before where I most wanted to go. A long time ago, I wanted to see the world; that is true. But things have changed. The *world* has changed. Ever since I escaped imprisonment, all I've been trying to do, every moment of every day and every night, is reassemble the pieces of my scattered existence. My body, my estate, my memories, my journal. I haven't had a thought to spare for what comes next. What is my place in all of this? Where do I fit in in this new century? I simply haven't decided. That is the truth. There is no need to descend into gloom."

His voice is unusually warm. He knows I'm upset, so he's

suddenly offering me honesty. But how can I believe it? After all, he hasn't said he'll stay.

Still, as his thumb slides from my ear down my neck, drawing small circles just above the collar of my sweater, a petting kind of gesture, I make myself face him. His eyes are dark again, the blood-glow dissipated; his proud jawline is illuminated by the silver of moonlight. He's breathtakingly gorgeous. Immortal, powerful...and still running away, *afraid*.

I've told him that I'm not that other Jonathan, that I'd never betray him the way he did—and I meant every word. But can I convince Dacian it's okay to stay? To trust me? To not hide from the world?

Can I be *enough*?

My heart curls in my chest and shudders with a thump. If he can hear it, he doesn't say.

Time keeps ticking, away and away and away. I lean into his touch, needing reassurance, something to hold on to so I won't break into pieces. I kiss him. Even if it's just for this moment and not for keeps, I let his tongue make a home in my mouth. And if I'm a little desperate when my hands pop the buttons of his jeans, he doesn't mention it and doesn't stop me. His fingers weave their way through my hair as I take him into my mouth.

In this world of shadows, Dacian is my anchor. If he disappears, I will become unmoored. Lost in the darkness without the light of his eyes to guide me, I may never find myself again.

Part Three

Till True Death Do Us Part

THIRTY

I spend the wee hours of the morning back in my dorm room, hugging my knees in my bed and trying to stop shaking uncontrollably. I struggle to distract myself from what Dacian told me, but I fail miserably. The fear that he'll leave, that I'll never see him again, zaps my body like tiny electric shocks.

I can't let that happen. I must do something to change his mind. But what? My words don't seem to be enough to convince him. No matter what angle I approach it from, Dacian's journal is key. It's the only reason he's still in Camden. If I want him to stay, I need to get my hands on it before he does.

I hide my face in my pillow. Wetness spreads under my cheek. This is so wrong. He trusted me enough to ask for my help finding it. How can I go behind his back? And what will I even do if I find it? Can I keep it from him just to make him stay longer? He'll be furious if he learns the truth. He'll think I betrayed him. The anger and contempt I saw in his eyes that first week of the semester will pale in comparison with what he'll feel for me then.

My mind spins and spins in circles as sobs wrack my body. Eventually, the pain dulls, and some clarity returns to me.

I don't need to decide what to do with the journal yet. I already promised Dacian I'd help him search for it, so I will.

That's the deal we struck, so technically, I won't be lying to him. But I need a plan. Between Dacian doing everything he can to find it and those who have his journal moving on to the final stage of their ritual, my time is running out. I have to concentrate.

I don't have any leads. But if Eric wasn't alone when he performed the ritual, the most likely suspects are his buddies, Mads Jr. and Grady. But can they really have killed Jeremy and Anita?

I remember Callahan flinging me across the room at the Welcome Week party—could that have been his vampire abilities manifesting? And his eyes—I thought I saw them glowing red. Was that real or a trick of the light? Just because I despise him and Mads doesn't mean it's okay to accuse them of murder. Drugging girls at parties is reprehensible, but it's a whole new level of atrocity to bleed someone dry and dump their mutilated body in the woods. And how are they feeding themselves in the meantime? Dacian said it doesn't take a lot of blood to sustain a vampire, but we're talking about at least two of them. Could their parties and drugs have anything to do with how they're getting their supply? Is Alessandra involved, too?

Dacian doesn't seem to suspect them, or at least he hasn't brought them up to me. But that makes sense, considering he's new here. There are two thousand students at Camden. He doesn't know everyone, and by killing Eric, he lost the opportunity to follow him to his murder buddies. That is where I have an advantage over Dacian. I know more about Eric and the legacies than he does. But how long will this advantage last? What if he asks me about my progress looking for his journal? Can I lie to him when he can hear my every heartbeat?

I'm going to have to be crafty. If I stick mostly to the truth, he might not notice I'm making other plans.

At least I can gauge where Dacian is in his search, but I can't say the same about Mads and Grady, if they are indeed the vampires we're looking for. How close are they to completing the ritual? How much time do I have left? Dacian never said what the final step was, just that it required preparation. Surely they intend to do it soon, though. With Eric suddenly gone, they might suspect someone is on to them. Unless they think he got scared and ran away. If only I could get close enough to investigate. The problem is that we don't run in the same circles. Heck, I actively try to stay as far away from them as possible, fully convinced that anyone who schmoozes with them is a low-level leech. It looks like I will have to hold my nose and sneak into one of their parties. But how am I going to stroll into their mansion? I am not a welcome guest. Every time they see me, they either try to run me over or punch me.

I puzzle over this conundrum for a few days but come up short until an opportunity strikes a week later.

"HAVE YOU HEARD?" Becky announces conspiratorially during one of our study sessions at the library. "After fall break, Alessandra Lucente moved in with Mads Jr. in that mountain mansion. It's just her and the three guys. How scandalous!"

Fiona wrinkles her nose in distaste. "I'm sure that place is nicer than our dorms, but who'd wanna share it with a bunch of dudes? It's probably like living in a frat house. Can you imagine the smell?"

"Ew, grody." Becky makes a gagging face. "But I heard she's helping them throw the biggest, baddest Halloween party ever."

I've been trying to finish my accounting assignment, only half paying attention to Becky's chatter, but my brain latches on to that last bit. I lift my eyes off my workbook. "The legacies are hosting a Halloween party?"

Becky nods. "Apparently, they already bought up all the alcohol in Camden. I'm going to the party at South Hall, but everyone there is complaining that they might have no booze because of the legacies."

Fiona rolls her eyes. "Wow, such tragedy..." They both laugh.

The gears in my brain begin to spin. I can't just walk into their house as myself, but Halloween means everyone will be in costume. This could be my chance to sneak in. If Eric had Dacian's journal, it might still be stashed in his room, ready for me to snatch it.

I hesitate. Is it safe to go snooping inside the potential vampire lair? Probably not, but the party should minimize the danger; I can't imagine them trying to kill me with so many witnesses around. As long as I keep out of their way, I should be able to search the place and get out before they could do anything to me. I'll need some help, though.

"Hey, can you do me a huge favor?" I quietly ask Fiona next time we're alone. "Can you come to the Halloween party at the mansion with me?" We're walking to the dining hall across the big green space, which is green in name only. A nor'easter knocked most of the leaves off the trees, and we're now approaching what is locally known as the stick season.

Fiona halts mid-step and looks at me as though I fell and hit my head. "Are you kidding?" she asks.

"Not really," I mumble awkwardly.

She narrows her eyes at me. "What's going on, Jonathan? Usually, I have to drag you by the ears when it comes to being social. Why on earth would you wanna go to the legacies' party?"

"Shh!" I make a gesture for Fiona to keep her voice down and nudge her to keep walking. I glance over my shoulder before I explain. I don't think anyone is eavesdropping on us, but it pays to be cautious. It's been a challenge to keep my plans secret from Dacian. Every time I've been alone with him since our night drive, I've gone straight to kissing him. It's easier to keep my thoughts blank and my mouth from blurting something when it's occupied. But I'm scared he might find out anyway. "Remember the stolen book we talked about?" I ask. "Don't tell anyone, but I think it was Eric Stockton who took it. I want to go to their house and search for it."

Fiona's jaw drops. "Are you being serious right now?"

"Well, you said it was an inside job yourself," I say defensively. "He was working at the library when it went missing."

"Yeah, but accusing Stockton of being in a satanic cult? That's lunacy!"

"All the more reason for you to come with me," I argue. "To prove me wrong."

"That doesn't make any sense!" Fiona says, flabbergasted.

"Please? For me? I'll be super quick, I promise." I do my best attempt at puppy eyes, which Fiona doesn't find cute at all. But after a little more pestering, she finally agrees.

"You're so gonna owe me for this one," she says.

And I will. In more ways than I could ever imagine.

THIRTY-ONE

Not having a costume or enough time to procure one on such short notice means I need to improvise. I put on my dark maroon hoodie—the closest thing I own to black—and borrow an old ski mask from Fiona. Yes, I'm going to the Halloween party as a burglar with every intention of stealing back Dacian's journal.

Fiona picks me up wearing her witch costume, and we drive to the top of the mountain to the legacies' mansion. When we arrive, the place is booming. I'm shocked by how gigantic the house is. Three stories tall, two wings, and a huge portico with marble columns, and it's already swarming with students. There have to be at least thirty cars in the long driveway, and even more parked on the front lawn.

"How are you gonna find the book? This place is huge," Fiona asks, trying to make herself heard over the blaring music.

The legacies must have spent a fortune prepping for this party. The entire house is decorated with red, blinking string lights, ghosts, dozens of hanging bats, spider webs draped over everything, and glowing jack-o'-lanterns in every corner.

"I...haven't really thought about that yet," I admit sheepishly.

"Well, you better start thinking now 'cause it looks like the hosts just showed up." She gestures with her chin in the direction of the stairs.

I look over my shoulder as Callahan and Mads Jr. descend the grand staircase wearing—my jaw nearly drops—Dracula costumes. A Molotov cocktail of emotions fizzes up in me.

Now that I know Dacian personally, this attire looks tacky at best and highly offensive at worst. I want to rip their cheap polyester capes off of them and burn them in a dumpster. However, the crowd surrounding me doesn't believe in high standards. Everyone explodes into cheers as the hosts make their entrance. I grit my teeth and try not to think about the significance of those vampire costumes. I need to get down to business.

"All right," I say, determined. "If you notice anything, give me a sign, okay?"

Fiona tips her head in disbelief. "So you want me as a lookout while you trespass? Being an accessory to a crime is a crime too, you know."

"Sorry." I sigh awkwardly. "But I'm gonna be quick. Just find me if something seems off, okay?"

Fiona reluctantly agrees.

We go in opposite directions, Fiona toward the kitchen and me deeper into the crowd of students. I'm scanning people's faces, trying to come up with a plan, when I notice Pixie Trish dressed up as—yes, of course—a fairy, complete with butterfly wings, a green wig, and a very short miniskirt. An idea sparks in me. It's risky, but I'm banking on the fact that she has a total of two brain cells. "Hey," I say, stepping in front of her.

Given my slapdash costume, it takes Pixie Trish a moment to recognize me. "What are you doing here?" she snaps, looking like she's getting ready to call for Grady.

"Wait," I say, lifting my hands in a pacifying gesture. "I was just wondering if you know where Eric is."

She narrows her eyes in suspicion. "And why would I tell you that?"

"Well, I've been thinking about what happened, and I want to apologize to him." It's an effort not to throw up in my mouth as I say this.

But she is still skeptical. "You should apologize to Grady first."

"I will," I say quickly. "I've just been worried about Eric. He's been out of class for a few weeks. He must be really sick if he's not even partying tonight. I might not have another chance to talk to him." I do my best to look remorseful, wondering if this stupid charade is gonna blow up in my face, especially if Pixie Trish is in on the fact that Eric is dead and Mads Jr. and Grady are covering it up.

But surprisingly Pixie Trish relents. "I think he's in his room. Last door on the second floor. He's, like, super contagious, though. He's been in there forever."

A massive wave of relief crashes over me. "Thanks," I say.

"You should definitely apologize to Grady too. He's still pretty pissed at you," Pixie Trish says just before I make myself scarce.

Once I'm sure neither Mads nor Callahan has spotted me, I dash upstairs.

There are plenty of people dancing on the landing and milling about in the hallway, including several couples making out. It's easy to remain unnoticed on the way to Eric's room. I double-check that no one is paying attention as I approach the door. Unease burrows under my skin as I step inside. This room belonged to a guy I watched die. I lock the door behind me and shake my head to dislodge the memory of Eric convulsing on the ground with Dacian's bloodied face hovering over him.

Inside, the room is a mess: clothes are strewn on the floor, the bed is unmade, and a couple of dirty mugs and plastic cups sit on the desk and the bedside table. The air is stale with the faint stink of cigarettes and dirty laundry. No one has been here in a while. Despite everything, I feel suddenly sad for the boy who lived here. In the end, Eric didn't have a single soul who cared enough to check on him.

Even his "best friends" don't seem to give a fuck where he is.

I free my face from my itchy ski mask and begin sifting through the clutter. Unbelievably, it takes only a minute before I find Dacian's journal sitting in plain sight on Eric's desk, buried in a messy pile of textbooks he probably never opened.

I pick it up. It has a weight to it, like I am holding a piece of Dacian's heart. It's bound in old, red leather. My fingers skim it gently. My chest aches with how much I want to know about Dacian, but another part of me—the more sensible one—whispers how wrong it would be to read someone's private thoughts without permission. Wouldn't it make me just like the person who stole Clay's letter and ruined his life forever? Or like Eric Stockton and—I'm increasingly convinced—Mads Jr. and Callahan, who used it to murder at least two innocent people? I refuse to be like them.

Then again, this might be my only chance to learn more about Dacian. I still haven't decided what I'm going to do with his journal once I'm out of here. I don't know how long I can hide it from him. What if he has already sensed what I'm up to? He might just take the book from me and leave. I may never see him again. That thought makes me want to tear my heart out and leave it bleeding on the floorboards.

Trembling, my hands flip open the journal before my conscience can interfere. My breath hitches, and despite everything, I smile at the sight of the familiar, elegant cursive. It's really his. A hundred years have passed, but he still writes the same way.

I let my fingers brush the letters. It feels like reaching out to his soul across time. I check the door—it's still locked. Downstairs, the party is raging so loudly that I can make out every word of "Sweet Dreams (Are Made of This)." I'll just peek at the journal and then slip out with it before the legacies catch me. Dacian can deal with them later. The fact that the journal is here is enough to connect Grady and Mads Jr. with the murders.

I skim ravenously through the entries, letting myself indulge in a few random passages. I wish I could absorb every word, every bit of Dacian's history. Almost everything the world knows about him is untrue; his very existence is considered fictional. It's both painful and cathartic to hold his real story in my hands.

I pause when my eyes catch a small drawing of a pentagram in the corner of one page. As I try to work out where I've seen the symbol recently, I read the words above it. My heartbeat quickens. Dacian was thinking about sharing the power of the shadows with Jonathan, and there were two ways to accomplish that. One was turning Jonathan into his progeny by making him partake of his blood, which Dacian didn't want to do as it would make Jonathan subservient to him. The only other way was the ritual, and he didn't know if Jonathan would go through with something like that. It says, *An offering of one is required for one to enter the realm of the shadows. To return with the power of many, an offering of many is required.* Then, Dacian recounts the massacre that served as the final stage of his own ritual.

A *massacre*.

My body stiffens. If Dacian had to do that, then that means the legacies...

My brain scrambles to put the pieces together. If Mads and Grady are indeed Eric's accomplices, they have already made their first offerings—they killed Jeremy and Anita. I would've been Eric's kill had Dacian not stopped him. But now comes the final stage: the offering of many. How do they plan to kill a whole bunch of people?

A cold dread loops around my throat. I strain to hear what's going on outside the door. The music is still thumping from the speakers below, but there's a noticeable change. The other noise I hear, the noise of people talking and laughing, is faint. I shut the journal and hastily walk to the door. With my heart pounding, I slowly open it and peek into the dimly lit hallway. Shit! On instinct, I jerk back, panicking—someone is there, and I think they saw me. It takes a moment to realize who it is: curly hair, witch hat, curvy frame. I stick my head back out again. "Fiona?" I whisper.

Fiona rushes down the hallway and slides into the room.

"Oh my god, Jonathan, finally." She sounds like she's been looking for me for a while.

"What's wrong?" I ask, shutting the door behind her.

Fiona looks shaken. "I honestly thought you were full of it before, but something very weird is happening downstairs. You know how you said to tell you if anything seemed off?"

"Yeah," I say, my sense of unease starting to multiply like germs in a festering wound.

Fiona's words come out in a rushed whisper. "It's probably 'cause I've read too many criminal statistics—like, about alcohol-related violence and date rape and all that awful stuff—but at parties, I never drink anything that doesn't come in a sealed container. But when I checked out the bar, I noticed there were no bottles, no cans. Everything was already mixed in coolers and punch bowls. And then I remembered Grady spiking that girl's drink, so I passed on the punch. But now, something is happening down there. People are starting to randomly pass out, dropping like flies one by one."

"Holy shit," I say.

How do they plan to sacrifice many people at once? This is how. The legacies have drugged the whole party because they're gonna use all those people for the final stage of the ritual. It's going to be a massacre.

"We need to get out of here." I push the words out through my tight throat.

"What's going on, Jonathan? Do you know something I don't?"

I look down, frantically trying to figure out how to explain any of this to Fiona. I can't betray Dacian's secret, but Callahan and Mads Jr. are about to commit mass murder, and even though their transformation is only halfway complete, we're no match for them in a fight.

"Something horrific is about to happen here," I say, hoping Fiona trusts me enough that she won't pressure me for more answers. "I can't explain, but please help me. We must find Dacian. He's the only person who can stop it."

Fiona draws back, alarmed. "Mr. Bathory? What does he have to do with any of this?"

"I really can't say. But I need you to trust me," I plead. "We have to go."

Fiona takes in my grave expression. "I hope you know what you're doing," she finally says.

I don't. But Dacian will.

I dash to one of the arched windows and check below, but we're out of luck. There's no rose lattice or gutter downspout to climb down, no balcony or porch we could jump to. Which means we'll need to go back to the first floor and use the front door to escape this mansion of horror.

I return to Fiona. "Let's go downstairs and hope we can make it to the front door without being seen."

She bites her bottom lip. "Wait—I saw a back door in the kitchen."

"Even better." I stuff Dacian's journal into the front pocket of my hoodie. It sticks out awkwardly; I really should've brought a bag or something, but it's better than nothing. I hope there are enough people still standing upright that we'll be able to blend in among them.

I reach for the door.

"Wait," Fiona says again before I can turn the handle. "I completely forgot about Becky."

I freeze. "What? I thought she went to a different party."

"She did, but she said it was boring because Mads Jr. did actually buy out all the alcohol in town, so she left and came here instead."

Damn. "I'm sorry, but we can't go looking for her now. The best way to help her is to find Dacian as soon as possible."

Conflicting feelings twist Fiona's features, but she follows me into the hallway.

My heart is thumping as we cautiously tread across the old, patterned runner. It's impossible not to notice that the house has gotten quieter. No chatter, no dancing. Someone has even turned off the music. Fiona and I exchange glances at the eerie new silence that hangs in the air. This isn't good. Without the cover of noise, it'll be more difficult to make our escape.

The dark, windowless walls of the hallway seem to close in on us. I motion for Fiona to crouch down when we get to the landing. I take a deep breath and peek around the corner.

What I see downstairs turns my blood cold. The floor is covered with bodies. Every single guest is passed out. They drugged them all. But that isn't even the most terrifying part. Mads Jr. and Callahan are standing in the middle of the foyer, each holding an unresisting body in their arms, gnawing at their exposed necks. I can almost hear the gurgling sounds as they tear through the skin and begin sucking the blood from their victims' throats.

Fiona lets out a horrified gasp beside me. "What the hell?" she mouths. Her shock reminds me of my own reaction when I stumbled on Dacian and Eric.

"I'm sorry," I mouth back, wishing I could explain. But all I can do is continue to watch as Callahan drops his victim unceremoniously to the floor. He licks the blood from his lips, but that does nothing to rid his face of the grotesque scarlet smears all over his jaw and cheeks. Blood is starting to pool around several bodies they've already tasted. For them, the real party is only just beginning.

Mads inhales deeply as though savoring the taste. "By the way," he says, "that book said they have to be dead for it to work. We've gotta make sure." With inhuman swiftness, he twists the neck of the guy he's holding. It lets out a loud crack that ricochets around the foyer.

Fiona claps her hand over her mouth to stifle a scream. I put my index finger to my lips, silently begging her to stay quiet.

"Right," Callahan grits out, then bends down to pick up the body of the girl he just drained. He drops her against his knee. The ease with which he snaps her spine like it's no more than a twig makes me want to vomit.

And I'm not the only one.

"Oh my god, can you guys just finish already? I'm gonna be sick!" a familiar voice complains from somewhere below. Both Fiona and I flinch as Alessandra steps into view. So she's involved in this too.

"Grow a pair, Lucente," Grady spits out before moving on to the next body.

Mads Jr. briefly lifts his teeth from the neck of a kid I recognize from my Latin class. Blood gushes down his chest in streams from his severed jugular. "Grady's right. What are you gonna do when I turn you? You should get used to it now."

"Maybe I'll have the stomach for it then," Alessandra scoffs. "It's not like you two were salivating for blood before you turned."

This catches my attention—so Alessandra is still human. Is there a reason for that? Or did she simply not want to get her hands dirty by participating in the ritual, so she's waiting for Mads to change her, like that somehow absolves her of responsibility for this bloodbath?

Instead of responding to her, Grady snaps another neck and drops the body with a thump. He methodically moves from the foyer to the living room to continue the carnage. Dark pools of blood spread across the floor, creating a red sea of death.

Alessandra makes a gagging sound as the blood flows toward her. She steps back, but it gets on her high heels anyway, so she makes a dash across the foyer to the guest bathroom, awkwardly maneuvering between the dead bodies. Grady laughs as she slams the bathroom door shut and begins to vomit into the toilet.

I turn to Fiona. "We have to make our move now," I whisper.

With Alessandra in the bathroom and Callahan and Mads busy in the living room, this is our only shot to sneak out of here unnoticed. My stomach twists at the idea of using murdered students as our distraction, but getting out of here alive is the only way to stop this madness.

It takes Fiona a moment to snap out of her shocked stupor and follow me.

I clutch Dacian's journal in my pocket as we slowly descend the stairs and carefully step over so many familiar bodies. Even Pixie Trish wasn't spared. Her green wig and butterfly wings stick out, permanently stained a deep red.

Fiona keeps her hand over her mouth as we tiptoe into the kitchen. This room is a big mess. A student crashed into a snack table as they fainted, spilling chips and spiked punch all over the tile floor. I wince and try to avoid stepping on anything crunchy. We're so close to the door. Getting out is all I'm thinking about when suddenly I feel someone seize my ankle. Petrified, I freeze.

Sprawled on the floor beneath me is Becky, dressed in a pink Care Bear onesie. She's gasping for air through the massive gash in her throat. I try to yank my foot free of her grasp, silently begging for her to stay quiet, but she's holding on for dear life. In the span of a few horrifying seconds, several things transpire at once. Fiona reaches the door. Realizing that I've stopped following, she looks back at me with wide eyes just as Becky finally gets enough oxygen into her lungs.

"HELP!" she croaks loud enough that the sound reverberates through the otherwise silent house.

I lock eyes with Fiona, and before she has a chance to react to her friend dying on the floor, I say, "29 Hollow Lane. *Go!*"

Fiona rushes out the back door. I jerk my leg out of Becky's grasp, but just as I do, heavy footsteps come my way...and then Mads Jr. bursts into the kitchen, his cheap vampire cape fluttering behind him.

"Well, well, well. What have we here?" he says as he skids to a stop on the bloody floor a few feet away from me.

Before I can run, Mads grabs me by the shoulders and hurls me through the kitchen and all the way to the living room. My body collides with an armchair, which is the only thing that stops me from crashing into the wall and possibly breaking my back. My vision doubles and I taste blood in my mouth. By the time my spinning surroundings resolve back into a single image, I find Mads gazing down at me with the excitement of a cat that has cornered a mouse.

"Hello, Evergreen. Are you trying to steal our book?" he demands, and I follow his eyes to Dacian's journal, which is miraculously still sticking out of my pocket.

"You're the one who stole it. I'm returning it to its rightful owner."

Surprise flashes on Mads' face as he realizes I know more than he thought I did. But his politician mask slips back on with practiced ease. He wags his finger at me. "Uh-uh. Let's keep things clear for posterity. *I* didn't steal the book—Eric did. I simply read what's inside. And speaking of Eric, what happened to him?"

I huff out a bitter laugh. "You tell me! He's supposed to be *your* fr—"

"Don't be fucking smart with him, Evergreen!" Grady roars before I can finish my sentence. He grabs me by the neck and lifts me up. My feet dangle helplessly above the floor. Staring at his face this close, I realize what a true monster he has become. Grady's pupils are dilated, and his irises are blazing red like he's possessed. His canine teeth are protruding from his mouth, their points sharp and dripping with fresh blood.

The pressure grows on my windpipe as he tightens his grip. He might just kill me. Panicking, I claw at his wrists, but he holds me in a death grip.

"Wait, Grady, don't kill him yet," Mads Jr. says.

Grady roars again but releases me. I cough violently as I collapse back to the floor. Black spots recede from my vision, and I catch my breath, momentarily relieved that my neck hasn't been crushed. But any notion that I might get away without further damage evaporates when, a second later, Mads adds, "So, Evergreen, are you gonna tell us what happened to Eric, or should we pull you apart piece by piece until you beg for us to let you die?"

Fear lurches through me. They have lost their minds. The ease with which they murdered their fellow students leaves me with no hope. The only thing I can do now is stall for time. If Fiona gets to Dacian quickly, I might still have a chance.

"Why are you doing this?" I rasp. "You already have everything you could possibly want. Why murder all these people?"

Callahan's face twitches, and for a second, I wonder if he's gonna ignore Mads and snap my neck.

Mads Jr. lets out a sigh. "Oh, Evergreen, Evergreen. What's money, what's influence, when you can have fucking *immortality*?" He practically shouts that last word, his eyes blazing with the same red glare as Callahan's. "No more of my shitty dad using me as a campaign prop when his ratings sink. No more stupid, *'What are you gonna do with your life, Archie? Behave like a future congressman, Archie! Smile like a senator, Archie!'* Fuck all that! Fuck rules, fuck society. This is real power. And with it, we can rule the world!"

Maybe it's the vampire transformation taking effect, but somehow, Mads' features become sharper as he speaks. His face elongates, and his grin stretches from ear to ear as though someone has widened his mouth to look like the Joker's. It's utterly horrifying and demented. Dacian never looked like this, even when he drank from Eric. He never sounded like this, either. But Dacian has more dignity in his pinkie finger than these two half-baked monsters combined.

I shake my head. "You really believe this crap, don't you? Being a vampire doesn't make you invincible. I bet you don't even know about the domain restriction. You're so used to your daddy bailing you out that you can't predict the most basic consequences of your actions. You've murdered five dozen students. The cops are going to be hunting you down for eternity. What good is immortality if you have to spend it in hiding?"

The sick smile slips from Mads' face, and Grady growls dangerously, but I'm not done. "And you're completely delusional if you think it's only the police you need to worry about. Because when *he* finds you—and I promise he won't stop searching until he does—you'll regret the day you laid your hands on what's his!"

For a moment, neither Callahan nor Mads responds. The living room is so deadly quiet as my threat sinks in that all I can hear is the thudding of my own heart. Maybe I said too much. But if I'm about to die, I want to tell these hell spawns what I think of them before I go.

"Well," Mads says, his voice so cold you can practically ice skate on it, "consider my earlier offer revoked. I'm gonna kill you very slowly, Evergreen, whether you tell me who took down Eric or not."

Callahan cracks his knuckles. "I'm gonna enjoy breaking everything inside you."

On instinct, I crawl backward as the two step toward me, but my back hits the armchair. I'm trapped. Grady grins his revolting vampiric grin, all teeth. I close my eyes, not wanting his face to be the last thing I see. I picture Dacian instead, his beautiful, noble features. I hope he won't be too angry about this stupid excursion of mine. I hope he will forgive me. Unexpectedly, I also wonder if I'll see Clay on the other side. Maybe I'll finally get to tell him I'm sorry I wasn't able to save him.

I brace for impact. But the surge of violence never comes. Instead—

"Who the hell is that?" Callahan hisses, annoyed and alert at the same time.

I open my eyes and zero in on the big arched window to my left and the shadow of a person hovering outside. My heart vaults into my throat. It's Dacian! Despite the sea of dead bodies around me, I feel lightheadedly happy to see him. But how did he get here so quickly? Did Fiona manage to get hold of him? It seems impossibly fast.

Haloed by the dim glow of the porch lights, Dacian looks like a human-shaped void. I think he's very angry.

Mads sneers knowingly, as though he's been expecting this all along. "Finally decided to show yourself, huh?"

"Here as summoned," Dacian replies. "Now, how about you step outside, Mr. Madison. Let's have a chat between equals. Mr. Evergreen has nothing to do with this. Leave him out of it."

But Mads only continues to grin. "I think Evergreen here has everything to do with this. I think you came here for *him*."

Dacian doesn't dignify that with an answer, but warmth fills my chest all the same. He's come to save me. He'll mop the floors with these monsters. At last, I feel a tiny flutter of hope that I might escape this horror show alive. But as I stare at Dacian's face, I realize that he doesn't look victorious yet. Instead, I see a swirl of worry in his eyes. Why is he worried? Oh, right—I need to invite him in.

"Dacian, please come inside!" I shout, expecting him to charge, to shatter the window and pulverize anything that stands between him and me.

Except that doesn't happen. What I hear instead is an explosion of laughter.

Awful dread makes my chest clench.

"You don't know anything, do you, Evergreen?" Mads cackles, nearly doubling over. Grady starts laughing too, a harrowing sound that makes me want to crawl out of my skin. "Not only do you have to be human—you have to *live* in the house in order to invite a vampire inside!"

I whip my head around to look at Dacian, but the question dies on my lips. With horror, I realize that Mads isn't lying. *Being what I am, there are places I cannot enter without invitation,* Dacian said. And I stupidly assumed that any invitation would suffice. From anybody.

"Now, let's discuss business, shall we?" Mads says to Dacian once he's gotten over his cackling fit. "What should I do to Evergreen as justice for you killing Eric? I'm assuming it was you who did it. There's no way that pussy could've taken him down. Should I skin him alive? Make you watch while I break every bone in his body? Or maybe…"

Nausea rises in my throat as Mads babbles on about various methods of torture he'd be thrilled to inflict upon me. Dacian keeps his face cold and focused, but I can tell panic is starting to seep through the cracks. A realization dawns on me. He didn't come here to save me after all; he must've known there was almost no chance he could do that while I was trapped inside. Still, he revealed himself to Mads and Callahan, hoping they might let me go. And now I'm going to die, and he'll be forced to watch.

"I'm sorry!" I blurt out, ignoring Mads' insane rambling, ignoring everything, focusing only on Dacian. "Coming here was a really stupid thing to do. I didn't think it through."

"It's all right." I see Dacian's lips move, but his voice is too quiet to reach me. His fingers touch the glass gently. There's nothing more I want in this world than to be able to touch them back. Instead, I clasp his journal. How could I have been such an idiot?

"Hmm, I really can't decide," Mads announces loudly. "I guess we'll just have to improvise."

Without warning, he pounces on me, yanking me up by the neck. I gasp.

"Jonathan!" Dacian shouts, losing his composure for the first time. He slams his fist against the window, but the glass might as well be made of diamond. It doesn't even rattle.

Mads bears his fangs, making sure we're in full view of Dacian. Callahan snarls hungrily behind me. My heart tumbles. This is it. I'm going to die a stupid, miserable death.

But before Mads can tear into me—

"Stop, Madison, or I'm gonna slit your girlfriend's throat!" Fiona yells.

Mads and Grady whip around in surprise.

I gape too. I can't believe what I'm seeing. Fiona is walking slowly across the foyer, pushing Alessandra in front of her while holding a kitchen knife to her neck.

A part of me is instantly terrified that Fiona didn't flee, that she's stuck in this murder house, risking her life for me. I'm the one who convinced her to come here in the first place. But another part is grateful that she didn't abandon me, that she came back like a true friend.

Despite the abject horror of the situation, Mads bursts out laughing like a maniac again. I don't know if he's drunk on blood or has simply lost his mind. "Onayemi! To think that a fucking equal rights nut would hold a blade in one hand and a hostage in the other—you're really something!"

To Fiona's enormous credit, she manages to keep her composure. "Only a privileged jerk like you would think any rights have ever been won by asking nicely," she says in a flat tone. "Let Jonathan go, and your girlfriend doesn't get hurt."

Alessandra whines, "She's gonna leave a scar on my throat! Please kill this bitch."

Mads takes a moment to assess the situation before replying. "Nice try, Onayemi. But who says I care more about her living than I do about Evergreen dying? He did get Eric killed. What do we say...bros before hoes?"

Alessandra's face reddens. "Maddie, that's not funny."

Mads raises a brow. "Who says I'm joking?" To Fiona, he smugly adds, "Do whatever you want with her. I don't care."

Fiona clenches her jaw. But her reply is not directed at Mads; unbelievably, it seems she expected this and is prepared for contingencies. "Told you this was gonna happen, but 'No, my Maddie ain't like that,'" she says to Alessandra, mocking her voice. "Now I've proven it to you—he's *exactly* like that. So here's the new deal. If you want to preserve your throat, invite Mr. Bathory in."

I don't know how Fiona figured it out, but she's driving a hell of a bargain. Being the only human who lives in this house, Alessandra is the only one who can invite Dacian inside. I wonder if the reason she moved in to begin with is that Mads smelled danger after Eric's death and wanted to make sure they were protected against other vampires. Ironically, now her presence has become a threat to them.

Mads takes several steps toward Fiona. "Why don't I just end this game and kill you both?"

"Maddie, please!" Alessandra shouts in disbelief, as the severity of her predicament finally sinks in. "I did everything you wanted. I lied for you. I even brought girls for you to drink from." But Mads Jr. is not swayed. To him, she means no more than the dozens of dead students sprawled on the floor.

Outside the window, Dacian rises into the air. "Invite me in, Ms. Lucente, and I can protect you from him."

Alessandra's shocked gaze darts from Mads to Dacian, taking in the faint shadows swirling around him. "You can?" she chokes out.

"I can." He gives her a shallow bow. "I am a creature of my word."

"That's a smart girl," Fiona encourages.

"Mads," Callahan warns menacingly, apparently fed up with the melodrama.

Mads shakes his head at Alessandra. "I'm sorry, but I can't let you do that."

"Maddie?" Alessandra whimpers as he steps forward, exposing his fangs with a sinister smile.

But Mads Jr. only scrunches his face in distaste. "You've outlived your usefulness, darling." The sudden viciousness that punctuates those words scares Alessandra stiff.

As though in sync, he and Grady lunge toward her and Fiona.

What unfolds next happens so fast that I can barely follow the action.

"Come in!" Alessandra shrieks in terror.

The window explodes in a blizzard of glass shards as Dacian smashes through it. Alessandra's scream dies abruptly, and she drops to the floor in two parts, the upper half of her body severed like a torn rag doll—either Mads or Callahan got to her before

Dacian could stop him. A pool of blood rapidly accumulates around the loose pile of her intestines. The void left by her dying scream is filled by two earth-shattering booms. The furniture splinters into wood chips as three black shadows dart around the room, colliding violently with each other like raging tornadoes. The sounds are so deafening that I cover my ears before they bleed.

Then, suddenly, everything stops.

As the dust settles, I numbly stare at the gruesome aftermath.

Fiona's eyes are wide, and she's crouching in the far corner of the room, paralyzed with fear. Dacian must have pushed her out of the way, choosing her safety over Alessandra's. I guess *I can protect you* doesn't mean *I will protect you.* One must be careful about word choices when striking a bargain with a vampire.

But neither Callahan nor Mads has escaped Dacian's wrath. Their mangled remains are scattered on the floor in pieces that don't even resemble human body parts—more like mashed pieces of meat. I nearly vomit at the sight of their exposed insides.

Dacian fiercely scoops me up with one arm, nothing like his gentle embrace when he held me in the woods. He grabs Fiona with his other arm and swiftly carries us both outside through the shattered window, setting us down in the gravel driveway.

THIRTY-TWO

"They're dead. Th-they're all dead. Even Becky," Fiona stutters.

She looked so brave standing up to Mads, but it seems reality has caught up with her. A tremor is starting to spread from her hands to the rest of her body.

"Not everyone," Dacian objects, his face grim. "Those two have completed the ritual. I merely slowed them down, but they'll rise again shortly."

This comes as a shock to me. How can those piles of human remains walk, let alone fight? But then again, they aren't human anymore, are they?

Dazedly, I examine Dacian. There's a weird steam coming off him and a squelching kind of sound. And his hands—I nearly recoil. It was too dim inside the living room to see that they were *gone*, smashed into shapeless pulp. His arms don't look right under the sleeves of his jacket either. Did he break his bones when he punched Mads? But no sooner do I have that thought than the damaged flesh of Dacian's hands starts to reshape itself, growing back anew right in front of Fiona and me. I blink, trying to reconcile what I'm seeing with what I've always believed about biology. Fiona is speechless too.

"Other than the people inside the house, does anyone know you went to this party?" Dacian asks her, not paying the slightest attention to his injuries.

"No. Just Jonathan," she replies, her lips still trembling.

"Good," Dacian says. "Drive back home, get rid of your clothes, and no matter what, do not tell anyone you were here tonight, all right?"

Cold understanding dawns on Fiona and me. I can practically see the headlines questioning how one of the few Black students in Camden and a gay scholarship kid whose ex-boyfriend was driven to suicide were the only two survivors of one of the biggest massacres Vermont has ever seen. We'd be blamed immediately. Unlike vampires, we can't just disappear into the mist.

Fiona exhales. "You're right. I have to go."

As she sets out to search for her car amidst the rows of vehicles left by the partygoers, Dacian turns to me. "Go with her," he says sternly.

His gaze flickers to the journal in my pocket.

"This isn't what you think it is!" I blurt in a panic. Although truly I have no idea what he's thinking—Dacian's face is a steel mask, devoid of emotion. But underneath it, he must be furious that I've betrayed him like this.

"We can talk about this later," he says. "Join your friend."

"I'm not leaving without you," I say firmly.

"Jonathan!" He glowers at me.

But I meet his intimidating gaze head-on. Without words, I try to convey that there's nothing he can do to make me leave short of physically removing me. I won't go without him. He's hurt. Steam is still rising from his half-regrown hands!

But it isn't only the fight he's about to face that terrifies me. What scares me is the possibility of Dacian disappearing after he's done with Mads and Grady. What if I never see him again? That's worse than being skinned alive by these two bloodthirsty monsters. Why can't he understand that?

Having found her car, Fiona pulls up behind Dacian. "You ready, Jonathan?" she asks.

I shake my head. "You go without me."

She frowns and doesn't leave, waiting for Dacian to weigh in. He's still glaring at me, but I hug his journal protectively and refuse to take a single step away from him.

Finally, he relents. "Go, Ms. Onayemi. Drive safely." He pauses, then says, his voice suddenly softer, "Thank you, Fiona."

It takes a second for Fiona to process that Dacian is thanking her for walking into a house full of vampires to save me. Solemnly, she nods, says, "Be careful," and speeds off into the night.

"How did you find us?" I ask as the lights of Fiona's car disappear around the bend.

"I will always be able to find you, Jonathan," he says meaningfully. I look down, shamefaced. And here I thought I could keep my whole journal retrieval plan a secret. "Now please, hide. I haven't fought another vampire in a long while," Dacian urges.

I wonder what he considers to be a long while, but his tone makes me instantly anxious. Just as I duck between the rows of the cars parked nearby, Mads and Grady burst out of the house, fully regenerated.

Without a moment's hesitation, Dacian takes them on. There's another series of loud booms, each making me jolt from its intensity. The force is so strong that many of the car windows shatter.

I crouch on the ground, maneuvering to get a better view. I need to check on Dacian.

At first, I'm completely disoriented. All I see is a violent collision of three shadows, bouncing and smashing into each other again and again. I can't understand what is happening at all. But after a few seconds my eyes seem to adjust to the vampire speed. It reminds me of seeing hockey for the first time and learning to follow where the puck was going.

Dacian punches Mads and then barrels toward Callahan. Mads' body flies back with so much force that it makes a crater in the Honda he collides with, knocking him out. But at the last moment, Callahan lurches to the side; Dacian misses and instead smashes into one of the marble pillars framing the house's portico. There is an awful, horrifying sound, and I don't know how much of it is from the pillar cracking in half and how much is from the impact Dacian's body takes. He collapses on the stone porch and coughs up blood.

For a moment, I can't breathe. I want to help him, but how can I? Callahan closes the distance between himself and Dacian in one giant leap, and stomps on his back with the force of a sledge-hammer. I hear more gut-wrenching cracks. I cover my mouth to stop myself from screaming.

Steam erupts from Dacian's spine. He must be trying to heal. But how long will that take? Callahan leaps into the air, about to descend on Dacian again, but just before he lands, Dacian rolls out of the way and springs to his feet.

I'm so consumed by watching him that I miss the moment Mads regains consciousness.

"Keep him busy, Grady," he calls out, panting. The metal door he slammed into creaks as he straightens up, his rib cage hissing with steam. "I can still smell that little rat. I'm going to catch it."

Horror pricks the back of my neck as I realize *I'm* the rat.

Dacian lunges to stop Mads, but Callahan gets in his way. Another boom shakes the air, causing a whirlwind of fallen leaves. But I don't see what happens next as I duck behind a Jeep, out of Mads' sight.

"Come out, come out, little rat," he says with glee.

The gravel and broken window glass crunch as he moves down the aisle of cars with deliberate slowness. He could rise up in the air and find me much sooner, but some people enjoy the hunt far more than the capture. Still, I only have a few seconds to figure out an escape route.

I gaze into the thick darkness of the trees. There isn't much distance between the Jeep and the woods surrounding the property. If I can disappear in there, maybe I can get away? But can I make it across the driveway in time? My heart hammers so loudly that I'm amazed it hasn't already given my location away.

"Come out, rat!" Mads rasps, sounding even closer.

Unable to think up a better plan, I pick up a piece of gravel and throw it at one of the cars at the far end of the row with as much force as I can. When it ricochets off the metal, I hear the patter of footsteps moving away from me.

It's now or never.

I make a mad dash for the woods. But just as I dive into the welcoming darkness, something yanks me by my hood. I nearly choke as Mads drags me back and tosses me onto the open driveway.

Pain radiates through my back as he leers at me, victorious. I have no idea what he's going to do to me. I pray that Dacian will intervene, but he's still fighting Callahan.

My whole body goes rigid, expecting Mads to tear out my throat with his teeth at any moment. But instead, he grabs my shoulders tightly and leaps into the air. Suddenly, the world becomes a blur as he pulls me upward with mind-bending speed. The temperature plunges as we climb.

By the time he stops, I'm terrified to look down—I feel nauseated just thinking about how high up we may be. When I look around, I can't see the horizon, just the night sky and distant stars. The air is so frigid that my panicked breaths come out in hazy puffs. And there's a sharp pain in my shoulders from the crushing grip of Mads' fingers. Why did he drag me up here?

"I know I said I'd skin you alive," Mads says, bringing his face closer to mine.

I flinch away from the deathly rotten stench coming off his teeth and his blood-smeared mouth. His pupils have shrunk into tiny black pinpricks surrounded by glowing, blood-red orbs. I can't believe how ugly he's become. "But I think this might be a bit more exciting, don't you?" He grins as he reads the dread on my face. "What goes up must come down!" He bursts out laughing, and before I can ask what the hell he means by that, he drops me.

The scream that leaves my body doesn't sound like my voice, or even a voice that belongs to a human at all. My stomach plunges, and my guts feel like they're being rearranged as I free fall. The wind that whips my face is so loud it nearly drowns out my thoughts: *This can't be happening. This can't be happening. This can't be!*

I flail my limbs desperately, causing my body to rotate, and I finally see the ground rushing toward me. It's astoundingly far away but approaching rapidly. I search the legacies' house as I plummet. But I can't see Dacian, just the quickly growing shapes of the parked cars in the driveway. My throat constricts as the realization hits. He won't save me this time. I'm really going to die. I await the ground in terror, too shocked to look away and unable to change anything. I can only hope that my death is instant and that my agony is short.

But just before I crash into the earth, a smoky shadow bursts into my peripheral vision. Then suddenly, my body jolts sideways as something—someone—catches me, the shadow materializing into a man. It's Dacian!

He carries me through the trees with the speed of a missile— we have too much momentum to decelerate. Branches hit my face and legs painfully, but it's nothing compared to the fate I've been spared.

"I've got you," Dacian exhales into my ear, his voice rough.

It takes several long moments for my mind to catch up to my body and realize I'm no longer falling. Dacian tightens his arms around me, and I cling to him with my frozen fingers, focusing on his words: *I've got you. I've got you.* As he navigates through the dense growth, slowing his pace somewhat, gradually, my hammering heart calms down too.

My eyes adjust to the darkness, but all I can make out is the looming black trunks of the trees surrounding us. No signs of human life, and Mads and Callahan don't seem to be pursuing us.

I take my time to recover my sanity, expecting Dacian to stop, but minutes pass and we're still flying. I thought he was trying to get away so we could regroup, but it's clear now that he isn't planning to return to the house.

"Where are we going?" I ask.

When he replies, his voice is dripping with barely contained anger. "I'm taking you away from the heart of their domain. I should've known better than to engage with you so close by—" He cuts off abruptly, struggling to contain his upset. "I forgot what it's like to defend someone so fragile."

My eyes widen. I don't know how I feel about being called fragile. I'm both offended and smitten with how protective he feels of me.

Before the fight started, I thought Dacian would easily tear the legacies to shreds. But now I'm not so sure. There is a fist-size chunk missing from his right shoulder. He's bleeding a lot. Steam rises from his flesh, but he's regenerating noticeably slower than before. And Dacian is no longer *flying*—it's more like long-distance jumping. He uses the trunks of trees and occasionally the ground to propel himself forward and upward. Why is that?

He fought two against one, and they had home-court advantage, where their strength was at full capacity. But that can't be the only reason Dacian is struggling. I wonder how long it's been since he properly *ate*. He told me he's been restraining himself from hunting and that fighting increases his need for blood. What if he doesn't have enough strength because he's starving?

A cold worry slithers around my throat. If this person, this being who walks the thin line between eternity and oblivion, born of the shadows yet carrying such a strong glimmer of light that it persists through centuries without diminishing or burning out, this man that I'm stupidly, irreversibly in love with—if *he* were to die, then I—

"Stop!" I demand. "Dacian, stop."

Confused but alarmed by the intensity of my voice, he immediately lands on the forest floor, kicking up a storm of dead leaves.

My legs feel much shakier than I expected when he sets me on the ground in front of him.

"What is it, Jonathan?" he asks, a crease between the perfect arches of his brows. "If you're going to insist that I take you back to that house, I'm telling you right now that I will not listen." He sounds adamant, and he looks ready to grab me and carry me away again.

I look down, not quite able to meet his faintly glowing eyes. "It's not that. I...I want to *help* you," I say. My body buzzes nervously.

I'd never offered anything like this before. I wonder what it'll feel like, if it'll be painful, or if there's some kind of vampire magic that will make me not feel anything—or even make it pleasant. I wait for Dacian to say something, to acknowledge my offer, but seconds tick away, and he's silent as a tomb. Of course, nothing is ever straightforward with him. I guess I'll have to be more direct.

I lift my eyes and tip my head, giving Dacian a full view of the left side of my bare neck. "I want to help you," I repeat slowly. "I can do this. For you."

Dacian's eyes flash bright red. "No," he says sternly.

My heart falls. "Why not?"

He shakes his head. "Not like this."

"I don't want them to kill you," I say, my voice rising in despair. But that does nothing to convince him.

He stubbornly takes a step back. "I am very hard to kill, Jonathan, in case you've forgotten. Once you're safe, I will go back and—"

"I already told you I'm not leaving you!" I shout, swiftly closing the distance between us again, grabbing the lapels of his jacket. He all but confessed to me before that I make him hungry. So why is he refusing my offer? Refusing *me*? Am I not good enough for him? "Take my blood," I say, holding his gaze. "Or not, if you don't want it. But if you dare to leave me behind, I'll chase you right back into that horror show, I promise you."

Dacian stares at me, stunned, but an unmistakable spark of

desire, of hunger, flashes in his eyes at the mention of the word *blood*, betraying what he really wants. "You're mistaken," he whispers. "It's not that I don't *want it*."

The way he says it makes my insides flutter. A strange relief washes over me. He's not rejecting *me*. Instead, he seems worried about what it will mean if he crosses this line and drinks from me.

I pull down the collar of my sweatshirt. "Take it," I repeat in a soft, reassuring voice. "It won't change anything between us. I'm offering it to you willingly."

Dacian's red eyes flicker at the sight of my exposed skin. He swallows, his lingering hesitation crumbling in the face of his own irrepressible need. "This isn't really the best place," he manages to say after a moment.

"Oh. Where is?" I ask, suddenly self-conscious. From all the vampire stories I've read, I've always assumed they preferred the neck.

Dacian leans in. Heat flashes over my face when he replies, his velvety voice caressing my ear, "Your thigh. It is a bigger artery."

I am now very aware of his hand hovering over my hip. I lick my lips and grab hold of my belt buckle. A tremble runs through my hands.

But Dacian stops me, his sure fingers over mine. "Thank you, but that will have to wait until another time. America may be the land of fast food, but I savor my meals. Neck is all right for tonight."

My breath hitches in my throat. There is a promise there. It's full of want, tamed for now, but when all of this is over, when we're alone again in the tangle of sheets with all the time in the world and nothing keeping us apart...

I nod. "All right."

I hear Dacian's murmured confirmation as he circles his arms around me and his mouth inches closer to my neck. I shiver in anticipation, but the first touch that comes is not that of fangs piercing my flesh. It's Dacian's lips pressing softly to the skin below my ear—once, twice—then he moves down, following the pulse in my vein.

Unhurriedly, he kisses me like there's nothing more he wants in the world than to simply be with me. My eyes close. My body turns pliant in his embrace, lulled by the gentleness of his touch. It makes me forget about everything—the rest of the world, the fight with the legacies, even the offer I made just moments ago—until a sharp pain pierces my skin. It explodes across my neck just above my shoulder. I gasp, and my arms go stiff around Dacian, instinctively trying to shove him away, but a second later, the hurt subsides, and I'm overtaken by a rush of warmth. It flushes over my entire body, and suddenly every sensation is amplified: the feel of Dacian's tongue on my neck; the strong clasp of his arms, every muscle defined like he's carved from marble; the quiet and infinitely erotic sucking noise that his mouth makes. It leaves me dizzy and breathless.

My legs fold, but he holds me up, stopping me from collapsing, and lowers me carefully onto the carpet of fallen leaves. There's a shimmer all around him now as steam rises from his wounds, all the damage mending right in front of my eyes. He's like a celestial body that has descended to Earth, his own sun and moons illuminating the voluptuous darkness that envelops us.

He pulls away after what could be moments or millennia. With his eyes closed, he takes a deep breath and then slowly exhales with contentment. The forest seems to sigh along with him.

"How do you feel?" he asks.

His shimmering eyelashes lift, showing the intoxicating scarlet irises underneath. I truly don't know how to answer. All I know is that I need him. Every cell in my body yearns to be close to him, to crash into him and erase all the distance between us.

Clumsily, I reach for his lips, but he leans away. "You wouldn't like the taste," he whispers, self-conscious.

"I don't care," I half growl, unapologetically drunk on him, and kiss him anyway—on the corner of his mouth until I can wrestle his face toward me. His resistance lasts for only a moment before he gives in and kisses me back, my tongue colliding with his in a mad urge to embrace each other.

The taste is sharp with lingering undertones of metal, but I barely notice it. A million sensations and thoughts swirl in my head as Dacian's hands find their way underneath my sweatshirt, fingers splayed possessively around my waist. He's so much warmer to the touch now that he's eaten, almost feverish. I want him to keep going, to yank these clothes off of me and touch me everywhere. But Dacian pulls away.

"I... I should go back and find them before they kill again," he says, visibly struggling to convince himself.

We both know he's right, though. The consequences of letting Mads and Grady escape are too great, not only for Dacian but for anyone else they might encounter.

I try to do the right thing and order myself to get up, but my fingers stay clasped around his jacket.

His lips curve up. "Thank you, Jonathan," he says as he helps me to my feet.

"I'm yours," I say, swaying a little. "I will always be yours."

There is a fondness in his eyes when he replies, "I will let you rethink that invitation when you feel a little more yourself again."

I want to argue that I haven't felt more like myself in a very long time, but instead, I gasp as he scoops me up in his arms again and springs off the ground.

"Try not to move too much," he warns me, covering my head with his hand. Before I can ask what he means by that, Dacian zooms through the air like a supersonic jet, and my heart flips.

The world blurs into a canvas of rugged black lines with a streak of silver that is Dacian's shimmer. His warning not to move proves unnecessary because I *can't* move. My body is pushed into him like I'm on an airplane taking off.

It took him several minutes to travel a safe distance from the legacies' house, but it takes only a few seconds for him to return to it. The ground shakes on impact when he lands; the little pieces of gravel around his boots shoot up into the air.

"Stay by me," he says as he puts me down on the path leading to the front of the house. His eyes narrow as he senses danger.

Mads and Callahan are still here. Alerted by our arrival, they quickly emerge from the house, each holding a jerrycan. Are they trying to set the place ablaze to destroy the evidence of what they've done?

"Look, the old fuck is back," Grady growls.

"And he brought his little rat back too," Mads adds. "Didn't go splat-splat after all." He fixes me with a look of cruel amusement. My stomach feels queasy. My shoulders ache from his grip, and my throat is still scratchy from being forced to skydive without a parachute.

Grady puts down his gasoline can. "Haven't you learned your time is over? It's our world now. Leave while you still can, old man."

"If your little rat runs fast enough, we'll even spare him," Mads taunts. They both laugh—a horrendous, screeching sound.

I can't believe their audacity. Did they just tell Dacian to surrender? Do they know who they are talking to? A small dark corner of my soul hopes he obliterates them just for that.

But Dacian doesn't respond to their insults, doesn't move a muscle. I glance over at his oddly impassive face; something feels off. At first, I can't pinpoint what it is. It's nothing physical, just a feeling of deep unease, the kind of ominous, skin-crawling pull you feel while gazing into a dark tunnel. But moments later, I start to hear it—the *howling*.

I peer into the woods. The sound is coming from far away but seemingly from every direction at once, and it's rapidly increasing in volume. It isn't long before Mads and Callahan hear it, too, and stop laughing.

"What the hell is that?" Grady grits out.

By now, the howling isn't the only thing out of place—the woods appear to be reacting too. The trees start to shiver, their dark branches vibrating as though in anticipation of something closing in. *A lot* of something. But no matter how long I stare at the woods, nothing appears there.

I look down at my feet and almost stumble. "What the…"

Dacian is still next to me, as still as a statue, except for his shadow—which is *moving*. Mine is cast behind me, where it should be, by the glow of the house's lights, but Dacian's is defying the laws of physics by lifting off the ground and slithering in front of him. And it's not just *his* shadow; plumes of shimmering black mist crawl toward him from the forest, curling around him as though summoned. A gathering of darkness.

Mads and Callahan bare their bloody teeth at Dacian.

"I don't know what this illusion is, old-timer," Mads warns him, "but it ain't going to save you. Your chance to escape has passed!"

Even still, Dacian's gaze seems far away, and the cloud of shadows starts to swirl in front of him like a vortex, its tendrils blazing through the night air and forming strange, dangerous shapes. The hairs on my neck stand up. His shadows have *teeth*.

The howling around us becomes impossibly loud. Driven to rage, Mads and Callahan lunge at us. I flinch, ready to get hit, but the legacies never reach us. Two massive shadow wolves jump from Dacian's vortex and barrel at them like cannonballs. Either unable to react to such speed or simply caught off guard, Mads and Grady can't evade them. The impact sends their bodies flying. They slam back into the porch. The remaining pillar supporting the portico gives out, and the whole thing crashes down on top of them.

Knowing vampire strength and healing ability, I expect them to recover quickly, but Dacian's shadows never give them a chance. The wolves bite their way through the collapsed overhang, shredding marble and wooden planks until they reemerge with the legacies' wrecked bodies in their mouths. They spit them onto the gravel as half a dozen more dark wolves spring out of the vortex and encircle them, snarling like hounds of hell. Steam erupts from Mads and Grady as they try to heal.

Grady manages to get on his feet and swing at one of the wolves, but the moment his fist connects with it, he screams. His arm goes right through the shadow as it turns into mist, only to rematerialize around his limb a split second later, all teeth and rage, shredding his arm into chunks of muscle and splintered bone. He howls in excruciating pain.

Mads tries to mount an attack as well, but Dacian's wolves are relentless. They pounce on him, flickering between thin mist and their corporeal shapes. They tear Mads and Callahan apart limb by limb. This isn't a fight. It's an execution.

Dacian doesn't call them off until the legacies' bodies are nothing more than a pile of gory mush and shattered bones. Only then does the snarling finally cease. The wolves retreat into the vortex, and then it collapses with a swoosh, slithering back into Dacian's shadow.

He steps forward. I'm too stunned, too shaken to follow him. Dacian walks up to the pile of gore and reaches down to lift Mads Jr. by what's left of his neck. Nausea roils up my throat. Chunks of flesh hang off his face, yet impossibly, he's still breathing. "Plea...ple..."

I struggle to decipher the gurgling noises that come out of the remains of his mouth. A plea to let him live?

But Dacian is unyielding. The ice in his voice could freeze the ocean. "You don't know what I am," he says, sounding suddenly sinister and unfamiliar. "You don't know where my power comes from. I have been as I will be. And you will return to ash."

A shiver runs over the back of my neck as I catch sight of Dacian's mouth. He's smiling. It's the same sickening, malicious expression I glimpsed in the memory from his past, where he stood on top of a mountain of corpses, blood streaming from his hands and madness raging in his eyes. I remember his cautionary words about the magic that created him and how difficult it was for him to hold on to himself.

He pulls Mads' head off his spine with a loud crack. Then he reaches down and effortlessly rips Grady's head off too. He carries them by the hair toward the house.

I snap out of my stupor. "Wh— Where are you taking them?" I ask, my mouth refusing to form the words on the first try.

Dacian looks over his shoulder. "I'm going to burn them," he says matter-of-factly. "That is the only way to truly kill a vampire."

The image of Dacian's skull being locked up in a box for ninety years flashes in my mind. That's why he couldn't die—they only burned his body, not his head.

"Wait! What about all the students inside?" I call after him.

Dacian doesn't turn around this time. "Everyone is dead."

Numbly, I sit on the lawn and watch Dacian finish up what the legacies started. He picks up the jerrycan, pours out the rest of the gasoline, and sets the place ablaze. It only takes a few minutes for the fire to engulf the old mansion.

Satisfied, Dacian returns to me.

Unlike Mads Jr. or Callahan, there's no blood smeared on his face, no trace of the deadly battle he just engaged in. Outwardly, Dacian looks impeccable. However, there's still something disturbingly wrong about him, as though the wicked shadows he summoned have released their grasp on the legacies and sunk their hungry teeth into his soul instead. For the first time in a long time, I find myself fearing what he is.

"My diary, Jonathan," he says, extending his hand expectantly.

I stand up. I thought there would be a price to pay for going behind Dacian's back to retrieve his journal, but he sounds eerily calm. An alarming suspicion sprouts in me.

"What are you going to do with it?" I ask.

He doesn't bat an eye. "Burn it to ash."

My heart tumbles. "No," I say automatically, shaking my head.

"No?" he echoes in disbelief.

"You can't do that," I say. "We don't burn books, Dacian. You, of all people, should know that."

But my attempt at reasoning with him fails spectacularly. His face changes, suddenly all sharp angles, and he towers over me. "That is no book. It is my diary, Jonathan," he snarls, his mouth twitching furiously. "Give it to me."

My body stiffens at the sheer violence in his words. I can see the points of his slightly elongated fangs peeking out from behind his lips. The fire rages behind him, casting him in an ominous light. But I wrap my arms around my front pocket protectively. "I'm sorry," I say. "I can't."

Violence flashes in his eyes. "How dare you!" he roars, and without warning, he shoves me. What would have been a small push had it come from a human, sends me twenty feet backward into the nearest tree. Pain explodes across my back when I collide with its trunk. For a second, my vision blacks out. As I struggle to get over the shock of what Dacian has just done to me, his blurry silhouette leaps over and grabs me by the neck. He lifts me up, pressing me into the tree.

"Why do you want the diary?" he hisses into my face. I've never seen him this angry before, and it's chilling. This isn't the Dacian I know. This is something else.

I gasp for breath, chasing spots out of my vision.

"Because without it, there will be no truth left about you!" I wheeze desperately. "The whole world will forever think of you as a monster."

"Well, maybe they're right. Maybe I am a monster!" he exclaims, glaring at me with his scarlet eyes.

"But you aren't!" I choke out stubbornly. "If you were, you wouldn't have saved me. You wouldn't have come here at all. Why risk your life for your journal or to fight Mads and Callahan? Real monsters don't care about other people."

Surprise registers on his furious face. His grip on my neck slackens a fraction. But still, he does not concede. "One good deed is not enough to change what I've done."

My throat aches, and I struggle for air. I don't know if I can get through to him when he's like this, but I mustn't give up trying. Everyone he's ever met gave up on him. But I won't be like them.

"You're right—one good deed is not enough," I agree as my eyes begin to sting. Smoke fills the air around us. "But this isn't judgment day, Dacian. You still have years of deeds ahead of you, possibly centuries. Are you saying those don't matter? Nobody is proud of everything they've done, but you have to live with all of it. It's called being human. Each choice, good and bad, gets you closer to who you really are. Your book is still being written. If you're going to burn it before your story is finished, you'll have to toss me into the flames with it because I'm not letting go!" I cry out desperately. Tears are rolling down my face now.

Dacian's eyes widen. For a moment, he just stands there, frozen. The fire crackles loudly behind him, and the house makes an anguished screech as a section of the roof caves in.

"I could never do that," he finally whispers.

His grip on my neck loosens. His thumb slides up to gently hold my jaw. The violent glare fades from his eyes, leaving them unbearably sad, like everything he's been running away from for centuries has caught up with him at once. "What would you have me do, Jonathan?" he asks mournfully.

My lips tremble from trying to stifle my sobs. "Let me be the keeper of your story. I promise your truth will be safe with me."

A bright swirl of embers erupts and disappears into the dark sky as he considers.

Then he pitches forward, his arms encircling my shoulders. His lips draw near my ear. "Very well, Jonathan," he whispers.

Still shaking and deadly tired, I collapse into him, let myself feel the warmth of his embrace. This is the Dacian I know. He's back. My fingers grab hold of his jacket, terrified to let go. Whatever just happened, we can talk about it later. Or not at all. Right now, all I want is to get out of here and put this carnage behind us.

But as the words leave Dacian's mouth, my vision turns wobbly. Before I can fully register that he's using his powers on me, I'm too far gone to protest. My eyelids fall shut, and I tumble into the deep, cold darkness.

When I wake again, it's morning. I'm tucked into my bed with Dacian's journal on my bedside table next to the box of Clay's letters, but Dacian is no longer here. I can feel it in my bones, even before I rush to his house and find it boarded up and empty. Even before the announcement of instructor change for Gothic lit lands in my mailbox. He has left just like he said he would. In the end, nothing I did was enough to change his mind.

THIRTY-THREE

The first few days following the massacre don't feel real.

It's like I'm watching my life happen to someone else, like I wasn't there in that mansion, one of only two humans to survive the deadliest Halloween in the history of Camden.

The police return to campus, and this time, it's not just local cops. The FBI, national and local news, and flocks of true crime fans all descend on Camden. Crying parents, shocked students, and baffled authorities are everywhere.

I hide out, mostly in my dorm or in the library, until things quiet down. Once the police finish their first round of questioning, the swarms of reporters grow bored and move on to the next American tragedy, and as they leave, the exodus of students and faculty begins.

"My parents are pulling me out of school for at least a month," Fiona says. We're in my room, sitting on the edge of my bed. My door is tightly shut. This is the first time I've seen her since the night of the massacre, since we promised to tell nobody where we spent Halloween.

"They've invited you to come too," she adds quietly, but she already knows my answer, and she knows it's better this way.

"I think I'm gonna stay here," I say.

She nods. For a moment, she's unusually silent.

"About that night..." I start.

Fiona turns to me sharply. "We can't ever talk about this, Jonathan. Ever. You understand?"

I'm taken aback by how intense her voice is, bordering on panic.

I couldn't believe how fearless she was when she strode into that murder mansion and stood up to those bloody vampires to save me. But just because she was brave doesn't mean the experience didn't affect her. She saw her roommate killed and couldn't do anything to stop it. She must be traumatized and grieving. Besides, Dacian was right—it really isn't safe to talk about it. Five dozen kids' lives ended in that mansion. The authorities will look for the killer, and when they don't find one, they'll need to save face and find someone to blame. Even if all evidence of Fiona's and my presence at the party has been destroyed by the fire, we can't afford to be reckless.

"Okay," I acquiesce, though it breaks my heart that the victims will never see justice and that their families will never know what happened. But no matter how much I want the truth to prevail, some secrets must remain secret forever.

But not everything hidden must stay that way.

"There's something else," I say tentatively. "Something I've never told you about my life before Camden. But I want to tell you now."

"Go on," Fiona says hesitantly.

"My ex-boyfriend, Clay, he...he didn't dump me. He killed himself," I finally confess.

As my story spills out of my mouth, something inside me fractures. My eyes begin to burn as pain floods my chest. After days of silence, of no contact with Dacian, the inescapable reality that he's gone is setting in, and I don't know how to handle it. I'm beginning to question everything that led me to this point, every decision I've made and its consequences. I used to be so sure that I was doing the right thing. But if that's the case, then why am I so alone?

"Now all I have left of Clay is this box of letters, and I don't know what to do with them," I say, my voice starting to crack. "I couldn't burn them like he wanted me to. But maybe keeping them is wrong. Maybe all my noble intentions are actually just me being selfish because I don't know how else to live my life." Tears stream down my face freely now. I don't even know who I'm talking about anymore—Clay, or Dacian, or maybe both.

Fiona waits for my sobs to subside before she replies, "There's this concept in logic called survivorship bias. It's an error that occurs when you look only at success stories, when you draw conclusions from studying only the so-called 'survivors' of a process. They coined the term after World War II when engineers were studying bomber planes that returned to the U.S. bases from the front lines. They were trying to figure out which parts of the planes needed to be reinforced. But at some point, it occurred to one of the guys that what they should really be looking at were the planes that had never made it back. Because those planes had been hit in their most vulnerable places, and *those* were the parts that needed reinforcement. If we concentrate only on those who survive, our understanding of the world gets distorted, and we make mistakes going forward. It applies to history too. You can't draw the right conclusions if you hear only one side of the story."

"But Clay is dead," I say, sniffling. "There is no one to speak for him anymore, other than his letters." *And Dacian is no longer here*, I don't say aloud. *And maybe I'm the one who drove him away.*

"That's exactly why I think you're doing the next best thing," Fiona says softly. "You're keeping the letters because they're a piece of the truth that would otherwise be lost forever. You're making sure they are never forgotten. I know it's not an easy choice to stick with, Jonathan.

"You know, my mom's family immigrated to the U.S. in the late fifties, but on my dad's side...well, his ancestors were brought here on slave ships. They are doing this project at Emory, using cargo notes to create a database with all the information we have about those ships so people like my dad can look up which ships their ancestors were trafficked on. And yes, it's very painful to look at. But should we turn away just because it's difficult to confront? Should we let the dead stay dead and move on? Or do those people deserve to be acknowledged?" Her sad eyes glisten.

I throw my arms around Fiona's shoulders and squeeze tightly. "Thanks. For everything," I say. "For coming back and saving me. For sticking around. For being a true friend."

She sniffles, returning the hug. "Call me, okay?"

"I will," I promise.

A MONTH PASSES QUIETLY, but Fiona doesn't return to Camden. I don't think she ever will. I wonder if I would leave too, if I had a place to go. But Camden is all I have, even though everything here reminds me of *him*.

To cope, I bury myself in my studies. My dreams are so empty that most nights I don't feel like sleeping at all. I stay up and read, and read, and read. Not just class assignments—novels too. I try to remember as many titles as I can from Dacian's stacks of books. Reading the same stories he read is like a ritual that keeps me connected to him in some nebulous way, even though he has chosen to stay far away from me.

It also helps to pass the time as I wait, which is the one thing I do the most.

I don't know what I'm waiting for, exactly. For the seasons to change? For this clawing ache in my chest to go away, to get buried underneath the snow like the piles of fallen leaves?

It's unclear, but still I wait. And wait. And wait.

Thanksgiving passes. I spend it alone in my dorm with my books. The first snow falls, resetting the colors around me to a blank white slate, as though this place is ready for the start of something new, or at least the death of something old. Some of the students who left campus trickle back in. Maybe they were unable to transfer somewhere else, or maybe they realized that every college has its tragedies, so why bother hightailing it to somewhere new?

Finals are approaching. But as time crawls forward, my heart remains suspended, unable to move on. Everything that mattered to me before has faded. Only reading still holds my interest in this endless procession of monotone days.

One chilly December morning just before finals week, I check my campus mailbox. As I sort through the stack of class correspondence and holiday flyers, I find two strange letters. The first one is from the Oxford Office of Admissions. I stare at it for a moment, mystified. I check the name on the envelope, wondering if I got someone else's mail by mistake, but it's addressed to me.

I open it and skim the contents. I don't understand. I start over from the beginning, this time reading slowly and carefully, and yet it still doesn't make sense to me. Words like *congratulations* and *your transfer application has been accepted* jump off the page. There's a mention of my requested major, which is conservation with a special emphasis on books, and information about a private scholarship I've been awarded so I can pursue my studies full-time. At the end there's a phone number to contact the Office of Admissions. Also in the envelope is a welcome brochure detailing the next steps I must take in order to enroll for the spring semester.

I gape at the letter. Is this real? But how could it be? I never applied. I never even told anyone that Oxford was my top college choice. There was no point, considering my financial situation. Yet somehow, it's all taken care of—my scholarship will even cover room and board. Am I dreaming?

Suddenly, a memory comes back to me. There's one person I *did* tell that early October afternoon on the bench by the pond. My pulse speeds up. It bounces in my rib cage with an irregular rhythm as I move on to the second letter. My hands shake. The cream-colored envelope is luxuriously thick and expensive, not your average post office stationery. But there is no return address on it and no sender, only a name written in the most beautiful and achingly familiar cursive—*Jonathan.*

My throat constricts. I clutch the letter to my chest as I stumble out of the mail room, not trusting myself to open it in front of other students. I don't make it back to my dorm, though; I'm not that patient. I find the first empty bench on the green, wipe the snow off it, and sit down to read.

My dear Jonathan,

I have started this letter so many times, only to find myself unable to put into words the things that must be said.

I am not a good man. I have countless regrets and crimes I must atone for. The rest of my eternity may not be long enough to accomplish that. In the end, I couldn't even stop myself from hurting you. To this day, it remains one of my biggest regrets.

I've had some time to contemplate what you said that night.

I spent centuries in the shadows, yearning to be found and set free. But it turns out that it is easier to remain unseen than to bear the possibility of being rejected for what I am. After all, becoming your true self is not a gate one simply opens. Instead, it is a long road to travel, mostly uphill and in bad weather. I must come to terms with these truths. Yet I know now that the only way to move forward is to try.

I hope you will forgive my impudence in contacting Oxford on your behalf.

I've always wished someone would come along and show me the world, but I'm beginning to realize that maybe I should be the one showing the world to someone else. And I hope that someone can be you. If you will still have me, I am yours.

Love,
Your immortal
D

BY THE TIME I finish reading Dacian's letter, my fingers are trembling, and my eyes are blurred with tears. I wipe them with the back of my hand to avoid accidentally marring the beautiful ink. Flurries start to fall from the shimmery gray sky as I sit on the bench, not able to move, just holding on to the letter like it's a lifeline. Conflicting emotions swirl inside me.

I want to punch him for disappearing without a trace, for using his powers on me without my consent, for leaving me alone all this time when I could do nothing but wait.

But then, after I punch him, I'm going to kiss him. I will kiss him senseless. I will kiss him and never stop kissing him for all eternity, every inch of that stubborn, infuriating, unbearable, and beautiful vampire.

But first, I need to make a phone call and buy a suitcase, because I, Jonathan Evergreen, am going to Oxford.

THE END.

Acknowledgments

The idea for this book came unexpectedly when I was watching the movie Renfield. It's not a particularly great movie (let's be honest,) but I just remember thinking how much I love vampires and why the heck haven't I written some yet? Fifteen minutes later, I had the basic plot for Love Immortal.

Despite how quickly the initial idea came, it was by far the hardest book I've ever written. Putting it into an academic setting definitely played a part. I think I got too traumatized in school; I still regularly have nightmares about midterms and finals, and revisiting that mind state for a year it took to write Love Immortal turned it into more of an endurance test than I had been prepared for. As much as I love Jonathan and Dacian, I am incredibly happy that they are finally out of my head. All grown up and off to college :) I don't think I will be writing academia any time soon.

Love Immortal would not have been possible without the generous contributions of time and talent from the following individuals:

James Bird and Adriana Mather,

copy editor Alison Cherry,

proofreader Laura Samotin,

cover artist ZeldaCW,

cover designer Valerie Gomez,

voice actor James Fouhey,

my potbelly pig Sheldon, who was listening to my edits even on his last day on earth, all the Friends,

and my wonderful readers who continue to give my stories a shot.

Thank you!

Kit